Going to
the Chapel

Going to
the Chapel

ROCHELLE ALERS
GWYNNE FORSTER
DONNA HILL
FRANCIS RAY

St. Martin's Paperbacks

GOING TO THE CHAPEL

"Stand-in Bride" copyright © 2001 by Rochelle Alers.
"Learning to Love" copyright © 2001 by Gwendolyn Johnson-Acsádi.
"Distant Lover" copyright © 2001 by Donna Hill.
"Southern Comfort" copyright © 2001 by Francis Ray.
Excerpt from *Rhythms* copyright © 2001 by Donna Hill.

ISBN: 0-312-97894-4

Printed in the United States of America

St. Martin's Paperbacks edition / June 2001

St. Martin's Paperbacks are published by St. Martin's Press, 175 Fifth
Avenue, New York, NY 10010.

10 9 8 7 6 5 4 3 2 1

Contents

Stand-in Bride   1
  BY ROCHELLE ALERS

Learning to Love   89
  BY GWYNNE FORSTER

Distant Lover   167
  BY DONNA HILL

Southern Comfort   235
  BY FRANCIS RAY

Stand-in Bride

ROCHELLE ALERS

Your love delights me, my sweetheart and bride.
Your love is better than wine; your perfume more fragrant
than any spice.

—SONG OF SONGS 4:10
GOOD NEWS BIBLE
TODAY'S ENGLISH VERSION

1

Kindergarten teacher Lisa Barnett could hardly contain her joy. It radiated from her large, clear brown eyes; was mirrored by the grin curving her wide, lush mouth; and it was apparent from her jaunty step as she pushed through the revolving door leading into the Barnett Savings and Loan Company.

The lending and mortgage institution had been a financial landmark in Savannah, Georgia, for three-quarters of a century. Her grandfather, Albert James Barnett, had petitioned the state for a charter to establish a bank for the city's African-American population, because most of them had opted to save their money in strongboxes or tin cans rather than deposit their meager savings in the city's White-owned banks. The charter was granted, and what had begun with half a dozen depositors the first month had grown to more than twenty thousand over seven decades, with assets totaling more than one hundred million dollars.

As a Savannah Barnett, thirty-year-old Lisa had grown up with every comfort her family lineage afforded. She had attended private schools, was presented to Savannah's Black society, and had graduated at the top of her class from an elite private women's college. She was well traveled, having visited more than a dozen African countries, as well as most countries in Europe and Asia.

But it was France that had enthralled her: the country, its people, the food, the language—and Sebastien deVilliers. She'd met the tall, spare, bookish-looking Frenchman the summer she turned twenty-seven. She wasn't certain why she was drawn to him, because he was the antithesis of the men she'd dated back home. Sebastien was charming, sensitive, sensual, and artistic. But what mattered most was that she had fallen in love with him. And it had taken three years for her to conclude that she loved him enough to accept his proposal of marriage.

Her peach-colored leather sandals made soft slapping sounds on the cool marble floor as she made her way past the tellers, customers, and the young man and woman sitting behind massive mahogany desks on the platform. She nodded to both, her smile still in place. At that moment nothing could dispel her ebullient state of mind.

The elderly woman who sat at a desk outside Gerald Barnett's private office looked up from her typing. Peering over the top of her glasses, Ethel Woodson recognized her boss's daughter.

"Good afternoon, Lisa. Looking for your daddy?"

Lisa nodded. "Good afternoon, Mrs. Woodson. Do you think he can spare me a few minutes?"

Mrs. Woodson glanced at the buttons on her telephone. "He just finished with his call. Do you want me to tell him that you're here?"

"No, thank you. I'd like to surprise him." What she didn't say was that what she wanted to tell her father would not only surprise him, but probably also shock him.

Rapping lightly on the door, she pushed it open, and walked into a large office carefully decorated with massive mahogany pieces of furniture from a bygone era. Though the bamboo mini-blinds were partially closed against the strong rays of the late-May afternoon sun, the diffused light still bathed the teak-paneled walls with a warm golden glow. Ribbons of gold formed a halo around the head of the middle-aged man sitting at a conference table.

Gerald Madison Barnett rose to his feet, when he saw his daughter walk into his office, extending his arms. Since Lisa had only recently moved out of the house they'd shared for nearly three decades, he marveled at how adult she now appeared. He had hoped she would set up her own residence after she'd graduated college, but she had balked, saying she didn't want to move out and leave him because she feared he'd be lonely. What his only child hadn't realized was that even though he'd been divorced for twenty-eight years and hadn't remarried, he may have been alone but he definitely wasn't lonely.

Lisa moved into his protective embrace, her arms going around his trim waist over a crisp, stark white shirt. Raising her chin, she smiled up at her father. And it wasn't for the first time that she could not believe how handsome he still was. He would celebrate his fifty-fifth birthday in December; he controlled his weight by carefully monitoring his diet and swimming laps year-round in the enclosed pool he'd built adjoining a wing of the house. Although she had moved out of the expansive house and set up her own co-op in downtown Savannah, she returned to take advantage of the pool at least twice each week.

Gerald's deep-set dark brown eyes crinkled as he smiled. "I thought we were scheduled to share dinner tomorrow."

Pulling back in her father's protective embrace, Lisa tilted her delicate chin. "We are. But I couldn't wait until tomorrow to tell you my news."

Lifting an eyebrow, Gerald let his smile fade slightly. Lisa's expression was so like the woman he had once fallen in love with, married, and subsequently divorced when their daughter was only a few weeks past her second birthday. She bore an uncanny resemblance to her mother—a woman who had walked out of their lives, never to return. He had become mother and father to his daughter, permanently sacrificing female companionship to remain a single father.

"What news?" His soft, deep voice was layered with a drawl that had come from his spending all his life in the South.

Her gaze shifted to the middle of his chest. "I'm getting married."

His grip on her tightened before he pulled back, his eyes widening in apparent shock. Running a large, well-groomed hand over his face, he shook his head. "To whom?" he asked through his fingers.

"Sebastien deVilliers."

Gerald's hand dropped to his side. "Who the hell is Sebastien?" His voice was dangerously quiet.

Lisa felt her joy dissipate as if someone had poured a pitcher of ice water over her head. Her father had never raised his voice at her—he didn't have to. Whenever he spoke through clenched teeth, she knew he was angry. *Very* angry.

Taking a step backward, she lifted her chin in a gesture of defiance. At thirty she didn't need Gerald Barnett's permission to marry. All she wanted was his blessing.

"He lives in France."

Gerald felt his knees shaking, and managed to retreat to the chair he had just vacated. Sitting down heavily, he stared at the stack of papers awaiting his signature on the highly polished table. He forced himself to unclench his teeth.

Waving a hand, he indicated a chair facing him. "Sit down, Lisa. I think I'm missing something here."

She complied, taking a matching leather chair and resting her elbows on the smooth, curved mahogany arms. The ribbons of light threading through the bamboo slats cast a golden glow over her pecan-hued face and glinted off the golden streaks in her light brown, chemically relaxed, shoulder-length hair. The warm, flattering light fired pinpoints of amber glints in her large expressive eyes.

Lisa folded her hands in her lap. She didn't know why, but suddenly she felt like a little girl instead of an independent thirty-year-old woman who had set up her own household, earned her own money, and answered to no one about her whereabouts. Yet Gerald Barnett's command that she sit down facing him harkened back to a time when he would chastise her for an action that went against everything she'd been taught as a Savannah Barnett.

"When did you meet this fellow?"

Her head came up quickly. "His name is Sebastien, Daddy. He's French—"

"I would assume that because of his name, and the fact that he lives in France," Gerald retorted, interrupting her.

Lisa's taut nerves tightened even more. "Please don't be rude, Father!"

Leaning forward, Gerald glared at her. His daughter only referred to him as *Father* when she was close to losing her temper. Well, it was taking all of his self-control to keep his own temper from exploding.

He nodded, acquiescing. "I'm sorry. Please continue."

Lisa pulled her lower lip between her teeth, chewing it until she was composed enough to form her thoughts. "I met Sebastien when I went to France three years ago."

"What does he do for a living?"

"Daddy," she wailed softly. "You promised not to interrupt."

Gerald's expression softened. "Sorry, Princess."

Letting out an audible sigh, Lisa smiled at her father. She had softened him up. Whenever he called her *Princess* she knew he would agree to anything she proposed.

"We hung out together that summer. He took me everywhere. We became wonderful friends. Yes, *friends*," she emphasized when a muscle in Gerald's lean jaw throbbed noticeably. "We kept in touch with phone calls and letters after I came back. Then we stopped communicating altogether about six months later."

"And now you're getting married?" Gerald asked after a pregnant pause.

She nodded, her professionally coiffed hair moving sensually over the shoulders of her peach-colored linen sheath dress. "We met again when I went to Rome last year during our winter recess. He was on holiday with his parents and sister—they had elected to spend Christmas in the Eternal City because they wanted to celebrate Christmas Eve Mass in St. Peter's Square. We took it as divine intervention that we were reunited in time to spend New Year's Eve together. His family invited me to join them for a midnight dinner, but Sebastien and I opted to bring in the new year in a café not far from the Spanish Steps. We wound up strolling the streets of Rome until the sun came up. I was scheduled to return to the States on the second, so we decided to spend New Year's Day together.

"Daddy, he's the most wonderful, sensitive, caring man I've ever known. Except for you," she added quickly.

Closing his eyes, Gerald drew in a deep breath. "Do you love him, Princess?"

A bright smile softened her lush mouth. "More than I thought I could ever love a man."

He opened his eyes, the piercing dark orbs pinning her to the seat and not permitting her to move. "Does he love you?"

"More than anything or anyone in the world."

He smiled for the second time since his daughter entered his private sanctuary. "When and where is the wedding?"

"I want to be married here in Savannah."

Gerald nodded. "When?"

"The last Saturday in August."

"That's only three months away."

"I know, but it's the only time that Sebastien and his family can get away for holiday."

"You know I promised I'd buy you a house for a wedding gift. Three months doesn't give you and your fiancé much time to look at properties."

Lisa glanced over her father's head. She felt the heat of his gaze on her face. "I don't plan to live in Georgia. I'm returning to France with Sebastien. He's in the process of restoring a family-owned seventeenth-century château, which we plan to turn into a bed-and-breakfast."

Gerald's right hand came down hard on the tabletop, startling Lisa. "Dammit!" The single word exploded from his mouth. "How dare you come in here and tell me you're moving as if we were discussing the weather!"

She stood up, her own temper flaring. "I dare because I'm your daughter. I dare because I thought you would be happy for me."

Unable to stand, Gerald closed his eyes, shaking his head. He'd wanted to see his daughter married, but he never thought her becoming another man's wife would result in her living an ocean away, on another continent.

His shoulders slumped in defeat. It was the first time in her life that Lisa had seen him looking so wounded. Moving around the table, she knelt at his side and curved slender arms around his neck, pulling his head against her shoulder.

"Be happy for me, Daddy. Please."

Gerald savored her closeness, her delicateness. Didn't she know she was all he had? All he had ever had since his ex-wife, her mother, walked out on them because she did not want to be a mother?

Reaching up, he covered both her hands with one of his. "I'm trying, Princess. You know I raised you to be strong, independent. But not so independent that you would consider moving thousands of miles away."

"It's only across the ocean." She dropped a kiss on the top of his thinning, graying hair.

"I'd have to sit up half the night to wait to call you."

"E-mail me, Daddy. That's what Sebastien and I do."

"It's not the same as talking to you," he said stubbornly.

"We'll still be communicating."

"I suppose you're right." Pushing to his feet, he pulled his daughter to his side. "Why the rush? Are you pregnant?"

A rush of deep color suffused her face. "Of course not."

"Well, I had to ask. After all, you did visit Europe during your Easter break."

She patted his chest. "We were very careful, Daddy."

Gerald stared down at her upturned face, knowing he could not stay angry at his own flesh and blood. "I wouldn't mind a grandchild or two."

Lisa laughed, the low, sultry sound reminding him of her mother. "Let me get married first."

"What type of wedding do you want? Large? Small?"

"I want something small and intimate. No more than sixty people. And I want Langdon Bridals to handle everything."

Katherine Langdon, owner of Langdon Bridals, was the most sought-after wedding consultant in the city. Most engaged women contracted with her more than a year in advance.

"That may not be possible, given the time frame," Gerald said.

"Please talk to her, Daddy. Tell her that I want it small, simple, but very elegant. I want my wedding to be the wedding of the season."

Gerald's lips parted in a smile under a neatly barbered mustache. "I'll ask, but don't get your hopes up. If she refuses, then you'd better have a backup plan."

"She won't refuse. What woman can refuse you?"

Throwing back his noble head, Gerald let loose a full, deep-throated laugh. "You really know how to get over on your old man, don't you?"

"I'm not trying to get over on you, Daddy. How many women in Savannah have tried to get you to marry them? The word is that you get more action than many men half your age. And don't tell me it's because you're a bank president. Just accept the fact that you're hot." Rising on tiptoe, she kissed his cheek. "Call me later and let me know when I can get together with Ms. Langdon."

Gerald stood motionless, watching his daughter walk out of his office. Within the span of fifteen minutes she'd turned his world upside down. He, Gerald Madison Barnett, who had maintained complete and utter control of every phase of his life, suddenly felt as if he were drifting in the middle of the ocean on a leaking raft.

His daughter planned to marry within three months and move with her French husband to Europe. Sinking down slowly to the leather chair, he braced his elbows on the table and covered his face with his hands. He sat in the same position for another ten minutes before he pressed a button on his speakerphone and asked Mrs. Woodson to get him Langdon Bridals.

2

"Mr. Barnett, I have Ms. Langdon's assistant on the phone. Her name is Rita Grady."

"Thank you, Ethel." He picked up the receiver to the telephone next to his left hand. "Good afternoon, Ms. Grady. May I please speak to Ms. Langdon?"

"Good afternoon, Mr. Barnett. I'm sorry, but Ms. Langdon

is off on Mondays. Is there something that I can perhaps help you with?"

He'd wanted to speak directly to Katherine Langdon. "Is it possible for you to check Ms. Langdon's calendar for the month of August?"

"I don't even have to look at it because I know that she's booked solid for August." There was a slight pause and the sound of pages turning came through the earpiece. "She has one Sunday open in late October."

"That's much too late."

"I'm sorry, Mr. Barnett. But if you'd like to speak to Ms. Langdon, then I suggest you call her tomorrow morning. She's usually in before eight. Would you like me to leave a message that you called?"

Gerald's forehead furrowed in a frown. "No, Ms. Grady. That won't be necessary. Thank you."

"Thank you for calling Langdon Bridals. Have a good evening."

"You do the same." He replaced the receiver on its cradle, his lips compressed in a thin, hard line. Lisa was his only child, his princess, and from the day she was born he'd tried to give her everything she wanted—within reason, of course. And it was within reason to give his daughter the wedding she wanted—a celebration planned by the very best wedding consultant in the city.

Moving from the table to a computer workstation, he typed in the name "Langdon Bridals." The information on the account appeared on the screen. Not bothering to glance at the balance, Gerald noted Katherine Langdon's personal information, writing down her address and telephone number. Then he buzzed the branch manager and told him that he was leaving for the day. He didn't have to tell Ethel Woodson or the branch manager to call him if there was a problem they couldn't handle. It was understood that they contact him by pager or cellular phone.

Five minutes later, he was behind the wheel of his spacious Mercedes-Benz sedan, driving in a westerly direction to the neighborhood where Katherine Langdon resided. Spanish moss hanging from massive ancient oak trees provided a moody background for the humid late-spring afternoon. He was born and raised in Savannah—as were his parents before him—but there had never been a time when he tired of the city's sensual, tropical lushness. It reminded him of a woman early in pregnancy. There was just enough ripeness in its beauty to entice the most jaded traveler.

He maneuvered up and down several wide boulevards until he turned down a street shaded on both sides with trees meeting in an arch. Katherine Langdon lived within walking distance to Savannah's historic district, with its waterfront and twenty-one squares spaced at regular intervals throughout the business and residential districts of the city. He parked along the street in front of a red-brick town house. Picking up his jacket off the passenger seat, he slipped it on, then made his way to the entrance of the well-preserved structure.

Katherine Langdon loved Mondays. It was her only day off. And she took advantage of the coveted twenty-four hours to remain in bed beyond six A.M., prepare a full breakfast, and catch up on her reading.

She shifted to a more comfortable position on a cushioned lounger on a second-story veranda, not bothering to open her eyes, savoring the cooling breeze from the slowly moving blades of an overhead fan. She'd spent most of the afternoon dozing in the humid air, too relaxed to get up and return to the cooler interiors of her town house triplex. Two formal weddings and a bridal shower in three days had tested her emotionally and physically. But she would get a reprieve of sorts next weekend: Langdon Bridals was only scheduled to coordinate a wedding breakfast Saturday morning and a restaurant wedding Sunday afternoon.

Despite her fatigue, Katherine loved her career as a wedding consultant. It had taken eight years to achieve a successful enterprise whose reputation was based on unabashed perfection. Planning a memorable bridal shower and wedding was the ultimate goal of Langdon Bridals. She always made it a practice to work out the smallest details with her custom-

ers, thereby avoiding unnecessary complications. Careful
planning became the perfect reflection of the guest of honor
and her own personal style.

A soft sigh escaped her parted lips at the same time the
downstairs doorbell chimed melodiously throughout the three-
story structure. Her eyes opened as she listened for a second
ring. Vertical lines appeared between her large, heavily lashed
cinnamon-brown eyes. Sitting up, she swung her legs over
the side of the lounger. She could not imagine who had come
to her home; she wasn't expecting any visitors. And she knew
it wasn't the mail carrier because her personal mail was always delivered to her business address.

Securing several silver-streaked strands of black that had
fallen over her forehead in the elastic band that held back the
rest of her hair, she made her way down the curving wrought-
iron staircase to the first level. The bell chimed again as she
walked into the spacious entryway.

Slowing her step, she stopped and peered through one of
the many panels of glass flanking the solid oak door. A slight
frown furrowed her smooth forehead when she recognized the
man on the other side of her door as Gerald Barnett.

She couldn't imagine why the president of Barnett Savings
and Loan Company had come to her home. If there was a
discrepancy with her business account, why hadn't the bank
manager called her?

Taking a deep breath, she opened the door at the same
time Gerald had raised his hand to ring the bell a fourth time.
His expression mirrored surprise as he stared down at her.

At first glance Gerald hadn't recognized Katherine Langdon. Her usual sleekly coiffed hair was piled atop her head
in seductive disarray, while several ebony-and-silver strands
trailed along her long graceful neck. She had elected to wear
a pair of fitted khaki capri pants with a navy blue tank top.
Both garments revealed more of the conservative wedding
planner's flesh than he'd ever seen before. Whenever their
paths had crossed, it was usually at the weddings of relatives
or business associates. She was always recognizable because

of her trademark uniform: black silk slacks and a matching mandarin-style tunic.

His gaze shifted from her questioning stare to travel down the length of her slender body to a pair of expertly groomed narrow feet before returning to her large brown eyes.

"Miss Langdon, I'm sorry to disturb you at home," he said, the words rushing out seemingly of their own volition. "But I needed to talk to you."

Katherine placed a hand against her throat. "Is there something wrong with my account?"

Shaking his head, Gerald offered a comforting smile. "No. I haven't come because of a banking matter. What I'd like to discuss with you is of a personal nature."

It was Katherine's turn to raise her naturally arching eyebrows. She opened the door wider. "Please come in."

Gerald Barnett walked into the entryway, the warmth of his tall body and the lingering clean scent of his seductive aftershave wafting in her sensitive nostrils. She and the bank president had interacted only once in the fifteen years since she'd become a resident of Savannah, even though she'd observed him from time to time whenever he was a guest at some of the elegant weddings Langdon Bridals had orchestrated.

When she'd first sought a loan to establish her business, the loan officer had declined her request because she had been recently divorced, lived in a rental unit, and claimed a savings account with a modest balance of only thirty-five hundred dollars. He'd stated unequivocally that because she didn't have enough collateral, Barnett Savings and Loan Company viewed her proposal as "high risk." Unwilling to accept his decision, Katherine had written a letter to Gerald Barnett himself, requesting a review of her application.

He'd called her and set up a meeting. After she outlined her business proposal, which included a five-year projection, he'd approved the loan. Gerald's instincts that she was a good business risk were validated, because she'd paid off the loan in five years instead of ten, and had subsequently purchased the three-story town house several years later.

Katherine led him through the entryway into a spacious sitting room set off from a formally decorated living room. She gestured to an armchair covered in a floral print—large pink flowers on a sea-foam green background. The green hue was repeated in plush wall-to-wall carpeting and the wallpaper, which was dotted with tiny pink-and-white apple blossoms. Cherrywood tables, lamps with full leaded-crystal bases, and ivory sheers at the tall windows invited one to come and sit.

Waiting until Katherine sat on a club chair with a matching oversize ottoman, Gerald sat down. His gaze swept around the room again.

"It's lovely. Your home," he added quickly. It wasn't that Katherine Langdon wasn't lovely, because she was that and more. But he hadn't come to admire the woman, only to solicit her services.

"You said you needed to talk to me," she said, deciding to be direct. She was more than curious to discover why the bank president had come to see her at home instead of at her shop.

He nodded. "It's about my daughter, Lisa. She just got engaged."

Katherine smiled, the gesture crinkling her large eyes at the same time an elusive dimple winked in her right cheek, and Gerald wondered why he hadn't noticed it before.

"Congratulations, Mr. Barnett."

"You *can* call me Gerald."

"I will if you don't insist on addressing me as Miss Langdon."

It was his turn to smile, and the expression softened the sharp angles in his lean face. He inclined his head. "Then Katherine it is."

"Am I correct in assuming that you want me to assist in planning your daughter's wedding?" He nodded again. "Has she set a date?"

"The last weekend in August."

"Next year?"

"No. This year."

Katherine shook her head and more hair escaped the elastic band, a curl falling down over her high, rounded forehead. "I'm sorry, but that's impossible. I'm booked up until late fall."

Leaning forward on his chair, Gerald gave her a long, penetrating stare. "Can you make an exception?"

"I'd love to, Gerald, but my schedule will not permit it."

"Does that mean that your decision is written in stone, Miss Langdon?"

Her gaze narrowed as she glared at him. It was the same statement she had made to him after his loan officer had rejected her application. Gerald Barnett was throwing her very words back in her face.

Tilting her chin in a defiant gesture, she peered down her nose at him. "No, it isn't, Mr. Barnett." They were back to being formal.

A smile parted his lips. "Then you're ready to negotiate?"

Vertical lines appeared between her eyes. "Do you mean am I ready to be blackmailed?"

Gerald's grin widened. "Blackmailers usually aren't the ones paying, Miss Langdon."

"Touché," she whispered.

And he would pay, she mused, her expression brightening noticeably. Rising gracefully to her feet, Katherine moved over to an antique secretary and picked up a clothbound book and a fountain pen. She didn't know how she knew, but she felt the heat of Gerald's dark eyes on her back. She turned quickly, catching him staring. She returned his direct stare, neither willing to look away. The impasse ended once she returned to her chair.

Opening the book, she uncapped the pen and wrote the name *Barnett* and the date across the top. "How many people do you expect to invite?"

Crossing one leg elegantly over the opposite knee, Gerald leaned back against the cushioned softness of the comfortable chair for the first time. He had scaled the first hurdle. Katherine Langdon was willing to listen to him.

"Lisa claims she doesn't want any more than sixty people."

Katherine wrote the number 60. "What's the groom's family name?"

"I think she said it was deVilliers."

The wedding consultant's head came up quickly. "You *think*?"

"He lives in France. I've never met him," Gerald added by way of explaining why he couldn't confirm his future son-in-law's surname.

"If I'm going to coordinate your daughter's wedding, then I think I'd better talk to her."

"Does this mean you're going to do it?"

Katherine wanted to tell him no but knew she couldn't. If it hadn't been for Gerald Barnett approving her business loan she wouldn't be in this meticulously decorated sitting room discussing his daughter's upcoming nuptials with him. She'd still be in a small rental unit, sitting at a sewing machine, putting together pieces of fabric for wedding gowns. His signature had changed her world and life forever.

She nodded. "Yes, Gerald, I'll do it. But it's going to cost you."

"How much?"

Quoting an inflated figure, she waited for an expression of shock to cross Gerald's face. And she had to admit that the man wasn't handsome as much as he was attractive. His face was too lean, claimed too many sharp angles to be classified as handsome. Much to her surprise, he reached into the breast pocket of his expertly tailored suit jacket and withdrew a billfold. He unfolded a check, borrowed her pen, and filled in the amount.

Her shock was apparent when he extended the check to her. It was obvious that he'd written the check earlier. He'd been *that* confident that she would accept his offer.

She recovered quickly, taking the check and the pen from his outstretched fingers. She handed him a business card. "Have your daughter call me as soon as possible. I'd like to set up a meeting where we can discuss all of the details she'll need to put on a very elegant wedding."

Gerald took the card, a slight smile curving his strong,

masculine mouth. "Thank you." Standing, he moved closer to Katherine, offering his hand. She placed her palm on his outstretched fingers, the delicate warmth of her touch radiating up the length of his arm. His hand closed over hers as he tightened his strong, protective grip.

"Thank you," she said after he'd pulled her gently to her feet. Standing beside him in her bare feet made her aware of his towering height. She stood five-six, so she estimated that he stood an inch or two above the six-foot mark.

"It's been a pleasure meeting you again, Miss Langdon."

She flashed a dimpled smile. "Same here, Mr. Barnett."

He nodded. "I'm certain we'll get to see each other quite a few times before my daughter marries. There's no need to see me to the door. I'll let myself out."

Without giving her an opportunity to respond, Gerald turned on his heel and walked out of the sitting room, leaving Katherine staring at a pair of broad shoulders.

3

Katherine stood motionless, staring at the check in her hand and berating herself for accepting it. If it had been anyone other than Gerald Barnett, she would've rejected him or her without batting an eye. Even though she'd inflated the amount to discourage Gerald, it was apparent that he would pay any fee she charged just to have her coordinate his daughter's wedding. And it wasn't that she needed his money. Not now. What she needed was more time, time for Langdon Bridals, and a lot more time for herself. It had been months since she'd had two consecutive days to herself, time to visit family members and friends . . . time to share dinner or a movie with a man.

Her gaze narrowed when her thoughts strayed to men. She'd married at thirty-three, was divorced at thirty-nine, and in less than three months she would celebrate her fiftieth birthday. She'd had one serious liaison after her divorce, but that ended four years ago when Paul Shelton, a psychology professor, was offered a position as department head at a small, private Ohio college. He'd asked her to marry him, but she'd rejected his proposal. At that time she wasn't ready to commit to marrying again. What she hadn't realized until after Paul left was that she hadn't been willing to give up a very successful business enterprise to start over in another state.

She stared at the check, experiencing a modicum of guilt at the amount. It was three times what she usually charged for a small wedding. Shrugging her bared shoulders, she slipped the check between the pages of the book. Her clients paid her well for her expert services, and because Gerald Barnett wanted to solicit her unique skills and precious time, then he would pay dearly for it, she rationalized.

Walking over to the secretary, she placed the book on its smooth surface. Her mind was churning with ideas for Lisa Barnett's upcoming wedding. She loved coordinating the smaller, more intimate gatherings because she could add the special touches that usually weren't appropriate with larger weddings.

A slow smile softened her expression. Yes, she thought, Gerald Barnett would get what he'd paid for—and then some.

Lisa Barnett and her first cousin, Meredith, were buzzed into Langdon Bridals several minutes before ten o'clock. The elegant shop, located on the first floor of a two-story town house, was in the heart of downtown Savannah. Her father had given her Katherine Langdon's business card and told her to call the wedding consultant. She hadn't been able to contain her shriek of excitement when she literally jumped into his arms and kissed every inch of his face. He'd done it! He had convinced Ms. Langdon to coordinate her wedding. After she'd recovered her composure, she called Langdon Bridals and set up an appointment.

She smiled at the woman sitting behind an exquisite reproduction of a Louis XVI desk. The desk was the centerpiece of a space resembling a European salon in its mix of patterns, furniture, and accessories. The walls, covered with hand-

painted Oriental rice paper, added to the effect. A large bouquet of snow-white flowers in a crystal vase rested on an
antique drop-leaf table in a corner, while soft light from table
lamps cast a warm glow on varying shades of muted greens.
A trio of pale green, silk-covered love seats were angled along
a wall to form the impression of a continuous bank of seating.

"Good morning. I'm Lisa Barnett. I have an appointment
with Ms. Langdon for ten."

Rita Grady returned Lisa's smile. She'd recognized the
woman the moment she'd stepped through the door. Even
though they were the same age, the bank president's daughter's path had never crossed hers: Lisa had attended an ex-
clusive private girls' school while Rita had been enrolled in
Savannah's public schools system.

Katherine's assistant was a stunningly beautiful young
woman with flawless sable-brown skin, a delicate oval face,
shiny, straight black shoulder-length hair, and exotic features
that hinted of other bloodlines in addition to her African-
American ancestry.

"Ms. Langdon is expecting you. I'll let her know you're
here." Pressing a button on an intercom, she announced Lisa's
arrival in a quiet professional tone. With her practiced smile
in place, Rita gestured to her left. "Ms. Langdon's office is
down the hall, the first door on the right."

Lisa nodded. "Thank you." She turned in the direction the
receptionist had indicated, Meredith Barnett two steps behind
her; seconds before they entered Katherine Langdon's office,
they held hands briefly for emotional support.

Katherine rose to her feet, her gaze on the two young
women. They were on time, which was a good sign. "Please
come in and sit down, ladies. We have a lot to discuss, and
very little time in which to plan everything."

Lisa and Meredith walked into the office and sat down on
two chairs facing a table that doubled as a desk. The table
held a thick book with samples of invitations, another book
with swatches of fabric, and a third with samples of menus.

Katherine stared at the taller woman. Her resemblance to
Gerald was startling, even though her features were softer and

distinctly more feminine, she'd inherited his coloring and deep-set dark eyes. There was no doubt she would make a beautiful bride.

She opened her mouth to begin her orientation, but was preempted when Lisa said, "I'd like to thank you for accepting me as your client. I'm aware that twelve weeks is hardly enough time to plan for a wedding, but the moment Sebastien proposed to me I knew I wanted to be a Langdon bride. This is Meredith Barnett. She's my cousin and will be my maid of honor—and my only attendant."

An expression of complete surprise froze Katherine's features. She didn't know why, but she'd thought the other woman was Gerald's daughter. Recovering quickly, she picked up a pen and opened a book with "Barnett–deVilliers—August 28" written across the top of the page.

Lisa Barnett looked nothing like her father, she thought, so it was apparent that she must resemble her mother. Gerald's daughter claimed a flawless golden complexion and large, expressive, clear brown eyes. Her coloring was the perfect foil for her light brown, golden-streaked shoulder-length hair.

"You're right," Katherine said. "Twelve weeks isn't a lot of time, but if we plan carefully, then you can have everything you want. You've selected Saturday, August 28, but I have to tell you that I have another wedding for that afternoon. Which means that you'll have to schedule an evening ceremony and reception."

Leaning forward on her chair, Lisa gave Katherine an incredulous look. "A nighttime wedding?"

"It can be very elegant. A candlelight service at your church at 8:00 P.M. can set the stage. And because it's too late to book a room at a banquet hall or restaurant, I'm going to suggest a reception on the lawn of your father's house under the stars."

Lisa's jaw dropped. "What if it rains?"

"The alternative is having it indoors. You're only inviting sixty guests, so space should not prove an insurmountable problem."

Katherine had driven past the property where Gerald Barnett lived a few times, and estimated that the expansive two-story, plantation-style structure could easily accommodate twice that number.

"I like the idea of having an outdoor reception," Meredith said, speaking for the first time.

Lisa frowned at her cousin. "You do?"

Meredith gave her a challenging look, raising her eyebrows. "Yes, I do."

"What about mosquitoes?" Lisa continued, her voice rising slightly.

"Stop it, Lisa," Meredith chided softly. "You want Ms. Langdon to plan your wedding, so you have to stop second-guessing her. She knows what to do."

Katherine let out an inaudible sigh of relief. Lacing her fingers together, she tilted her head, giving the younger women a narrowed look. "Well, Mes. Barnetts, do you want a wedding?"

"Yes," the cousins answered in unison.

Running her fingers through her hair, which was parted off center, Katherine tucked several strands behind her left ear. She opened the book of sample invitations. "First, you'll have to select your invitation and response cards. And I also need to know if you want Langdon Bridals to select your gown and your attendant's."

"I want you to handle *everything*," Lisa said.

Katherine mentally estimated how long it would take for her dressmaker to sew two gowns. She made a notation on the page.

"Before you decide on the fabric and the styles for the dresses, and the menu selections, I need to know if you want a theme that also includes the French culture."

Lisa bit down on her lower lip for several seconds. Then the intelligent clear orbs crinkled in a smile. "I think the menu should reflect both cultures."

Katherine raised her delicately arching eyebrows. "Just the menu?"

"That's enough," Lisa said with a finality that indicated she had made her decision.

Katherine wanted to tell Lisa that she was making a mistake, but held her tongue. She was being paid to give the bride what she wanted, and it was apparent Lisa Barnett wanted a traditional American wedding.

The three women spent the next four hours selecting an invitation, its inscription, and the accompanying response card. They thumbed through the book with sketches and photographs of wedding gowns, selecting a bride and an attendant's dress, then finally settled on a menu, which included several French dishes.

The session ended when Katherine gave Lisa and Meredith each a printed checklist. Her expression and tone sobered noticeably. "I want you to pay close attention to the dates on this list. Everything, and I mean everything, must be completed by these dates. You *must* go for your fittings as scheduled, or don't expect to wear your dresses on August twenty-eighth. You must also make an appointment with the hair and makeup consultants two weeks before the wedding ceremony to make certain they know what hair and skin types you have."

She turned her complete attention to Lisa. "As soon as you leave here, contact your minister. That is, if you decide you want a religious ceremony. Have your father call me so that I can schedule a time to come see his house. I also want you to call my assistant every Wednesday with an update. Rita will not call you unless there is a change in the schedule I've outlined for you. Do you have any questions?"

"No." Again, the Barnett women replied in unison.

Katherine offered a comforting smile. "Well, ladies, we end our first session. Feel free to contact Rita if you encounter a problem. If it's something she can't handle, then I'll step in. But I also want you to understand that your wedding is one of many that I'm coordinating. I'll try to make myself available, but if I don't get back to you right away it doesn't mean I'm ignoring you."

Lisa rose to her feet, Meredith following suit, and extended her hand. "I understand. Thank you again."

Taking the proffered hand, Katherine nodded. "Thank you for choosing Langdon Bridals for your wedding."

Waiting until the women walked out of her office, she slumped against the cushioned back of her chair. Closing her eyes, she took a deep breath. Her first session with Lisa Barnett had taken four hours, more than it usually took with a prospective bride, her mother, and attendants. She prayed silently that it was not an indicator that this bride-to-be would present a problem—a problem she could not afford, given her time frame.

The day after Lisa Barnett walked into Langdon Bridals, Katherine awoke to what was to become "the day from hell." An oppressive humidity and a lightly falling mist descended on Savannah like a damp shroud. She gave up with applying a light cover of makeup to her moist face, opting instead for a shimmering lip gloss. She swept her hair up and secured it in an elastic band. An ice-blue linen blouse with a pair of matching slacks was returned to the closet in exchange for a cap-sleeve chocolate-brown shift in the same fabric; low-heeled brown pumps replaced a pair of bone-colored mules.

Forgoing her usual cup of herbal tea, fruit, and slice of wheat toast, she decided leave her house earlier than usual and order breakfast after she reached her office. Agreeing to coordinate the Barnett–deVilliers wedding had forced her to rearrange her already tight schedule. She pulled an umbrella from a tall wicker basket positioned in a corner of the entryway and walked the short distance from her town house to her office.

Rita tapped on the door to Katherine's office to get her attention. "I'm going to call it a day, unless you have something else for me to do."

Katherine glanced up from the purchase order from one of her favorite caterers, looked at the clock on the table, then

smiled at her competent assistant. It was after six o'clock—
more than an hour past Rita's quitting time.

"There's nothing that can't wait until tomorrow. Thanks
for staying and helping me out."

The telephone had rung steadily all day with calls from
frantic brides and their anxious mothers. One mother sobbed
into the receiver that her daughter had gone off her diet and
couldn't fit into her wedding gown. The wedding was scheduled for two weeks away. Rita managed to calm the woman
down long enough to transfer the call to Katherine, who told
her to bring the gown to the dressmaker, who had been instructed by Langdon Bridals to always leave an ample seam
for just such predicaments. Another call resulted in a change
in the menu when the groom's father was diagnosed with high
blood sugar.

After a while Katherine instructed Rita to activate the
voice mail and screen the calls. All were eventually returned,
in order of importance, and it became one of those rare occasions when both women spent the majority of their day on
the telephone.

Rita waved her hand. "Think nothing of it. Remember that
Mr. Barnett will be here between six-thirty and seven."

Katherine nodded. "Thank you for reminding me. Enjoy
your evening."

"You, too."

Gerald Barnett's secretary had called earlier with a message that he had flown up to Atlanta for a meeting, but was
expected to return to Savannah on an afternoon flight. He was
to meet her at Langdon Bridals before taking her to his home
for a survey of the property.

Turning her attention back to the invoice, Katherine ticked
off an item with a red pencil. The caterer had listed black
truffle instead of chocolate truffle. Her client would be more
than surprised to find fungi on her daughter's bridal shower
dessert tray instead of small balls of chocolate rolled in pow-
dered cocoa and nuts. It took another fifteen minutes of careful perusal of the rest of the menu before she determined it

was correct. She placed a call to the caterer, informing them of their error.

Ten minutes later she stood in the rest room adjoining her office, staring at her reflection in the mirror over the basin. The stress of the day was clearly visible. The lines framing her mouth and the puffiness under her eyes indicated fatigue. She had worked all day without stopping to eat. She hadn't ordered breakfast, and when Rita called for a lunch delivery she hadn't stopped long enough to enjoy the Caesar salad. What she had done was drink several cups of coffee and half a gallon of distilled water.

After splashing water on her face, she patted it dry with a fluffy terry-cloth towel, and then applied a light cover of moisturizer from the jar on a shelf near the basin. The shelf held a profusion of creams and lotions, along with her favorite fragrance. The bathroom was constructed with a shower stall, commode, and bidet, which Katherine had insisted upon when the architect drew up the plans for the space that would house Langdon Bridals. She brushed her hair, securing it in the elastic band, hoping to survey the Barnett property quickly. Before returning home she planned to stop at one of her favorite seafood restaurants along Factor's Walk and enjoy a leisurely dinner.

4

Gerald offered his driver a weary smile before ducking his head and slipping onto the leather seat at the rear of the limousine. The door closed behind him with a solid thud.

His day had not gone well. His flight to Atlanta had been delayed earlier that morning because of heavy fog, which put him ninety minutes behind schedule. The board members of a small, failing savings and loan association had waited for him before they began the meeting, but had in their own way chastised him for something that was beyond his control—the weather.

They'd made him pay by openly rejecting his offer to

merge Barnett Savings and Loan Company with their bank. Most had viewed his proposal as a takeover rather than a merger. Gerald had spent most of the time trying to convince them that it would not be a takeover. He'd proposed a merger of the boards, with a Barnett member determining the majority, and a name change from Southern Trust to Barnett Southern Trust. They refused to change their position—not even when he offered to lend them the thirty million dollars they needed to stay afloat.

Before adjourning the meeting, he rose to his feet, nodded politely, and said, "Gentlemen. You know where to reach me if you change your minds." He'd made a silent promise that he would not return to Atlanta for another meeting with them. If they changed their minds, then they would have to come to Savannah. And if they *did* decide to have Barnett Savings and Loan Company bail them out, then the stakes would be a lot higher.

Glancing at the gold watch on his left wrist, Gerald grimaced. It was almost five o'clock. Airport delays had put him two hours behind schedule. He would have just enough time to shower and change clothes before he met with Katherine Langdon. Recalling her delicate beauty elicited a smile from him—his first natural smile of the day.

The doorbell at Langdon Bridals rang at six forty-five. Katherine's pulse quickened once she realized she would come face-to-face with Gerald again. She didn't know what it was, but there was something about the banker that intrigued her. He'd become one of Savannah's most eligible African-American bachelors and was known to date several women at the same time, yet appeared unwilling to commit to any of them.

She made her way down the carpeted hallway to the reception area. Gerald's face showed clearly on a closed-circuit monitor on Rita's desk. Reaching for a button under the desk, she pressed it, disengaging the lock on the front door.

He pushed open the door and walked in. He did not resemble the man who'd come to her home the day before.

Gone was the tailored business suit; in its place was a sky-blue golf shirt with a contrasting navy blue collar and matching bands on the sleeves. Tailored navy blue linen slacks and a pair of highly polished black loafers completed his winning casual attire. Seeing him without a jacket made her aware that despite his broad shoulders Gerald was very slim. There wasn't an ounce of excess flesh on his tall frame.

His eyes crinkled in a beguiling smile. "I hope I haven't kept you waiting."

Katherine returned his smile, enchanting him with the dimple in her right cheek. "Not at all," she replied truthfully.

Even though Rita's day usually ended at five, hers sometimes continued for several more hours. And it was only after the office closed for the day and the telephone stopped ringing that she was able to accomplish most of her tasks. The only exception was when she scheduled evening appointments for those who were unable to come during regular daytime business hours.

Glancing around the reception area, Gerald noted the carefully chosen furnishings. Langdon Bridals was as meticulously decorated as its owner's private residence. His gaze shifted, and he stared at Katherine with a gleam of interest in his eyes, enthralled at what he saw. Her bare face radiated a healthy glow that enhanced her understated beauty.

Why hadn't he noticed that before? Why, he asked himself, hadn't he noticed *everything* about Katherine Langdon? But that would change now that she was coordinating his daughter's wedding. Interacting closely with Katherine would give him the opportunity to become familiar with her.

Katherine was strangely flattered by what appeared to be Gerald's interest in her, but carefully schooled her expression not to reveal her own curiosity.

"Give me a minute and I'll be right with you." Her voice was soft, controlled.

He nodded, watching as she turned and made her way down a hallway and disappeared into a room. He was still standing in the same position when she returned, carrying a leather case. He held out his hand, and wasn't disappointed when she gave him the case. He waited while she pushed several buttons on a panel on the wall near the front door, activating a sophisticated security system. He preceded her as she closed the door; it locked automatically.

He startled her when he reached for her hand, threading his fingers through hers. "I'm parked around the corner."

Katherine couldn't conceal the shiver of excitement that raced through her as he held her hand in his strong, protective grasp. The rain had stopped, but the cloying smell of damp earth, flowers, and the haunting scent of Gerald's aftershave lingered in her sensitive nostrils. At that moment everything about him seeped into her, making her aware that the tall man walking alongside her had touched a part of her that she'd withheld from every man except one—her ex-husband. Gerald Barnett looked nothing like the only man she'd loved unselfishly. There was no physical resemblance, yet both claimed a masculine sensuality that she found hard to resist. A sensuality that silently announced that she was its feminine complement.

Gerald rounded the corner, walked another twenty feet, and stopped next to a black, late-model Mercedes-Benz sedan. He released Katherine's hand, then reached into a pocket. He disarmed the alarm and unlocked the doors with a press of a button on a remote device. Leaning over, he opened the passenger-side door. Waiting until she was seated and belted in, he closed her door, and opened the rear one to place her case on the seat behind her. Circling the car, he took his own seat behind the wheel. The warmth of the automobile's interior intensified the delicate subtle fragrance of her perfume.

Slipping the key into the ignition, he went completely still. The scent of her perfume reminded him of a woman from his past—a woman he thought he'd forgotten. He had given the perfume to a woman who at one time he'd loved more than anything. Lisa's mother.

Starting up the Mercedes, he shifted into gear, and pulled away from the curb in a smooth, continuous motion. A muscle in his jaw twitched as he concentrated on the road in front of him. It wasn't until he maneuvered around a double-parked sport-utility vehicle that he realized that not only did Katherine Langdon smell like Elaine, but that she also reminded him of her.

"How is Lisa coping with the list that I gave her?" Katherine asked after a comfortable silence.

Gerald chanced a quick glance at his passenger before returning his attention to the road in front of him. "She's doing quite well, thanks to Meredith. Together they've finalized the guest list, sent off the wedding announcement to all the local newspapers, and made arrangements with Reverend Dixon for an eight o'clock ceremony."

Katherine nodded. "That's good. They're scheduled to meet with the dressmaker tomorrow morning."

"How were you able to pull everything together so quickly?"

"I've created an inflexible timetable. If I have to make allowances, then it's only for a forty-eight-hour period. If I go into a third day it's certain to spell disaster. It also helps that I've developed a very efficient partnership with several caterers, dressmakers, printers, and photographers."

"You run your business like a drill sergeant."

Katherine raised her eyebrows, giving him a long, penetrating look. "Is it not the same with your bank?"

"There are laws that govern the banking industry."

"And I've set up my own set of laws for Langdon Bridals. It's not vanity that permits me to say that I'm the best in Savannah. Why else would you have sought me out, Gerald?"

He laughed, the low, rumbling sound bubbling up from his chest. "You're right about that, Katherine. And if you weren't the best I never would've agreed to pay you that outrageous sum you quoted."

A wave of heat flooded her cheeks. He knew she had overcharged him. "You didn't have to pay it."

He grunted. "And not permit my daughter to be a Langdon bride? I don't think so, Ms. Langdon."

It was Katherine's turn to laugh, the sultry sound floating over Gerald like silk. He realized that she had a wonderful voice—soft and caressing.

"You paid it because you've spoiled your daughter."

Gerald nodded in agreement. "You're right about that. I would've gladly paid ten times that amount to make certain that Lisa gets her wish."

Katherine felt as if Gerald had chastised her. She had no right to judge him as a father. There was no doubt Lisa Barnett was used to getting her way, and if it hadn't been for Meredith's intervention, their initial consultation would've become even more difficult.

"I don't mean to sound ungrateful."

"There's no need to apologize. It's not Lisa's fault that I've been an overindulgent father."

"If I had a daughter I'd probably want the same." There was a wistful tone in Katherine's voice.

Gerald glanced at her again. "You never had any children?"

She looked out the side window, staring at the occupants of passing automobiles. "No," she said after a prolonged silence.

What she didn't say, couldn't say to Gerald, was that she and her ex-husband hadn't had any children because two years into their marriage he was too intoxicated to do more than pass out in bed. The few times she managed to get him into bed before he emptied his nightly bottle of scotch proved futile. After awhile she gave up altogether.

Ray came to her a year after they were divorced, clean and sober for the first time in years. He'd confessed that he'd been too frightened of the notion of becoming a father, because he believed he'd inherited his father's proclivity for physically abusing children. His confession had stunned her, and after he'd left her apartment she cried bitterly for what they could've had and shared. His disclosure changed her because she threw all of her energies into starting up her own business. It had taken years of hard work and sacrifice, but in the end it had paid off.

"Did you ever want any?" Gerald asked.

"Yes."

"It's not too late, Katherine."

Her head came around and she stared at him, her expression saying, *You must have lost your mind.* "Surely you jest, Gerald. I'm going to turn fifty in a few months."

"I'm not talking about you giving birth. Have you ever thought about adopting an older child?"

"No."

"I did," he admitted. "It was after Lisa left home to attend college. I suppose I was going through the empty-nest syndrome at the time."

"And why didn't you?" she asked.

"I would if I'd been married. Children, especially those who have been in foster care for a long time, need two parents for stability."

"It still isn't too late."

Gerald shook his head. "Ten years ago I would've agreed with you. At fifty-four I'm ready to bounce a grandchild on my knee, not chauffeur my son or daughter to a soccer or Little League baseball game."

"If you decide to marry, I'll give you a big discount," she said glibly.

"How much of a discount?"

"Twenty percent."

"Make it twenty-five and you have a deal," he countered with a wide grin.

She flashed her own smile. "Deal."

The moment Gerald assisted Katherine from his car she was overwhelmed by the size and beauty of the place he called home. The design was completely Southern in tradition: a formal façade symmetrically graced with columns, balconied windows, dormers, dentils, and cupolas. It was a modern structure with an old-house look; a carriage house—one of two two-car garages—was connected by a porte cochere. Looking around, she could visualize tents set up for dining and dancing.

Holding her hand gently within his protective grasp, Gerald led her around the house to an exquisite garden. A knowing smile softened his mouth as he watched her eyes widen in surprise. The garden had become a source of pride for him. Setting aside more than four acres, he'd contracted with a landscape architect for beds of aromatic herbs, annuals, perennials, an orchard of fruit trees, two small ponds, and a waterfall.

"Come," he said in a mysterious tone.

Towering oak trees, swathed in Spanish moss, stood like sentinels along the path as they ventured farther into a green jungle of wildflowers growing in abundant abandonment.

Katherine followed his lead, down solid slate steps that reminded her of the cantilevered balconies of Frank Lloyd Wright's masterpiece home, Fallingwater.

A slight gasp escaped her when she saw the man-made waterfall cascading over large rocks. Variegated ivy trailing over the rocks added to the spectacular sight. The waning sunlight and encroaching evening shadows had turned the landscape into a fairy-tale setting.

"It's unbelievable." Her voice was a whisper.

Gerald smiled at her awed expression. "Let me show you something that is truly unbelievable. The architect added something that wasn't in the original design as a bonus."

They retraced their steps, her shoulder brushing against his arm, and walked past the orchard of peach, pear, and cherry trees. An arch covered with blooming Cherokee roses led to a slate path and beyond to a freestanding pergola supported by four massive marble columns covered in English ivory, tiny white roses, and grapevines. A white wrought-iron table with four chairs sat under the shadowy profusion of leaves and flowers. Several stone benches were placed near a matching outdoor grill.

Katherine concluded it was the perfect place to either begin or end a day.

"Will it do?" Gerald's warm breath swept over her ear.

Her gaze shifted from the pergola to his impassive expression. "It's perfect. I think the reception should be held right here."

"But you haven't seen the inside of the house."

She wanted to say that she didn't need to see the house's

interior. The grounds were magnificent. Strategically placed palm trees and acres of rolling manicured lawn with the lush garden would provide the perfect setting for a fairy-tale wedding reception.

"Come with me, Katherine," he said in a quiet voice, extending his hand and holding her gaze with his purposeful one.

Katherine studied his face, feature by feature. There was an open invitation in his dark eyes. There was also a silent challenge she was unable to resist—only because she didn't want to.

5

Katherine and Gerald walked into the house through a grand foyer framed by massive columns, which led into a living room that was lightly furnished to keep it open and airy. An oak-plank floor complemented a custom chenille sofa and what she recognized as a Nancy Corzine wooden armchair. Silk draperies, tied back to expose the view from gracefully bowed windows and topped with transoms, provided a vintage look.

"If it rains, then everyone can come in here," Gerald said.

He led her into an area he always referred to as his "gathering room." This space adjoined the bathing pavilion with the indoor Olympic-size swimming pool. The postless windows afforded the room a sense of unending space; disappearing windows brought the outdoors inside whenever two twelve-foot-wide sliders were pocketed back into the walls.

Katherine still hadn't recovered from the unique design of the custom-built house when she found herself in the middle of an ultra-modern kitchen painted in vibrant aqua tones that featured a stove hood that was faux-finished for an aged copper look. The room's focal points were its marble backsplash and custom-finished maple cabinets. A slight smile curved her mouth. The caterers would love working and serving from Gerald's kitchen.

"It's perfect," she said, repeating what she'd said earlier when viewing the outside of the house. "Inside and out."

Gerald nodded. "I believe it'll do. Of course, Lisa would prefer having her reception at a banquet hall."

"That's because she grew up here and probably doesn't see its exquisite beauty the way an outsider would."

"Would you like a tour of the other rooms?"

Katherine glanced at her watch. It was almost eight and her hunger pangs were intensifying with each passing minute. "Perhaps another time."

"Have you had dinner?" Gerald didn't want to take her back home—not yet.

"No, I haven't. But—"

"Please have dinner with me," he said quickly, interrupting her. "I'm certain I can throw something together in under an hour."

She shook her head. "Thank you for offering, but maybe another time."

She'd wanted to accept his offer to share dinner, but didn't because of her own uneasiness. There was something about Gerald that drew her to him, and there was something else that told her that becoming involved with a client's father was not good business practice. And it wasn't the first time that a bride's or groom's male family member had expressed an interest in her. She had successfully parried their advances with subtle hints that she made it a practice not to mix business with her private life; however, Gerald was the first man who had interested her in a long time.

She had also forgotten how long it had been since she'd permitted herself to share a man's bed. There hadn't been anyone since Paul Shelton. She counted quickly to herself. It had been almost four years since she'd enjoyed the intimacy that came from sleeping with a man. Her gaze swept over Gerald's solemn expression, wondering if he was aware of her erotic thoughts.

He angled his head. "Monday?"

"Monday," she repeated, confusion clearly mirrored in her gaze.

"Aren't you off on Mondays?"

Realization dawned. He wanted her to share dinner with him on Monday. "Yes, I am."

"Would you, Katherine?"

"Would I what?" she asked.

"Share dinner with me." The four words were forced from between Gerald's teeth. It was obvious that Katherine wasn't going to make it easy for him.

She recalled the number of women she'd seen Gerald with at various restaurants over the years, and suddenly she didn't want to be added to the mounting list that he squired around the city.

"It will give us the opportunity to discuss Lisa's wedding plans," he added smoothly.

A slight smile parted her lips. "You're right." She decided to accept his offer, but it would be on her terms. "What time do you want me to meet you here?"

His eyebrows lifted. "Here?"

"Yes. You said you'd cook for me."

Gerald wanted to take Katherine to one of his favorite restaurants outside the city limits. He wanted to sit, eat, drink, and feast on her delicate beauty. And he wanted to uncover whether he was drawn to her because she reminded him of Elaine: What he feared most was that after more than thirty years he might still be in love with his ex-wife.

A slow smile softened the sharp angles in his lean face. "What would you like for me to prepare for you?"

Katherine gave him a saucy look. "Surprise me."

His smile faded. "You really like surprises?"

"Yes, I do."

Throwing back his head, Gerald laughed. "I like you, Katherine." He reached for her hand.

She felt a warm glow flow through her with his touch and compliment. "Thank you, Gerald. I think I'm beginning to like you, too."

"Are you sure you don't want a tour?" he asked, stalling for more time.

"Monday," she reminded him.

"Monday," he repeated.

Tightening his grip on her slender fingers, he escorted her out of the house and to his car. What he didn't realize as he drove her back to downtown Savannah was that he had already begun counting the days until he would see her again.

Katherine overslept for the first time in years. It was the ringing of the telephone that woke her half an hour past noon. Reaching for the receiver on the bedside table, she mumbled a garbled greeting.

"Hello," came a cheery male voice.

She rolled over on her back, all vestiges of sleep disappearing. "Good morning, Gerald."

"I'm sorry to disappoint you, but it's already the afternoon."

Katherine looked at the clock beside the telephone. It was twelve thirty-five. She pushed herself into a sitting position. "Where has the day gone?" she mumbled. Things were probably going smoothly at the office for Rita because she hadn't called her.

"The day is waiting for us," Gerald said. "I'm calling to ask you what you'd like to eat."

A sensual smile curved her mouth. "I thought you were going to surprise me."

"What if I prepare a seafood appetizer, and filet mignon and steamed vegetables as the main course?"

"That sounds wonderful. I'll bring dessert."

"That won't be necessary. I have dessert."

"Will it keep?"

"Yes. Why?"

"We can eat it another time." She'd ordered a sinfully decadent praline dessert from a renowned Savannah pastry chef to finish the meal.

Gerald's sensual laugh came through the wire. "Will there be another time for *us*?"

"Of course, Gerald. Remember, tonight is a business meeting."

There was a pregnant silence before he spoke again.

"You're right. What time do you want me to pick you up?"

"There's no need to pick me up. I'll drive myself."

"My daddy taught me that a gentleman always picks up and drops off his date."

Katherine bit down on her lower lip to keep from laughing aloud. "This not a date, Gerald," she reminded him.

"If you say so," he countered glibly. "Do you swim?"

"Yes, I do. Why?"

"Why don't you come over early and take advantage of the pool?"

"What time will we sit down to dinner?"

"Seven."

"Is five too early to come to swim?"

"You can come now."

A slight frown creased her forehead. "Where are you, Gerald?"

"I'm home."

"Did you play hooky?"

"I damn sure did," he admitted, laughing softly. "I happen to have a very easy boss."

She laughed. "Then we have something in common because I also have a wonderful boss."

"I'd say you're quite lucky, Katherine."

"So are you, Gerald."

"Come over whenever you want."

"I'll see you later."

"I'll be waiting for you."

Katherine hung up, wrapped in a cocoon of anticipation. A week had sped by quickly, each day dawning and ending with an increasing eagerness that she would see Gerald Barnett again. It had taken only six days for her to reach the conclusion that she was flattered by his interest. She wanted him to find her attractive—attractive enough to continue to see her even after Lisa's wedding.

What she had to remind herself was that she didn't want things to move too quickly. Not the way it had been with Ray. She and Raymond Proctor had fallen in love at first sight and married a month later. All of the requisites for dating and courtship were forgotten as she ignored her brother's warning to wait to get to know the talented musician better. Even after she'd lived with Raymond she was never given the opportunity to know her husband that well. Only after he'd revealed the trauma of his turbulent childhood did she finally understand why he'd sought to drown his anguish in alcohol.

No, she told herself as she swung her legs over the side of the bed. It would be different with Gerald. Not only was she older, but she also had had much more experience with the opposite sex.

6

Gerald opened the door to a low-slung, two-seater convertible sports car, waiting until his daughter was seated and belted in before he closed the door. Bending, he kissed her forehead. "Drive carefully, Princess."

She smiled at him through the lenses of her sunglasses. "I will, Daddy. I'll call you later."

Nodding, he moved away from the racy automobile as she turned the key in the ignition and backed out of the driveway. He'd awakened that morning feeling more alive than he'd been in years. Knowing that he was going to see Katherine later in the afternoon had him feeling like a teenage boy about to embark on his first date. First there were butterflies in his stomach, then the nervous anxiety that what he'd planned to prepare for dinner would turn out to be a total disaster. After he'd swum more than half a dozen laps across the pool he found his anxiousness waning; in its place was the usual calm that made him the confident man who had become one of Savannah's most prominent residents and businessmen.

His gaze narrowed as he watched Lisa drive away. She slowed, stopping and coming abreast a kiwi-green updated Volkswagen beetle. He saw her wave to the driver before accelerating. A slow smile parted his lips as the green car came closer and he recognized the driver as Katherine. If he'd been allowed three guesses as to what model car she drove, he would've failed miserably. She seemed more like the BMW, Lexus, or even the Mercedes-Benz type. Her choice of automobile revealed a bit more about Katherine—she wasn't as staid as he had first perceived her. She drove up beside him, stopped, and put the Volkswagen in park.

Smiling, he leaned into the open window. "Turn it off. I'll have someone garage it for you." He opened the door, extending his hand.

Katherine placed her fingers on his outstretched palm, permitting him to pull her gently to her feet. Tilting her chin, she smiled at him. "Thank you."

Moving closer, the heat from his body competing with the sun, Gerald pressed his lips to her cheek. "Thank you for coming."

Katherine pulled her hand from his loose grip. He was too close, too virile, and the pressure of his mustache felt strange against her flesh. She thought not seeing Gerald for four days would diminish his effect on her, but she was mistaken. She'd tried rationalizing it was because he was who he was that she felt apprehensive. After all, he was president of the bank where she had her personal and business accounts. He had knowledge of every check she wrote and how much her deposits totaled on any given day. With the stroke of a computer key he could pull up everything about her private life. And she hadn't wanted to be that vulnerable. She felt naked, exposed, and the last man who'd seen her that way was Ray. She'd come to him on her knees, begging him to give her a child. His response was a drunken leer, then laughter. The laugh was so maniacal that she hadn't been able to move to escape the frightening sound. When she forced herself to stand, she walked out of their apartment and checked into a motel. She spent two days in the small room without eating or drinking. When she finally emerged she had lost five pounds and was almost dehydrated. She returned home a different woman, informing Raymond that she was ending their marriage, and a week later he was gone.

After Gerald's call earlier that morning, she'd spent almost forty minutes trying on various swimsuits, modeling each one in front of a full-length mirror. The first one was cut too high on the hip, the second revealed too much cleavage, while the third one was just too tight. She finally settled on one with a halter top and a rounded neckline that flattered her trim body. She had to remind herself that Gerald had invited her to his home to share dinner and his pool, not his bed.

Reaching behind the driver's seat, Katherine picked up a small Styrofoam box from the floor and a sail bag off the rear seat. "The dessert should be refrigerated before it melts."

Gerald took the box from her. "What is it?"

"Praline parfaits."

He raised his eyebrows. "From Henri Fouche?"

She nodded. "The one and only. I've arranged for him to prepare the desserts for Lisa's reception." The exquisitely prepared sweet concoction had become all the rage in Savannah.

"You're an incredible woman, Katherine, because my brother asked Monsieur Fouche to prepare desserts for my father and stepmother's anniversary dinner last year and he turned him down flat, saying that his clients placed their orders with him six months in advance. I had to practically sit on Lenny to keep him from punching out the supercilious little twit. Of course *we* all remember when he was Henry Franklin before he went to Paris to become a pastry chef."

Katherine was aware that Henri was overly impressed with his own artistic creativity; however, the fact remained that he was the best pastry chef in Savannah, if not the state of Georgia.

"I've maintained a very fragile professional relationship with Monsieur Fouche."

"You're probably the only one who does get along with him."

His assumption was correct. Since she'd started up Langdon Bridals she'd made it a practice to develop a professional relationship with every vendor—and that meant having to concede wherever possible to please her clients.

Gerald led the way to his home, she falling in step beside him while giving him a sidelong glance. He was dressed in a stark white T-shirt, faded jeans, and white deck shoes. It

was the second time she'd seen him in casual clothes, and
she decided she liked him better that way. The business suit
made him appear too sedate and sober.

Minutes later they entered the expansive kitchen. Katherine left her sail bag on a bar stool, while Gerald put her
dessert in the refrigerator. She watched his fluid motions as
he turned and closed the distance between them. There was
something so direct and intense in his gaze that she found
herself holding her breath. He stopped only inches from her,
his gaze moving slowly over her face.

Gerald stared at Katherine, committing everything about
her to his memory. He'd spent the past few days trying to
remember the exact color of her eyes, the shape of her mouth,
the gold undertones in her flawless complexion, and the
glossy sheen of her salt-and-pepper hair. The only thing he
had memorized was her smile and the enchanting dimple in
her right cheek.

"Would you like to take the tour now, or swim?"

"I'd prefer seeing the house first." Katherine suspected
he'd invited her to his home under the guise that it would be
a business meeting, and she wanted to dispense with that first.

Grasping her fingers, he led her up the winding staircase
to the second story. She followed Gerald in and out of rooms
that were exquisitely decorated, each one claiming its own
personality. His library was a handsome retreat with a cof-
fered ceiling, applied wall moldings and aged-looking,
French-doored cabinets. The custom-made desk had a
hand-tooled leather top and bamboo legs. Table lamps with
pewter bases and linen shades offset the other furnishings in
a purely masculine room.

The upper level contained four bedrooms, each with adjoining baths; however, it was the master bath that caught her
by complete surprise. Mirrors of polished stainless steel
mounted on jade-green marble countertops enclosed the entire
space, while mitered windows came down to the countertops
without interrupting the spectacular view of the garden.

She jumped slightly when Gerald moved behind her, his
warm breath feathering over the back of her neck. Closing

her eyes, she savored the sensual smell of his cologne.

"Gerald?" She didn't recognize her own voice.

"Yes, Katherine?"

She took a deep breath to slow down her runaway pulse. "You're too close."

He moved even closer, the solid muscles in his chest pressing against her back. "I like being close to you," he said in a whisper. "I like looking at you, and I like smelling you. It's been a long time since I've been with a woman who's worn that perfume. A very, very long time."

She closed her eyes. "How long, Gerald?"

He placed his hands on her shoulders, his fingers caressing the delicate bones of her clavicle under her blouse. "Not since Lisa was a baby."

She wavered, trying to comprehend what he'd just told her. He was attracted to her because she reminded him of another woman. And she knew that woman was his daughter's mother. Her fingers curled into tight fists.

"Why did you really invite me to your home, Gerald?"

Tightening his grip on her shoulders, he turned her around to face him. His expression was so severe he could've been carved out of granite. "I invited you for two reasons. One is to discuss my daughter's wedding plans, and the other is to uncover why I find myself so attracted to you."

Katherine was taken aback at his candor, and it was several seconds before she could bring herself to respond. "Do I remind you of your ex-wife?"

Gerald stared at Katherine as if he were photographing her with his eyes. She did not physically resemble Elaine, yet both women claimed the same sensual magnetism that drew him in—and he was helpless to resist.

Shaking his head, he said, "No. You look nothing alike. The only thing you share is that you're wearing the same perfume she wore."

"Had you given her the perfume?"

Lowering his head, he pressed his lips to her forehead. "Yes."

Unconsciously she wound her arms around his trim waist

while burying her face against his solid chest. "What happened, Gerald?"

Closing his eyes, he swallowed to relieve the dryness in his throat. He'd made it a practice never to discuss his ex-wife with any woman. Everyone he had become involved with since his divorce had asked why he was raising his daughter as a single father, and he always said that he didn't want to talk about it.

He didn't know why, but after so many years, he wanted to talk about it now.

"She just walked away."

Pulling back, Katherine stared at him. Even though Gerald had closed his eyes she knew they were filled with pain. His words were filled with pain.

"Why?" Her voice was low and comforting.

He opened his eyes, staring at her—unblinking. "She couldn't deal with being a mother. She said she loved being married, but she didn't want children. Lisa wasn't quite two when our divorce was finalized. After that I never saw or heard from her again."

Vertical lines appeared between Katherine's clear brown eyes. "Didn't she tell you she didn't want children before you were married?"

He shook his head. "No. But if she had told me I probably wouldn't have married her. I always wanted a child—children."

It was Katherine's turn to close her eyes. She inhaled deeply, filling her nostrils with the natural scent of Gerald's body mixing with the subtle fragrance of his cologne.

"It's as if we married the wrong partners. Your ex didn't want children and neither did mine."

Gerald froze, nothing moving. Not even his eyes. "I thought you couldn't have children."

She offered him a sad smile. "It had nothing to do with my not being able to conceive." Slowly, methodically, she told him about Ray, his alcoholism, and his fear of fathering a child.

Gathering her closer, Gerald rocked her from side to side.

"I'm sorry, darling," he crooned against her ear. "I'm so sorry," he repeated.

Katherine was successful in stemming the flow of tears welling in her eyes. She didn't want to cry—she had done enough of that to last her two lifetimes. It was her past and with every sunrise she looked to her future.

Pushing gently against his chest, she pulled back and smiled through the moisture turning her eyes into large pools of sparkling sherry. "I think I'm ready to swim a couple of laps now."

It wasn't until nearly an hour later, when Katherine stood under the warm spray of the shower, that she remembered Gerald's endearment. A secret smile softened her lips. He had called her *darling*.

The word had flowed so easily from his tongue, making her wonder how many other women he'd called darling. Turning her face up to the water, she washed her hair with a special shampoo that would prevent the chlorine from turning her gray hair a greenish-yellow shade.

She had to admit that she was enjoying sharing her day off with Gerald. He hadn't heated the pool, but allowed the sun coming through the frosted glass to heat it naturally. When she'd dipped her toes in the water she'd pulled her foot back quickly. It had been too cool for her comfort. Gerald had noticed her reluctance and turned a switch to heat the water.

Waiting for a rise in the water temperature provided her an opportunity to observe him. What she'd suspected when seeing him in his casual attire was confirmed when he stood on the deck in a pair of swim trunks. He claimed a swimmer's body: wide shoulders, long, ropey arms, flat middle, and muscled legs. She managed to complete two laps before quitting, then sat on the deck, feet dangling in the water, and watched Gerald crisscross the pool with the speed and silence of a torpedo.

He'd walked up the steps leading out of the pool, his chest barely rising and falling with the exertion, and showed her where she could shower and change her clothes. He told her she would find him in the kitchen.

Forty minutes later, her blow-dried hair pulled back in an elastic band, and dressed in a tangerine-orange, loose-fitting tank dress, Katherine made her way to the kitchen. Gerald was standing at the countertop, placing portions of chilled shrimp, lobster, and crab legs on a large platter.

"Who's going to eat all that?" she asked, the question startling him.

He smiled at her, his teeth showing whitely under his neatly barbered salt-and-pepper mustache. "You think this is a lot?"

She closed the distance between them. "It is if we're going to have an entrée."

Tilting his head, he stared at the platter, then shrugged his shoulders under the short-sleeved, black, V-neck silk sweater he wore with a pair of black linen slacks.

"Whatever is left over can be used for a salad."

"Who taught you to cook, Gerald?"

He smiled, covering the platter with plastic wrap. "My mother. She'd always wanted a girl, but after three sons she decided to give up. My dad used to complain that she was going to make sissies out of us because she taught all of us to cook, sew, and do laundry. She said she never wanted her sons to marry because they couldn't take care of their own basic day-to-day needs."

His expression stilled and grew serious. "She didn't live to see any of us marry, but Lenny, George, and I never forgot what she used to call her domestic survival training."

"Didn't you say that your father just celebrated an anniversary?"

He nodded. "I was seventeen and my mother had been dead a year when Daddy married Virginia. Daddy is completely helpless without a woman. But, it's been a wonderful marriage for them, because they celebrated their thirtieth anniversary last year."

Katherine stared at Gerald's strong profile, wondering why

he hadn't remarried. Hadn't he wanted a mother for his daughter?

"If it hadn't been for your domestic survival training, would you also have remarried?"

Shifting to his left, he stared down at her. "No, Katherine. It has nothing to do with whether I could take care of my daughter and myself. When Lisa was a baby I hired a live-in nanny for her. I've always had a cleaning service clean my house, a landscaper for the outdoors, and a caretaker to make certain everything is in working order. I haven't remarried because I haven't found the woman I'd want to share my life with." He noticed the slight smile playing at the corners of her lush mouth. "What's so funny?"

"I can't believe you haven't found the right woman. You've dated practically every single black woman in Savannah from forty to sixty."

Throwing back his head, Gerald laughed, the sound coming from deep within his chest. When he recovered, he shook his head. "Wrong, Katherine. I haven't dated you."

Her eyes widened as she curved her arms around her body in a protective gesture. "Do you want to?"

He moved closer until they were only inches apart. "Yes, I do."

Her eyelashes fluttered. "I don't intend to be one of your women, Gerald."

Reaching out, he pulled her arms away from her body. "You won't. Contrary to what you've seen or believe, I don't have a harem. You're the first woman I've invited to my home since my marriage ended."

"But . . . but I've seen you with other—"

He placed his forefinger over her lips, stopping her words. Seconds later his mouth replaced his finger, increasing the pressure until her lips parted under his surprisingly gentle kiss. The caress of his lips on hers pulled her into a slow heated intimacy she had forgotten existed.

Without warning, he pulled away, his deep-set gaze fusing with hers. "The *first*, Katherine. Have I made myself understood?"

Running her tongue over her lower lip, she tasted him again. She wanted to ask why he hadn't invited other women, but decided to wait. If she agreed to date Gerald, then there would be time for him to answer a lot of her questions. Her eyes crinkled in a smile.

"Yes, you have, Gerald."

He returned her smile. "Where would you like to eat?"

"How about under the pergola?"

He ran his finger down the length of her nose. "I was hoping you'd say that."

7

The soft buzzing sound of the intercom punctuated the soothing strains of cool jazz coming from the speakers of a mini stereo system on a shelf in Katherine's private office. Reaching over, she pressed the button on the intercom.

"Yes, Rita?"

"Mrs. Russell and Mrs. Thompson have arrived."

Closing her eyes, Katherine counted slowly to three. She opened her eyes and picked up a folder with the names "Russell–Wilson" on the tab. The bride's mother and twin sister had tested the limits of her professional patience; however, it would end in another three weeks when Trina Russell exchanged vows with Representative Galvin Wilson, Savannah's most popular member of Congress.

"Please send them in, Rita."

Rising to her feet, she walked to the door to greet the tall, thin, blond women. They swept into her office, the scent of an expensive perfume trailing in their wake. Katherine waited for them to sink down on the cushioned softness of a love seat before she sat opposite them on a matching armchair.

Opening the folder, she handed each of them a photocopy of a tentative menu for a bridal shower. "I'm going to have to have your final approval on the menu tonight."

Mrs. Russell was hosting a bridal shower for her daughter, but hadn't been able to decide whether to have an evening gala sit-down dinner or a sumptuous luncheon. Katherine had finally convinced her to consider the luncheon because she and her husband had already decided on a formal black-tie wedding with a sit-down dinner reception for three hundred invited guests.

"Are you sure these selections will be enough?" Mrs. Russell asked after she'd perused the sheet of paper.

"More than enough," Katherine confirmed. She'd listed mushrooms Florentine, "wedding" chicken salad, Salade Nicoise, croissants and sweet butter, double chocolate torte with chantilly cream, lemon sherbet to cleanse the palate between courses, champagne, white wine, espresso, café au lait, and tea.

"Do you have an alternative menu?" Tiffany Thompson asked. She tucked a flaxen curl behind her left ear and the three-carat diamond ring and band of diamond baguettes on her ring finger gave off brilliant blue-white sparks.

Katherine was grateful that she hadn't had the pleasure of planning Tiffany's wedding. If there was any credence to "good twin, bad twin," then Trina and Tiffany were it. Trina was mild-tempered, easygoing, while Tiffany was the total opposite.

Katherine's temper flared, and she bit back the virulent words poised on the tip of her tongue. She forced a smile. "I could suggest a tricolor pasta salad with a vegetable medley, with Caesar, Greek, and Waldorf salads, honey Dijon chicken, an assortment of breads, an apricot upside-down cake, white wine, specialty coffees, and tea."

"I prefer that menu," Tiffany said, smiling at her mother.

"So do I," Mrs. Russell agreed after a noticeable pause.

Katherine sighed aloud. Personally, she preferred the first menu. The selections were more elegant and in keeping with the warmer temperatures. But she was paid to give her clients what they wanted—and she would.

"I'll call the restaurant and give them your selections."

The three women stood up. Mrs. Russell extended her hand. "Thank you so much, Miss Langdon."

Katherine took the proffered hand. "You're quite welcome. I'll call you in a few days."

She waited until she was alone, then flopped down on the love seat. She kicked off her shoes, pressed her head against the cushion, and closed her eyes. She was still in the same position when Gerald walked into her office. She hadn't heard him; his footsteps were muffled by the carpet, but she recognized his cologne.

Gerald stared at Katherine, his gaze softening when he noticed the length of the lashes resting on her delicate cheekbones. There was a fragility about her that he hadn't noticed before. Bending slightly, he pressed a kiss to her silken cheek.

Katherine opened her eyes. "How did you get in here without Rita announcing you?"

He sat beside her. "I told her that I wanted to surprise you."

"I should fire her for not adhering to the rules."

"If you do, then I'll hire her to work for me."

"You wouldn't?"

"I would." He brushed his mouth over hers. "I came because I couldn't stay away from you."

Trailing her fingers along his jaw, she smiled. "You're shameless, Gerald Barnett."

His eyebrows lifted. "Why? Because I'm honest about how I feel about you?"

She sobered quickly. Gerald had been forthcoming about his feelings while she refused to disclose her own emotions.

They'd been dating for a month. Gerald came to her home on Mondays to pick her up, and they usually spent the entire day at his house. They shared brunches, swam in the pool, and went for walks in the garden. One Monday it rained all day and they stayed in the gathering room, reading and listening to music. Their relationship was simple and uncomplicated.

Lacing her fingers through his, she stared at his large hand. "I don't want things to move too quickly."

He frowned at her. "If we move any slower we'd come to a complete standstill."

"You know what I mean, Gerald."

"No, I don't, Katherine."

"We're dating—"

"I see you one day a week," he said, interrupting her.

"And that's the only day I can claim for myself."

A warning voice whispered in Gerald's head that he was being unreasonable. He wanted more from Katherine than she was able to give him, but it had been a long time since he'd been attracted to a woman with whom he felt compatible.

"Forgive me for being selfish. But . . ." His words trailed off.

"But what?"

Shaking his head, Gerald forced a smile. "Nothing," he lied.

If he hadn't stopped himself he would've admitted to Katherine that he was falling in love with her. And it wasn't a love that was filled with an unbridled passion, but one that was peaceful, comforting, and secure.

Lisa had fallen in love and planned to marry her French fiancé in eight weeks, while he found himself fantasizing about marrying her wedding consultant. He'd lain in bed the night before, thinking about Katherine. He loved her smell, her soft voice, the texture of her skin, the perfect fit of her body whenever he held her against his own. She'd permitted him to kiss her, but whenever he made an attempt to caress her body she pushed him away.

Pulling her head against his shoulder, he dropped a kiss on her hair. "Do you plan to work late tonight?"

"No."

"Will you share dinner with me?"

"Where?"

"At The River's End in Thunderbolt."

Katherine stared up at Gerald, the smoldering flame in his eyes sending a warming heat through her. Each time she saw him, the pull was stronger, and she knew she had to stop fighting her emotions—had to stop denying that she was falling in love.

"Give me a few minutes to freshen up."

Rising, Gerald pulled her up with him. Cradling her face between his hands, he kissed her mouth. "Thank you. I'll wait outside for you."

Katherine nodded. She'd also agreed to go to the restaurant with him because she was tired—tired of not wanting anyone to know that she was dating Gerald Barnett.

She retreated to her private bathroom, where she brushed her teeth, applied a light cover of makeup, and ran a wide-tooth comb through her hair. Peering closely at the mirror, she saw a middle-aged woman with smooth, flawless golden-brown skin. She still found it hard to believe that she would soon celebrate her fiftieth birthday. She was only five pounds heavier than she'd been when she graduated high school, and if it hadn't been for her graying hair she suspected she could easily pass for a woman in her late thirties.

After putting on a jacket that matched her lemon-yellow dress, she retrieved her handbag from a credenza. She closed the door to her office and made her way to the reception area.

Katherine smiled at her assistant. "I'm finished for the day. Have a good evening."

Rita stared numbly at her boss as she opened the door and walked out. It was only four-thirty. Since she had come to work for Langdon Bridals she had never known Katherine to leave the office before her. A bright smile creased her face. Perhaps Mr. Barnett had something to do with . . .

Her thoughts broke off as she shook her head.

"Couldn't be," she said softly.

Katherine picked up her cup of latte, staring at Gerald over the rim. They'd spent the past two hours dining and watching shrimp boats and luxury watercraft sail gently down the Intracoastal Waterway.

"We have to come back again when it's dark. The moonlit harbor sky is unmatched anywhere in Savannah," Gerald said. His voice was a seductive velvet murmur.

She took a swallow of the deliciously brewed coffee. "I'd like that very much."

"I like you very much, Katherine."

She laughed, the sound reminding him of a tinkling bell. "And I you, Gerald."

Her admission seemed to shock him as he leaned back in his chair. The glow from the lighted candle in the middle of the table reflected off the sharp angles that formed his face. The pristine whiteness of his shirt collar enhanced the rich dark color of his skin.

"Do you really, Katherine?"

She lowered her gaze in a demure gesture. "Yes."

A slight smile curved his mouth. "Thank you."

She returned his smile, placing the cup on its saucer. "You're welcome. Thank you for dinner."

He shook his head. "No, Katherine. I should be the one doing all the thanking."

"For what?"

"Your beauty and your company."

She sat, unable to move as Gerald stared back at her in a waiting silence. And there was no mistaking that he wanted her. It was the first time she recognized lust in his gaze. She studied the lean dark-skinned face, knowing that what she felt for the man sitting opposite her had nothing to do with reason.

How could one reason with love?

One couldn't.

She'd answered her own question.

Tearing her gaze away, she picked up her handbag. "I'm ready to go home now."

She stood and walked out of the restaurant to the parking lot, leaving Gerald to settle the check.

The drive back to Savannah was accomplished in complete silence. Katherine stared out the side window while Gerald concentrated on the road. He found a parking spot several doors from her town house.

"Don't," he warned when she placed her hand on the door handle. "I'll see you in."

She didn't want him to see her in. She wanted to get away from him as quickly as she could. Maybe with some distance between them she could make sense of her jumbled thoughts.

She wanted Gerald—wanted him in her life and in her bed. But then she was frightened—frightened that she would eventually want something from him that he wouldn't be able to give her. And she suspected that something was marriage.

Paul had asked her to marry him, but she'd turned him down; but it was different now because *she* was different. Dating Gerald was a reminder of how sterile her social life had become. If it weren't for her business she would be a hermit. Her family lived in Macon, she had no close girlfriends to confide in. What she had was Langdon Bridals and nothing else to take up the empty hours.

She waited until Gerald came around the car and opened the door. He helped her out and curved his arm around her waist as they walked the short distance to her building. He took her keys, unlocked the front door, and stepped into the entryway. Soft, golden light from a table lamp illuminated the space. She walked in, holding out her hand for her keys.

Instead of giving her the keys, he placed them on a table. Turning, he gathered Katherine in his arms, pulling her flush against his body. He lowered his head, pressed his mouth to the side of her neck, and breathed in her essence. He wanted her so much that he was unable to stop his hands from shaking.

"Katherine." Her name was a groan.

She felt his hardness throbbing against her thigh as her desire rose to meet his. Rising on tiptoe, her arms curving around his neck, she searched for his mouth, drinking in the sweetness of his kiss. The kiss deepened as he took her mouth with an almost savage intensity.

She dissolved into a morass of fiery desire when he kissed the side of her neck before he moved behind her to run his tongue along her nape.

She went limp in his arms just as a sweep of lights flooded the entryway. The light reminded her where she was and what she was doing. They were making love with the front door open.

"Gerald." His name came out in a hoarse whisper.

Her voice penetrated the fog of desire pulling him under

where there was no escape. His head came up and he stared
at her wild-eyed expression.

"What's the matter?"

"Close the door."

8

Gerald tightened his hold on Katherine's waist, took a backward step and closed the door with his shoulder. Bracing his
back against the door, he pulled her to his chest, lowered his
head, and covered her mouth with his, devouring its sweetness.

Katherine curved her arms under his, abandoning herself
to the forceful domination of Gerald's mouth. She had been
kissed many times, but never the way he was kissing her.
Every nerve in her body tingled from head to toe. His mouth
moved lower, to the side of her neck, as he breathed in the
scent of her bared flesh.

Her breath came in long, shuddering gasps when Gerald
cradled her hips with both hands, pulling her against his groin.
Once again, there was no mistaking his arousal as he pressed
his thighs against hers. She drank in the comfort of his
strength, his devastatingly masculine appeal, and his obvious
virility.

She shivered noticeably as his fingers inched up her thighs,
gathering the fabric of her dress and leaving her flesh burning.
Surrendering completely to his masterful touch, Katherine
collapsed against his chest, and would've fallen if he hadn't
supported her sagging body.

Gerald registered the soft ringing sound before Katherine
did. She eased back, staring at him as if he were a stranger.
The sensual mood had been shattered by a telephone call. She
attempted to extricate herself from his embrace, but he held
onto her as he reached for the tiny cellular phone on his belt.
Flipping it open, he pressed a button.

"Yes?"

"Daddy!"

He went completely still. "Lisa?"

"Daddy . . ." Her voice trailed off as sobs came through the earpiece.

Gerald's pulse raced uncontrollably. "Are you all right?"

"I don't know."

"Where are you?"

"Home."

"I'll be right over." He ended the call, slipping the phone into the breast pocket of his jacket.

Staring at Katherine, he shook his head. "I'm sorry."

She offered him a comforting smile. "That's all right. Go to your daughter."

Lowering his head, he kissed her gently. "I'll call you later."

She waited until the door closed behind Gerald's departing figure before she collapsed on the straight-back chair next to the table.

She sat, eyes closed, her chest rising and falling heavily, unaware of the minutes slipping away while enjoying the waning passion Gerald had aroused in her. Her breasts felt full, heavy. Every fiber in her body tingled with desire—a desire she hadn't felt in years. A desire she wanted to share with him.

Lisa opened the door to her father's ring, collapsing against his chest. "I . . . I hate her," she said, her voice breaking.

Gerald anchored a finger under her chin, raising her face to his. Lisa's eyes were red and swollen. "What's the matter, Princess?"

"Sebastien's mother. I hate her, Daddy."

A slight frown creased Gerald's forehead. "Hate is a strong word, Lisa." He reached for the handkerchief in his pocket and blotted her tears.

She sniffled, smiling through her tears. "I don't really hate her even though she's embarked on a crusade to work my last nerve."

"Come sit down and talk to me." He grasped her fingers

gently, easing her to sit beside him on an off-white love seat covered in Haitian cotton.

"Why the nine-one-one call, Princess?"

Pulling her lower lip between her teeth, Lisa took a deep breath. "Sebastien called and said his mother was angry because Noelle wasn't going to be in the wedding. She's threatening not to attend if I don't include Noelle."

"Isn't Noelle her daughter?"

"Yes. Madame deVilliers says it's a French custom that all of the children be attendants."

Gerald lifted his eyebrows at this disclosure. "How old is Noelle?"

"Sixteen. I'd hardly call her a child, Daddy," Lisa said disdainfully.

He shrugged a shoulder. "She's not a woman, Lisa."

"She's not quite an adult. But she's certainly no child."

"You're going to have to compromise, Princess."

"How? What she's asking is impossible. They live an ocean away."

"You have a wedding consultant, Lisa. I suggest you talk to her."

Lisa shook her head. "Miss Langdon is good, but I don't believe she's a miracle worker."

"That's not for you to decide. I want you to call her tomorrow and tell her your problem."

"What's going to happen if she can't do anything?"

"You won't know that unless you make her aware of your dilemma."

Tunneling her fingers through her hair, Lisa shook her head. "Okay, Daddy. I'll call her. But if she can't help me, then I swear I'll elope before I let that woman ruin my wedding."

Gerald shifted on the cushion, quick anger rising in his eyes. Lisa looked and sounded so much like Elaine that he thought he was reliving a scene from thirty years ago. Instead of facing adversity, his ex-wife had walked away from her responsibility, and he hadn't tried to stop her. He wouldn't permit that to happen again—not with his daughter.

"If you elope I'll disown you," he threatened. His voice was quiet, yet held an undertone of repressed rage.

Lisa's eyes widened as she stared at her father. This was a Gerald Barnett that she had never seen before. She no longer recognized him as the indulgent man who had given her any and everything she'd ever wanted or asked for.

"You wouldn't, Daddy."

He stood up, glaring down at her. "Just don't test me, Lisa."

Turning on his heel, he made his way across the room and walked out of her apartment, slamming the door violently behind him.

Gerald drove aimlessly around downtown Savannah with unseeing eyes. He finally parked, staring into space, and it wasn't until his anger abated that he realized he was back on the street where Katherine lived.

He wanted to go to her and unburden his heavy heart. He wanted to tell her that he was frightened of losing his daughter the way that he'd lost his first love. Closing his eyes, he sat in the car and lost track of time.

The soft ringing of the telephone on the bedside table pulled Katherine from a deep, dreamless sleep. She groped for the receiver and mumbled a slurred greeting.

"Hello." There was a pregnant silence on the other end. "Hello?"

"Katherine. Please don't hang up."

She sat up and stared at the clock when she heard the familiar masculine voice. It was 10:45.

"Gerald?"

"I'm sorry for waking you."

"What's the matter, Gerald?" Her voice was soft, comforting.

"Nothing," he lied smoothly. "I promised I would call you."

She laughed softly. "You're not a very good liar, Gerald."

"How would you know?"

"I know a little something about you."

"Care to tell me?"

"You like me, Gerald Barnett."

"That's obvious," he said, laughing. "I've said it enough."

Katherine sobered quickly. She knew intuitively Gerald hadn't called her just to engage in idle chatter. "How's Lisa?"

"She'll call you tomorrow."

"What about?"

"I'll let her tell you."

"Aren't you going to give me a hint?"

"I can't, Katherine. Lisa is a grown woman who will become a wife in less than two months, and it's time she handled her own problems."

What he wanted to tell Katherine was that for the first time since Lisa's birth he felt that he'd failed as a father. He'd protected his daughter and fought her battles. He hadn't permitted her to stand up for herself. She should've been able to confront her future mother-in-law as to how she wanted her wedding.

It was he, not Lisa, who went through a period of mourning when she left home to attend college. He'd called her so often that she'd had to remind him that she was a woman, not an infant to be monitored constantly.

Her reprimand made him stand back and think. She was right. It was during that time he'd begun dating again, and when Lisa graduated college and returned home he'd suggested she set up her own household.

"Whatever her problem, I'm certain Lisa and I will be able to work it out," Katherine said confidently.

"Thank you."

Her soft laughter came through the earpiece of his cell phone. "You're quite welcome."

Gerald stared at the lighted dials on the dashboard as cooling air from the car's vents swept over his face. "Do you have anything planned for the Fourth?"

There was a slight pause from Katherine. "As a matter of fact, I do. I'm going to Macon to see my family."

He forced a smile he didn't feel. He wanted to see her

more than one day a week. He wanted to see her every day and every night.

"I'm sorry I woke you up. But thanks for listening."

"Good night, Gerald."

"Katherine?"

"Yes?"

"I love you."

She heard the softly spoken three words, then a break in the connection. She held the receiver to her ear until a sharp piercing sound forced her to hang up.

How could he confess to loving her, and then hang up?

She lay in the darkness, smiling. He loved her and she loved him. A gentle peace filled her, but it was after midnight before she was finally able to close her eyes and sleep.

9

Katherine woke the next morning, blissfully happy and filled with a newly awakened sense of contentment that hadn't been there when she'd fallen in love with Ray. What she felt for Gerald was different—different because there wasn't a sense of frantic urgency, different from her relationship with Paul because with him there had been no passion between them— only mutual respect.

Pushing herself into a sitting position, she stretched her arms over her head, and then left the bed to begin her day.

Lisa Barnett walked into Katherine's office at nine o'clock. There was a slight puffiness under her eyes that hadn't been there during their prior meetings. And judging from her frantic telephone call to Gerald the night before, Katherine assumed the younger woman had been crying. Offering her a comforting smile, she directed Lisa to sit on the love seat.

"How can I help you this morning?"

Lisa launched into a discourse about her future mother-in-law's discontentment because she hadn't included Noelle deVilliers in her wedding party. "How can she be an attendant when she's not coming to the States until a week before Sebastien and I marry? What about her dress?"

"Her dress is not a problem," Katherine said.

Lisa's expression mirrored surprise. "It isn't?"

"Not with E-mail."

"E-mail?"

"I'll be right back," Katherine said, rising and walking out of the room. She returned minutes later with a white envelope.

"This is the pattern for your maid-of-honor's dress. If you want your future sister-in-law to wear the same design but in a different color, then I can scan the pattern and E-mail it to a dressmaker in France, who can make the necessary adjustments."

Lisa's eyes widened until they resembled silver dollars. "It's that easy?"

Katherine nodded. "It's that easy. What's Noelle's coloring?"

"She's a brunette with dark blue eyes and very fair skin."

"How fair?"

"Peaches and cream. She happens to be a pretty girl."

"Contact Noelle and have her select a dressmaker ASAP. I'll need an E-mail address to send the pattern. You'll also have to decide what color you want for her dress."

Lisa smiled for the first time in hours. "I think she would look wonderful in a peacock blue."

Katherine nodded in agreement. The soft blue shade would be a perfect complement to Meredith Barnett's burnished gold. "Once Noelle sets up her appointment at the dressmaker's I'll become involved. I'm going to request that the completed garment be shipped to the States rather than have your fiancé's family bring it with them. I've heard too many horror stories about airlines losing or misplacing luggage."

Tunneling her fingers through her hair, Lisa closed her eyes, exhaling.

"You're incredible, Miss Langdon. How can I thank you?"

Katherine reached over and patted her shoulder. "Just continue the tradition of being a beautiful Langdon bride."

Lisa's smile was dazzling. "That shouldn't be too difficult.

After all, I'll be wearing a Langdon original wedding gown. Thank you again."

"You're welcome, Lisa."

And there was no doubt that Gerald's daughter would be an exquisite bride, Katherine thought after Lisa's exit. She had selected a sleeveless dress with the rich pattern of a Chantilly lace bodice enhanced with silver threads, beads, and embroidery. Subtle ruching at the waistline added shape, and underneath a strapless silk Mikado skirt fell into pleats at the hip, while pearls edged the hemline. And because Lisa stood five-three and weighed 105 pounds the gown's design was certain not to overpower her petite figure.

Katherine's entrée into the wedding business had begun as a dress designer. She'd left Macon at eighteen to enroll in New York's Parsons School of Design. A month into her sophomore year she was hospitalized with pneumonia and missed more than six weeks of classes. Her parents convinced her to come back to Macon to convalesce, and once she returned to college it was to transfer her credits to the Savannah College of Art and Design. She fell in love with the sensual lushness of Savannah, and after graduating promised herself that she would return to the city to live. She did return; now, after fifteen years as a Savannahian, she still loved her adopted hometown—and found herself in love with one of its most prominent African-American men.

She wanted to spend the Fourth of July holiday weekend with Gerald, but on the other hand she couldn't disappoint her parents. Even though she called her mother and father a couple of times a week, they always complained that they didn't see her enough; she'd stopped trying to explain that spring, summer, and fall were her busiest seasons.

This upcoming Fourth offered her a temporary respite. No one had scheduled a bridal shower or wedding; however, if she hadn't been committed to going to Macon, it would've provided the perfect opportunity to share more than one day with Gerald. She planned to leave Friday and return Sunday afternoon to avoid the Monday holiday traffic.

The buzz of the intercom captured her attention; she rose

from the love seat and made her way to the desk. "Yes, Rita?"

"I have Jake Collins on the phone. He says he's returning your call. Before I transfer him I want to let you know that Tresses called to say your stylist can fit you in for ten-thirty."

Katherine picked up the receiver and pushed a button on the telephone console. "Hello."

"What's up, Kat?"

She winced at the sound of the gravelly voice. Jake of JC Catering was the only person who referred to her by that name. "I wanted to talk to you about your new waitress. I noticed that she served on the right and picked up on the left. I just wanted to know if she'd been told that the process is the reverse."

"I've gone over it with her over and over, but she just can't seem to remember her right from her left. I've thought about letting her go."

"Consider putting a bracelet or a ribbon around her left wrist when she's serving, then reverse it when she's picking up to clear the table."

Jake's laugh came through the wire. "You're a genius, Kat."

"I just don't want complaints from my clients, Jake."

"I hear you. Look, Kat, I'll see you later."

" 'Bye."

Katherine ended the call and retrieved her handbag and car keys. She had to get her hair done for a bridal shower dinner later that evening.

Three hours later Katherine returned to Langdon Bridals, her hair swept up off her neck in a sophisticated French twist and her fingers and toes professionally groomed and shimmering with a soft rose-pink color. She came to a sudden stop when she spied a large bouquet of exotic flowers in a vase on Rita's desk.

She smiled at her assistant.

"Beautiful flowers."

Rita arched a professionally waxed eyebrow. "They're not for me. The card has your name on it."

A slight frown puckered Katherine's forehead as she plucked an envelope off the colorful cellophane wrapping. Opening the sealed envelope, she withdrew a small card. Her gaze moved over the bold, slanting, handwritten missive: *Thank you for being YOU. Love, GMB.*

Her lips parted in a soft smile. *And thank you for being you, Gerald,* she mused. Her gaze shifted to the profusion of lilies, orchids, birds-of-paradise, and roses, then to Rita's questioning expression.

"Please put them with the others." She tucked the card into her handbag. "Did I get any calls?"

Rita shook her head. "No. It's been very quiet."

"If that's the case, why don't you take off early?"

"Are you certain you won't need me?"

"Very certain."

"Then I'm out of here." She picked up the vase of flowers and placed them on a table in the reception area as Katherine retreated to her office.

Katherine sat down at her desk, picked up the telephone, and dialed the number to Barnett Savings and Loan.

"Mr. Gerald Barnett, please."

"Please hold. I'll connect you to his executive assistant."

She was placed on hold for a full minute before a strong, authoritative feminine voice came on the line.

"Mr. Barnett's office."

"This is Ms. Katherine Langdon. I'd like to speak to Mr. Barnett, please."

The woman's voice changed, becoming softer, less intimidating. "Please hold, Ms. Langdon. Mr. Barnett said to put you through whenever you call."

A smile tugged at the corners of her mouth. It was apparent she'd made Gerald's A-list only because she was responsible for his daughter's wedding.

"Katherine?"

She closed her eyes at the sound of his soft, drawling voice. "Gerald. I want to thank you for the flowers. They're beautiful."

"You're beautiful, Katherine."

She felt a shiver ripple through her with his compliment. "Thank you."

The soft whisper of his breathing came through the wire. "I meant what I said last night."

Closing her eyes, Katherine bit down on her lower lip. "Yes."

"Yes, you remember? Or yes, you know?"

Opening her eyes, she stared at the pattern on the wallpaper. "Both." She hardly recognized her own voice. "Gerald?" she asked after a prolonged silence.

"Yes, darling?" Again the word slipped so easily from his lips.

"We need to talk."

Again there was silence, this time from Gerald. "When am I going to see you?"

"Sunday. I should be home by six."

"I'll be waiting for you at your place. Unless you'd prefer to come to mine?"

"No," she said quickly.

"Have a safe trip."

"Thank you. Good-bye, Gerald."

"Good-bye, darling."

She ended the call, an expression of satisfaction shining in her eyes while her body vibrated with an indefinable feeling of rightness. She wasn't certain of a future with Gerald, but that no longer mattered, because they'd reached the point where their relationship had to be resolved.

The tense lines ringing Gerald's mouth eased when he spied Katherine's car as she slowed and pulled into a parking space along the curb next to him. He'd spent the past few days reacting like an automaton, speaking only when spoken to, eating and sleeping only because they were necessary for his survival.

He'd called himself ten thousand fools for telling Katherine that he loved her, but seeing her smile as she waved at him through the windshield lessened his concern that he'd acted like a love-struck adolescent.

Moving around to the driver's side, he opened the door, extended his hand, and helped her from the small green car. He gathered her close and she curved her arms around his neck and pressed her lips to his smooth-shaven jaw. Shifting his head slightly, he brushed his mouth with hers, breathing in the scent of her sensual perfume.

"Welcome home," he whispered.

"Thank you," she whispered back.

Katherine stared at Gerald, unable to conceal the deep feelings he'd aroused in her. Spending four days away from him and Savannah had given her time to reexamine her reaction to the man she'd fallen in love with.

She'd asked herself over and over if she was drawn to him because of his lineage, wealth, influence, or was it out of gratitude for her loan approval? The questions had attacked her relentlessly, keeping her from a restful night's sleep until she finally confided in her brother.

Fifty-five-year-old school psychologist Robert Langdon, Jr., married father of three and grandfather of four, had earned the reputation of being brutally honest. He told Katherine that she'd married Raymond because at thirty-three her biological clock was ticking, and had only become involved with Paul because he'd permitted her to control their relationship. However, Gerald was different because he was more demanding. And that aggressiveness made her feel vulnerable.

She'd listened silently, and then cried on her brother's shoulder, finally acknowledging she should've heeded his warnings in the past. He dried her tears, kissed her tenderly, and urged her to follow her heart.

Threading her fingers through Gerald's, she buried her face against his chest, as early evening shadows turned the street into an emerald forest, communicating without words that she'd missed him.

They headed for her town house, unlocked the front door, and stepped into the entryway. Realization dawned as they shared a smile.

Katherine's gaze shifted to Gerald's waist. "Where's your cell phone?"

Cradling her face between his hands, he dropped a kiss on the end of her nose. "I decided to leave it home."

Her fingers curled around his wrists and she pressed a kiss to the palm of his left hand. She boldly flicked the tip of her tongue over the flesh, eliciting a gasp from him. It was her turn to gasp as he pulled her closer, his head lowering as he trailed his tongue down the side of her neck.

His tongue, the soft brush of his mustached mouth, and the heat and strength of his athletic body jolted Katherine into an awareness that she had continually rejected advances from other men because she'd been waiting for Gerald. He'd changed her and her life when he approved her loan, when she'd opened the door after he came to her home unannounced, and when he kissed her for the first time. And now, when she'd invited Gerald to come to her home to talk—talk to her heart.

"Gerald?"

"Darling?"

"Let's go upstairs and talk."

Needing no further prompting, Gerald swung Katherine up in his arms and headed for the staircase.

10

Katherine directed Gerald to her bedroom, feeling as if she'd entered a surreal world—one where she saw rather than felt him making love to her. Slowly, methodically he unbuttoned her blouse, slipped it off her shoulders, holding her hostage with his penetrating gaze.

Gerald's chest rose and fell in unison with Katherine's, his breathing deepening with each article of clothing he removed and discarded. Her blouse, slacks, sandals, bra, and finally her silken panties lay in a heap on a chair beside the queen-size, wrought-iron bed. Bending slightly, he curved his arms under her shoulders and knees and placed her on her bed as if she were a piece of fragile crystal.

Katherine closed her eyes, counting off the seconds as Gerald undressed himself, then lay down beside her. He held her hand, waiting until both their pulses slowed before he moved over her and kissed her tenderly. She opened her eyes, smiling at him smiling down at her.

Wrapped in an invisible warmth, she opened her arms to her lover, and he loved her relentlessly, his hands and mouth branding her flesh with his passion. Their world stood still, the rising sounds of straining desire filling the bedroom as Gerald paused to slip on protection; then dammed up passions escalated the instant he eased his hardness into her warm pulsing body.

Everyone and everything else ceased to exist for Gerald and Katherine as they each offered the other a love that left them awed by an ecstasy neither had ever experienced before.

Their naked bodies still moist from their lovemaking, they lay side by side, holding hands, sharing the peace and contentment flowing between them.

Gerald pulled Katherine into the curve of his body. He held her until her breathing deepened and the soft whisper of her breath brushing his throat indicated that she had fallen asleep. He closed his eyes and minutes later joined her in that sated sleep reserved for lovers.

Katherine displayed a dimpled smile as she supported her arms on the brass railing of the sloop, watching the buildings along Factor's Walk grow smaller and smaller. She felt another source of heat compete with the warmth of the setting summer sun, and leaned back against the unyielding strength of Gerald's body as he came up behind her.

"What a wonderful birthday gift."

Gerald had called her earlier that morning, asking that she pack a bag with lightweight clothing for an overnight trip. It wasn't until they'd boarded the sleek forty-foot sloop docked along the Savannah River that she realized that she would celebrate her fiftieth birthday sailing.

Turning in his embrace, she stared up at the face of the man she had come to love completely. Rising on her toes, she curved her arms around his neck, pulling his head down.

"I love you," she whispered, openly confessing her love for the first time.

Gerald went completely still, his gaze fusing with Katherine's. He'd waited patiently for her to utter the words he'd longed to hear for weeks. He'd confessed his love for her, in and out of bed, his heart aching whenever she thanked him. He didn't want her thanks but her love. He wanted her in his life—forever.

He examined her salt-and-pepper hair pinned up off her neck, the mysterious glow of her clear, heavily lashed brown eyes, the rounded tip of her pert nose, and her mouth—a mouth that offered him a sensual sweetness he was helpless to resist. Lowering his head, he kissed her passionately, stealing the breath from her lungs.

He loved everything about Katherine—her face, body, and the ecstasy she was able to arouse in him just by sharing the same space. She was perfect—in and out of bed.

Tightening his hold on her waist, he pressed his mouth to her ear. "Marry me, Katherine."

Her head came up slowly and the moisture filling her eyes turned them into pools of shimmering liquid sherry. Her lower lip trembled slightly as she smiled through her tears.

She loved Gerald; the love offered a sense of peace she had never experienced before—a love that was gentle, comfortable, and without limits or boundaries.

It had taken fifty years, but everything was right in her world. Closing her eyes against his intense stare, she whispered, "Yes, Gerald. Yes, I will marry you."

A week before Lisa Barnett's wedding, Katherine was introduced to Jacques, Veronique, Sebastien, and Noelle de-Villiers. Their connecting flight from New York had touched down at the Savannah airport, where they were picked up by Gerald's driver and whisked off to a downtown hotel. It took thirty-six hours before their circadian rhythms were able to adjust to the different time zone.

She'd shared dinner with the Barnetts and deVillierses on The First Lady, one of the old-fashioned riverboats that plied the Savannah River. It had become a festive occasion when Sébastien slipped a stunning sapphire and diamond ring that had belonged to his maternal great-grandmother on Lisa's finger to seal their betrothal.

Her own gaze had lingered on the exquisite platinum and diamond bangle on her right wrist, which was a constant reminder of the night she'd celebrated her fiftieth birthday with Gerald. They'd spent hours on deck dining under the stars. The sloop's crew of four was nearly undetectable during the trip down the Savannah River. They were served incredibly delicious gourmet meals prepared by a master chef and catered to by a silent waiter who seemed attuned to their every need. It was well past midnight when she and Gerald retired to their cabin and a session of lovemaking that left both gasping for their next breath. She had fallen asleep in Gerald's protective embrace, and when she awoke hours later, she'd discovered his gift on her wrist.

Three weeks later they completed the medical examination requirement for a marriage license, and because there was no waiting period in Georgia before or after the issuance of the license they decided to wait before setting a date. They also wanted to wait until after Lisa and Sebastien married before informing them of their impending nuptials.

Rita announcing the arrival of Lisa and Madame deVilliers followed the buzz of the intercom. Katherine stood and waited for the two women. She directed them into a space that had been set up as a sitting room/solarium. Massive potted palms, ferns, and exotic flowering plants hanging from baskets suspended from the ceiling took full advantage of the bright sunlight pouring through floor-to-ceiling windows.

Veronique, petite and professionally coiffed, claimed a perfect face and body for a middle-aged woman. It was evident that she was extremely high maintenance.

Her light blue eyes crinkled attractively in a smile. "Your shop is so chic, Miss Langdon. It reminds me of a French drawing room," she said in slightly accented English.

Katherine returned her smile. "Thank you. And please, call me Katherine."

"Bon."

She invited Lisa and Veronique to sit on plush armchairs, then brought them up-to-date on everything she'd planned for the wedding. Lisa's satisfaction was apparent when she smiled, but the same couldn't be said for Veronique. A slight frown creased her pale forehead as her eyes narrowed slightly.

"I'm sorry I wasn't consulted about these plans," she said in a haughty tone.

"But I told you what I wanted, *belle-mère*," Lisa countered.

"What *you* wanted, Lisa?" Veronique asked. "Have you forgotten that you're not marrying an American?"

A rush of color suffused Lisa's face. "Have you forgotten that Sebastien and I are marrying in *America*?"

Veronique tilted her chin while looking down her nose at her future daughter-in-law. "That is your first mistake."

Sitting up straighter, Lisa glared at Veronique. "There was no way I was going to wait six months to marry Sebastien because of your country's residency requirement."

Spots of bright color dotted the older woman's translucent cheeks. "You have not only insulted me, but also my family and my country. You have deliberately ignored our customs. You did not include our custom of postnuptial fireworks. And we do not serve monstrous cakes that no one eats, but cream puffs we call *croquembouches*. My chef would've put the *croquembouches* into a peanut brittle re-creation of our chateau."

Katherine, stunned by the virulent exchange, decided it was time to mediate. "Veronique, we do not serve peanut dishes because of potential food allergies."

The silver-haired woman turned, her eyes shooting laser-blue sparks. "I did not ask you for your opinion, *Miss Langdon*."

Lisa jumped up. "Stay out of this, Miss Langdon! I don't need you to defend me."

Katherine rose, her temper exploding. "I'm not being paid to defend you, but to coordinate your wedding. I specifically asked you if you wanted a French-American theme, and you said no. The only inclusion is a few dishes for the reception dinner."

"I didn't say no."

"I hope you're not calling me a liar, Lisa." Katherine's voice was soft and layered with repressed rage.

Veronique stood up. "One thing I know about Lisa, and that is she is not a liar, Miss Langdon."

Katherine held up her right hand. "I think we should end this meeting right now."

"I think not!" Lisa shouted. "My father's paying you to—"

"Your father isn't paying me to take insults," Katherine said, interrupting her. "This meeting is over. Now!" Walking over to a small round table, she pressed a button on a telephone console. "Rita, please see Madame deVilliers and Miss Barnett out."

Turning, she walked out of the room, down a hallway, and into her private office. She closed the door, biting down on her lower lip to keep the expletives from spilling out.

It was another ten minutes before she'd regained control of her temper. She opened a checkbook, ripping out a blank check. Her hand raced across the negotiable document as she filled in the payee, amount, and then scrawled her signature.

Walking out of her office, she made her way to the reception area. "I'm going out," she flung at Rita.

Rita's large eyes widened when she saw her boss's expression. "Will you be back?"

"Yes."

The door closed with an angry slam and Rita knew exactly who had set Katherine off—Lisa Barnett. The young woman had left Langdon Bridals in tears while her future mother-in-law attempted to console her.

Long, determined strides took Katherine across the marble floor of Barnett Savings and Loan. The woman who usually sat at the desk outside Gerald's office wasn't there. She opened the door leading to his private office.

Gerald's head came up quickly, the words to the letter he was dictating to Mrs. Woodson dying on his lips. Ribbons of sunlight streaming through the bamboo mini-blinds bathed the space in gold, reflecting off his stark-white shirt.

She noticed everything about him in one sweeping glance: his close-cropped, thinning, graying hair; deep, rich, red-brown coloring; his broad shoulders, trim waist, and the exquisite tailored perfection of his suit trousers.

He wasn't the man she had fallen in love with, the man she had promised to marry, the man she wanted to spend the rest of her life with. He was Gerald Madison Barnett, bank president.

A sensual smile curved his mustached mouth. "Mrs. Woodson, you can use my usual closing."

Gathering her steno pad and pencil, Mrs. Woodson smiled at Katherine as she stood and walked out of the office, closing the door quietly. Katherine reached into her purse and handed Gerald the check as he came around the desk.

"What a pleasant surprise," he said softly, ignoring the paper in her hand. He pulled her against his chest and pressed a kiss to her forehead.

Her body was rigid. "Take the check, Gerald."

He plucked the check from her hand, his forehead furrowing in confusion when he noted his name and the amount. "What's this for?"

"It's a refund."

Gerald released Katherine. "A refund for what?"

She met his confused gaze with her angry one. "It represents the balance on your daughter's account."

His deep-set eyes narrowed. "What the hell is going on, Katherine?"

"I'm through, Gerald. I'm through with the Barnett–deVilliers wedding."

"You can't!"

"Don't tell me what I can't do, Gerald. I've had enough of your daughter and her attitude. You may be an expert in running a bank, but you've failed—and failed miserably—at being a father. You've raised a spoiled minx who has no respect for others. The greatest gift you can give her is a course in parenting before she has her own children."

Gerald felt Katherine's rage as his own temper rose. "You can't walk out four days before the wedding."

Rising on her toes, Katherine thrust her face close to his. "Watch me."

"I'll sue you!" he shouted.

"Don't threaten me," Katherine said. She handed him a business card bearing the name of another local wedding consultant.

Turning on her heels, she walked out of his office, head held high. She didn't see the stunned expression on Mrs. Woodson's face as she made her way out of the bank with unseeing eyes. It wasn't until after she'd returned to the privacy of her own home at the end of the day that she broke down and cried.

She cried because she'd gone against everything she'd believed in. She'd made the biggest mistake of her professional career. She'd blurred the lines between business and pleasure: She'd become involved with her client's father.

11

Ignoring the doorbell, Gerald pounded violently on the door to Lisa's co-op, sharp pain radiating from his fist and up his arm. Instead of his temper cooling during the time it took for him to call Lisa and for his driver to drop him off at her housing complex, it had escalated. He'd raised his daughter to be independent and outspoken, not insulting or insolent.

Just when he thought his life was in order, perfect, it had thrown him a vicious curve. His daughter and the woman he'd fallen in love with and planned to marry in a few months had exchanged virulent words, resulting in him having to choose between them.

He loved Lisa more than anyone or anything in his life. He was all she'd had from the moment her mother rejected her, resulting in his becoming father, mother, counselor, and confidant.

The door opened and Lisa fell against his chest, crying

hysterically. Gerald gathered her tightly, his right hand moving up and down her spine in a comforting gesture. His anger eased with her tears. He held her until her sobs subsided to sniffles, then escorted her into the living room.

Sebastien deVilliers's tall, lanky form rose from the love seat, an expression of uncertainty on his delicate, angular face. "She called me to come over," he said in flawless English.

Gerald nodded. He approved of his daughter's choice of husband. The French government employed Sebastien to oversee the restoration of landmark buildings. He'd also noticed the young architect's infinite amount of patience with Lisa.

"I'd like to speak to my daughter—alone."

Raising her head, Lisa stared up at her father. "I'd like Sebastien to stay."

"And I would like to stay," Sebastien stated firmly.

Gerald's gaze did not waver as he glared at his future son-in-law. "No." The single word, though spoken softly, registered the same impact as a whip striking its target.

Lisa jerked away from Gerald. "Daddy!"

"Enough!"

Lisa knew her father well enough to know he was close to losing his temper. She looked at Sebastien. "Go back to the hotel. I'll meet you there."

"Are we still going through with our plans?" he asked in rapid French.

"*Oui*," Lisa replied.

Sebastien inclined his head to Gerald. "*Bonjour*, Monsieur Barnett."

"*Bonjour*, Sebastien," Gerald mumbled under his breath. He wanted him gone so he could talk to his daughter.

Too wound up to sit, he walked over to the French doors leading to the patio and stared at the wrought-iron table with seating for four, while Lisa saw her fiancé to the door. She hadn't sold the apartment, but had decided to lease it to a colleague who was looking for a larger place to live.

"Daddy?"

Turning, Gerald stared at her. There was no mistaking the apprehension in her voice.

Closing the space between them, Gerald grasped her hand and led her to the love seat. The rapidly beating pulse under his fingers reminded him of the runaway heartbeats of a tiny bird he'd once found after it had fallen out of its nest. His own heart turned over in pity, but he told himself that he couldn't permit his love for his daughter to blind him to her faults. Katherine's statement that he'd failed as a father was branded on his heart and in his brain.

"I never thought I'd ever say this, Lisa, but I'm ashamed of you."

"I'm sorry, Daddy," Lisa said, resting her face against Gerald's chest.

"It's not me you should be apologizing to."

Lisa nodded. "I know there's no excuse for me screaming at Miss Langdon. It's just that I can't take any more of trying to appease Sebastien's mother and her going on about how weddings are conducted in France. All I want is a small wedding for my family and close friends, not an extravaganza where the entire village is invited to witness a civil ceremony after the religious one. She won't stop about the postnuptial fireworks and that fact that the French don't have toasts at the reception, and on and on. She even complained that there is no post-wedding feast of cider and crepes the following day as an ongoing tribute of the next generation joining the family line."

"I'm afraid I'm going to have to agree with Veronique."

Lisa pulled back, an expression of complete surprise on her face. "How could you, Daddy?"

"Because I do," he said in a tone that dared her to challenge him. Katherine had told him that she thought Lisa was making a mistake when she refused to incorporate some of the customs of a French wedding with those of an American.

"The moment I leave here I want you to call Miss Langdon and apologize to her for your rudeness," he continued. "I'll contact her later and ask that she change her mind and follow through with your wedding."

Lisa let out a loud gasp. "She quit?"

"Did you expect her to take your insults? You're a thirty-year-old woman. It's time you acted like one."

Closing her eyes, Lisa pressed her forehead to her father's shoulder. "You're right, Daddy. I have been a little off the hook lately."

Gerald wanted to tell Lisa she was entitled to premarital jitters, but he decided not to. It was time for his daughter to accept responsibility for her own behavior.

He kissed her forehead. "I'll talk to you later."

"Okay."

Nodding, he stood up and made his way out of the apartment. Glancing at his watch, he noted the time. The board members of Southern Trust were expected to arrive in Savannah within half an hour. He hoped this meeting of the combined boards would finally result in the merger he'd been anticipating for months.

His driver opened the door to the spacious car, and Gerald slipped onto the rear seat. Then he did what he hadn't done in a long time: He prayed. He prayed that he wouldn't lose Katherine Langdon—the one woman he wanted to spend the rest of his life with.

Katherine cradled the fragile china cup with both hands and stared into the black liquid. Raising the cup, she took a sip of the fragrant brew, savoring its soothing properties. She was back in control.

After she'd returned from Barnett Savings and Loan, she told Rita to handle all calls. The only exception had been a call from Lisa Barnett, who spent more than ten minutes apologizing profusely for her behavior. She and Lisa discussed alternatives to include more of a French theme, and before ringing off Katherine told her that she would commit to seeing the Barnett–deVilliers wedding plans to their conclusion.

She'd hung up calling herself ten thousand fools, knowing she had to go through with her original agreement because she had never reneged on a contract since starting up Langdon Bridals. Now what she had to do was resolve her relationship with Gerald. But that would wait until tomorrow.

The chiming of the doorbell shattered the silence, and she knew intuitively that it was Gerald. Rising, she made her way on bare feet across the cool tiles of the kitchen floor and through the narrow hall that led to the entryway. The light from a table lamp provided enough illumination for her to discern the outline of Gerald's tall body through the glass panel. She unlocked the door, opened it, and seconds later she found herself swept up in a possessive embrace.

"Gerald." Her voice was muffled against his throat as she pushed against his chest. "We have to talk."

Easing back, he held her gaze. He had never seen her look more sensual. Her hair swept up off her neck in seductive disarray and a revealing floor-length silk lounging garment in a shimmering cherry red made him want to sweep her up in his arms and climb the staircase to her bedroom. Sharing her bed had elicited a renewal of sexual desire he hadn't had in years.

Cradling her face between his palms, he brushed his mouth with hers. "Are we still getting married?"

Katherine felt the movement of his erratic breathing as her own stopped momentarily, catching in her throat. "Shouldn't you be concerned about Lisa's wedding?"

"No," he said softly. He had shredded her check, then had Mrs. Woodson put it in an envelope addressed to her business location. "There is a ninety-nine percent certainty that Lisa's going to marry Sebastien. What I'm concerned about is the two of us. I haven't had a woman in my life for more than thirty years, and I've never regretted that decision. But what I will regret for the rest of my life is not fighting to keep you."

Curving her arms under his shoulders, Katherine rested her cheek over his heart, listening to the strong pumping sound under her ear. "Lisa called me earlier and apologized," she began in a quiet voice. "Now it's my turn to apologize. I've had many difficult clients over the years, but I've never dropped any of them. I know I overreacted with Lisa because I'd permitted myself to become involved with you. And one of my unwritten policies is never to become personally involved with a client's family member."

Gerald dropped a kiss on her fragrant hair. "No, darling. There's nothing for you to apologize for. You've helped me see what I couldn't see for years. I've been giving Lisa mixed signals: Grow up and be independent, but don't worry because Daddy will fight your battles and solve all your problems. That ended today. And I have you to thank for that."

His words and his nearness gave Katherine a comfort she had never known. She loved Gerald, wanted to marry him, and grow old in his arms.

"What are we going to do, Gerald?"

Bending slightly, he picked her up effortlessly. "We're going upstairs to talk and set a date for our wedding. Then I'm going to tell you silently how much I love you."

She gave him a sassy grin. "I won't mind if you make some noise."

"What do you want me to say?" he asked, heading in the direction of the curving staircase.

"Moan good for me and I promise to scream for you," she whispered close to his ear.

Throwing back his head, Gerald laughed. "You've got yourself a deal, Miss Langdon."

The day of Lisa Barnett's wedding proved to be a predictable Savannah summer day—hot and humid. An early morning thundershower washed away the haze, leaving a blue sky with puffy white clouds in its wake.

Katherine left her bed at six, feeling invigorated. Lisa and Sebastien's rehearsal at the church and the subsequent rehearsal dinner held at Gerald's house had become a festive affair.

One of Gerald's teenage nephews, who had been recruited to partner Noelle de Villiers as a groomsman, teased the young French girl relentlessly until she joined him and the other young adults in their antics. It was apparent to everyone that Lisa and Sebastien were very much in love with each other, much to the delight of their parents.

The prenuptial gathering had provided Katherine with a glimpse of the people who would eventually become part of her family. She and Gerald planned to marry the last Sunday in October—the date she had originally selected for his daughter's wedding.

She'd called her parents and brother, swearing them to secrecy. She and Gerald had agreed to wait a week before making a public announcement that they intended to exchange vows at the small Macon Baptist church she'd attended when living there.

Her smile was bright and her step was light. Her lips were pressed shut so no sound of hysterical joy would burst out. She would save the joy—for her own wedding.

The crowd in the historic African-American church grew restless as the minutes inched past eight. Katherine pushed back the sleeve to her black silk tunic and glanced at her watch. It was eight-twenty and there was no sign of Gerald, Lisa, or Sebastien. Meredith and Noelle had broken with tradition, arriving at the church without the bride.

The dimmed lights, dozens of burning candles, string quartet playing Bach and Beethoven sonatas, and countless baskets filled with bouquets of pale peach peonies, cream and burgundy roses, baby calla lilies, and rich red berries created an ethereal setting that was certain to become the wedding of the season.

At eight-thirty Katherine felt the beginnings of what she was able to identify as panic. What if something had happened to them en route? Had they become involved in a traffic accident?

She walked over to Rita. "I'm going to my car to call Gerald."

The assistant raised her eyebrows, nodding. Katherine had never referred to Mr. Barnett so casually before. "What do you think happened?"

"That's what I'm going to find out."

She headed for the back of the church at the same time the doors opened and Gerald strolled in, elegantly attired in formal wear. Her gaze widened when she realized he had come alone. She gripped the back of a pew to support her sagging knees. In the wavering light she couldn't quite make out Gerald's expression, but one thing she knew was that he wasn't smiling.

Standing at the altar, he faced the assembled guests as the musicians put down their bows. "Ladies and gentlemen, I regret to inform you that you will not witness Lisa Barnett exchange vows with Sebastien deVilliers this evening because they've eloped."

There were choruses of gasps, whispers, and a strangled cry from Veronique as she collapsed against her husband's shoulder. Katherine stared at Gerald, unable to believe what she'd just heard.

Gerald held up his right hand for silence. "I'm certain everyone, myself included, came here tonight for a wedding." Heads bobbed in confirmation. "We'll, I'm not going to disappoint you good people."

Heads turned and all gazes were glued on Gerald's long, fluid stride as he retreated to the back of the church and grasped Katherine's hand.

Her heart pounded relentlessly in her chest as she shook her head. "No, Gerald."

He pulled her closer. "Unclench your teeth and smile, darling. You and I are going to be married."

Amid gasps of shock and surprise, Gerald signaled for Meredith and her partner and his nephew and Noelle to precede them up the red carpet, while Katherine glanced over at the deVillierses. Jacques touched his wife's eyes gently with a handkerchief, taking care not to muss her professionally applied makeup.

It wasn't until the quartet began the familiar strains of the wedding march that Katherine realized that she was about to be a stand-in bride.

Katherine did not remember Gerald escorting her along the carpet to the altar. It was as if she had floated over the colorful surface to the front of the church.

Rev. Dixon nodded to the couple as he cleared his voice to begin the ceremony. She repeated her vows trancelike, her gaze fused with Gerald's. There was no blessing or exchange of rings, but before she and Gerald kissed each other for the first time as husband and wife, he smiled at her, holding her cold fingers within his warmer grasp. "Your love delights me, my sweetheart and bride. Your love is better than wine; your perfume more fragrant than any spice."

His soft drawling voice floated clearly to the back of the church, and all of the love and emotion Katherine felt for her husband overflowed. Her cheeks were moist with tears as he gathered her to his chest and kissed her mouth gently.

Standing on the steps of the century-old church, Katherine pulled on her husband's arm, garnering his attention. The bright spotlight from a video camera and the intermittent flashes from cameras, along with the hail of rice and flower petals, had pulled her from her momentary state of shock. She was now Mrs. Gerald Barnett.

"I need to go home and change. I don't want to be photographed in work clothes."

It was as if Gerald noticed her black silk tunic and matching slacks for the first time. "I'll send everyone to the house to wait for us. I don't think they'll miss us for a couple of hours."

Katherine placed a hand over his satin waistcoat. "It won't take me a couple of hours to change."

"Maybe yes, maybe no." He gave her a leering grin.

"No, Gerald. We'll have plenty of time for that tomorrow."

His eyebrows met in a frown. "Why tomorrow?"

"Remember, French receptions usually end well after midnight."

He had forgotten. Even though his daughter had eloped with her French husband, Lisa had compromised with Veronique by extending the reception into the early hours of Sunday morning.

Gerald's regular driver drove them back to her town house, where she called her brother and told him to pack for an overnight stay in Savannah. Before he could question her sanity, she told him to bring his wife, children, grandchildren, and their parents to help her celebrate her marriage to Gerald Barnett. However, when Robert reminded her of the two-and-a-half-hour drive between the two cities, she promised that the celebrating was certain to last well past midnight.

She changed her black undergarments to off-white, before slipping into an ivory silk floor-length slip dress with an overdress of matching organza with embroidered flowers along the rounded neckline and hem. Gerald sat on a padded stool, watching her as she slipped on each garment. She presented him with her back and he stood and buttoned the many covered buttons running from the nape of her neck to her waist.

Lowering his head, he breathed a kiss on the back of her neck. "I love you, Katherine Barnett."

Turning, she curved her bare, scented arms around his neck. "Not as much as I love you, Gerald Barnett."

"I think not," he whispered, pressing his mouth to hers.

"I think so," she argued softly, moving closer. Staring up at him, she said, "Had Lisa given you any indication that she'd planned to elope?"

Gerald shook his head. "No. She did threaten once that she was going to elope when Veronique chastised her for not including Noelle in the wedding, but I told her that I would disown her if she did."

"Have you decided to disown her?"

"No, darling. Lisa's one half of what makes me who I am, and you're the other half."

Katherine laughed, the low, smoky sound he'd come to look for and love. And he wanted to make her laugh many more times before he closed his eyes on this world.

"You're a big pussycat," she teased.

"You're right about that because you're the only woman who's been able to make me growl."

Pulling out of his loose embrace, she flashed a sensual smile. "Let me touch up my makeup before we leave."

Gerald also wanted to return to his home. He was anxious to change out of the cutaway coat and into a white dinner jacket.

A satisfied grin tugged at the corners of his mouth. It seemed as if both Barnetts had gotten their wish. It was ironic that father and daughter would celebrate wedding anniversaries on the same day.

It was close to midnight when Katherine's family arrived. Priceless champagne flowed from several fountains; a live band alternated with prerecorded music, the music spanning several generations, while most of the assembled danced under the starry night sky.

She introduced everyone to Gerald, and then gave her brother the keys to her town house. "I thought you'd prefer staying at my place rather than at a hotel."

Robert Langdon cradled his sister's face between his large hands. His smile said it all. He was proud of her. "You did good, baby sister."

Katherine was beginning to feel the effects from the countless glasses of champagne thrust at her whenever someone offered a toast as the clock inched toward one-thirty. Veronique and Jacques, having recovered from not seeing their son exchange vows with his American fiancée, danced nonstop.

Katherine had requested Etta James's "At Last" as her special song when she shared her first dance with Gerald, while he chose Nat King Cole's "Unforgettable."

One of the waiters tapped Gerald on his arm and informed him that he had an overseas telephone call. "I'll get Jacques and Veronique," Katherine said when he stared at her. The overseas call had to be from Lisa and Sebastien.

The two couples retreated to Gerald's library. Veronique

sat down on a chair, while Jacques stood next to her, one hand resting on her shoulder. Gerald pulled Katherine against his side as he picked up the telephone receiver resting on the desk's leather surface.

"Hello."

"Hi, Daddy. Who was that that answered the phone?"

"Where are you?" Gerald asked, deliberately ignoring his daughter's query.

"I'm in Paris. Did you find my note?"

"*Oui*, Madame deVilliers, I did find your note." Everyone sat up straighter. "You know what I said I'd do if you eloped."

"Yes. You said you'd disown me; but after I thought about it I knew you were just kidding."

He raised his eyebrows. "You did?"

"Of course. I . . ." Her voice was drowned out by the sound of exploding fireworks. "What's that noise?"

"Fireworks, Princess. We're celebrating a wedding."

There were several seconds of silence before Lisa's voice came through the receiver again. "Whose wedding? Don't tell me you're celebrating without the bride and groom being there?"

"Wrong, Princess. There is a bride and groom. Katherine and I were married tonight."

"Miss Langdon? You've been seeing her?"

"Yes. She's no longer Miss Langdon, but Mrs. Katherine Barnett."

"I can't believe it. You and Miss Lang . . . I mean Mrs. Barnett. . . . Dammit, Daddy, I can't call her Mrs. Barnett if she's my stepmother, can I?"

"It'll be up to Katherine how she wants you to address her. Your in-laws are here. You want to speak to them?"

"Yes."

He extended the telephone receiver to Veronique. Dressed in a becoming raspberry satin sheath, she rose and took the telephone.

"*Bonjour*, Lisa." The sky may have indicated night, but the clock said it was the next day. Veronique's expressive eyebrows lifted as she listened to her daughter-in-law attempt to explain why she and Sebastien had eloped. "It's all right, daughter," she said in a comforting tone. "No, I am not disappointed. We still have Noelle. That is, unless *she* decides to elope. Look, *ma petite*, kiss Sebastien for me. Jacques and I want to get back to the celebrating. I have changed my mind about American weddings. They are simply wonderful. *Adieu*." She returned the phone to Gerald and walked out of the library on her husband's arm.

Gerald put the receiver to his ear. "Princess?"

"She just dissed me, Daddy."

"I'm about to do the same, Lisa. My wife and I still have to cut the cake. As soon as Katherine has a free week we'll fly over and visit you and Sebastien."

"I'd love that. Daddy?"

"Yes?"

"I love you. And tell Katherine I love her for loving you."

"Why don't you tell her yourself?"

Katherine took the proffered telephone. "Good morning, Lisa."

"Good morning. Would you mind if I called you *Mother*? I'm certain Daddy told you that I never really had a mother."

She felt her eyes well with tears. "Of course I wouldn't mind. In fact, I'm honored—I always wanted a child."

"It looks as if we all won: I married Sebastien, and now that my dad married you, I have a mother and you a daughter."

"How right you are. Good-bye, daughter. I'll see you soon."

"Good-bye, Mother."

Katherine replaced the telephone on its cradle, and then turned to Gerald. The brilliance of the diamonds on the bangle circling her wrist sparkled under the recessed lights as her fingertips traced the outline of his wing collar.

"How long do you think we have to wait before we're grandparents?"

Pressing his forehead to hers, Gerald kissed the tip of her nose. "I hope not as long as it took for me to find you."

"Was the wait worth it?"

"Oh yes, Katherine Langdon Barnett, more than worth it. How does it feel to be a stand-in-bride?"

"Very, very good," she said as their lips met in a sweet joining that promised forever. Hand in hand, they walked out of the house and back to the festive celebrating.

It probably would become the most talked-about wedding of the season not because of its elegance, but because of the woman who'd managed to land one of Savannah's most eligible African-American bachelors.

Learning
to Love

GWYNNE FORSTER

1

"Go right in, Dr. Braxton," Professor Adejonko O. Kuti's secretary said. "He's expecting you."

Sharon Braxton had been in the offices of other Columbia University professors, but she hadn't previously seen a brass knocker on an office door. But there it was, along with a brass plate inscribed *Dr. Adejonko O. Kuti, Professor of Economic Development*.

Hmmm, she thought, *bet he thinks well of himself.* She thanked the secretary and tapped gently on his door.

"Come in."

She hesitated. His voice projected a deep vibrancy, like distant thunder, but impatient and a little arrogant, and she had a sudden feminine urge to see the owner of that voice.

She opened the door, stepped inside and stood there. Waiting. Professor Kuti did not glance up from the reading matter on his desk.

"Have a seat," he ordered, still engrossed in the papers before him, but she remained standing.

Accustomed to a generous amount of deference herself, Sharon bristled, but if she was going to get his help in setting up her project in Nigeria, she'd have to hold her tongue. However, after several minutes, her patience expired.

"Dr. Kuti," she said evenly, "your secretary gave my assistant an appointment for me to see you here at your office on March twenty-seventh at ten o'clock in the morning. Today is March twenty-seventh, and it's ten o'clock in the morning."

Without moving his head, he raised his eyes as if in reprimand, and then his head snapped up in a classic double-take. Slowly, as if by means other than his own, he raised himself from his chair and stared at her.

Sharon sucked in her breath and thanked God for the presence of mind not to gape at the man. She thought of holding her wrists in order to slow down her pulse. His six foot, five inch height, smooth dark skin and copper-brown eyes weren't all that unusual—nor were his finely chiseled cheekbones and aristocratic nose and lips—but he had a masculine persona that jumped out at her and lassoed her as tightly as any cowboy ever roped a calf.

At last, he spoke. "Won't you . . . uh . . . have a seat?" He pointed to the chair beside his desk, but she sat instead in an armchair that faced him from across the room. No point in letting him have all the advantages.

"Thank you for agreeing to see me, Dr. Kuti. You're aware that much of the financial and other international aid to developing countries is wasted by inefficiency and duplication of effort. Different Western countries and international agencies are pouring money and experts into the same country for the same purpose, but very little is accomplished. As the United Nations Assistant Secretary-General in charge of this project, my job is to eliminate this waste. I've developed a plan, and I want to try it out in Nigeria. As a UN officer, I can do it without too much interference, but you'll agree that I'll be more successful if I have your support."

He fingered his square chin and seemed to muse over what she'd said. "Nigeria is a big country, and it's very complicated, probably too much so for a foreigner to understand. You have to focus on a specific area."

So she was in for a lecture. Well, she hadn't been a student in years, and she didn't plan to act like one. "I'm focusing on Yorubaland."

He sat forward. "*Yorubaland?* You're the person in charge of . . . of this?" he asked as though the idea was ludicrous.

She knew that when it came to the status of women, Africa made the United States look like a perfect paradise. Still, she hadn't counted on having to tussle with that. She raised an eyebrow. "I'm in charge of this and much more, Dr. Kuti, as I'm sure you know. I need a letter of introduction to someone in Yorubaland who can make people listen. A letter from you can open the doors I want opened. How about it?"

She had the feeling that he wasn't really listening to her, that he was reacting to her on some other level. He made a pyramid of his fingers and took a deep breath. "Miss Braxton, you'll never get all these international aid providers to cooperate. It's a waste of time. Besides, you're asking a lot. My people don't appreciate things foreigners start, and they aren't used to taking orders from women, so—"

The nerve of him! "*Dr.* Braxton," she corrected him. "I don't give orders, Dr. Kuti. I collaborate with local officials."

She wished he wouldn't stare at her that way, as if he were trying to find something inside of her. Yet his gaze wasn't harsh or unfriendly. It was all she could do to keep her mind on her reason for being there.

"It will be hard on you. As a troubleshooter, you have to go into the villages and talk with the elders. Women don't do that."

She crossed her legs at the knee, leaned back in the chair and waved her hand, dismissing the idea. "This woman does." Maybe he needed a challenge. "You're an expert on development and you're a Yoruba." When he didn't so much as flicker one of his long, black lashes, she added, "I'm sure you care about your country . . . and your tribe."

"Yes. Yes, of course," he said, as if his thoughts were elsewhere. "You'll . . . uh . . . You'll hear from me."

Refusing to be dismissed, she stood and walked toward his desk. When he rose to his full height, she imagined him resplendent in an elegant dashiki striding like a colossus across the mountains of his homeland. As she usually did when terminating an appointment, she extended her hand and when he took it, frissons of electricity shot up her arm. The man held her hand and stared at her as though perplexed.

She pulled herself together as quickly as she could and made herself smile. "Thank you for your help. I hope to hear from you soon."

"My secretary has your phone number?"

She nodded. "Thanks again." She didn't hold out much hope for his help, but if he wouldn't write that letter for her, she'd succeed without him. It wouldn't be the first time.

———

Long after the door closed behind Sharon Braxton, Adejonko O. Kuti stood as she'd left him, staring at the spot she'd vacated. Dumbfounded. *In the name of Olórùn.* Inarticulate, practically speechless, fumbling for words like a college freshman in a public-speaking class. He was thirty-three years old, had earned two degrees at Oxford and a Ph.D. at Harvard University, and he'd lived, worked or traveled in seventy countries. But she'd reduced him to putty. Perspiration beaded his forehead as he dropped himself into the chair. He'd never felt this . . . this hunger . . . this . . . He threw up his hands as a dreadful thought came to him: The feeling wasn't going away. *Was this the reason why men in these so-called developed countries chased a woman as if she were the only one left on earth?* Maybe he'd been away from home too long.

He buzzed his secretary. "Call Adedeji over at the UN and find out what he knows about Sharon Braxton."

"She's an Assistant Secretary-General, Professor Kuti."

"I know that, and I've read some of her work, but . . . Call Ade and ask him."

"Yes, sir."

If he played it straight, he'd give her a letter to his father, Fadipe A. Kuti, an Oba, one of the crown princes of the Yoruba tribe. His father was honest, though he certainly benefited from the disarray of international funding and the projects of the do-gooders who streamed through Western Nigeria. But if he sent a letter to his father with an American woman, United Nations officer or not, his father would conclude that his elder son was interested in a foreign woman, and he'd have a fit. When he ran his hand over his hair and ground his teeth, on the left side of his jaw, Kuti knew he was admitting to frustration. He'd have to think hard about giving Sharon Braxton that letter.

Several days later he told his secretary to telephone Sharon, not because he'd decided to help her, but because he couldn't get her out of his mind. Tall, slim and lovely with big, soft-brown eyes, and the sharp mind that he liked in a person. Maybe if he saw her again, he wouldn't like her. She agreed to have lunch with him the next day, and he hardly slept that night. Knowing she caused his restlessness, he tried to harden himself against her; the elder son of a royal chief did not grovel before a woman.

"I'll come to you this time," he told her in what he considered a magnanimous gesture. It didn't escape him that she accepted his courtesy as if it were her due. *American men must have a hard time with their women.*

He walked into her office and looked around at the trappings of status. The kind of accommodations he'd expect a senior man to have and, without thinking, he said something to that effect.

"Don't tell me you're a male chauvinist, Dr. Kuti, because if you are, we aren't going to get along." She rose from her chair, walked to meet him and extended her hand. "Have a seat."

Her fingers sent electric currents plowing through his body, and he stared at them, wondering at their power. "Thanks. I never know what to say to you American women."

When she grinned, he suspected that his face bore a telltale, sheepish expression. "Afraid I can't help you with that," she said. "Now, if you want to know about development strategy . . ." She let it dangle, a mischievous smile playing around her big brown eyes. Eyes that projected warmth and wickedness. Then her face bloomed in a full smile.

His palms bore the prints of his nails. With his heart beating at twice its normal rate, he might as well give up. *What on earth did the woman do to him?*

"What can I do for you?" she asked, and he appreciated that she didn't sound the least officious, even if she *had* caught him off guard with the unexpected softness. Maybe she was needling him, or maybe he was going crazy. He didn't know which. Wrapping himself in his normal dignity, he looked her in the eye.

"I thought we'd eat across the street at the Ambassador Grill and . . . discuss a few things."

He watched, mesmerized, as her eyebrows came up slowly and her unpainted lips curved into a grin. "You're kidding.

We're on my turf, so you're my guest. We'll eat in the Delegates Dining Room."

He stared. Maybe he'd misunderstood her. "Shall we go?"

A long shapely leg swung from her knee, rhythmically, bobbing and weaving like a snake. He shook his head. Clearing it. "To the Delegates Dining Room?"

In spite of himself, his fingers brushed over his short hair and he ground his teeth. "But *I* called *you*."

Her grin widened. "I know. You can get even with me sometime."

Enough of this nonsense. "And I will, too, lady. Trust me, I will get mine."

"Be glad to accommodate you. Let's go."

At least she only nodded to or smiled at the people who greeted her as they walked to the dining room. The women in his world would have stopped to chat, impressing him with their importance and prominence. She let him finish eating before mentioning her plan for Nigeria. He listened to the details. She intended to implement a pilot program in Yorubaland, testing a method of obtaining collaboration among national and international groups that were helping to develop the region. If the plan succeeded, she would introduce it in other underdeveloped countries.

"I have to leave for Nigeria in three weeks. I'm not used to failure, Dr. Kuti, but—"

"Call me Jon. I admit the plan's a pretty good one, but you can't expect . . . well, they're used to dealing with men, and I'd hate to see you—"

Interrupting him, she leaned forward. "I'm Sharon. Don't mention this gender business to me again, Jon. I'm where I am because I'm good at what I do, but I can't accomplish much in the six months I'll be there unless I have the cooperation of local leaders."

She looked him in the eye only briefly, then aimed her gaze somewhere over his shoulder. Maybe she liked him, too.

"Now then, are you going to help me or not?" he heard her say, though the words came to him as though from a great distance.

He shook his head, clearing it. "All right. I'll write some letters, and I'll send copies to you and to the United Nations office in Lagos." A glance at his watch brought a surprise. He looked around the nearly empty dining room and marveled that the time had gone so quickly.

"I have to be going. I . . . uh . . . We ought to get together at least once more before you leave. Going to Nigeria with no knowledge of the politics of the place is like . . . I mean, Sharon, you could be walking into a hornet's nest."

Her hesitation made him hold his breath, because he wanted to see her again. When she said, "Thanks, Jon. I'll take all the advice you're willing to give me," he decided that Sharon Braxton would need a lot of advice.

Advice, huh? She'd done her homework and had enough information on the people of Western Nigeria to enable her to accomplish her goal. How much "advice" did she need? She went back to her office, walked over to the window and looked down on the East River. What was it about that man that made her want to play with him, to tease him until he got mad enough to . . . to give in to her—all the way? She didn't believe he'd hold still for it, but she'd love to stroke him into . . . *Girl, you're getting pretty fanciful.*

She heard her buzzer. "Phone for you, Dr. Braxton. He says it's personal."

Her eyes widened. What "he" had something personal to say to her? Her brother would identify himself. "Sharon Braxton speaking."

"Jon here. It occurred to me that your office might not have information on separate villages. If you'll tell me which ones you'd like to visit, I'll get a contact for you and tell you a bit about them. Would that help?"

She recovered from the sudden sound of his rich *basso profundo* and told herself that no matter what he looked like, sounded like and acted like, he was just a man. *Yeah. Right. And thinking about him sends you into a tailspin.*

"Jon, I'd like that."

"Good. Have your secretary send me your Nigerian itinerary, and I'll take it from there. We can go over it the next time we meet."

She thanked him, but he didn't fool her. They didn't have to meet in order to discuss it, but if he needed an excuse to see her, she didn't mind, and what he'd suggested could only help.

"Okay. I'll do that this afternoon," she said.

She hung up. So she interested him as a woman. Or did he consider her a challenge, a hill to climb? Not that it mattered. She didn't let her libido lead her by the nose. Then her mind's eye conjured up his image, and she sucked in her breath and released a mild expletive. She wasn't going to lose her head over a man, and certainly not one who didn't appear to hold women in high regard. But, *Lord*, he was so much *man*. Power, self-confidence. He exuded it. And the man could get to her. She had to watch herself around him.

During the next week, they met several times for lunch, usually at Jon's instigation and for reasons related to her project that he said were important. But by the time she was ready to leave for her six-month stay in Nigeria, Jon had stopped fabricating reasons to see her.

"You're leaving tomorrow," he said after phoning her one morning. "How about lunch?"

She went to lunch with him at a restaurant of his choice, because she shared his passion for Italian food. "What about dinner tonight?" he asked, not waiting for their lunch to arrive.

"I'm not sure that's a good idea. Besides, I have to finish packing." She knew it wasn't a good idea. She'd seen so much of him in the past two weeks that he'd eased his way inside of her, and she hadn't wanted that.

He leaned back in the booth and stared at her, exposing a bit of himself for the first time, as his copper-brown eyes darkened with emotion. "As efficient as you are, I know you've already finished packing." Then he leaned forward. "My cards are on the table, Sharon. I'm going to miss you, and I mean plenty. What do you say to that?"

What *could* she say? "Whatever I say will get me into trouble."

He handed her letters to the Secretary of the Interior, the chiefs of two Yoruba townships and the head of the Economics Department at the University of Ife at Ile-Ife, seat of Yoruba culture. "I've also sent letters to the United Nations Resident Representative in Lagos. If you need anything, phone me."

She thanked him. "Surely, with these recommendations, I won't have any problems."

"I said, if you need anything, and I mean *anything*—from a paper clip to a Mercedes—phone me, and I'll see that you get it."

She couldn't move her glance from his hypnotic gaze. Icy marbles battled for position in her stomach, and her breathing accelerated. "We're skating on thin ice, Jon. I'm grateful for—"

"I don't want gratitude from you. I want to spend this evening with you, having dinner, seeing a play or a movie. Or maybe listening to some music. And as for thin ice, where I come from, there isn't any."

He could manage a sense of humor even when he was serious, and she liked that. "Dinner, then. I have to turn in early."

He took a pad from the inside pocket of his jacket. "Where do you live? I'll pick you up at your place at seven-thirty."

Which meant he'd change clothes, and she should dress. "One-eighty-five West End. I live in Lincoln Towers."

His smile robbed her of her breath and she grabbed her chest. "Wonderful. I live on Sixty-eighth Street between Columbus and Central Park West. We're neighbors." The smile lit up his face, and she couldn't help catching his mood as he radiated happiness. "We'll have a lovely evening," he promised.

"What do you wear to dinner?" she asked.

"A dark suit, but if you feel like dressing up, I'd love to see you in a dress. Your suits are nice." He seemed to think about it for a few seconds. "I'd say they're elegant, but . . ."

He leaned forward, excitement mirrored in his copper gaze. "Let's make an evening of it. What do you say?"

Caught up in the magic of his enthusiasm, she reached across the table and grasped his hand. "Yes. Let's. I'll expect you at seven-thirty."

His fingers wrapped around hers and he gazed into her eyes. Suddenly frantic as rockets exploded in her head, she jerked her hand from him and rubbed her treacherous fingers. His smile didn't comfort her, for it held a troubled shadow.

"I'll . . . We'd better go," she said. "I have to put my desk in order and check my travel documents."

He stood, reached for her hand as she attempted to stand, and she had no choice but to touch him again. "Till this evening."

She nodded and walked away as fast as she could.

She left her office sharply at five and took a taxi home. So he was tired of her "nice" suits, was he? After a leisurely bath scented with Fendi bath oil, she patted herself dry, looked in the full-length mirror, liked what she saw and sprayed Fendi perfume where it counted most. Over her red bikini panties and bra, she slipped on a skin-tight, strapless red silk evening dress, put diamond studs in her earlobes and red lipstick on her lips. Then she brushed her hair down below her shoulders. *Tired of her Oscar de la Renta suits? She'd show him.*

The doorman rang her on the intercom at exactly seven-thirty. "Dr. Kuti is here to see you."

"Thanks, Norm. Please send him up." Down, girl, she said to herself when her pulse threatened to run out of control. Maybe she shouldn't have put on her "scud missile," as she called her dress. What would he think?

I hope I'm doing the right thing, Jon said to himself as he stepped into the elevator. He hadn't had this kind of relationship with an American woman, and this particular female was probably full of surprises even for an American man. He rang the doorbell and stepped back. In his culture, standing close to the door after knocking was considered poor manners. The door opened and she smiled at him. At least he thought she did. She hit him like a bolt of thunder, addling him. Pure woman. A shimmering goddess. He could do nothing except stare at her.

She stepped out of the door into the hallway and grasped his arm. "Come on in. I won't bite."

That comment was what he needed to restore his aplomb. "Maybe not with your teeth. You're dynamite." He handed her the box of a dozen red roses that the florist assured him every woman wanted and waited for her reaction. Her fingers trembled as she opened the box. Then she gazed at the roses for a while before slowly raising her eyes to his.

"Thank you. They're beautiful, and I love flowers. Roses are my favorites."

"That means you're pleased?"

"Yes. I love them."

"I . . . uh . . . You're . . . I like you in that dress."

"I hope you do. Otherwise I'll make you wait while I change into one of my *nice* suits that you're tired of seeing."

He had to smother a laugh. "I remember saying something like that, and if it's the reason you're wearing this dress, I congratulate myself on my tactlessness."

He caught her staring at him before she diverted her gaze. "You look like a prince in your royal blue dashiki."

"Thanks. We call it an *agbada*. I wasn't sure you'd appreciate my wearing it, but we're living it up, as my roommate at Harvard used to say, and this is my tuxedo."

"Well, trust me, it makes a statement, and a regal one at that."

Their reservation was at "21," one of New York's most famed restaurants, and the red roses he'd ordered rested in a crystal vase on their table. It pleased him that she mouthed a thank you as the waiter changed the candles and lit new ones. He liked the fact that she always told him at once that he'd pleased her, that she didn't let him stew over a thing. A thoughtful woman. He could get used to her. Men had watched her as they walked toward their table, and that pleased him, too. He didn't mind being the envy of men; in fact, he was accustomed to that. They finished an elegant meal and stepped outside the restaurant.

"I know you're flying tomorrow morning, but could we walk a couple of blocks before I take you home?" When she agreed, he said, "You aren't always this agreeable, are you?"

"Good heavens, no. I certainly am not."

"Then why? I'm getting the impression that I'm more attractive at night than I am in the daytime. Or . . . was it the roses?"

"It's because you're wonderful company, and you haven't said one male chauvinist thing all evening."

A groan escaped him, and he didn't care if she heard it. "Why didn't I keep my mouth shut while I had things going my way?"

"You mean things aren't going your way now? Let me tell you, they are, because I'm strolling with you on this concrete in these spiked heels. You're way ahead."

"I don't see how you stand up in them?"

"Habit."

In the taxi to the apartment house in which she lived, he wanted to hold her hand, but he wasn't certain how she'd take it, so he let himself sit on one side of the cab while she sat on the other. At her apartment door, he didn't suggest prolonging the evening, though he didn't want to leave her. The last American woman he'd taken to dinner had expected to spend a few more hours enjoying his company. Intimate hours. But he knew that even the slightest suggestion of such to Sharon Braxton would torpedo their embryonic relationship.

"I'll take you to the airport tomorrow morning," he said. "What time does your flight leave?"

"Ten-twenty, but you don't have to—"

He grasped her arm, because he needed so badly to touch her. "I don't have to do much of anything apart from my work at Columbia. I want to take you to the airport, and I'll be here for you at seven."

At her hesitation, cold tendrils of apprehension plowed

through him. "Is there another man you want to take you tomorrow morning?"

She looked him in the eye. "No, there isn't."

"Then I'll be here."

She studied him for several seconds, then she opened her apartment door, reached back and kissed his cheek. "Thanks for a wonderful evening." By the time he recovered from the shock of her unexpected behavior, she had closed her door. But one day it would open, and remain open.

At six-thirty the next morning, Sharon asked the doorman to send someone up for her bags. Somehow, she didn't think Jon would appreciate acting as her porter. But when he arrived, his first words were, "Where are your bags?"

"One of the handymen took them down for me. I made coffee. Do you have time for a cup?"

His smile of appreciation gave her a good feeling as he strolled into her home for the first time. "I'd love some coffee. All I've had today is a glass of water." He glanced around. "This is . . . it's elegant and so . . . I guess the word is feminine." His left eyebrow lifted in a way that suggested deep thought. "You are a many-sided woman."

"I take that as a compliment. Sit there, why don't you, while I get us the coffee. Is a mug okay?"

"You can give it to me in a pot."

Now that was something for the imagination—the famed Dr. Kuti drinking coffee from a pot. "Be right back."

He drank the coffee quickly. "That was wonderful, and I'd ask for another one, but we'd better be going."

He'd hired a limousine to take them to the airport, and she could see that he was accustomed to luxury as he relaxed in the Lincoln Town Car's sumptuous leather seat. His long, tapered fingers strummed the space between them on the seat and she wondered what was causing his agitation. Did he want his hands on her? Goose pimples popped out on her arms as she imagined how those hands would feel on her body.

"The only advantage to getting out this early in New York

is the absence of traffic. We're almost there, and I can eat."

"You like food, I presume."

"Food is the second most gratifying thing in a man's life."

"I see."

"You're not going to ask me what's number one?" A smile played around his lips, and she knew he was baiting her.

"Nope. I'm not going there."

His laughter, deep and resonant, seemed to come from the depth of him, and it showered her with pleasure. "Wise woman."

After she checked in, he suggested they have breakfast. "Are you going to wait till I have to go through security?"

"I have a pass from the consular office, so I can stay with you till you have to board. Let's eat. Airline food isn't fit for pigs."

Then he took her hand and she looked up at him, aware that the wonder of their electrifying connection mirrored itself on her face. Gently, he squeezed her hand, took her small carry-on case and headed for the food court holding her hand as though he had the right.

"That stuff's full of cholesterol," she said, eyeing his sausage, bacon, eggs and thickly buttered biscuits.

"Yeah. I know. It's the worst habit I've picked up since I left home. Soul food is rightly named. Now, if I just had some fried ham, redeye gravy and grits . . ." His copper-brown eyes took on a dreamy cast. "That's what I call food."

She shook her head in dismay. "And the same man can dine on smoked salmon, caviar, confit of goose and other gourmet delights with an expression on his face that says he's in heaven."

"Sure. Good food is just that no matter who created it." He picked up a strip of bacon and held it to her lips. "Have some. You can afford the calories."

She bit off a piece. She loved bacon, but had sworn off it. "I thought you liked me in that red dress. If I eat what you're eating, I'll split it."

"If a woman is fat, we Yoruba say her husband is prosperous."

She couldn't help staring at him. "That must be the richest region on this planet."

He dabbed at his lips with his napkin, drank the remainder of a glass of water and gazed at her. Suddenly, as if her remark had just registered, he bared his white teeth in a wide grin. Then he laughed. "There's a lot to be said for a woman who can get into that red dress. We'd better go through security. Where are you sitting?"

"Business class."

"Good. At least you'll be comfortable."

They checked through security and went to the business class lounge to wait for the flight. She couldn't understand why he'd become so silent, almost pensive.

"Do you wish you were going home?"

He lifted his shoulder in a quick shrug. "In some respects, yes, but I'm comfortable where I am."

So much for that enigmatic reply. "That's my flight number," she said. Once more, he took her hand, as they walked to the gate.

"I'm going to miss you."

"And you don't want to, do you?"

"I'm not sure, but that's past the point. Remember what I told you. If you need anything, I want you to call me. Promise?"

He was so serious, so . . . All at once, he locked her into his arms in a powerful grip, lowered his head and seared her mouth with his hot lips. Wildfire shot through her, and she clung to his shoulders.

"Kiss me?"

It was phrased as a request, but it sounded like a command, and she parted her lips for his foraging tongue. Her trembling body betrayed her when he slipped his tongue into her mouth, tightened his hold on her body and loved her. She pulled his tongue deeper, feasting on it as if she were starved. And she was starved for a man's loving, she realized. This man. The realization shocked her, and she broke the kiss.

When she looked up into his eyes, eyes now stormy with desire, she knew he was no less stunned than she. Nothing had prepared her for such a reaction to him, or to any man. She lowered her gaze, aware that she reciprocated the desire that his eyes communicated.

Still holding her body loosely in his arms, he looked into her eyes and let her know that his cloak of dignity never deserted him. "I wasn't prepared for that, and I don't suppose you were. I'll be in close touch with you. Take perfect care of yourself." His fingers stroked her right cheek, then he walked away.

2

He hadn't staggered since he was knocked senseless playing rugby at Oxford, so he measured his steps carefully until he was seated in the limousine he'd rented to take them to the airport. He passed his hand over his eyes several times, making certain that he was awake and in his right mind. As was general among his people, he'd grown up believing that sex was for a man's physical relief, and he'd always behaved that way. He knew American women expected the same gratification as a man, but those he had known planned their own game and played their own tune. Sharon Braxton responded to him honestly, and he couldn't help wondering about the others. He stretched both arms out on the back of the seat, laid back his head and closed his eyes. Maybe the difference was him; he'd never felt that way in his life. Intentionally or not, she'd made demands of her own, and he'd wanted to meet them. It was a good thing that six months and over five thousand miles separated them; she couldn't be a permanent fixture in his life, because she would never accept the conditions he'd have to offer. But the thought of not having her—of any other man knowing her—made his belly contract until he thought he'd double up from the pain.

By late April, over three weeks after her arrival in Nigeria, Sharon had settled in her job. It pleased her that the United Nations Resident Representative had located her at the University of Ife in Ile-Ife, the heart of Yoruba culture. From there, she could easily visit Yoruba villages and small towns outside the direct sphere of government influence. Of the more than one hundred and fifty tribes in Nigeria, the Yoruba was one of the largest and was the most thickly settled in that region.

Since she didn't have a phone in her house—most people didn't—she hardly expected a personal call from Jon, though there were times when she'd have given most anything to hear his voice; for that matter, any friendly voice. She didn't have a clue as to where her African ancestors came from, but she decided soon after getting off the plane that they hadn't come from Nigeria. The only people who identified with her were foreigners from other Western, developed countries.

She sent her driver with a letter to a local chief—the most certain way to get a message delivered—whom Jon had also written, asking him for an appointment.

"He'll see you tomorrow, sir," her driver told her when he returned.

On the verge of stamping her foot, she told herself to ease up. Exasperated at his insistence on calling her *sir*, she glowered at him. "Aluko, you are to address me as *madam*. If you don't, I'll have to get another driver. Do you understand?"

"Yessir, madam."

She threw up her hands in disgust. Then it occurred to her that, to a Yoruba, *sir* was probably a part of the word "yes" when speaking to one's foreign employer. She gave up. He could call her whatever he liked.

After a successful meeting with the chief, in which he promised his full cooperation in her pilot program, she stopped along the road to buy bananas, grapefruit and papaya. She hated bargaining, but if you didn't bargain, you thought yourself superior to the seller, since bargaining was a form of socializing. She wished Jon had remembered to caution her about that, because she was sure she'd hurt the feelings of some of the market women from whom she purchased fruits, vegetables, fabric and art objects.

She put the fruit in a basket she'd purchased in Ibadan,

the largest Yoruba town, turned toward her car and stopped. At least twenty small children, whose ages she couldn't guess, stared up at her as if she were a Martian. Their smooth dark skin, large eyes and colorful clothing made her wish for a camera.

"*Oyinbá,*" they said in unison. She waved at them on her way to the car.

"Aluko, what does the word *oyinbá* mean?" she asked her driver.

"White woman, madame."

When she could close her mouth, she said, "That couldn't be right."

"Yessir, madame. It means white woman."

"But I'm black."

"Not really, madame. Africans are black."

"Well, knock me dead."

"Sorry-o, madame."

At her office in the university's humanities building, she found a note that Dr. Kuti wanted her to telephone him collect, and she went to the dean's office to make the call.

"Would you please excuse me?" she asked the dean's secretary. "This is a personal call."

The girl's eyes widened. "*Personal?* You're making a personal call to Dr. Adejonko Kuti? He's the *àkóbí* of the Oba, Chief Fadipe Kuti."

Apprehension settled in her chest, and she took a deep breath. "What does all that mean?" she asked the still-wide-eyed woman.

"He's the first-born son of a royal chief. When his father dies, *he* will be the royal chief, the Oba." She fanned herself. "Dear me!"

Sharon recovered from her shock and gave the secretary a level look. "This is still a personal call."

Alone, she dialed his number. So Jon was the Prince Charles of Yorubaland. He could at least have warned her, but he hadn't, and for not doing so, she deserved a piece of his hide. No wonder he'd assured her he'd get her anything she needed.

"Hello, Jon. This is Sharon."

"I know who it is. Why haven't you returned my other calls?"

"Your other calls? This is the first notice of one that I've received. Who answered when you phoned me?"

"Never mind. I'll take care of *that*! How's your project coming along?"

"Fair. Contacting each village personally is so time-consuming. But you're been a great help. You know, I haven't even started on the international aid providers, and since I've been here, I've discovered a number of local groups that give important services. Getting them all together is going to be a problem. How are you?"

His deep voice, so warm and strong, gave her a sense of protection, although thousands of miles separated them. "I'm the same, with the exception that you're not here."

"Sorry 'bout that. You're not here, either."

"Does that mean anything to you? My not being there?"

She had to remember that if you gave him an inch, he used it as if it were a mile. "You're a smart man, Jon, and you know I'm not likely to dig a hole for myself. Why didn't you tell me you were royalty? That secretary almost passed out when I asked her to excuse me because my call to you was personal."

He chuckled, and she didn't remember his having done that before. "I can imagine she did. By now, she's told everybody on the campus."

He didn't seem annoyed, but she needed to be sure. "Does that bother you?"

"Not one bit. I've thought of you a lot, Sharon. Too much, in fact."

Her pulse quickened at the suggestive words, but her tongue reflected her natural tendency to be impudent. "Serves you right. A nice guy would have warned me that dropping his name every place I went would have people genuflecting as though I were the Snow Queen from the Great North."

His laughter rolled to her across the miles, warming her and forcing her to remember that magic moment when he held her close and claimed her with his lips and his foraging tongue.

"Do you miss me at all, Sharon?"

She didn't want to cross that road. He was a prince, and she knew she'd never settle in Yorubaland. Being a foreigner wasn't fun, especially in an African country where she wasn't considered black.

"Did you hear me? I said, do you miss me?"

She took a deep breath and released it slowly. She didn't want to commit herself, but if he touched her at that moment, he'd know the truth. "A little," she said, wanting to give him something.

"Only a little?"

She was doggoned if she'd tell him how she longed to be with him. Still, an odd and surprising plaintiveness in his voice got to her. "Well . . . more than a little."

"Thank you for that. I think of the minute or two when I had you in my arms and you responded to me so honestly. Sharon, something happened to me, something that I was not one bit prepared for."

"And you think *I* was prepared for *that*?"

She imagined that lights sparkled in his copper-brown eyes when he said, "How'd you make yourself say that? That's the first encouragement I've had from you."

He wasn't serious. "Jon, back up a little. Didn't I wear my red sheath when you took me to dinner?"

"Hmmm. I guess you'd call that encouragement. Quite a bit, now that I think about it."

"Good. And did I kiss you back or didn't I?"

The sound of his long, heavy intake of breath reached her through the wire. "Yes. You kissed me, Sharon, and if you don't kiss me again, I want a description of that kiss to cover my grave."

She ran her fingernails across her brow. Better not answer that seriously. "Who'd write it?"

"I already have. I'll call again Friday at about this time. Good-bye."

" 'Bye."

She stared at the receiver. Hadn't the Yoruba ever heard of sweet names? She'd have to teach him.

At home in his apartment on New York's East Side, Jon was dealing with a level of frustration that was alien to him. He knocked his fist into the palm of his left hand. She missed him more than a little, did she? And while she was barely missing him, he was losing his common sense over her. What had happened to his well ordered, predictable life? He stuffed his socks in his shoes and kicked them under the edge of the bed where, along with most of his other shoes, they couldn't be seen.

For reasons he didn't examine, he wondered how Sharon would react to his untidiness, considering the American fetish for neatness. He stripped, showered, dried himself and crawled into his king-size bed. The elder son of Fadipe A. Kuti, the Oba, had to marry a Yoruba woman; he shouldn't even consort with a woman not of his tribe.

"Oh, hell." Muttering his favorite American oath, he grabbed the sheet, but stopped himself from ripping it apart.

Time and distance hadn't tempered his appetite for Sharon. If anything, his longing to be with her had deepened with the passage of time. He rolled over and phoned Adedeji, his friend and tribal brother.

"*Kú irólé*. Good evening, Ade. This is Jon. Are you alone? I need some straight talk."

"Sure. Ellie's watching TV. What is it?"

"Ellie's American. Is she so different from Yoruba women? I've dated American women. You know that. But I've never . . . those relationships were . . . there wasn't an interest. I hate to ask these questions, but—"

"I know. Sharon Braxton. I saw the two of you leaving 'Twenty-One,' and my first reaction was *trouble*! They're different, man. You have to learn everything all over again, but don't worry. Once Ellie knew I was eager to please her, all the birds flew in formation like a squadron of U.S. jets."

Jon frowned. "I gather 'eager to please' are the operative words here. Am I right?"

"Right. And once you get things straightened out with her, you'll have to deal with the Oba, and *that* will definitely test your mettle. Your father is fair, but he's tough. I'd rather have the job of handling the woman; the rewards are fantastic."

Adedeji held a very senior United Nations post, and Ellie, his wife, was a respected television reporter. For the first time, he wondered about their plans for the future.

"Mind if I ask where you and Ellie are planning to retire?"

"Not at all. As Americans, our children will live here, and we want to be near them. We'll go home on vacations. I'm not sure you could do that."

Didn't he know it! "I may never have to face it, but I needed to know what I could be up against."

"Plenty," Adedeji assured him. "You'd face an army."

"I know. I'd appreciate your confidence."

"Kè." Indeed!

He'd thought time and her absence would ease Sharon out of his system, but it hadn't. His desire for her had become a driving need, a hunger that he didn't even consider assuaging with another woman. If he couldn't find his way out of the passion that gripped him with the power of unbreakable tentacles, he was in for it. As the elder son, his father deferred to him, but he nonetheless expected him to carry out his duties as royal prince and heir to the Oba-ship of the Egba Yoruba. If his father thought he had other ideas, there'd be hell to pay. He'd never gone up against his father, had never contemplated it, and it startled him to realize he'd do it if he had to.

He slept fitfully and, by daybreak, he knew he was going home. He wasn't teaching summer school and didn't have another class until mid-October. If he had to defend himself before his father, he'd rather do it in person. By the time the news of his relationship with Sharon reached the Oba, it wouldn't bear the slightest resemblance to the truth. Besides, he needed to see her. If she missed him a little, perhaps he could encourage her to need him. Hell, he was just digging a deeper hole for himself, but he couldn't help it; he had to see her.

Two days later, he was on a British Airways flight to London. From there, he'd get a plane to Lagos.

Sharon leaned against her car, folded her arms and regrouped. She had not come all the way from Ife to Ejigbo in heat so insufferable that the air conditioner in her car was all but useless, only to have a cola-nut-chewing twerp tell her she couldn't see the village head.

The man wouldn't get the better of her, she decided, walking back to the compound. "What do you do here?" she asked him, hoping to get a good handle on her opposition.

He grinned and immediately wiped the pleasant expression from his face. "I'm in charge of contracts and financing," he said in a tone that demanded respect for his status.

"And I'm Assistant Secretary-General of the United Nations in charge of coordinating the aid you're receiving. Either I see the chief, or you've had your last bundle with the UN's logo stamped on it."

His Adam's apple bobbled furiously and he swallowed several times. "We heard Dr. Braxton was coming, but—"

"*I* am Dr. Braxton, and you know it, because I gave you my card."

"But I thought—"

"I will certainly report you to the Oba. You can count on that."

His obvious trembling verified for her the reputation and power of Jon's father. "Come," he said. "I will take you to my chief myself." Because she didn't trust him, she called Aluko, her driver, and asked him to accompany them.

The old man listened while she outlined her program and told him why it was needed, but he gave her no assurance. Rather, she had the sense that he was in some way culpable with regard to the waste of international aid to his village.

"I am at your service," he said, "but I will have to have the agreement of the Oba. My cousin, the Oba."

In other words, she had probably wasted the day. She didn't despair, though, because the finance officer would repeat her threat. Still, it was a long shot. She headed back to

Ife feeling as if she were wasting six months of her life. She
stopped to buy fruit from a woman who always sat by the
road and with whom she traded. The children were used to
her now, but they still gathered around her. A few touched
her gingerly, as if to see if her skin was different from theirs.
"Dash, mammy," they all said at once. *Dash* meant give me
something, and it was a custom she disliked, one practiced
throughout Yorubaland.

She got back to her house and sank into the nearest chair,
grateful for the air conditioning. Almost at once a car drove
up bearing the university's logo. She opened the door and
greeted the dean's messenger.

"I have a cable for you from Dr. Kuti, ma'am," he said,
appraising her with an interest he hadn't previously shown.
"Do you want me to wait for a reply?"

From those words, she didn't have to be told that he knew
not only the sender but also the contents of the cable. "No
thanks. If I want to send a reply, I'll drive over to the office
or to town. Thanks for bringing it."

Without moving from the front door, she read, "I've just
arrived in London, and I'm leaving tonight for Lagos. If you
get this before five o'clock your time, call this number. Otherwise, I'll see you in a day or so. Jon Kuti." Below, she saw
what was obviously a London telephone number.

Her heart took off like a runaway train. She had to sit
down and calm herself. Fearing that what she'd seen had been
wishful thinking, she read the cable again and folded it to her
breast. After some minutes, she looked at the paper and recognized fate; as much as she longed to see him, she wasn't
likely to resist his overtures.

She relaxed in the chair, her eyes closed and her heart
pounding. *Oh, my Lord. It's four-thirty, and I don't have any
idea where Aluko is.* Too bad. She grabbed her purse and the
car keys, got in the Peugeot 404 and headed for the university.
"I need to make a call to London, Miss Abeodun," she said
to the dean's secretary.

"I know," she said, "and it's personal."

Sharon looked at her in a withering reprimand. "Would

you care to answer it for me, since you've obviously read it?"

Miss Abeodun had the grace to appear sheepish as she rushed from the office.

Sharon could hardly control her shaking fingers as she dialed the number.

"Adejonko Kuti."

She found her voice with difficulty. "Jon, are you really coming tomorrow?"

"Yes. What is your home address? I'll stop there on my way to see my family."

"You won't stay a while?"

"I'd love to stay with you indefinitely, but I know that question implied something you didn't mean. Furthermore, if I'm in Nigeria twenty-four hours without checking in with my folks, they'll feel slighted. Where do you live? I don't want to greet you in your office at the university."

"House 43 on Road Fourteen, the university campus. Around what time do you think . . . Never mind, I'll stay home all afternoon."

"Knowing how dedicated you are to your work, I take that as encouragement. I want to see you, Sharon."

Joy suffused her, and she had to tell him the truth. "Me, too, Jon."

"My plane lands in Lagos at seven in the morning. I'll get a car and a driver at the airport and head for Ile-Ife."

"I'll be here."

He hung up without saying good-bye or . . . Didn't he know any words of endearment? Darn it, she had to tell him about that habit. Driving home, she acknowledged she had to clarify her thoughts about Jon. Although she cared a lot for him, maybe more than was good for her, that didn't mean she should lose her head. In the short time she'd been there, she'd seen enough of the Yoruba to realize she wasn't ever likely to be one of them, and that if she was considered Jon's woman, she might lose the progress she'd made on her project. Still, if she was honest with herself, she'd admit that if he opened his arms when he walked into her door, she'd be inside them in a split second.

At twelve-forty the next afternoon, a white Mercedes drove up to Sharon's door and stopped. "I'll be back in a few minutes," Jon said to the driver. "Then we'll go over to the staff club and find something for you to eat."

"Yes, sir. Take your time."

He loped up the four short steps and reached for the bell. Then he saw her. Her smile, wide, glowing and welcoming, took his breath away. He couldn't speak and didn't try. And as if by some magic she had divined the turbulence and power of his emotion, she took his hand and led him into her home and into her life.

Sharon hadn't been sure how she should greet him, so she opted for honesty and let him see the flame for him that struggled to flare in her heart. She looked up at him, bigger than he'd seemed in New York as he towered above her in a tan, short-sleeved business suit that Yoruba businessmen favored. It seemed as if her heart were sinking, or maybe she was drowning as she looked into his sparkling gaze.

Coming to herself, she managed to say, "Hi."

His long fingers gripped her hand, communicating strength and, yes, affection, but his silence unnerved her, for he gazed into her eyes, yet didn't utter a word.

"You must be tired," she said, flustered at the awkwardness of the situation. "Sit down, and I'll get you some food and something to drink."

But he didn't sit down. Instead, he continued to look at her, and a smile that he obviously tried to force didn't make it to his eyes. "Are you glad to see me?" he said at last.

"Yes. Yes, I'm . . . I'm happy to see you."

"Then I'll be back in half an hour."

"You'll be—"

"I want to get my driver settled. Believe me, I'll be back."

He walked out, and she stared at his broad back as he ran down the steps. Then with his hand on the door of the car, he turned and looked at her, his whole face glowing. She felt the muscles of her face trying to make themselves return his smile, and knew that they failed as the shock of that look on his face reverberated through her whole system. He'd said he would be back. The Mercedes drove off, and she closed the door.

She looked down at her white sandals and eyed her pink T-shirt and white linen shorts in the mirror. She doubted that a Yoruba woman would greet him dressed that way, but she wasn't Yoruba, and she couldn't allow him to forget who she was. He liked soul food, so she'd made biscuits and had the cook fry chicken and make lemonade. That, along with sliced tomatoes and potato salad, should be enough even for his big appetite. She doubted she'd eat; just the sight of him had taken her appetite. She set the dining room table for two and waited.

With her heart in her throat, she opened the door as the Mercedes rolled to a stop at her doorsteps. He didn't behave as she thought, or maybe hoped, he would. Appearing nonplussed, he stood inches away from her, gazing into her face.

"Seeing you in my homeland, in the place where I roamed as a child . . . I'm rarely at a loss for words, but now . . . Well, you can't know how you've touched me."

She rubbed her arms from her shoulders to her elbows, trying to bolster herself with her usual aplomb. "Had you always planned to come home for the summer?"

Evidently tired of the shadow-boxing, neither of them saying what they felt, he stepped closer. "I'm in Nigeria only because you're here. Can I . . . Come to me, Sharon, and let me hold you." He opened his arms in invitation.

Tension gathered within her as she stared at the dark desire in his mesmerizing eyes. "Jon. Oh, Jon." As if her feet had wings, she sprang into his arms, and her fingers found their way to his nape as she offered him her parted lips.

Then his mouth was on her, trembling in uncontrollable passion as his tongue pressed to her lips begging entrance. Fiery ripples spiraled down her arms and legs as she anticipated the feeling of having him inside of her. She opened her mouth and took him in, tremors streaking through her and settling in her feminine center while he possessed every niche and every centimeter. As though starved for her, he pulled her lips into his mouth, claiming all of her. But she needed his hands all over her, and when her nipples pained her and ached for his touch, she twisted against his chest, yearning to have him caress her breasts with his fingers and lips. She couldn't stand it.

He plunged his tongue into her again and again, trying to assuage his hunger for her. Shocked by the tremors that rippled through him, he stepped back a little, lest he harden against her; he couldn't allow himself do that. But she moved into him, letting him know that she was bereft of his nearness, and he nestled her in his arms, stroking her, caressing her arms and shoulders, unable to get enough of her.

"You did miss me, didn't you?" he asked.

"Yes. I missed you."

She buried her face in his shoulder, as though unwilling to look at him. Surely, this woman wasn't shy. But she seemed to have cooled off, as if she had expected more than he'd given her. He knew she hadn't wanted him to take her to bed, so . . . He remembered Adedeji's words.

Anxious now, he held her to him in a fierce caress. "You mean an awful lot to me, Sharon. I've never felt for anyone what I feel for you. When you kissed me just now, I had the sense that you needed more than I gave, that you were frustrated. Tell me what you want and what you need."

When her arms tightened around him and her soft lips grazed his neck, he thought he'd explode, but control came naturally to him. "Remember that I have to learn your ways."

She stepped back and smiled, almost bewitching him again. "I'm not the first Western woman you've . . . uh . . . gotten close to. Am I?"

He shook his head. "There've been a few, but I was killing time; I wasn't really interested. Those were different relationships." He pointed to his heart. "With you, I feel something deep in here, and it's a first with any woman anywhere."

She took his hand and walked with him to the dining room. "I'd better feed you if you haven't eaten since you got off that plane this morning."

Was she evading him? "And what I just told you doesn't interest you?"

She had a way of smiling at him that sent hot little needles shooting through his veins. "Jon, don't you know I care for you?"

"Then, what is it? There's something. I felt it, just now."

Her eyes sparkled, and with lips soft and sweet she reached up and kissed him beneath his jaw. "Honey, don't you Yoruba men know any sweet, loving names to call a woman you . . . you care for?"

Now that was something to think about. "You mean sweetheart, baby and things like that? I thought that only happened in your television situation comedies. It never occurred to me that those silly people were behaving the way they thought everybody else in the country behaved, that it's normal."

Her fingers gripped his arms. "But I don't want you to call me sweet names unless you mean what that implies."

"Olùfé. Mi Sharon. Olùfé tèmi." As he said it, he wanted to melt into her, to make her a part of him, but he moved away. He might be besotted with her, but he still owned his soul.

"What does that mean?"

"Maybe someday I'll tell you."

Her eyes narrowed, and he knew it wasn't his Sharon he was about to deal with, but Dr. Sharon Braxton.

"Okay. Mind if I ask Miss Abeodun in the dean's office what it means?"

If they had needed a way of breaking the ice, that did it. He looked at her fists on her hipbones and the upward, defiant tilt of her chin and nearly doubled up in joyous laughter. He didn't know anybody else capable of giving him so much joy.

"I wouldn't do that if I were you," he said. "I feel what it means, but I'm not ready to articulate it. Can you accept that?"

She worried her bottom lip, and a frown creased her forehead. "Do I have a choice? I'd better feed you before you become totally unreasonable."

He looked at the table, seeing that she had replicated her

way of life in what, for her, had to be difficult circumstances. He sat down and reached for the glass of lemonade.

She slapped his hand, surprising him, and his head snapped around. "We have to say grace," she said.

"Every time?"

"Every time."

"I should think the Lord would find that monotonous."

"Well, he doesn't. Who do you pray to?"

"Allah. God. *Olórùn*. I don't leave anybody out. Besides, my father claims they're all the same being. But . . . just in case. Ah, you remembered my passion for soul food. This is wonderful. Who cooked it?"

"I made the biscuits, potato salad and lemonade. Jimma fried the chicken."

"With your recipe, no doubt. Nigerians don't cook chicken this way."

He drank his lemonade and got up from the table. "I'll be back in a minute." He'd almost forgotten the gift he'd brought her. "I hope it's the right one," he said, handing her the package that he'd purchased at Saks Fifth Avenue. The red velvet rose tucked beneath the silver bow was meant to say that she was special, and he watched the expression on her face with anxiety.

"It's so beautiful I don't want to open it." Her hand caressed his wrist. "Thank you."

When she gasped, he figured he'd done the right thing.

"How did you . . . why did . . . Oh, Jon, thank you so much. I looked for some here, but I couldn't find any, and I brought only a little with me. How did you know which scent I wear?"

"I told your secretary I needed to get some for someone and that I had liked what you wore. Are you pleased?"

She leaned over and kissed his cheek. "Of course I am. There isn't a bottle of Fendi perfume in Lagos. I looked everywhere."

He let his fingers go to the side of her face and stroked her, gingerly at first and then with the affection he held for her in his heart.

"Why would you need this stuff? I wasn't here." He'd meant it to be amusing, and her laughter thrilled him. A woman without a sense of humor could be a bore.

"Now," he began, when they were back in the cooler living room. "Tell me about your work. Are you making the progress you hoped for?"

"Most of the international agencies and foundations will attend the first meeting, but I'm getting less cooperation from the locals. Some of the junior chiefs of small chiefdoms seem scared to open their books and show how they apply the aid they receive. I also suspect their accountants of padding their own pockets, but if I try to prove that, I'll make enemies that I don't need."

He sat forward with his elbows on his thighs and cupped his chin with his hands. "Just as I expected. What about those people I wrote?"

"Fine. They're no problem."

"Give me a list of the foot-draggers, and I'll see that they get in line."

"You weren't sure my plan is what's needed, but you're willing to help me. Why?"

He stroked his chin, leaned back and locked his hands behind his head. "I was raised to be honest. It's important to me, and I don't want any dealings with a dishonest person. I've known from the beginning that your plan is precisely what we need, but I was equally certain that you couldn't pull it off, because my people aren't used to dealing with women officials. And God forbid a woman should give a man an order."

"When they're slow to cooperate, I threaten to withhold all aid in the future. Most of the time, it works. But I guess some will have to be convinced. Thanks for your support."

He got up and gave in to his penchant for pacing the floor, his head down and his hands behind him. "I don't want you to fail."

"Why?"

"Because it's good for my people, but mostly because I ...I want you to be happy." He glanced at his watch.

"Sharon, I have to be in Ogbomàba before nightfall. It's four o'clock, which means I have three hours."

"Then you're not staying." It wasn't a question.

Tension gripped him, and he wondered if she could hear the mad thundering of his heart. "Let's have an understanding about this. You aren't asking me to share your bed, and the way I feel, I wouldn't consider staying here in any other circumstances. Minutes after my plane landed, my folks knew it. Our custom dictates that I go there the day I arrive, but I'll see you tomorrow."

"I'll be in Lagos tomorrow and for the next six days."

"Which hotel?" She told him. "Then I'll go to Lagos. I have a flat there overlooking the lagoon. You'll like it. Come kiss me, so I can get out of here."

She sashayed to within inches of him. "Sharon, huh? What happened to *Olùfé*?"

She pronounced it perfectly. How could she make him feel the way she did? His lips burned with the impulse to kiss her until he lost himself in her. *"Fetísílè,"* he told himself. *Pay attention, man. You're teetering on the edge.*

He pointed to his chest. "She's still here. I'll call you at your hotel tomorrow night. Kiss me?" Her arms eased around his neck, but she didn't part her lips until he asked entrance. Then he slipped into her mouth and spirals of unbearable tension snaked around him as her body became a blaze of liquid fire, torching, burning, but never consuming the way he longed to have her ravish him. He felt a rush of blood and a tightening of his groin and moved her from him. Her lashes swept up swiftly, and he held both of her shoulders, making sure that she didn't move closer to him.

"Olùfé," he whispered softly, and made himself leave her.

For a long time, Sharon stood as he'd left her, rooted to the spot. What was she supposed to think? The average American man wouldn't have considered leaving her, family customs or not. He was right in thinking she hadn't wanted them to make love; she hadn't gotten to that point, and after hearing that his heart and head weren't in sync, she knew he also hadn't reached the point of commitment. With so much against them, maybe they never would.

The next morning on her way to Lagos, she told Aluko to stop at the library. If she didn't reach Lagos until sundown, she intended to find the meaning of that word.

"I want your best Yoruba–English dictionary," she told the librarian.

"It's a reference book, so you'll have to use it here," the woman said.

Olùfé, loved one, she read. And then she saw *Olùfé tèmi.* Was that what he'd whispered? Love of mine? She said the words aloud. Yes. She closed the book with trembling fingers and placed it on the librarian's desk. *Lord, please don't let us wind up hurting each other. But how can we miss?*

In Lagos, she checked into the Ambassador Hotel on Ikoyi, called the United Nations office there and reported her room and telephone number. After going over her notes and making necessary phone calls, she set out with her driver to find a bookstore and her own Yoruba–English dictionary.

The village children followed Jon's rented Mercedes to his father's compound. He had brought chocolates, uninflated balloons, ballpoint pens and books. As soon as he'd distributed the presents, he opened the gate and went inside where the Oba, his father, tall and regal in his flowing *agbada* and matching *filà,* awaited him at the front door of the main house. He knelt and prostrated himself before his father in homage, as was the Yoruba custom. He had often thought this reverence for one's elders was the reason for so little conflict between generations. The Oba tapped him on the shoulder as evidence of his satisfaction.

"*Kú àbò, mi bàbá.*" Greetings, my father.

The Oba beamed with pride. "*Kú àbò, àkóbí omokùnrin.*" Greetings, my first-born son. "Now, come tell me how long you will be with us." They walked inside, and the Oba motioned Jon to sit down.

He'd been expecting that question, but he didn't have an answer because he didn't know when Sharon would leave.

"My plans aren't definite. Only thing certain is that I have to be back at Columbia University the middle of October."

Fadipe Kuti leaned back in his thronelike chair—a place that only he ever occupied—and looked hard at the son he adored. "How much of this indecision is due to Sharon Braxton?" He raised his hand to forestall an answer, signaling that he had more to say. "Yes, I've heard rumors, plenty of them, none of which I like."

His father never left doubt as to where he stood on any issue, but when you were the Oba, why should you?

He accepted his father's warning, and he could do no less than reply in kind. "I'm sorry, *Bàbá*, but you surely don't plan to choose my friends."

"Nonsense." The Oba snorted. "If you followed her here, it's because you're involved with her. You know your duties and responsibilities here, and they cannot include any woman who is not Yoruba. Do you understand?"

Jon straightened his shoulders and looked his father in the eye. "Perfectly. We're stuck in the nineteenth century, and I'm supposed to stay back there along with the rest of this tribe."

The Oba squeezed and pumped his left fist and Jon noticed that he ground his teeth, but he wasn't retracting a single word. Among his people, if you gave a man an inch, he would then demand a yard.

At last, the Oba stood—signaling his rising anger and calling attention to his authority—and raised his right hand. "I don't want to hear any more of these rumors."

Better not to declare war, Jon decided as he recalled an old African proverb, until he had a reason and intended to fight. And Sharon hadn't given him a solid reason.

"Right now, it's a moot point, *Bàbá*. I'm going to spend some time in Lagos."

"But you will stay here with us for a few days?"

"I want to be in Lagos tomorrow, but I'll come home to see you often. *Iyá*?" Mother?

"She's in Oshogbo. Asàbi is expecting her baby any minute now."

"I'll see her on my way to Lagos tomorrow." Asàbi, his sister, was younger than he and already had five children. He thought she was overdoing it, but when it came to family planning, his brother-in-law lived in the dark ages. He spent a few minutes with his paternal grandmother at her house a few yards from his mother's house, stopped to say hello to his cousins, the children of his father's brother who'd died in an accident and whose widow his father inherited as a third wife. Then, he ate some bananas and a slice of papaya and went to bed. Tomorrow, he would begin the task of whipping his tribesmen into line, beginning with his own kin—some of whom had not only refused to cooperate with Sharon but had been obstreperous.

3

Not a dictionary to be had anywhere, but for one-fifth its price in the States, one could buy the best cognac at most any store, Yet, English-language books published outside of Nigeria were at a premium. One more indication that she had a tough job before her. She shrugged. If she'd drunk camel's milk in Mongolia in order to get her job done, this was a piece of cake. Nigerians loved red, or so it seemed considering how many women wore it, so she put on a short-sleeved red linen suit, got her briefcase and went down to the conference level of the hotel. Arranging to have the meeting there had increased her status with the locals, and many invitees who hadn't planned to come were attending. Nonetheless, key figures stayed away.

At intermission, she walked out into the corridor hoping to persuade the head of the Women's Home Economics League to see things her way. She'd no sooner gotten the woman's agreement to cooperate than the sound of his voice sent darts zigzagging through her limbs. She spun around. They'd been together the day before in her house in Ife, but how different he seemed now.

"You scored well in there this morning," he said. "How are you?"

He stood close, yet he seemed miles away. Elegant in a pale-green brocade agbada and *filà*, this crown prince of the Egba Yoruba stood out among those of his tribe as a diamond among chips of zircon. When she realized that his gaze held no intimacy, she stepped back, and the meaning of her move did not escape him. Anger furled up in her; Sharon Braxton was no man's back-street woman, she told herself, recalling the old movie. She didn't want or expect him to kiss her; such was, after all, inappropriate at a business gathering. But he didn't have to act as if he barely knew her, either.

"I think I'll be able to pull it off if I can get the minister of commerce to clear the docks of all that merchandise stuck there."

Sparks of anger flickered in his eyes. "You mean the import/export office doesn't clear the imports for entrance? Or is the guy levying tariffs on international aid?"

"He doesn't permit entry. In some cases, he's held goods there for a year. If he processed the things, the recipients would receive their goods on time, wouldn't be inclined to hoard and would be willing to lend to others when they had a surplus."

"I see. That ought to be straightened out by the end of the day. Are you comfortable at this hotel?"

"Yes. Uh . . . if you'll excuse me . . ." She had to get away from him. What had happened to her warm, sweet Jon? "I'll . . . Jon, I'll see you around."

"What are you talking about, you'll see me around?" The words came out calmly, and he kept his expression neutral, but his eyes darkened in a thunderous glare.

"Exactly that." She went back in the meeting room and took her place on the dais, hoping he'd leave. But he sat through the remainder of the afternoon session, though he didn't intervene. At the end, she gathered her papers, skipped the obligatory chatting and made her way out of the meeting room as quickly as possible. She'd fallen hard for him. Had she made the biggest mistake of her life?

Her steps quickened. She didn't know whether he'd followed her, but she got into the elevator alone, let the wall take her weight and blew out a long breath of air. She wouldn't be surprised to learn that the insides of her veins had shriveled up. She made it to her room on the eleventh floor, kicked off her shoes and pulled off the red suit. Since she hadn't taken time for lunch, she ordered soup and a sandwich. Gazing out of the window, she tried to imagine what explanation he'd give her for his strange behavior. *Cut it off right now, girl, before you're so far under you can't get out.*

At the knock on her door, she slipped on a robe, took a pen and the equivalent of a tip from her pocketbook, shoved the pocketbook under the pillow and opened the door.

"*Jon!* I'm not dressed for company."

"I'm not company." He walked past her, turned and stopped. In her bare feet, she stared up at him, and though he loomed taller than ever, she was not intimidated.

"Then what are you? Downstairs there, you treated me as if I were someone you hadn't previously met. If you can't explain that, please leave."

"It was not the place for familiarity."

"Have you forgotten who I am? I know that. But you were so impersonal. And don't tell me you were pretending disinterest; not even James Earl Jones is *that* great an actor."

He took a step toward her, and she moved closer to the door. "Then I'm a better actor than he is. With half a dozen of my kinsmen milling around, I didn't dare give them gossip to take back to my father."

"Don't tell me your father still puts you across his knee and paddles you."

His expression turned menacing, and she knew she was close to his tolerance limit. "Strike back if you need to, but don't insult me. If you knew our customs, you would apologize for that remark." He removed his *filà* and ran his hand over his tight curls. "You mean everything to me, and you ought to know that."

"I'm replacing the thoughts I had about you. You're not

going to kiss me in private and act as if I'm a case of cholera when we're around other people."

"Sharon, please be reasonable. How should I have behaved? You're a high-ranking UN official, and I'm—"

"That's the problem, isn't it? We're dealing with who you are when you come home, where you're royalty. Well, maybe nobody told you that Prince Charles danced the boogaloo with a little black gal in the Caribbean just because she asked him to dance. And CNN flashed it all over the world. Didn't demean his status one bit."

On a roll now, she put her hands on her hips and looked at him from beneath her long lashes. "It wouldn't have affected your niche in Yoruba society if you'd taken my hand for a second and told me you were glad to see me. In fact, considering the number of your tribesmen there who'd already indicated an interest in going off somewhere with me, being attentive to me might have elevated you in their eyes."

He shook his head, a sadness mirrored on his face. "Sharon, do you think me so fickle?" He put a letter in her hand and moved toward the door. "Your program deserves to succeed, and it will. I'm going back to New York tomorrow. There's no reason for me to stay here."

"Don't go." She bit her tongue, for the words were out of her mouth before she realized she would say them.

He stopped beside her and gazed down into her eyes, his own clearly troubled. "Why should I stay if you have no faith in me, if you doubt my integrity? I came to Nigeria because I needed to be with you, near you, and I won't stay unless we can be together." He looked down at her bare feet. "Do you walk around barefooted when you're at home?"

She nodded.

"So do I. Can we get back on track?"

A knock on her door brought a questioning look to his eyes. "I ordered some food. When you knocked, I thought you were the waiter."

She opened the door and stepped aside to let the waiter

come in. He put the tray on the desk, and she signed the check and tipped the man. "May Allah bless you," he said and closed the door.

"Would you like half of my sandwich?" she asked Jon.

"The only thing I want right now is you in my arms."

Her hands went to her sides, rubbing up and down furiously in what he had to know was a case of nerves fueled by passion and desire. Immediately, she anticipated his touch, his taste and the way she would feel in his arms. His eyes darkened, and she knew he read her thoughts and recognized her need for intimacy with him.

"Sharon, *mi Sharon. Olùfé tèmi.*"

Tremors rocked her, and she tried not to hear the thundering tumble of her heartbeat. As if of their own volition, her arms reached out to him. *"Jon. Mi Jon. Olùfé tèmi."* Excitement sparkled in his eyes. "I looked it up in the dictionary," she said.

Then he had her in his strong arms, caressing her and loving her. Wanting and needing more, she parted her lips, and in a second she felt his tongue inside of her, searching, claiming her until he anointed every part of her mouth. He locked her to him, splayed his big hands across her hips and held her. Her breasts began to ache as they had in Ife when he'd kissed her until she couldn't stand more. Didn't he know?

She eased away from him. "You asked me what I needed, and I . . ." Without thinking, she rubbed her hand across her left breast. "Honey, my breasts ache. Can't you . . . Oh this is terrible."

He put his arms around her and brought her back to his body. "Are you saying that . . . that they're sensitive?"

She buried her face in his shoulder and murmured, "If you stroke them, toy with them, you can practically control me." She didn't look at him. She couldn't.

"Well, I'll be. If there's anything else—"

She poked him in the chest with her index finger. "That isn't a weapon you can use at will. Only with my permission."

He laughed. "Thanks for the warning. I'll concentrate on getting your permission."

"I'm hungry. I'll share my sandwich."

"I had lunch. I'd like us to plan on having dinner together whenever we're in the same town. Okay?"

"Fine with me," she said, biting into the chicken sandwich. She remembered the letter he'd given her, opened it and read:

Everything waiting for import clearance will be admitted by day after tomorrow. In the future, no more than one week will elapse between receipt and clearance of goods.

It was signed by a trade official.

"This is wonderful. All right if I read it at the meeting tomorrow morning?"

"That's why I gave it to you. You've done a great job in explaining the importance of this plan, and most of the key people I've spoken with support it. Your opposition is coming from a few who're accustomed to getting kickbacks, and you're about to make them work for a living."

"Tell me about it. This place runs on *dash*. The guy couldn't find my restaurant reservations last night. I took a couple of U.S. dollars out of my pocketbook and held them in my hand where he could see them. His eyes sparkled. 'Why, Madame, I must have overlooked it. Come with me.' "

"Doesn't surprise me. I have a few more arms to twist, so I'd better leave. Be here for you at seven. *Olùfé*. I want to hear you say that in English."

She finished chewing her mouthful of chicken and winked at him. "When the occasion arises."

He let out a sharp whistle. "Another *cunjie* woman. See you tonight."

"I'll have to close my business," a man told Jon that afternoon.

Jon narrowed his eyes and told himself to keep his temper in check. "You don't have a business. You have a scheme for robbery, and I intend to report you to the *Oba*. You know the consequence if you continue."

"Yes, sir."

"One more of these gougers, and I can concentrate on my reason for coming here," Jon said to himself. At least he didn't have to go far to find him; the key people had all come to the meeting either to cooperate or to protect their interests.

"And if I process the supplies as you ask, will you speak to the Oba on my behalf?" the next culprit asked him.

"I said I'd do it. You'll get your extra ten meters of land." He raised his right hand to discourage Ojo's obsequiousness. He hated to see a grown man bending and bowing to another one. Ojo wasn't dishonest. His problem was his limited intellect, he did the best he could with what he had, though that wasn't an awful lot.

He walked swiftly toward the front door of the hotel to discourage anyone who might want to waylay him. At his apartment, he showered, stretched out and took stock of his day. He wouldn't have believed that Sharon would walk away from him, torpedoing their relationship, but despite what she felt for him, she would. Knowing that had shaken him.

After much indecision, he decided to wear one of his American summer business suits to dinner. When she saw him, her eyes widened, and a smile claimed her entire face, rocking his very foundation.

It surprised him that she greeted him in the lobby rather than allowing him to come to her hotel room for her. Surely, she knew he would never crowd her. He walked to meet her, and his right hand reached out to her automatically, it seemed. As he looked down at her, longing to embrace her, he understood why he'd displeased her during the morning meeting's intermission.

"Hi," she said. "No *agbada*?"

He couldn't help smiling. She'd prepared herself for his Yoruba regalia. "I have a feeling it made the wrong statement earlier today."

She tilted her head to the side and appeared to study him.

"You're wrong about that." She took his hand, turned it palm up and gazed at it, piquing his curiosity.

"Are you a palmist?"

From her expression, one would have thought he'd asked if she were a murderer. She shook her head. "No, indeed. I'm just checking your labor record. Studying is the hardest work you've ever done."

"Now that's a laugh. You wouldn't believe what I did during the summers of my years at Harvard. I washed dishes in restaurants, delivered packages on my bicycle, and when I got fired, I stood on State Street and played my flute. I made so much money with my flute that I was tempted to skip the next semester."

She stopped walking and stared at him as if in awe. "Really? You must be good at it. Did you study?"

Caught up in her enthusiasm, he grasped her arm and walked with her across the lobby. "I started playing the flute while I was at Oxford, but since I came to the States, I've studied seriously."

Her eyes lit up and she tugged at his arm, bringing him closer to her. "Play for me sometime?"

He loved her voice, her gestures, the way she half-smiled when thinking of a pleasant thing. She got to him without trying.

"Well? Will you or won't you?"

"Of course I will. By the way, I have to attend a government reception tomorrow night, and I'd like you to go with me. Will you?"

"You've been here two days and already you have a government invitation? How'd they know you were here?"

"Word of mouth is the way news travels fastest in this country. Nigerians like to be in the know, and we prove that we are when we can pass on the latest gossip."

"I'm impressed. What do I wear?"

"Any dressy street-length dress. It's informal. How about it?"

They ate dinner in the hotel dining room, and as they left, he said, "I want to see you to your room, and after we get there, I want to kiss you. But not in the hallway."

She stepped on the elevator in front of him, turned and raised an eyebrow. "I doubt I'd get promoted to Under Secretary-General just by strolling into the Secretary-General's office and telling him I wanted a raise. Honey, I'd be more subtle."

"Sure, but indirect doesn't always work with you."

Her wide grin told him she was pulling his leg, but he didn't want his leg pulled; he wanted her in his arms.

"Nothing works with me all the time. I saw an old Mae West movie not long ago, and I almost doubled up with laughter when she told this knockout of a man that being obvious didn't cut it, and that a little imagination would get him what he wanted."

"What was funny about that?"

He stood still gaping at her, and she sashayed over to him, closed his mouth with her fingers and said, "What's the matter, big boy? Don't you know how to kiss?"

They reached her door, and he took her plastic key, opened it and walked in behind her. "Don't you try that with me."

"No?" Her fingers trailed along the lapel of his jacket, then stroked his tie and roamed from his shoulder to his elbow before he stopped her.

"I see you're using your imagination, Sharon. Now I'm going to use mine."

Before she could digest his words, he'd lifted her off her feet, pinned her to the wall and wrapped her legs around his hips. She saw the wildness in his eyes and, giddy with anticipation as to how far he'd go, she looped an arm around his neck and pulled him tight to her body. Then she felt the full power of his virility as he surged hard against her and plunged his tongue into her welcoming mouth. More of him. She had to have more of him as frissons of heat ignited her nerve ends and settled in her feminine center.

"Jon," she moaned. "Oh, Jon."

The fingers of his left hand stroked her right areola, and she cried out with the pleasure of it, gripping him to her with all the strength she could muster. Powerless to control her driving need, her hips undulated against him, and he pressed her shoulders to the wall. Shock reverberated throughout her system when he stared down into her face, his own unreadable. And then she read the question that formed in his eyes and knew he'd made up his mind to take whatever she was willing to give even though he hadn't asked for it.

She dropped her head to his shoulder, and he eased her to the floor. "*Mi Olùfé*, I'm sorry. I took advantage of you," he whispered.

"I had no business challenging you that way."

His laugh bore no mirth. "If you knew how hungry I am for you, you'd cut a wide swath around me. Sharon, we have to decide where we're going with this thing. I came here because I couldn't stay away, but I hadn't thought past just needing to be with you. Now, well . . . I don't know."

"I think we'd better avoid these . . . er . . . clinches."

When that grin spread all over his face, she wondered why she'd bothered to say the words. "Easier said than done. Besides, I can't see myself *wanting* to avoid them. I'll be here around eight tomorrow evening."

"Ring my room, and I'll come right down."

His eyes lit up and a grin formed around his lips. "Not a bad idea, all things considered. Sleep well."

But she didn't sleep well. How could she? Nothing could have stopped him from making love to her but an unwillingness to commit himself. She didn't doubt that he'd known women, any number of them. But he cared about her and, even if he didn't, he wouldn't attempt to misuse a woman of her status. His battle was with himself, and she hadn't decided to help him.

"What do you mean, 'wait for you in that other room'?" she said to Jon shortly after they arrived at the reception.

"Please." His smile didn't fool her. Something about that didn't smell quite right, but she put an enigmatic expression on her face, walked into *that other room* and stopped in her tracks. Yoruba wives sat side by side in chairs against the

walls, wearing their fine *kábà*, skillfully wrapped dresses and
headgear that matched their husband's *filà* and *agbada*. She
stared at them, their hands lying casually in their laps and
their mouths closed as if they were alone.

The expletive she released under her breath was anything
but mild. "Don't you even think it," she said to nobody in
particular, whirled around and went to find Jon. She didn't
have to look for him; he appeared immediately as if he'd been
expecting her.

"You care to step outside where we can't be overheard?"
she asked him, aware that her voice trembled. Without a
word, he inclined his head toward the reception room.

"Didn't you know when you invited me that I wasn't going
to hold still for that?" He seemed pained, but she didn't care.

"I confess I'd forgotten about this custom, and when I
remembered it, the minister had already seen me. So I had to
greet him."

"I'm leaving this second."

"You can't be alone outside at night in this town nor any
other. I'll excuse myself, and we'll go."

"All right, but if you're gone more than ten minutes, I'm
leaving."

When he'd walked in there and seen only men, the nerves in
his belly had declared war on him. He'd had no choice but
to present himself to the minister and pray that Sharon would
forgive him. He got back to her as quickly as he could.

"It's a ridiculous custom, one of a number that I'd forgotten about. Trust me, I detest that business of segregating
men and women socially."

"I'm glad to hear it," she said. "I worked with those same
men yesterday and this morning, but I'm too stupid to carry
on a conversation with them after eight in the evening."

He reached past her to open the car door, but she opened
it herself, and he didn't comment, because he knew she was
fit to eat nails.

"Sharon, the purpose of that custom has nothing to do with

anybody's intelligence; it's intended to enforce the superiority of men."

"How do I know you're different?"

"You don't, so you'll have to go on what you know of me. My telling you won't mean a thing."

"One more message like that one and we're casual acquaintances. Period."

She walked briskly past him as they entered the hotel. At the elevator, she stopped, indicating that she didn't want him to go any further.

"Are you telling me you can walk off from me for good and not look back? Don't I mean anything to you?"

Tears shimmered unshed in her eyes, but he knew she didn't want comforting. "Yes. You mean something to me. But Jon, I know my worth as a human being, and I am not about to walk into a roaring furnace if I know that's what I'm doing. I wouldn't forget you, not ever, and breaking off with you would hurt. But I'd do it in a second, before I'd compromise myself and regret it later."

"I once told you that I have never felt for any person what I feel for you. I've never loved a woman, Sharon, until now. And I love you. I won't ever ask you to violate your principles, because I know I won't abandon mine."

"But isn't that what you asked me to do tonight? You knew I'd see red."

"But I also knew you wouldn't sit there if you decided you didn't want to. I was watching for you."

She sagged against the wall beside the elevator door. "I was going to ask you to go with me to a party at the Consulate tomorrow evening, but maybe that's not such a great idea."

He had to touch her somewhere, so he settled for a finger at her elbow. "I'd love to go with you."

She looked at him for a long time, and he gazed into her eyes to let her know he could stand her scrutiny. "I won't give you up easily," he said.

"I know you won't. Call me tomorrow around noon."

"When are you going back to Ife?"

"Day after tomorrow if I can find my driver. I haven't seen him all day."

"Don't worry, the drivers always check in with the bell captain." Unable to resist, he leaned forward and quickly kissed her lips. "Dinner tomorrow night?"

She nodded. " 'Night."

He watched the door close. Did he love her enough for the sacrifices he'd have to make? Edward VIII gave up the British throne for Wallis Simpson, a niggling voice reminded him, and a shiver streaked down his back. Edward VIII didn't have to face the Oba of the Egba Yoruba after he did it. His father would be outraged. In fact, considering the speed of Nigerian gossip, he was probably on his way out of his mind right then.

He loved her. He'd said it in Yoruba and now in English. And what was she going to do about it? She knew she loved him. Loving him was easy, but putting up with the customs of his people was not, and she knew she'd never do it.

As if to make that point, she chose wide-legged, black chiffon pants and a dusty rose halter top to wear to the Consulate with him. Observing herself in the mirror before leaving her hotel room, she said a word of thanks that her full bosom didn't sag when she wasn't wearing a bra. She met him in the lobby and handed him her stole, which he threw around her shoulders. She brushed a kiss on the side of his mouth.

"Hi. I think I can make a first-class American man out of you," she said.

"You may have to."

She eyed him quizzically, but he didn't elaborate. "You look beautiful as always," he said.

"Thanks. You look great yourself." If she'd known he'd wear an *agbada*, she might not have dressed so daringly. At the Consulate, he stayed close enough to support her if need be, but not enough to suffocate her or interfere with her conversations. He was exactly want she wanted in a man. Intelligent. Successful. Handsome. Kind. Generous. And so loving. Her gaze caught a tall man in Yoruba attire, and she couldn't help staring at him, for he strongly resembled Jon. *They're brothers*, she realized as Jon joined the man and walked toward her with him.

"Sharon, this is my brother, Olu."

"I'm glad to meet you, Sharon. Actually, I accepted this invitation because I figured you'd be here, and I had to meet the woman who's got my brother spinning like a top."

She liked Olu at once. "Where'd you hear about me?"

His smile did wonderful things for his dark eyes. "Where? Where *didn't* I hear about you? By this morning, we must have had a hundred calls about you, half of them concerning your obvious devotion to each other. You live up to your notices, I can tell you that. Our father wants to meet you."

Both of Jon's eyebrows shot up. "Did he send you here to tell me that?"

Olu obviously wasn't intimidated by Jon's severe scrutiny. "Definitely not. He's confined his reaction to pacing the floors and the grounds; by now, I suspect he's pacing the walls."

Jon gave a short laugh. "I knew you spelled trouble the minute I saw you."

"How long did you stay in the States, Olu? Your speech says you spent a lot of time there."

"Yeah," Jon said. "When he got back here, we thought he was one our cousins whose ancestors left here on a slave ship. He's completely Americanized. You two are fellow alumni. Olu got his bachelor's at Yale and his medical degree at Johns Hopkins."

Sharon tugged the stole around her shoulders, certain, when she couldn't understand Olu's quizzical look, that she'd worn the wrong outfit. She'd rather her appearance had been more conservative when she met Jon's brother. She shrugged. She'd pleased herself, and that was what counted. "I'd love to meet your father, Olu. I've heard so much about him."

Olu didn't smile when he said, "Good. I don't think this is something Jon wants to assert himself over. *Bàbá* knows we are men, and he treats us that way, but I think he would *command* Jon to bring you to him—and, father aside, no one disobeys his Oba's command."

"Jon hasn't said he wouldn't take me."

His half-laugh wasn't meant to soothe. "No. But I'm looking at him, and as they say back in the States, he's got his back up."

"Not to worry. He'll bring me."

"What makes you so sure?" Olu asked her.

"Because I will ask him to bring me. That's why."

She grasped Jon's fingers, as cold as if they were ungloved on a New York winter day, and knew he had a lot at stake. So did she.

"I'll see you tomorrow morning before you leave for Ife," Jon told Sharon. "I'd better not go in tonight. You're setting up meetings in each town now, and in every case, you have to contact the chief first. Give me your itinerary when we meet for breakfast, okay?"

"There'll be at least twelve town meetings. I expect the chiefs will cooperate, because they all attended the conference and voted for the plan. You know, this seemed a lot simpler when I was sitting in my office in New York."

"I can imagine. It's to your credit that you're pulling it off with style."

"Do you think your father sent Olu here to warn you about me?"

"Not in this world. According to an old African proverb, 'Only an eagle announces his death.' If my father planned to make trouble, he wouldn't send someone to warn me."

"You'd disobey him?"

He shrugged. "I've done it many times."

"From what I've heard of him, it doesn't sound as if he'd hold still for sass."

His eyes widened. "I never said I confronted him, and I certainly didn't sass him, but I have a mind just as he has. It's different among my people, Sharon. Fathers defer to their first-born sons. He is the center of his father's life. His pride." Jon fingered his chin as if in deep thought. "The son obeys out of respect for his father and his culture," he went on, "but he does not cower. And the father will not risk losing that son, no matter how great his pain. Yet, if they disagree, the conflict will be there, and they have to resolve it."

"Hmmm." She raised her arms to him, her gaze glued to his mouth, and he worked at getting a grip on his common sense. "Kiss me?" she asked.

His fingers splayed across her back—made naked by the top she wore—caressing her flesh as he longed to do, and he swallowed the moisture that accumulated in his mouth. He brushed her lips quickly, knowing that if he slipped inside of her mouth, he'd probably crash the door in his eagerness to get her alone and inside of her.

"Olu's waiting, and if I stay with you another second, I won't leave you tonight. See you around eight."

"That was quicker than I thought it would be," Olu said. "You're in deep. I don't think I'd want to make your footprints, because you have some tough decisions ahead of you."

He let out a long breath. "Maybe. Maybe not."

His brother stopped walking, and he felt Olu's hand grip his shoulder. "Be careful you don't underestimate the power of what you feel for this woman, and don't forget that 'a loose tooth will not rest until it is pulled out.' "

"I know that; it's a question of priorities, nothing else."

Olu's voice was that of a man who conceded, who rested his case. "Yeah? That's problem aplenty. *Bàbá* is getting on in years, and he looks forward to your return home to take your rightful place as Oba to our people. I'm with you whatever you do, but—"

"I'm glad to know you're prepared to understand. I love Sharon, and she loves me. If she said she didn't, I wouldn't believe her. Olu, the fire igniting us is so intense . . . I didn't dream I could feel this way about anybody or anything. If you've never experienced it, it's the best I could ever wish for you."

Jon turned on the light beside the door as they entered his apartment. For that second, the darkness had seemed ominous, and he knew that wasn't a good sign.

"And you say *I'm* Americanized," Olu said. "I think I'll stay here for a couple of weeks. My office is covered, and I need a rest."

Jon couldn't restrain the laugh that bubbled up in his throat. "In other words, you don't want to be around if I do the unthinkable and *Bàbá* bursts an artery."

"I don't have to tell you that you're damned if you do and damned if you don't. As *Bàbá* always says, 'there is no cure without a cost.' Wake me up before you go out tomorrow."

"Sure thing. I'm leaving here at a quarter of eight."

"Forget I said that. Good night."

He was through pretending for the benefit of others. From now on, he'd let the chips fall where they may. She sat at a table facing the door of the hotel's coffee shop, and her brown eyes sparkled when she saw him. He reached the table, leaned down and brushed her lips with his own, and her radiant smile blessed him for it.

"You light up this room," he said, and meant it. "I have to stay here for another week, and I'll stop by Ife to see you on my way home."

"When am I going to meet your father?"

He hadn't thought she'd bring that up so soon. He looked steadily at her. "Have you ever heard of Pandora's box?"

She had the nerve to laugh. "Sure. I've opened it many times."

"Then you have an idea as to what you can expect."

She sobered, reached across the table and took his hand. "I know this probably won't be fun, but I long to meet the man who raised you, because I know I probably won't understand you fully until I do."

"You're probably right. He carries our culture with him. I don't. You'll meet him when you convene the town meeting in my hometown."

"Which one is that? I don't want a surprise."

"Ogbomàba. You won't encounter any problems there."

"With the town meeting? I don't expect I will, but—"

"Don't cross that river before you get to it."

He walked with her to her car, where Aluko sat with the

engine running and the air conditioner blowing. "I'll see you in a few days." Drat the luck. If he kissed her in her driver's presence, she'd fall in the man's esteem, so he had to content himself with holding her hand for a second.

"Plan to stay a while," she whispered.

"Do you recall my answer when you made that suggestion before?"

She nodded.

"Look for me Friday evening."

4

"I've wasted five good minutes of my life trying to figure out what kind of mood he'll be in and how he'll act when he gets here," Sharon said to herself. "This is not my style."

After the cook finished his morning chores, she gave him the rest of the day off. Around three, she set out what she planned to cook and prayed the electricity and water wouldn't go off before she finished it. She managed during the frequent power and water outages in Ife by keeping a good supply of candles, several large jugs of water, plenty of fresh fruits and roasted peanuts and the battery of her laptop computer fully charged at all times. She put a tray filled with a dozen pillar candles on her bedroom dresser, set the table for two with white linen, candles, porcelain and flatware, and a vase of the calla lilies a neighbor had given her.

Getting together a decent meal in Ife was no mean feat, so she'd bought essentials while in Lagos. She put the pork chops in the oven and prepared the remainder of the meal, which she'd cook later. Then she headed for the shower. Heaven forbid the water should go off while she was full of bath oil. Her luck held. She dressed in a burnt orange caftan and white sandals, brushed her hair down and hung a pair of dangling gold earrings in her earlobes. A glance at the lipstick brought a laugh. She ignored it. What was the point?

At six o'clock, she sprayed Fendi perfume where it counted most, went downstairs, put the potatoes in the oven and started the green beans to steaming. She glanced around the living and dining rooms. It didn't rate with her New York co-op, but it worked. Twenty minutes later, the Mercedes rolled to a stop at her doorstep.

A second after she opened the door, she was tight in his arms.

"You wouldn't believe how long a day this has been. Minutes moved like hours. Kiss me."

She kissed him quickly and would have moved away, but he stopped her, a frown marring his handsome face.

"Honey, I don't think we'd better start this right now. I planned a nice evening for you, and if you start this—"

Honest and open as always, his face showed his disappointment. "I stand corrected. Just cue me in on the program."

He looked at the glass of scotch and soda that she handed him and raised an eyebrow. "I'd love to have that, but I don't drink and drive."

She smothered a laugh. This guy was smooth. "I made you a nice dinner. So, here."

He accepted the drink and took a few sips. "I thought that comment would yield a hint about this . . . er . . . this program of yours."

As if she didn't know that. But she was ahead of him. "Don't worry," she said. "I figured out your angle. Ready to eat?" She lit the candles on the table.

"Sure I am. The scent of this food is making me ravenous."

She uncorked a bottle of wine, and he filled their glasses. He hardly spoke while they ate, and she saw no need to force conversation. After his second helping of lemon meringue pie, he sat back in his chair and gazed at her. "This was wonderful. Is there anything you don't do to perfection?"

"I can't sing." She said it in jest, but he didn't laugh.

"Shall we clear the table? I hope you're going to leave the dishes for the cook."

So he was in a hurry, was he? Well, she was traveling rather fast herself. "I'll stack them in the sink, and—"

"I'll do that. You sit down."

Points in your favor. Instead of sitting down, she tripped up the stairs, brushed her teeth and lit the candles on her dresser.

"Got any toothpaste?" he asked when she came down.

She fluffed the pillows on the living room sofa and didn't look at him. "In the bathroom upstairs. If there's anything valuable in your car, you'd better bring it inside. Theft is the way some people around here make a living."

From his expression, she knew he hadn't missed the cue, and when he came back in the house, she heard him lock the door and bolt it. A few minutes later, he sat beside her on the sofa. "Sharon, I can't hold it back. I want to make love to you so badly I can't think of anything else."

"Why don't you find out whether I'm interested?"

He pulled her into his arms, but immediately gentled his touch as he gazed at her with copper-brown eyes that burned with the fire of desire. Then his mouth came down on hers, demanding yet trembling, and she could feel the excitement, the untamed man in him. Feral and a little wild. Heat surfaced in her, and her breath shortened. His tongue skimmed her lips, begging entrance. She took him in, eager for the taste of him, and she thought she'd go mad as he darted here and there, teasing, tantalizing, until she pulled him deeper and feasted on his tongue.

She wanted to slow him down, but her own eagerness fired him, and his hands roamed her back and her buttocks while he plunged his tongue in and out of her mouth. Tremor after tremor rolled through her, and when her tell-tale breasts began their siege on her senses, she placed his hand on her left one. His long fingers stroked her sides, her breasts and finally cupped her buttocks.

"Jon. Honey, I'm . . . I'm—"

He swallowed her words. Springing up, he lifted her and locked her to him, suddenly unleashing his passion as never before, as his lips covered her mouth, his fingers tightened on her buttocks and he rose hard and massive against her in an onslaught that rocked her senses. Currents of electricity plowed through her, firing her feminine center.

"I need you. Need you," he whispered.

"Upstairs."

He picked her up, dashed up the stairs and headed like a homing pigeon to her bedroom. Her caftan dropped to the floor, leaving her breasts bare, and he stunned her by not looking at them. Immediately, he threw back the covers, laid her in bed and joined her.

"Do you want me to use a condom?"

"Yes."

Whoa. Something was missing. "I'm not ready, honey," she whispered.

He frowned. "What? What is it?"

Now how was she going to handle this? She'd studied the Yoruba culture, but she didn't know how they made love.

"Will you . . . let me lead you this first time?"

He wrapped his arms around her and looked down into her eyes, his face as serious as she'd ever seen it. "Whatever you want or need, I want to give it to you in whatever way you need it. Just show me."

She ran her fingers lightly over his pectorals and gave him the surprise of his life. Then she suckled him until he moaned.

"Kiss me?" she asked him.

His kiss was hot and wild as he plunged in and out of her mouth, showing her what he wanted, but she took his hand and placed it on her breast, and he stroked and toyed with the nipple until her keening cry filled the room.

"Please. Please kiss them."

His head snapped up, and he stared down at her. Then a smile crawled over his face and he bent his head and slowly began to suckle her. Then, as if he'd discovered he liked it, he went at it vigorously, until her hips began swinging beneath him. Frantic, she took his hand, guided it to her feminine folds and stroked gently. In seconds, he had her at fever pitch, and she thought she'd die for want of him. No longer able to restrain herself, she took him into her hands and caressed him lovingly.

He jerked upward. "*Olùfé.* Oh, love," he moaned. "Stop it or I'll explode. Tell me when."

With her other breast in his mouth, he teased and suckled

while his now-talented fingers worked their magic at her gate of love until love's liquid spilled over his fingers.

"Now, darling."

"Are you sure?"

"Yes. Yes, I'm sure." She shielded him and led him to her portal.

"Look at me, Sharon." He stared into her eyes and plunged home, electrifying her nerves and every atom of her body. His hips moved with rapid and powerful strokes, claiming and branding her as his own. She didn't know her flesh from his; he was everywhere. In her, around her and all over her. She gave herself up to him and moved to his rhythmic beat until the tightening and pumping began and she exploded in ecstasy, locking him within her in a joyous release.

"Jon. I love you. *I love you.*"

Seconds later, he shouted, "*Olùfé tèmi*. My love. You're mine. Mine!" and splintered in her arms.

After a long time, he raised his head from her breasts and gazed into her eyes. "The feeling. Oh, love, the feeling! I think I've just been reborn. Will you be hurt if I thank you?"

"Why . . . no."

His smile nearly took her breath away. "Do I have a lot more to learn? I've never before had a serious affair with a European or American woman, and let me tell you, it's different. I'm happy. What about you?"

"Honey, I'm on cloud nine. I couldn't have asked for more."

"But I'll find a way to give you more. I understand a lot of things now, and I suspect I didn't scratch the surface. But you're my woman, and I'll see that you're happy in bed and out of it."

"That's a tall order."

He grinned cockily, and she hugged him and kissed his neck. "Tall order? I'm a tall man." He stroked her nipple. "Now this . . . This boggles my mind. Around here, breasts are for feeding babies. Period."

"Were. And mine are beautiful. You didn't even look at them."

A sheepish grin floated over his face. "Believe me, that's in the past."

He rolled over with her, wrapped her legs around him and took her breast into his mouth. Fully in command now, he rocked them to the stars.

Later, unable to sleep, Jon tried to imagine living without the woman in his arms and knew he'd never give her up. He hadn't known he could feel as he had when she held him in her body, and when she exploded all around him, he'd nearly lost consciousness. And she loved him. She'd shouted it repeatedly. He was in for it, but it wouldn't be the first time he'd swum in troubled waters. Small comfort; he'd never gone up against his father, Fadipe A. Kuti, Oba of the Egba Yoruba.

Four weeks and four successful town meetings later, Aluko put Sharon's bags in the car and asked her, "Where to this time, Madame?"

"We'll be in Ogbomàba this week. Remember?"

The drive to Ogbomàba took them past banana, papaya and cola nut farms and over roads filled with potholes. Farm women sat beside the roads in the broiling sun selling their produce while their men sat beneath shade trees playing *ayo*, a game similar to checkers. She closed her eyes, as if that would blot out the implications of what she saw for her relationship with Jon.

When she entered the small but neat boardinghouse to register, Jon waited for her beside the reception desk. His kiss surprised her, for she hadn't thought he would make such a statement in his hometown.

"Can you come with me right away? My father is waiting for us."

"I need ten minutes." After checking in, she changed into a yellow cotton short-sleeved coatdress and white mid-heel sandals.

He smiled his approval. "I can't believe there's a man alive who wouldn't love you. You're . . . You're wonderful."

"Thanks, but what I am right now is nervous."

"Don't be. My father's a gracious man."

When they got out of Jon's rented car, she looked toward the big white house, and her heart took a tumble. Standing on the porch in front of the door stood an *agbada*-clad man with such self-assurance that he could only be the Oba. Jon took her hand and walked with her to his father. To her amazement, he released her hand, stepped back and prostrated himself on the carpeted porch. Then he stood, put an arm around her shoulder and addressed his father.

"*Bàbà*, this is my Sharon."

Not knowing whether she should offer to shake hands, she put her palms together as if in prayer and bowed slightly.

The Oba nodded in approval. *"Kú àbò, Omo mi. S'álafià l'e dè."* Greetings my child. I hope you arrived in good health.

Her face must have expressed the concern she felt at his greeting in Yoruba, for he smiled. "My son has fine taste, it seems. Come in, both of you. Our food is waiting."

At the end of the meal, she figured there was little of her public life that the chief didn't know. What he hadn't already known, he didn't hesitate to ask her. An engaging man, as tall and as handsome as his sons, the Oba had an elegance, an air of authority that commanded respect and compliance, and she recognized it as a trait in Jon that she hadn't previously labeled.

"Ask Nedega to show Dr. Braxton around our compound," the Oba said to a servant. He looked at Sharon. "There's much to see here."

She understood that he wanted to speak with Jon alone, so she smiled, bowed slightly and followed the servant.

"Now, let us get to business," the Oba said, as he led Jon into what looked like a throne room, but which was in fact the place where he received petitioners and other guests.

"Why have you brought Sharon to me, *omokùrin mi*?" My son.

"I can't give her up, *Bàbá*. I love her, and it isn't a love that you can wave your hand at. I'm never going to forget her."

The Oba stared at him, his lips thinned and eyes narrowed. "Surely you are not telling me you want to marry her when you know I have agreed with Chief Olusanya that you will marry his younger daughter. I have betrothed you to her."

So it was going to be war, but he'd stand his ground. If he didn't, he'd lose Sharon. "But I was not a party to that agreement."

The Oba clenched his teeth and pounded the floor with his silver cane. "No. But you haven't opposed it, either. Besides, you don't need to make an issue out of it. You marry Adelle and take Sharon for your second wife and live with her, though you will have to give Adelle children or her father will be outraged."

"Sharon won't hold still for that, and I won't give her up," Jon said, his deep bass voice unsteady but his tone profound. "I can't do that, *Bàbá*."

"Then you will persuade her to accept you as *orogùn*." A co-wife.

Jon shook his head, squared his shoulders and looked the Oba in the eye, fully cognizant of the meaning of his father's words. *Take it or leave it.* "That can never be," he said. "Never, *Bàbá*. Never."

The Oba banged his silver staff on the floor with such force that a lamp toppled from its pedestal and crashed on the Persian carpet, the veins standing out in his face and neck so prominently as to distress Jon. He didn't remember having previously been the object of his father's rage, and it was not a comfortable position.

"How dare you!" the Oba hissed. "I'm not familiar with this word, 'never.' " He stood and faced his son. "You have disappointed me. I cannot accept your marriage to this woman, except as *orogùn*, your second wife."

Jon didn't know Sharon had returned to the room until he heard her say, "Are you cra . . . ?" Catching herself, she sat down. "I'm sorry, sir. All this is a moot point, anyway." She didn't look at Jon, because she knew his pain had to be greater than hers, if that were possible.

"Marriage is not on my mind," she told them, blinking back the tears. She was damned if she'd let them see her cry. "I came to Nigeria to implement a United Nations project, and thanks to Jon and probably you also, sir, I'm succeeding in that. After I visit the remaining towns on my list and convene the concluding conference in Lagos, I'm going back to New York."

"You are a charming woman, attractive in many ways," the Oba said, "and I can see why Adejonko loves you, but he is the heir to the chieftaincy, and he must marry one of his own people."

She didn't see how she'd have gotten through the polite exchanges that followed if Jon hadn't been there with his arm always tight around her. For once, she couldn't fight for what she wanted. Jon would make his own decisions. One thing was certain, though; she would never share him with another woman, and being wife number two was as inviting as a drink of hemlock. After the Oba excused them, she told Jon as much.

"He'll come around," Jon said. "I don't want any wife but you, and I would never think of asking you to be the second *anything.*"

She shrugged at the hopelessness of it. "If you say so."

He was less hopeful than he'd led Sharon to believe, because flexibility wasn't something he'd often observed in his father. Reminding himself that he had an alternative, that he could break off relations with his father, painful as that would be, he set about convincing him.

"If I marry Sharon, one of your grandchildren may win a Nobel prize, *Bàbá.* Sharon is brilliant, and our children would be, too."

The Oba rolled his eyes toward the sky and patted his right knee in impatience. "Geniuses have been known to sire idiots; there's no telling what the two of you together would give me."

"They'd be good-looking, *Bàbá*, You can't dispute that."

"Your children would be good-looking if you begot them with that toothless cunjie woman out on Ondo road. All of my descendants are handsome."

It wasn't funny, but he could hardly hold back the laugh. He tried another tactic. "You could visit us in New York, attend the symphonies at Avery Fisher Hall, visit the planetarium and, especially, the Metropolitan Museum of Art. New York is full of art. It's everywhere."

"Yes. And fifty percent of it is fake African masks and statues, not to speak of all the phony Kente cloth all over Harlem."

He'd forgotten momentarily that his father had spent a summer in New York during the early 1960s. "Oh, come on, *Bàbá*," he pleaded. "You would enjoy being away from here during the rainy season." He leaned forward. "You could go fishing in the Florida Keys, and you could visit Disneyland, sir."

"What? So an oversized rat can give me a guided tour? Nonsense!"

A tap on the door, and Olu walked in. He'd never in his life been so happy to see another person. His brother greeted the Oba according to custom, patted Jon's shoulder, sat down and poured himself a cup of coffee. "Am I in the middle of something?"

The Oba picked up the gold-plated staff that lay beside his chair, one of many that he treasured, spread his knees and braced both hands on the symbol of authority.

"Your elder brother is trying to shorten my days."

"He loves Sharon, *Bàbá*. This isn't something that he can stride away from as he's done about previous things that mattered to him. We love our women, but I can see that his is a different love. He's welded to her. She's part of him."

The *Oba* stood, closing the subject. "The way to deal with trouble is to walk away when you see it coming. He had that chance. Every man has it."

He had to give it one more try. He loved his father and his family, and he couldn't break with them. He walked outside, where children of friends and neighbors played in the compound, and strode over to his grandmother's house.

"I hear you have an American woman. Your father has not agreed to your marrying her, so what are you prepared to give up?"

He looked at the kind old eyes, their whites brown with age but their twinkle still bright. "Everything."

"And you won't regret it?"

"I don't know. I *do* know I don't want to live without her."

"When you decide one way or the other, bring her to me."

As he walked out, he met his father about to enter the house. So he'd come for counsel as well. "*Bàbá*, I can't give her up. I won't. Look . . ." He ran his hands over his hair. "You'd love visiting us in the States. I could arrange for you to tour the White House and meet the President."

What had he said to put that scowl on the Oba's face? "*You want to kill me*? I could only take one wife to the White House, and the two I left behind would be working roots on me for the rest of my life. No, thank you."

"I see. You won't change your position. I'm going to marry Sharon. If she'll have me, that is."

The Oba's eyes widened, the veins of his forehead standing out prominently as he gasped and, with trembling hands, grabbed the pillar to steady himself.

"*If she'll have you?* Who is she? The Queen of Sheba reincarnated? *What living and breathing woman wouldn't want to marry the first-born son of Chief Fadipe A. Kuti, Oba of Ogbomàba?* I want you to bring her here to me."

"I'll ask her."

She'd had about as much of the Oba as she could handle for one day. "Jon, this is redundant. Neither of us is going to budge an iota," she said as they walked out of the boarding-house.

"I haven't asked you to budge. He wants to see you. Why not find out what he has to say? I've given him my position."

Cold marbles rolled around in her belly, but she refused

to let him see her quake. "You've told your father what you will do?"

His arm snaked around her waist and tightened. "Yes. Let's go. Do you love me, Sharon?"

She gazed up at the face she loved, its expression somber. "I love you. No matter what happens here, I will always love you." She could barely put one foot in front of the other as they walked to his car.

"I just needed to hear you say it."

"I'll finish here week after next, sir," she told the Oba, "and then I'm going home. That will solve everything."

"It solves *nothing*. My son has defied me."

Her head snapped up. *"Jon!"*

The chief waved a hand. "He will marry you no matter what I say—"

"If you'll have me," Jon said, doing the unthinkable and interrupting his father.

"Sit. Sit," the *Oba* said to Sharon, who, in her excitement at learning of Jon's decision, had jumped up from her chair. "You have a Yale University Ph.D.," the Oba continued, "Good. Good. You will be the first member of our tribe to hold such a degree from Yale. We will have a tribal wedding."

"Just a minute, sir. Jon hasn't asked me to marry him, and if he wants me to he has to propose properly." Her long lashes flew up, and she gaped in surprise as Jon knelt before her. "Will you be my wife, my only wife, and the mother of my children?"

She slipped to her knees beside him. "Oh, yes. For as long as we live."

"So this is the habit of American men, is it? Unbelievable," the Oba said. "Well, we will have tribal wedding rites."

"Tribal wed . . . No, sir. I'm going to be married by a Protestant minister in a Protestant church."

The Oba narrowed his eyes and took in a long and deep impatient breath. "Young woman, you do not speak to me in that tone. I said it will be a tribal wedding, and it will be a tribal wedding."

And they came to the place where two seas met. Jon recalled the biblical passage that he'd learned at Oxford University and wondered if he was about to lose all that he'd just
gained. Sharon had as much tenacity as his father.

"But, sir," she said, "it's my wedding, and I have a right
to choose what form it takes."

Though his father stared at Sharon, he saw his admiration
for her, grudging though it seemed. "Sharon, I am not only
Adejonko's father; I am the Oba. You remember that."

"Yes, sir. I meant no disrespect, but I am used to standing
up for my rights."

"Hmm. Yes, I can well imagine. But you remember what
I said."

Jon gazed at the two of them, his loved ones. Shedding
another coat of his culture, he acknowledged that in all things,
he stood with Sharon. He could remind his father that, as the
elder son, he deserved some deference, but he didn't. He
loved the old man. He also loved Sharon, and he'd stand with
her.

He regarded his father with understanding. "*Bàbá*, Sharon
is Christian, and she must have a Christian marriage."

"All right. All right. We will have both, but tribal rites will
be first."

He knew his face bloomed when she grabbed her chest as
if to prevent her heart from flying out of it, and her face shone
with happiness.

"Yes, sir," she said, her face wreathed in her smiles.

"Now, *omobìnrin mi*, my daughter. How may I reach your
father, your uncle or your brother?"

"My father is deceased, sir, but you may contact my
brother. She gave him Cannon's E-mail and postal addresses
and his telephone number.

Three days later, she received a cablegram from Cannon
stating that he would be flying the next day to Lagos and that
he'd rent a car and driver to take him to *Ogbomàba*. When
she showed the message to Jon, a lazy smile curled around
his lips.

"This is going to be interesting," he said, offhand. "By the way, I'm going back to New York along with you."

"You're not giving up the chieftaincy, are you?"

"Probably. I am not going to ask you to abandon the success you've worked so hard to achieve, because I don't think you should, so it will depend on when the occasion arises. Besides, I'm tenured at Columbia, and I'm happy there. Olu is up to the task."

"I wonder why Cannon's coming so soon?" she said. "Oh, well, I guess the Oba invited him to our wedding, but don't I get to set the date? I need a dress, for goodness' sake." She remembered later that Jon didn't answer those questions.

"My mother has been visiting my sister, Asàbi, who recently had a baby, and she arrived home about an hour ago. Let's go see her."

"*Iyá*, Mother. This is my Sharon."

Sharon hadn't seen such a slim, elegant woman since she left Lagos. Flawless, porcelain dark skin and Jon's copper-brown eyes that smiled a welcome.

"I have heard so much about you. Everyone speaks so well of you," Leda said, and opened her arms to Sharon.

She stepped into them eagerly, glad for an understanding female presence. She could see that their greeting pleased Jon, and it was obvious, too, that this woman loved her son.

"I have no idea what tribal marriage rites involve," Sharon told her. "Will you help me?"

"Of course I will."

"I can't believe *Bàbá* yielded," Jon said to his mother.

"A shepherd does not strike his sheep," she replied. "If he had persisted, he might have lost you. Remember: In your thirty-two years, you have never before confronted him. He accepts now that you are your own man. I am happy for him and for you."

"Sharon and I love each other, and I would never have surrendered my right to be with her."

Leda regarded Sharon with a smile that was warm and genuine. "You are fortunate and blessed that a man is willing to give up for you all that my son would have sacrificed. I'm glad he found you."

"Thank you. I didn't know what to expect of this meeting with you, but you've made me more comfortable than I've been since I entered this compound."

Leda's copper-brown eyes twinkled mischievously as Jon's so often did. "We women understand each other. Now, *omobìnrin mi*, my daughter, you must perform *dá àna*, the traditional marriage customs. They are simple. We have dispensed with most of the old ways, but in families such as ours, my son's Ìyàwó, bride, should visit all of his relatives for one night. They entertain you to show the family's good will."

Sharon stifled a gasp. "How long does this take?"

"Four or five weeks. But Jon cannot accompany you. One of my husband's unmarried daughters will go with you. You may begin as soon as you are engaged."

She looked at Jon. "I thought we became engaged when I said yes."

"It is official as soon as your brother arrives," Leda said. "From that time until you complete the *dá àna*, you and Jon may not lie together."

"What does that mean?" she asked Jon when they sat in his car in order to have privacy.

"Just don't lose your temper. It'll soon be over. For a traditional ceremony, there must be an exchange between my father and your brother."

She withdrew from him. "I'm not going there, Jon. I'm not saying one word, but if it's what I think it is, we're in for it. I'm just going to sit back and watch the fireworks."

"Yeah. If Cannon's at all like you, things ought to liven up around here."

She glared at him. "Anybody would think you're merely a bystander."

Laughter rumbled in his throat, and he hugged her to him. "I am. This is between our parents or guardians. Male ones, of course. In this respect, we're still backing into the twentieth, not to mention the twenty-first century."

"You're enjoying this."

"It's more accurate to say I can hardly wait to see who wins."

She thought of Leda. Such an elegant, intelligent woman seemed out of place in that environment. "Your mother is educated, and your father has more than one wife. How is this?" she asked Jon.

"After her children—Olu, Asàbi and I—were born, she told my father she wanted an education, and he sent her to the University of Ife. She chose a second wife for him who took care of us while she studied. She has a degree in English and a master's in library science. Father inherited a third wife from his deceased brother, but he has not consummated that marriage, though he takes care of her and her children."

"And it's your half-sister who will go with me to visit the relatives?" He nodded. "I have to negotiate this five or six weeks with the relatives. I haven't finished my project," She reminded him.

"Then speak to *Iyá* about it. It's overdone, anyhow."

She wanted so desperately to be alone with him, to escape for a few minutes the tidal wave of Yoruba culture in which she seemed to be drowning.

"Can't we be alone somewhere other than this car just to sit and talk? Hold hands? Every eye is on us. Anybody who says Nigerians are promiscuous is out in left field."

He raised an eyebrow. "Don't get carried away. This puritanical attitude relates to women. Men who don't have several wives are likely to fool around when their one wife is pregnant, and often when she isn't."

He took her back to his mother. *"Iyá,"* Sharon said. "Mother. I have not finished my United Nations project, and I have to return to my office in New York according to schedule. I'd like to reduce the length of the *dá àna* to, at most, a week."

She had expected a cool reception to the idea, but Leda's warm smile told her she needn't have worried. "Then you will visit three of my husband's brothers and three of mine. Inez will travel with you in the Oba's chauffeured car. If you like, you may stay in my guest room while you're here. You'll be more comfortable, and you can at least have a few minutes of privacy with Jon."

Sharon thanked her and went with Jon to get her things from the rooming house. "That was easy. I thought she'd say no."

"She might have. But you began by calling her mother. That got her to eating out of your hand."

She was enjoying the comfort of her air-conditioned, beautifully furnished, sunny room in Leda's house when she looked out of the window and saw the gate to the compound open and a white Lexus roll in and stop. Seconds later, Cannon Braxton stepped out and headed for the big white house. She raced down the stairs to Leda's private sitting room.

"*Iyá*, my brother is here."

"Yes. I saw him get out of his car, but you must wait with me. When they've finished talking, he'll come here."

"Where's Jon?" She didn't like having her future planned when she wasn't given the opportunity to speak her piece.

"He's in the same position as you. He's with Olu, waiting for the outcome."

"I can tell you the outcome." Sharon said, fighting her temper.

"So can I, but it's a ritual we have to go through."

The Oba stood as his guest entered the room, a courtesy he reserved for foreigners and Obas of his rank. "Thank you for coming, Mr. Braxton. I'm Jon's father."

"I'm glad to meet you," Cannon said, extending his hand. "I didn't know my sister had marriage on her mind until I got your cablegram. What's this all about and where is she?"

"She's with my wife. You will see her as soon as you and I have settled this small matter. It is the custom in noble Yoruba families to pay a bride price to the bride's father or male guardian. What are you asking?"

"*What?* Man, you're out of . . . You're asking me to sell your son my sister? Where is this character? And Sharon?

That girl is out of her mind if she thinks I'm going along with this."

"Hold on, young man. I know this isn't your custom, but it is ours. I cannot bless this marriage without this exchange between your family and mine."

"Then for Pete's sake, don't bless it! My father would turn over in his grave if I went along with this. And I'd bet my neck Sharon didn't give you permission to give me anything in exchange for her marrying your son."

Fadipe took a deep breath and blew it out. "I gather you don't know who an Oba is. An Oba is a crowned head of his people. A king. Jon is my elder son and heir to this chieftaincy. One doesn't speak as you have to the Oba."

"I'm sorry, sir, but to an American like me, the idea is outrageous, and I cannot give my consent."

Fadipe rang for a servant. "Ask Dr. Braxton to come here. She is with *iyálé mi*. My senior wife."

"What's the purpose of this custom?" Cannon asked the Oba.

"When a couple marries, their families are wed as well. For us, marriage is indissoluble, and the bride price is compensation to the family for taking away its beloved daughter."

"The Yoruba divorce."

"Yes, but mainly Christian Yoruba. We are traditional. Sharon will have a Christian marriage after our traditional ceremonies."

"Cannon," Sharon exclaimed as she entered the room, and he rushed to greet her, picked her up and swung her around.

"What's going on, Sharon?"

"Jon and I fell in love when we met in New York. It got deeper here. I love him something awful, Cannon, and he loves me. But I know you aren't going to agree to *Bábà*'s terms, and I don't want you to." At his raised eyebrow, she explained her reference to her future father-in-law.

"Then you'll just have to settle for a Christian marriage and skip the traditional one."

"I don't think Jon will be happy doing that."

"Will you accept a token gift?" Fadipe asked Cannon.

"Like what? Look, sir. I'd like to meet Jon. I need to know the man who managed to sweep my sister off her feet. He must be exceptional."

"He is," the *Oba* said without hesitation.

Jon walked into his father's meeting room, and she gazed with pride at the man she loved, tall and regal in a gold brocade *agbada*. Less than half an inch shorter, Cannon walked to meet him, and her heart returned to its natural rhythm, for she saw that they liked each other even before they spoke.

"I can't go along with this bride sale, Jon," Cannon said after they greeted each other.

"I didn't think you would, and I haven't made it a condition for marrying Sharon. In fact, I don't have *any* conditions. I love her and want to marry her."

Cannon turned to the Oba. "You know what? I'm starved. If you want to give me something of value, I'd like a meal and a glass of fine wine.

"I bless them," he added, winking at Sharon.

Sharon looked at Jon and saw that he held his breath, as she did, while the Oba frowned in reflection.

"It doesn't please me, Mr. Braxton, but my son wants this woman. If they have your blessings, I give them mine, and you'll get a great meal."

Sharon dashed over to where Jon stood with a wide grin on his face. "Problem now is that we can't make love anymore until after we're married," she whispered.

He grinned at her. "There was supposed to be a bride price, too."

The success of the final conference in Lagos had her smiling for days afterward. She'd done what the skeptics at UN headquarters in New York said couldn't be done. Jon had helped, but it was she who had argued for the plan, and she'd won. Before leaving Lagos, she ordered a white wedding dress, tiara and veil for her Christian wedding, and a gold-embroidered *iro* and headpiece for her traditional wedding.

"I can't see her?" Jon asked Olu. "This is ridiculous."

Olu's eyes twinkled with merriment. "What's stopping you? Go over to Iyá's house, knock on the door and ask to see her. With luck, she'll be the one who opens the door."

"I agree," Cannon said, working on his second bottle of beer. "As a lawyer, I can assure you that most people ignore the law unless there's a penalty."

Jon stared at his future brother-in-law. "Right. See you." A few minutes later, he tapped on the front door of his mother's house.

To his surprise, Sharon answered the door. He didn't give her time to object to his being there. Starved and aching for her, he swept her into his arms, and she parted her lips for his foraging, impatient tongue. From the minute he touched her, his libidinous craving sent his blood racing through his veins, and his pulse took off like a runaway train. Without warning he rose against her hard and massive as he sampled her sweet mouth and felt the hard tips of her breasts against his chest. When he would have picked her up and carried her to her room, she moved away.

"Honey, you know what we're doing is against the rules. You have to wait until after our Christian marriage."

Studying the determined set of her jaw, he wished he could find something to kick. He ran his hands over his hair and gazed down at her. "It doesn't bother you that we can't make love?"

"Of course it does, but I'm disciplined. Besides, I start my *dá àna* tomorrow, and . . . if I'm going through this, I want to do it right. I'll see you in a week. Look after Cannon for me."

"Cannon is a man of the world. He needs looking after the way a fish needs swimming lessons. He'll be staying with *Bàbá*, Olu and me."

The next morning, with Cannon beside him, he stood on his father's porch and watched her get into his father's limousine with his half-sister, Inez. The driver tapped the horn for the errand boy to open the gate, and she headed for the unknown.

He turned to Cannon. "I can't imagine what I did that made me so lucky."

Sharon quickly learned that her dread of the prenuptial rituals had been unfounded. Each of Jon's uncles was a chief, though not an Oba, and they and their families greeted her with warmth and enthusiasm. She wished Jon could have shared the fun. At the home of his father's younger brother, Jon's cousins asked her to dance. She did the hula that she'd learned as a teenager one summer in Hawaii, and every woman in the compound, including two in advanced pregnancy, tied a rope around her waist and tried the hula. When she arrived at the compound of Jon's oldest maternal uncle, she learned that her fame as a hula dancer preceded her when the chief asked her to dance the hula.

"I'm not very good at it, sir."

"I heard differently. And anyhow, it isn't likely any of us will get to Hawaii to see the real thing."

The women and children worked at learning the Hawaiian dance, while the men watched, some drinking palm wine, others savoring French wines and cognacs.

Storytelling appeared to be an important part of the ritual, and at the home of each chief, the elders told family tales that served to orient her into Yoruba life.

At her last stop, the mother of Chief Ekti, Leda's youngest brother, told of an ancient kinsman, the *Oba Ewuare*, who, when his only sons were murdered, decreed that henceforth no one should have children. To ensure it, sex was banned for three years, and any man whose wife became pregnant would be killed—the child as well. All in his domain were to mourn for three years, The men, being true to their nature, eventually resorted to anarchy; and though forbidden to emigrate, they dispersed throughout the western region to form the Ishan region, a Yoruba stronghold.

Dumbfounded, Sharon didn't know whether she should laugh, cry or even applaud until Inez whispered, "We've heard it hundreds of times. It's supposed to be funny, so you should laugh." That didn't appeal to her, so she looked into the dictionary Leda had given her and went over to the old woman.

"*Ole se é, baba.*" Thank you, wise one. Everyone in the compound applauded, and the old woman took her hand and smiled.

She wasn't prepared for what greeted her on her return to the Oba's compound. News traveled fast.

Leda welcomed her and said, "Our families have fallen in love with you. We are all pleased that Jon has brought us such a wonderful bride. Now you must bathe and dress quickly. In a few minutes, Olu will come for you. He will take you to Jon, where you will receive the Oba's blessing. Then you will be Jon's wife. Here is your certificate."

She finished her ablutions, dressed in the gold-embroidered *ìro* and headpiece and went downstairs to wait for Olu. "Aren't you going with me, *Iyá*?" she asked Leda.

"No," she said and kissed Sharon warmly, "but Cannon will stand with you."

Thoroughly confused by the strange customs, she hugged Leda, grateful for her presence. Olu arrived wearing a richly embroidered gold lamé *agbada* and *filà*. "Do you have your certificate?" he asked.

She nodded, guessing that the occasion forbade friendliness or familiarity with her. He walked with her to the Oba's house. At the door, he said, "I'm out of line here, but I want to thank you for what you've given Jon. You will never regret this."

She couldn't find the words to tell him how his gesture of friendship touched her, so she tried to smile. He gave a thumbs-up sign and opened the door. A minute later, she stood with Olu before the Oba. Jon walked in accompanied by Cannon and the Oba stood.

"*Ki Olórùn só wa.* May God watch over you," the Oba said. "Sharon, go to your husband."

She thought her heart had stopped beating. "You mean . . . ?"

The Oba smiled. "Yes, Jon is your husband."

She wasn't one for shedding tears, and especially not in

public, so she sniffled as hard as she could. *What's he waiting for?* she wondered. Then she remembered the Oba's words and ran to Jon's open arms.

"My wife. My love." His kiss was dry and swift, but it telegraphed to her the special place she occupied in his heart.

"We have an hour before our Christian wedding, so go and dress. *Iyá mi* has arranged everything. Inez and my other half-sister will be your attendants, and my sister, Asàbi, will be your maid of honor. *Iyá* will give you my calla lilies. You will ride with Cannon, and Olu will ride with me. The others will ride in the limousine with *Bábà* and *Iyá*. I'll be waiting for you at the church."

She grabbed his sleeve. It was all moving too fast for her. "Where are we getting married?"

"At the Christ Episcopal Church. The minister is Reverend Ogunba."

"That name sounds familiar."

"Right. He's my mother's uncle. His son is a chief who attended both of your conferences. My mother is a Christian. Hurry. It's a bad omen to be late."

Leda and the bridesmaids helped her dress. She didn't mind the rush, or having these people she'd known only a short time attend her at her wedding. She felt their love and their enthusiasm and excitement at having her become one of them. She kissed the women, took a last look at herself in the mirror and turned to go.

"I'm an excellent photographer," Leda said, "and I'll take some good pictures for you. Our relatives have pictures of your *dá àna*, so you'll have a record of these days. You're a beautiful bride."

"Why is this Lexus moving so slowly?" Sharon asked Cannon as they motored to the church.

"Local custom. The bride is supposed to be reluctant to get married."

"Nonsense. I'm not reluctant. I've never been so happy in my life. Besides, it's stupid. I'm already married to him, and I have the paper to prove it."

"You'll get one to prove this one, too, and I'm going to register it with the U.S. Consulate before I leave. I came here hot under the collar, revved up about this whole thing. But it went well."

"What did you say to the *Oba*?"

"I don't think you want to know."

"Tell me."

"I asked him if he was crazy, and he retaliated by telling me I was talking to a king. He found out I didn't much care. Jon didn't care, either. He's a great guy, Sis. You could spend the rest of your life looking for his equal. Here we are."

He kissed her. "Love you, gal. Be happy."

Seconds after she entered the church she heard the strains of "Here Comes the Bride." Leda adjusted her tiara. "Go now," she said.

With Cannon beside her, she walked to meet Jon, who stood at the altar with Olu waiting for her.

The altar was bedecked with calla lilies and fern, and the setting sun cast a glow through the azure blue and yellow stained-glass windows. She looked up at Jon, and he winked as if to say, "We made it."

Jon placed a plain gold band on her finger, and she put a matching one on his. Inez surprised her with a beautiful contralto rendition of "Through the Years."

After asking their intentions and offering a short prayer, The Reverend Ogunba said in a loud voice, "Sharon Braxton and Adejonko Odukoya Kuti, I now pronounce you man and wife."

At last the tears came. Tears of joy so intense that she could hardly bear it.

"You may kiss your bride, Dr. Kuti," the minister said.

He gazed down at her for a long time, and then his lips brushed hers tenderly, as if he were afraid of bruising them.

"I love you, Sharon. I love you so much. So much," he said, in a basso that trembled. Tears glistened in his eyes and finally fell on his cheeks. "Do you love me?"

"Oh, yes," she said. "I love you. And I will for as long as I breathe."

Their relatives gathered around them, but they took no notice. His kiss was sweet on her lips, and their tears mingled in joyous communion.

Leaving the wedding, Fadipe A. Kuti, the Oba of Ogbomàba, relaxed in his limousine and smiled. He reached for his cellular phone, dialed the Mercedes dealer in Lagos and ordered a white Mercedes for shipment to attorney Cannon Braxton in Philadelphia, Pennsylvania. No one got the better of the Oba of Ogbomàba.

Distant
Lover

———

DONNA HILL

1

"Got everything?" Denise Hendricks asked, scanning Nina's bedroom for any forgotten suitcases.

Nina Benson took a breath, hands on her ample hips. "I think that does it. Don't believe the chauffeur missed anything." She stepped into her low-heeled, camel-colored mules, a perfect match for her free-flowing palazzo pants and spaghetti-strap top. She linked her arm through Denise's, snatched up her purse and prescription sunglasses. "Let's hit the road, girl."

"You sure the driver won't mind bringing me all the way back to the city from the airport?" Denise queried as they headed for the door.

Nina twisted her glossy lips. "Believe me, the Burns Corporation pays this limo company a hefty fee every month to take their employees and guests wherever they need to go. Don't even worry about it."

"You won't get any argument from me," Denise said, flashing a dimpled smile and the little-girl gap between her two front teeth. "I love what you did with your hair." She touched one of Nina's springy curls.

"Della convinced me to try something new, said it would be perfect for a Caribbean trip. I don't have to worry about it frizzing up in the water, or have it collapsing from the sun. And Mr. Reggie twisted my arm into having the color lightened. But I have to admit, I really like it. He was right as usual."

The spiral curls, rinsed in a soft auburn color, haloed Nina's somewhat round face, slenderizing it, giving it a more oval shape. When she looked at the finished product in the mirror, the night before, she could have sworn she looked ten years younger. And there was nothing wrong with that in her book.

"How is everybody over there? I need to stop in and get a manicure."

"Everyone's fine. Wild and crazy as ever. You know Chauncie's pregnant, right?"

"Get out!" Denise squealed, tapping Nina's arm.

"Yep."

"I know Della must be strutting like a peacock."

"And then some. Couldn't get her to stop talking about what she was going to do with her grandchild. Didn't sound like Chauncie and Drew were going to have much to do with the poor baby at all."

The women laughed.

"And you know Della," Nina commented. "Once she makes up her mind, that's it. You see what she's done with the shop. The minute it changed over from Rosie's Curl and Weave to Della's House of Style, there was no turning back. The business is thriving, her club is the hot spot of Harlem these days. That's a determined woman. *And* she has that handsome husband Matt to come home to every night."

"Hey, I'd let him add up my numbers any day," Denise quipped.

"Girl, you need to stop." Nina laughed. "But seriously, one of these days I hope to have what Della and Chauncie have. They done good, as the saying goes."

They stepped out of the front door of Nina's brownstone on historic Striver's Row. The immaculately kept homes were the pride of Harlem. Nina truly felt blessed to have lucked out to secure a mortgage that she could afford. Although she earned a solid six-figure income plus commission as the Senior Vice President of Development for the Burns Corporation, she knew she had Ross Burns to thank. It was no coincidence that her mortgage lender was not only a personal friend of Ross', but had also secured the financing needed to build the string of mini-hotels and resorts that the Burns Corporation was constructing throughout the Caribbean—the reason for her trip.

It was her job to set the negotiations, secure the purchase of the land, and ultimately oversee the development in St.

Michaels, Barbados—Ross' latest project. She'd never been to the island of Barbados, which gave her business trip an added benefit.

Nina settled back against the butter-soft leather of the limousine, thinking ahead to what the next sixty days would entail. She gazed down at the brilliant marquise diamond that sat at least an inch off the third finger of her right hand.

"This isn't an engagement ring," Ross had said to her over a candlelit table at the Russian Tea Room, two days earlier. "Just something to let you know how much I think of you, Nina. And to remind you I'm always here for you." He grinned that crooked, heart-stopping grin that made his onyx eyes sparkle. "And when you're ready, simply put it on your left hand."

"Ross." She shook her head helplessly, dazzled by his gift, and floored by his barely veiled suggestion of marriage. "I can't take this. It's too much. Really." She slid the black velvet box toward him, even as the glitter from the perfect stone beckoned her.

His expression, which only moments before had been filled with warmth and expectation, suddenly turned hard, almost mean.

"When I give a gift to any of my employees, I expect them to be gracious enough to accept it." The right corner of his mouth ticked. "It's not everyone who gets the attention that you do, Nina. I'm sure you're aware of that." His meaning was perfectly clear.

She thought of her beautiful home, her meteoric rise up the corporate ladder, the company car, the business account and the staggering salary. All to which she'd grown accustomed. Ross Burns had the power to make it all disappear—permanently.

Her stomach fluttered dangerously. She liked Ross, admired his brilliance, his determination. And there'd never been any doubt that he'd always taken a special interest in her. In the beginning she'd been naïve enough to believe that it was simply because she was good at what she did—the best. But deep inside she'd sensed the truth and had refused to face it, didn't want to accept the implications. Now this. She'd allowed herself to become slowly seduced by all that he offered, tangled now in a web of which Ross was the master spinner.

Nina took a shallow breath and forced a tight smile across her mouth. "Thank you, Ross. It's . . . beautiful."

His face lit up like a lamp had been switched on beneath his smooth chestnut brown skin. He reached for the box, opened it and took out the diamond, set on a platinum band. He took Nina's right hand and slid the perfectly fitted ring onto her third finger. Bringing her hand to his lips, he delicately kissed the inside of her palm. "To the future, Nina Benson," he had murmured.

"You okay?" Denise asked, nudging Nina from her thoughts.

Nina blinked, pushed the images aside and laughed self-consciously. "Yeah, just thinking." She glanced down at the ring.

"What are you going to do about that?" Denise quizzed, pointing to it.

"I've been asking myself the same question, Denise. There's more attached to this than Ross' benevolence."

Denise frowned. "What do you mean? You never did tell me the whole story."

Nina reached for a button in the armrest and the Plexiglas panel slowly rose with a gentle whir, separating them from the driver. Nina angled her body to face Denise.

"He tried to imply that all I have, everything I've accomplished, has been because of him. And that essentially, I owe him. This ring is a *symbol* of our ties together."

"Damn," Denise muttered. "And if you give it back it's a slap in the face to him."

"Exactly, and then everything else comes into jeopardy."

Denise's brows rose. "Your job," she stated more than asked.

"I'm pretty sure of it. That's what it sounded like to me."

"Ross doesn't seem to be that sinister, Nina. Because if that *was* the case then we'd be talking about sexual harrass-

ment. Especially if all these things are making you uncomfortable, and you feel your job is in jeopardy." She paused
for a moment, let her comment simmer. "Maybe he really
does care about you and did all those things because you *are*
important to him," she said cautiously. Hey, believe me, you
could do a helluva lot worse than Ross Burns. Most women
would give their right arm just to have him look their way."

"But what about how I feel, what I want?"

"How *do* you feel? Honestly."

Nina was thoughtful for a moment before saying, "Let's
face it, Denise, I'm no spring chicken anymore. Maybe that's
why it's been so easy for me to just 'go along' with the
program. Next year I'll be forty. I'll never see a size ten
again—a twelve on a bad day. My field of opportunity along
with my eyesight is narrowing every day.

"The thing is I don't know if I feel that way about Ross.
Sure, he could make all my financial fantasies come true. But
then what? When I slip between the sheets with someone I
want it to be a love connection, not a time bomb fastened to
my bank account."

Denise chuckled at the analogy. "You want my advice?"

"No, but when did that ever matter?"

"Exactly. Now, I say, relax and enjoy it. Give Ross a
chance. I mean, it's not like someone else is in your life right
now. But be honest with yourself, too. It's never too late to
say 'No, enough!' And if he threatens your job, or you because of it, you know what you'll have to do no matter how
ugly it is."

Nina sighed heavily. "Well, this time away will give me
a chance to think. Whenever I'm directly working on a new
project my head seems to clear, my thoughts are sharper."

"Hopefully when you get back you'll have everything in
perspective."

"Yeah, I hope so, too. To be truthful, I need to have my
program together before I get to Barbados."

"Sense some trouble?"

"Nothing I can't handle, I'm sure. But Mr. St. Michael
doesn't sound as if he's going to give in quietly and go away

with the nice, fat check I'm prepared to offer him. At least, that's the lowdown according to Ross. He told me in no uncertain terms to use whatever was at my disposal to close this deal."

"You know those island men, girl," Denise said in a mock Caribbean accent. "The men rule. They play hard and want their women hot and soft. So use what you got."

Nina rolled her eyes. "Believe me, I've heard all the rumors, and the old wives' tales about the size of their feet. But I'm going there on business, strictly. And Mr. St. Michael will need to be real clear about that."

Denise arched a brow. "Okay, now, just don't call me talking 'bout how Nina got her groove back!"

They both cracked up laughing.

2

The flight to Barbados was mostly uneventful, except for the musical lilt of island accents that floated throughout the jumbo jet cabin, clothing that burst with color and language that was often just as lively. Nina was actually disappointed when the stewardess closed the curtain of her first-class cabin.

Settling herself down with a glass of white wine and her laptop, Nina went over all the details of the deal she planned to offer Mr. St. Michael. He owned a three-mile stretch of land a stone's throw away from the breathtaking white beaches—the perfect location for the development of several dozen bungalows that Ross Burns' corporation was adamant about building. It would secure Ross' foothold in the Caribbean and solidly establish him as one of the premier developers in the area.

She had to admire Ross, she mused, studying the electronic version of what the completed project would look like on her computer screen. Ross had vision and an abundance of energy. When you were in his presence he made you believe anything was possible, and that you were the most important person in the world. His appearance only enhanced his win-

ning aura. He wasn't that pretty-boy magazine type of handsome. He had the classic African features of full lips and
broad nose. He had remarkable cheekbones; pearly white,
near perfect teeth; and bottomless black eyes that could be
soulful and warm or as cold as granite. With his exceptional
tastes in clothes and jewelry and his incomparable personal
style, Ross Burns could turn heads in a pitch-black room. Add
the tempting baritone that could easily switch from the hip-
hop lingo of the 'hood to the polished vernacular that his
Harvard MBA had afforded him, and you had the total man.

Nina closed her laptop, took a sip of her wine and sighed.
Yes, Ross was the personification of many women's dreams.
But was he hers? She didn't think so.

"Can I refill your drink before dinner, Ms. Benson?"

Nina's lowered gaze slid upward, blinked and focused on
the smiling honey-brown face of the first-class stewardess.
Absently she handed over her glass. "Yes, thanks."

She scooted a bit deeper into the oversized leather seat and
peered out of the window. Nothing to be seen for miles but
blue skies and puffs of cotton. She hoped that the weeks
ahead would be as smooth as this flight.

Whenever any of Ross' staff traveled to the Caribbean, they
stayed in the penthouse suite at the Hilton. Their every need
was met. The only thing Nina had to concern herself with
was planning for the meeting. One phone call would have her
bath run, bed turned down, dinner served to her specifications
and, if she wanted, her clothes laid out for her.

She looked around at the stunning interior of the suite.
Gold fixtures sparkled from the light streaming in from the
floor-to-ceiling wraparound windows. The bar was fully
stocked, a seventy-two-inch television and incredible stereo
system made their mark in the sunken living room. The sparkling blond wood floors were sprinkled with white silk and
rayon rugs and white leather furniture set on hand-polished
cane supports. It was like living in a fairy tale, even if only
for the moment. This is what her career—what Ross—had
afforded her.

She should be totally happy. Any woman in her place would be. She blew out a long breath as she folded her lingerie and placed them in the dresser drawer. Briefly she gazed at the splendor that surrounded her. Something was missing from her life.

3

Vincent St. Michael cut through the gentle blue waves, sleek as an eel, and burst above the water. His chocolate brown body glistened as if rubbed with coconut oil as he emerged from the ocean and strode toward his beachfront home. The hard muscles of his thighs contracted and retracted as he walked, the electric blue Lycra brief clinging to his body clearly defining his virility, accenting the taut stomach and broad hairless chest.

He grabbed a green-and-white–striped towel from the lounge chair on the deck and ran it across his face and close-cropped hair.

"Vincent . . ."

He looked up. His housekeeper Jade stood on the steps of the house, cordless phone in hand. Vincent instantly felt a pull in his groin and smoothly wrapped the towel around his waist.

Jade was everything a housekeeper should not be. Tall like a runway model, with a butterscotch complexion that always looked sweet enough to eat. A silky sheet of ink black hair fell below her shoulder blades, framing a heart-shaped face with a pert nose, a dimpled chin and exotic sloping eyes with thick, curly lashes and sleek, arching brows.

"Phone for you," she called out in what almost sounded like bells to Vincent's ears.

Jade held the phone in one hand, her other planted on her narrow hip, sensuously wrapped in an orange and green ankle-length fabric that was only held together by a knot at her waist. A matching strip of fabric covered her lush breasts, which threatened to burst free of the single bow that tied the cloth together in the back.

He knew how Jade felt about him, but he'd made a promise to his father's best friend to look after his daughter and keep her safe. Jade was twenty years old. Young enough to be his own daughter and old enough to make a grown man weep with desire. And as much as she had tempted him to cross that thin line, he never wavered.

"Thanks." He took the phone and walked back toward the lounge.

Jade continued to watch him from the doorway.

Vincent picked up his sunglasses, slid them on and stretched out on the chair before speaking.

"Yes. Good day."

"Mr. St. Michael?"

The voice was rich, soft and truly American. "Speaking."

Nina settled against the zebra-print pillows of the couch. "This is Nina Benson, from the Burns Corporation."

The corner of Vincent's mouth curved upward. *So, they'd sent a woman to do a man's job.* "Yes, Ms. Benson. What can I do for you?"

He had a British accent, Nina registered absently, laced with the lyrical cadence of the Caribbean.

"I just got in, but I was hoping we could possibly get together for dinner and discuss the deal we're willing to offer you."

"What happened to Burns? He's the one I've been dealing with."

Nina ignored the subtle slight. "When it gets to this point in the negotiations it's my ball game," she said in no uncertain terms.

"The Trojan horse," he murmured.

"Excuse me?"

"Nothing. What time?"

"Eight is good for me. I'm staying at the Hilton."

"I'll see you at eight." He depressed the talk button without saying good-bye, held the phone in his hand for a moment and briefly wondered about the person behind the voice.

Jade was suddenly standing above him. "Will you be here for dinner?"

Vincent squinted behind the sunglasses. "No. I'll be going into town tonight."

"To meet that woman who called?"

Her voice sounded tight, Vincent noted, but he would not be pulled in by her petulance. He'd fallen into that trap before.

"Yes." Simple. End of story.

"Fine." She spun away, a whiff of something soft blowing around her, and returned to the house.

Vincent sighed, and adjusted his long body on the chair. "Women," he mumbled before closing his eyes and drifting into a light sleep.

Nina dressed carefully for her meeting with Mr. St. Michael. She didn't want to appear too casual or too formal. After careful consideration she selected a pale lavender, linen and rayon tank dress with tiny white buttons running down the entire front length. The dress reached just above her ankles, with walking splits on either side. She added tiny diamond studs to her lobes, a light dusting of translucent power to her face to tone down her always-there shine and a faint coat of cinnamon lipstick. She gathered her curls on top of her head and fastened them with a rhinestone clip.

She faced herself in the mirror and was satisfied with the effect, in addition to the stylish camouflage that the dress provided for her more-than-a-handful breasts and brick-house hips. She walked toward the bed and felt her thighs rub together. One of these days she was actually going to use her membership to the gym and get rid of the extra fifteen pounds she'd gained, she thought.

The phone on the nightstand rang.

"Yes?"

"Ms. Benson, there is a Mr. St. Michael to see you," the front-desk receptionist announced in a tone that sounded like awe to Nina.

Quickly Nina peeked at the digital clock next to the phone. Eight sharp.

"Please tell him I'll be right down."

"Yes, ma'am."

"At least he's prompt." She snatched up her leather portfolio, checked to be sure she had everything she needed and headed for the door, picking up her hotel card key from the hall table on her way out.

Vincent was seated in the conversational grouping of wicker chairs that surrounded the indoor fountain and a profusion of tropical foliage in brilliant colors of turquoise, burnt orange, fuchsia and sunshine yellow. The receptionist pointed him out to Nina when she inquired at the desk.

Steeling herself, she began to approach him. He turned toward her as if he'd sniffed the air and recognized her scent. Nina hesitated an instant, startled and suddenly aroused by the totality of the man. Instantly he brought to mind images of African kings, regal, dignified, exuding such quiet power that only their presence was needed to wield their will. Dark, dangerous as the big cats that prowled and hunted on the countryside.

His skin was the color of the darkest polished mahogany and he had deep, almost brooding eyes, fringed with incredible black lashes. His face was a stunning study of hard planes, angles and soft lines. His hair, which he kept short, could only achieve that wave because nature had provided it. His attire was a simple ensemble of a soft beige cotton shirt, opened halfway down his chest, and matching wide-legged pants. But on him they looked like the robes of royalty.

Slowly he stood to his full height, which Nina guesstimated to be a solid six feet plus an inch or two. A lazy smile moved across his wide mouth like dawn breaking over the horizon. His dark, deep-set eyes crinkled at the edges.

Nina swallowed, forced her mind to clear and felt a trickle of perspiration wiggle down the column of her spine. She concentrated on putting one sandaled foot in front of the other.

"Mr. St. Michael," Nina greeted, extending her hand.

"And you are my Trojan horse," he murmured, his right brow arching in appraisal. He brought her hand slowly to his lips and placed a light kiss on her knuckles.

Nina fought down the shudder that weakened her knees. *Damn, damn, damn.* "That's the second time you've said that to me," Nina responded, easing her hand from his warm grasp.

"I'm sure you've read how the city of Troy was destroyed. They let down their defenses to allow the magnificent Trojan horse into their midst."

"Are you trying to imply that I'm dangerous, Mr. St. Michael?"

He chuckled. "As my Nana would say, 'Beware of strangers bearing gifts.' "

"Hopefully you won't always consider me a stranger," she replied in a voice she barely recognized as her own. *Why did she just say that?* She cleared her throat.

Vincent smiled, his lids lowered, almost covering his eyes.

"I can assure you that the deal my company is willing to offer is completely aboveboard. Everyone wins." *That smile again.*

"That remains to be seen, Ms. Benson." He paused, switching gears. "So, where would you like to have dinner?"

"I thought we could eat here in the hotel restaurant."

He slid his hands into his pockets. "I have a better idea. There's a wonderful little place just outside of town. I think you'll like it."

Nina looked at him a moment and knew she was going to have her hands full with this one. "I'm sure I will," she said finally.

He offered her his right arm. She slid her hand around taut muscle and their evening began.

4

The restaurant, or what posed for one, Nina thought—very suspicious of the building that resembled more of a hut than an eating establishment—was located between a cove of trees and a pebble-and-seashell walkway.

The almost-iridescent stones and shells of pale pink, sky blue and ivory crunched beneath her feet. It wasn't until they came closer that the tantalizing aroma of island cuisine assaulted her senses. Her stomach emitted an unladylike shout-out in response.

"I'm sure Clotie can take care of that," Vincent teased.

Nina felt her face heat with embarrassment, thankful for the shadows of the mango trees that shielded her mortified expression. "Clotie?" she asked, thankful for a diversion, while wondering if it was some sort of rare Barbadian delicacy.

Vincent pointed to the hand-carved wooden plaque that hung at a precarious angle above the door. "Clotilda's Place."

"My grandmother," he said reverently, and held the door open for her.

The outside of Clotilda's was certainly no indication of its interior. A dazzling mix of tropical plants hung from the bamboo rafters and seemed to sprout from the nooks and crannies of the candlelit room. What was most spectacular, however, was the view from beyond the bar.

Across the entire expanse of the back was a wall-to-wall window that looked out upon the bay. Twinkling lights and the ethereal silhouette of ships' sails could be seen in the distance, dotting the calm water.

Nina didn't realize she was holding her breath until Vincent gently tugged her arm, leading her to their table—right in front of the magnificent view.

"Would you like a drink before we order?"

Nina placed her purse on the table, glanced around quickly. "A glass of white wine would be nice."

Vincent grinned and Nina was certain the room was suddenly brighter. She blinked. "Did I say something wrong? They do serve white wine, don't they?"

Vincent leaned back, assessing her. It had been a long while since a woman captured his attention the way this woman did. There always seemed to be a string of them, passing in and out of his life like the sun on a cloudy day. None of them really wanted him, Vincent, the man. They wanted the riches he could offer, his name and family legacy. They wanted to know what it felt like to bed the *mystique* of Vincent St. Michael. What it felt like to have access to anything or anyone simply by knowing him. He'd grown weary of the game. Weary of pretending to care, weary of looking for something in their bodies he could never find: peace.

"You can have whatever you want," he said finally, in a tone so soft and low it sounded more like an erotic invitation to something far more heady than wine.

Nina felt herself stir, tingle, as if he'd touched some private place beneath her clothing. She tried to swallow, but her throat was suddenly dry. She reached for her glass of water and took a long sip, thankful for the simple act that calmed the sparks of electricity that popped between them.

Then, just as quickly as the inexplicable had seized him, reality settled like a hard lead ball in his gut. Yes, she was attractive, not like the slender island beauties he was accustomed to, but pleasing to the eye nonetheless. Yes, she possessed intelligence and an almost beguiling innocence that was unnerving. Yes, he'd like to touch her, assure himself that she was as soft and supple as she appeared. He'd like to put his mouth to hers, taste what he knew would be the sweetness of her lips.

All these things were true. But what was truer still was the fact that this enchanting woman in front of him was the enemy in a beautiful disguise. She was here to steal his family's land. Land they'd sweated and toiled on since being freed from slavery, generation after generation. He was the last of the male St. Michaels, the final stand. He was responsible for his family's future—in more ways than one—a responsibility he couldn't risk a moment forgetting.

Vincent cleared his thoughts and signaled the waitress.

Rita glided toward him, hips that he remembered well swaying beneath her multicolored wrap skirt. She eyed Vincent with a familiar gleam and a knowing smile on her very full mouth. Though neither of them had forgotten the insatiable passion they'd unleashed in each other, they both understood that their relationship would never move beyond the bedroom.

Rita placed her hand possessively on Vincent's shoulder. "Long time, Vincent, man," she cooed. "What can I get for you and your lady friend?" She graced Nina with a warm smile.

"The lady would like a glass of white wine to start. A rum punch for me. This is Nina Benson. Nina, Rita Pope."

"Pleasure," Rita acknowledged.

"Nice to meet you," Nina muttered, forcing a smile and wondering exactly what was the story between the two of them. From the looks that passed between them, it was plain that they knew each other *outside* of Clotilda's Place. But that was none of her business.

"Be back with your drinks." Rita swiveled away to the beat of calypso coming from the five-piece band.

Vincent quickly focused all of his attention on Nina. He linked his fingers together. "So, Ms. Benson, is this your first time in Barbados?"

"Yes, it is. I can hardly believe I've never been here before."

"Then I must show you around. It's truly a beautiful place. One of the few Caribbean islands not suffering from poverty and unemployment."

"Have you always lived here?" She sipped from her glass of water.

"Born not too far from here," he said. There was no need to elaborate that his family owned the town of St. Michael, and all the major businesses in it. "I attended school in England."

"Hmm. That explains the accent."

Vincent grinned. "Around 'ere dah'lin' it be you wit de ac'cent."

Nina flushed. "I guess you're right. What about your family?" She really wanted to ask him about a wife, children . . . significant other.

His knee inadvertently brushed hers as he adjusted himself in the chair and she nearly yelped at the contact.

"Are you all right?"

Nina cleared her throat. "Yes. Fine. Must have been a fly or something. Startled me," she concluded inanely.

Vincent studied her for a moment, and wondered if she'd felt the same thing he did, or if the charge that shot through his body and straight to his loins was only his imagination. He shook his head slightly. "I'm sorry. What were you asking me?"

Nina leaned forward and the light from the candle cast a soft glow around her face, illuminating her eyes. For an instant Vincent's breath caught in his throat and a fluttering sensation—similar to the feeling experienced when something important was about to happen—rolled through his belly. What in the world was wrong with him? He hadn't even had a drink yet.

"I, uh, was asking about your family," Nina repeated.

"My family has a home here on the island. My sister, Clarise, lives in New York with her husband and children. There are an assortment of aunts, uncles and cousins from here to England. And my grandmother, Clotilda, on my father's side runs everything from her window seat at the family est . . . home." He shrugged slightly. "What about you?"

"Hmm. I have a sister also and two adorable twin nieces," she said with a smile. "My parents relocated from New York to Florida about five years ago."

He glanced at the diamond sparkling on her finger. "I didn't hear you mention a husband."

"There isn't one to mention," she replied evenly.

He pursed his lips. "I suppose that leaves you plenty of free time to put these . . . deals together."

"My job isn't my life, Mr. St. Michael."

Rita returned and placed their drinks in front of them. "Decided on your meal?" She glanced from one to the other.

"How's the flyin' fish tonight?" Vincent asked.

"Mouthwaterin' as always," Rita tossed back with a bit more innuendo than necessary, Nina thought.

Vincent looked to Nina, brows raised in question.

"Sounds delicious." Her overenthusiastic tone made her sound like a cheerleader for the winning football team, she thought, embarrassed.

"And the sides?"

"Callaloo and sweet bread." Vincent closed the menu.

Nina displayed a tight smile and gave a nod of agreement.

"Be right up." Rita drifted away, leaving them with the soft scent of her perfume.

Vincent returned his attention to Nina and picked up their interrupted conversation.

"You were telling me how your job is not your life."

He ran his tongue across his lips and Nina instantly felt the seed of her sex throb in response. She recrossed her legs, brushing his knee, which sent another jolt shooting through her. This dinner couldn't be over fast enough, she thought, her brain completely on scramble. A trickle of perspiration slid languidly down her spine.

Nina took a deep breath and a sip of wine, having totally lost track of whatever it was he was saying. *Concentrate, girl.*

"Um, it uh, isn't my life," she said, reining in her thoughts. "I'm sure you do more than work."

"What do you do for entertainment?" Vincent asked, bypassing her last comment.

"Plays, museums, dinner parties . . ." She shrugged.

"Then I must take you out for some *real* entertainment—island style—while you're here."

"My visit isn't for pleasure, Mr. St. Michael. It's business." *Could she sound any more stuck up?*

Vincent grinned, and it immediately made Nina think of a predatory jaguar ready to pounce on its prey. *Lord, where was dinner?*

"Life is one long exercise without entertainment, Ms. Nina Benson."

Nina shifted in her seat. "Maybe . . . under other circumstances—"

"Then it will be my pleasure to change your mind."

"What makes you think you can?" she challenged, raising her chin a notch.

"Because I don't doubt anything I set my mind to do, and my goal is to show you another side of life. It will be so much more entertaining if you give in and let it happen." He raised his glass as if in a toast before bringing it to his lips.

Nina felt her entire body flush with heat. *Let it happen! Not hardly.* Although the idea was beyond tempting.

5

Nina lay restless in her canopy bed, the sheer net covering swaying gently from the breeze coming through the open terrace doors.

She closed her eyes. And saw Vincent. She opened them, and there he remained—full, virile and taunting.

Their dinner had been an assault of her senses, full of innuendo, double meanings and laced with sexual invitation. She barely remembered eating as she battled to stay a step ahead of the conversation or, at the very least, to keep pace.

Vincent St. Michael had the uncanny ability to twist her words, change the direction of the conversation, make her feel as if she was the most important person in the world, and that a sexual encounter between them was inevitable.

She turned onto her side, and in the moonlight, caught the sparkle of the diamond on her finger. Ross. He expected things from her: to cinch this deal and ultimately make a commitment to him. When she'd boarded the plane in New York she'd been certain of one, considering the other. And now, after one single candlelit dinner with Vincent St. Michael, she was no longer sure of anything.

Vincent braced his forearms on the railing of his deck, looking out onto the soothing stillness of the water, its mild crests appearing like ribbons of iridescent white drifting toward the shore.

He absently twirled a tumbler of rum on the rocks between his large hands. Nina Benson was trouble, he mused, bringing the glass to his lips. He could feel it in every fiber of his body. It was at once disturbing and thrilling.

Since the breakup with his childhood sweetheart, Serena, he'd been emotionally dead inside. He should have married her, had children with her, built a home with her. But he hadn't—afraid of losing himself in total commitment. So she'd left him, fed up with waiting, and moved to England. That was nearly ten years ago. He hadn't seen or spoken to her since. And he hadn't forgotten what could have been.

To fill the void, he dedicated himself to the family business: restaurants, boating, the business school, the art gallery and his art. His string of beautiful women ran from Barbados to Trinidad to Antigua. He'd left his mark and not a few broken hearts behind. They'd all been exciting at the time, a joy to look at and satisfying in bed. But none of them had been able to make him feel more than the first bursts of physical attraction. He wanted more. He was ready now.

"How was dinner?" The soft voice came from behind him.

Vincent glanced over his shoulder. The light from the moon and the pale glow from inside the house shot straight through the filmy dress that Jade wore, clearly defining the voluptuous curves of her firm, tempting body. He felt the stirrings of a powerful erection, took a sip of his drink and turned back to look at the water.

"I thought you were asleep," he said, his tone noncommittal.

Her arm brushed his as she moved beside him, her scent soft and sensual. "Couldn't sleep."

"Nice night. Easy for sleep," he said, easily slipping into the shorthand rhythm of the islands.

"If nothin' wanders on the mind, so."

"Happens. Comes and goes. Let the waves lull ya."

"Don't work tonight. Don't work many nights."

He cut her a look, sensing where the talk was headed. "Warm buttermilk with a spot of brandy. Nana lives by it."

Jade pursed her lips. It wasn't old family remedies she wanted, unless it was some mojo to open Vincent's eyes. She wanted him. Wanted him so bad there were times when she could scarcely breathe for the wanting. But he simply looked at her with no more desire in his eyes than if he were looking at a cold cup of coffee—and she couldn't take it anymore.

"Ain't buttermilk me needin'. Me want ya, Vincent, like a woman wants a man." She stood there proud, determined, yet with a deep sadness in her eyes. "But it won't gon' happen." She smiled weakly. "Me understands and don't hold it against ya none for not wanting me, ya know."

"Jade—"

She held up her hand. "Hush now. No need explaining it to me again. Ya made a promise and ya bound to keep to it. That's the kind of man ya be. And that's why I can't stay 'ere no more. Made plans to leave in the morning."

He turned fully toward her. "What? You can't do that. Where will you live? How will you take care of yourself?"

Jade smiled. "You forget the money Pop left for me. I'll be fine. Done found a nice place already."

"You've been planning this and you didn't talk to me about it? Where is this place? I want to see it and meet your neighbors." His protective instincts were in full force now.

Jade laughed, the sound like wind chimes stirred by a breeze. "Been wit ya for five years. You forget me not fifteen no more. A woman now, Vincent."

She stepped away from him, looked deep into his eyes as she slid the straps of her dress from her shoulders. The dress hung for a moment on the swell of her breasts before drifting down to pool at her feet.

The exquisiteness of her naked beauty rushed through him with such force that he couldn't move, couldn't think.

Before he had the presence of mind to react, Jade turned and walked back into the house, leaving her womanly scent, discarded dress and a visibly shaken Vincent behind.

6

Nina sat in the cushioned cane chair on the terrace of her hotel room sipping an early morning cup of herbal tea and watching the first of the beachgoers test the waters and lay claim to their patch of white sand.

She put her bare feet up on the opposite seat and thought about her evening with Vincent. For all her planning and preparing they hadn't discussed one thing about the proposed resorts or his thoughts about them. He had without effort kept her unbalanced and unfocused all evening—lulling her with island gossip and folklore. And her three glasses of wine topped with a potent tumbler of rum punch didn't help keep her head clear.

They'd made an appointment to meet later in the day and Nina was determined to keep it strictly business.

The phone rang. She picked up the extension on the terrace.

"Hello?"

"Nina, it's Ross."

Almost instinctively she removed her feet from the chair and sat up straighter. "Ross . . . how are you?"

"Missing you," he responded in a decidedly familiar tone. "The office is never the same without you. How was your meeting with St. Michael?" he quickly added, slipping smoothly to business mode.

She swallowed, thinking of the intense push and pull that radiated between her and Vincent at the restaurant. "Fine. Just the preliminary getting-to-know-you thing." She laughed lightly. "We plan to meet this afternoon for more formal talks."

Ross was silent for a beat too long and Nina could almost see the tight expression hardening his features.

"I see," he finally said. "I want this deal signed and sealed quickly, Nina. The contractors are ready and waiting on word from me to begin."

"I understand. And it will be. Have I ever let you down?"

"No. And I don't expect you to."

Her body tensed.

"I'll call you later tonight. You can bring me up to date. You will be in tonight, won't you?"

The question hung there, the glove of challenge thrown down between them. She knew what he was doing, what he was really asking, and she resented it.

"If not, I'll call you in the morning."

"I was thinking of coming down there in about a week or two," he said, tossing her a curve. "I could use a short vacation. And what better place to spend time with you than on a tropical island?"

"Your idea to *visit* me sounds more like you don't trust me to handle this deal."

He laughed. "Don't be ridiculous. If I didn't think you could handle it, I wouldn't have sent you. I would think you'd be happy to see a familiar face, especially when you'll be away from home for so long."

"Of course, whatever you decide to do is fine, Ross. It's your show." She rolled her eyes and held her tongue.

"So . . . I'll expect to hear from you."

"You will. Good-bye, Ross." She quietly hung up the phone, fighting the urge to hurl it onto the beach below.

Nina was ready and waiting for Vincent in the hotel lobby. She'd spent the better part of the afternoon going over her notes and planning her strategy. She wouldn't give him room to breathe, she thought, crossing her legs and scanning the guests moving in and out of the lobby.

Vincent watched her as he leaned casually against one of the marble pillars on the far side of the lobby floor.

He'd intentionally arrived early, staked out his territory and waited for her arrival. He wanted to see another side of her—the one where she was unguarded and vulnerable.

Throughout the night, images of Nina haunted him. Oddly enough, Jade's brazen display had ignited his desire for Nina. It was Nina's full-figured form that taunted him until the sun crested over the horizon, and it took all his willpower to keep from calling her, hearing her voice again. He'd waited as long as he could stand it, then it seemed as if something unseen pushed him through the doors of his home and to this place. And there was nothing he could or wanted to do to stop it. Not even seeing Jade drive off in a cab to her new home was enough to take his mind off of Nina Benson.

He couldn't recall ever feeling so captivated by a woman. Even the hot passion that flared between him and Serena had not kept him up at night, stalking the floors like a caged beast. Even the daily allure of the beautiful Jade had not mesmerized him to the point of distraction.

What was it about this Nina, this American, that had slipped beneath his skin?

What he must do was remember why she was there—to take his birthright, his family's land—and forget the inexplicable feelings of yearning creeping through his veins. He adjusted the jacket of his suit and approached.

"I hope I haven't kept you waiting too long."

Startled, Nina turned and looked behind her.

"My earlier meeting kept me longer than I'd anticipated."

A smile danced around the corners of his mouth, and the cool, clean male scent of him went straight to her head. Her heart hammered.

"No. Actually, I just arrived." She stood and picked up her purse. "I hope everything turned out well for you."

He came around the wide wicker chair. "Business meetings are what you make them."

She looked at him for a long moment. "Then let's make this one worth both of our time."

"That remains to be seen." He cupped her elbow. "My car is outside. I thought we'd take a tour."

She hadn't planned on that, nor had she dressed for it. Her plan was a simple across-the-table sit down, lay out her cards and play. But she had to remember this wasn't Wall Street or Madison or Park Avenues in New York. This was the hot, sultry tropics where everything and everybody moved at their own leisurely pace.

"Sounds wonderful," she finally said. "Where to first?"

"I was thinking of a tour of the beach."

"The beach?"

"I find it very relaxing. Helps me to unwind after a long day." He smiled. "And sometimes a short one."

This man was trouble from the word "go," Nina thought, not unkindly. But she was going to discuss business whether he wanted to or not. "I'd really like to see that land we want to purchase, so that we—"

"Nina Benson, look around you. Look at the beauty, the peacefulness. This is not the push and pull of New York. We take the time to enjoy life here on the island. You live longer. There's plenty of time to see the land, talk business, cut deals." He paused. "Come, my car is waiting."

Nina held her tongue and allowed him to lead her outside, wondering why she was letting him use his charm to distract her from the reason she was there. The truth of the matter was, it felt incredibly liberating to simply relax and enjoy. It had been more than three years since she'd had a real vacation. Although she traveled often, it was always business-related. What harm could it do to take just one more day? There was always tomorrow. Ross would just have to be patient—and trust her. The question that she was reluctant to address was: Did she trust herself?

7

The tour of the exquisite white beaches became an exploration of the antique and novelty shops, meanderings up and down the alleys and pathways boasting everything from tiny patchwork huts to sprawling homes that looked as if they were snatched from the pages of a fairy tale.

Before Nina realized it, twilight had fallen and the cloudless skies were filled with a cloak of sparkling stars that shimmered against the water.

For the first time in longer than she could remember, Nina actually felt relaxed. That ever-present sensation of her body running on overdrive had slowed to a gentle hum.

All throughout the day Vincent had been the perfect gentleman and expert guide, making sure that she caught a glimpse of the nuances of island life from the vendors who sold everything from fabric, polished stones and fully cooked meals to overflowing glasses of rum punch. Vincent filled her mind and her senses with colorful tales of his life in Barbados, the history of the island and its people, the gossip and fables that had been handed down from one generation to the next and secret whispers about lovers.

"Have you ever been in love, Nina?" Vincent asked suddenly as the car pulled up in front of her hotel.

She turned to him, thought about Ross, about her almost charmed life, recalled her unforgettable day and the possibilities of what a different kind of future could hold, and she knew the answer.

"No," she said softly, looking directly at him.

Vincent's gaze held her for a moment. "Neither have I."

The driver came around and opened the door, cutting off the electrical current that sizzled between them. He extended his hand and helped Nina from the car. Once on firm ground she turned, bent low and looked at Vincent.

"Thank you for a wonderful day, Mr. St. Michael."

"My pleasure. Perhaps you can call me Vincent now that we're better acquainted."

Nina's answer was a gentle smile before she turned and walked toward the hotel entrance.

"I'll see you in my dreams, Nina Benson," Vincent whispered as he watched every dip and sway of her departure.

Nina felt like she was floating as she entered her hotel room with what felt like a permanent smile on her face. She absently tossed her purse on the couch, stepped out of her shoes in the middle of the floor and glided toward her bedroom.

No sooner had she flung herself spread-eagle across the bed than the phone rang. Annoyed at the interruption of her momentary flight of fantasy, Nina started not to answer. But what was the point in that? she concluded. Whoever it was would invariably leave a message and she'd have to return the call anyway.

Rolling onto her stomach she reached for the phone.

"Hello?"

"Hey, girl. It's Denise."

"Dee!" Nina curled into a fetal position, ready for a gab-fest. "Girl, it's good to hear your voice."

"I was trying to give you a minute to get settled before I got all in your business."

They laughed.

"So . . . tell, tell. What's he like?"

Nina momentarily closed her eyes and a smile stretched across her face. "Whatever I thought Vincent St. Michael was, he isn't." She started from the moment they'd met, leaving nothing out and concluding with the day they'd just spent together.

"Wow," was all Denise could find to say.

"Exactly," Nina replied, twisting Ross' ring around on her finger.

"He must be something if he has you fumbling the ball. I've never known you to lose sight of the goal, Nina."

"Yeah, I know." She sighed heavily. "But it just feels good, at least for the moment, to simply unwind, have a man dote on me. Ya know?"

"Doesn't Ross do that?"

"Not in the same way. Ross is calculating. Everything he does is with the intention of getting what he wants. And that's not to say that his basic feelings aren't sincere, they're just suspect. Especially after our conversation at dinner before I left."

"Hmm. I see you have been doing some thinking. But what makes you think this Vincent guy doesn't have some ulterior motive as well?"

"Instinct. Woman's intuition. I don't know. He has nothing to gain by keeping this deal from happening, more if it goes through."

"I suppose . . ."

"I hear something in your voice, Dee. What is it?"

"Just be careful and don't let his island charm keep you from doing your job."

Nina pursed her lips, a sudden wave of annoyance rushing through her. "I know what I'm doing, Denise. I'm not some addle-brained kid on summer vacation," she snapped.

"Hey, take it easy. I'm just saying island men are notorious for having a laundry list full of ladies-in-waiting. I just don't want you to become one of them, that's all."

Nina rolled her eyes, but she couldn't entirely dismiss Denise's concerns. She'd seen the fire between Vincent and Rita at the restaurant, the reaction of the women they'd come in contact with throughout the evening. She'd wondered about his relationship with the ones who had responded to his smile with a light touch or a kiss on the cheek in more than a platonic fashion.

"I'll be careful," she said finally. "I'm here to do a job, and I'll get it done."

After dropping Nina off Vincent decided to spend the night at the family estate instead of going home. When he arrived he was surprised to find his Nana still awake and sitting in her favorite chair by the window. Other than the papery sound as she turned the pages of her Bible, the house was quiet.

The house held wonderful memories of his youth: running up and down the winding hills, swimming in the pond, chasing the chickens and geese and causing havoc with the servants when he and his numerous cousins would do everything from hiding the laundry to letting the farm animals in the back door. He couldn't count the number of times his Nana Clotie would demand that he and his running buddy Sam get a switch for a good behind-whipping for some misdeed or the other.

His Nana was a strict disciplinarian, but she handed it out as equally as she did her love. He couldn't remember a day of going without a hug or a kind word of encouragement. He was raised to believe that he could accomplish anything. And that being a Black man was no excuse for not achieving. Now with the sole responsibility of the family fortune resting on his shoulders, he knew he could not fail her. To do so would be to fail himself as well, and all he was taught to believe.

"What are you doing up so late, Nana?" Vincent asked as he entered the sitting room.

Clotilda turned her regal head of snowy white, her birch brown skin barely chronicling her near one hundred years. She smiled and her deep brown eyes seemed to sparkle with delight at seeing her favorite grandchild. She held out a delicate hand to him. "Vincent," she sang in the high-low accent of the island. "Come, son, sit beside your old Nana. You know I'm not long for this world," she said, adding her customary epitaph.

"Nana, you will outlive us all," Vincent said with a grin, taking a seat at her feet.

"What's troublin' ya, Vincent?" She stroked his cheek, the same way she'd been doing since he was a boy.

"Why must something be troubling me?"

She clucked her tongue. "Not'in' brings ya back home at this hour but trouble."

He lowered his gaze, still amazed that she could read him so well. He released a breath and the confusion that had kept him up at night . . .

"Always a woman," Clotie muttered when he'd finished, and patted his hand sympathetically. "What is it that troubles you so about her?"

He hesitated a beat. "She's the one who's come to buy the land, Nana."

Clotilda's sharp Indian features hardened beneath the tautness of her skin. Her eyes narrowed. "So they sent a woman," she said, looking out onto the rolling hills that resembled massive waves at high tide. She turned to her grandson, her gaze stern. "I told you in the beginning not to entertain the American company's notion of coming here. They'll swallow us up as they have all the family homes on the island with their big hotels and thiefin'." She wagged a finger at him. "I warned ya. But you want to be a numskull and do things your way. And here they be, right on our doorstep pushin' their way in. This is our home, Vincent. It belongs to this family.

You were entrusted with it to keep it safe for the next generation and their families." Her voice grew more and more strident as she continued. "It will be over my dead body that I will sit back and let dem take what's rightfully ours. Don't care none for how much money it gon' bring. Never enough to buy our heritage."

Clotilda took a deep breath, gripping the wooden arms of her rocking chair. She raised her hand and pressed her palm against her forehead. "Leave me be now. You need to go think and so do I. Your room is ready as always. Get some rest, we'll talk again." She waved her hand in a dismissive motion, and Vincent knew that his audience with her was finished.

He kissed her cheek. "I won't disappoint you, Nana. I promise you that."

She looked up at her beloved grandson, saw the determination mixed with turmoil in his eyes, and knew his choices would be much more difficult than he anticipated. Who was this Nina Benson? And what hoodoo had she put on her grandson?

As Vincent lay in bed that night, surrounded by all things familiar, he knew that nothing in his life would be the same again—no matter what decision he made.

8

Nina awoke the following morning with a new sense of purpose. Denise's comment of the previous evening didn't sit well with her at all. She knew why she was there and what she was there to do. Did both Denise and Ross suddenly think so little of her abilities that they questioned her actions? She'd show them she was just as sharp, just as committed as she'd always been.

By nine A.M. she was showered, dressed and ready for her day. She pulled out her folder of notes from her briefcase and reviewed the step-sheet for the offer the corporation was willing to give. It was a sweet deal. Vincent stood to make a handsome amount of money when it all came together, including a percentage of the profits in the first three years. How could he resist something like that? She took a sip of her herbal tea. The key was getting him to sit down and listen to the proposal.

She scanned through her notes for Vincent's number, picked up the phone and dialed. It was answered on the second ring.

"Enterprises. Good morning."

"Yes, good morning. This is Nina Benson, I'm trying to reach Mr. St. Michael."

"I'm sorry, Mr. St. Michael is not here."

Nina frowned. "Is he expected later?"

"No, Miss, I'm sorry, he's not."

"Is there any way to reach him?"

"Mr. Vincent doesn't want to be disturbed today, Miss. He's in the country."

"Do you think he'll call in for messages, then?"

"Perhaps. No tellin' with Mr. Vincent."

"I see. Well, if he should call for messages, would you please tell him that Nina Benson called and she would like to speak with him. It's very important."

"I'll be sure to tell him, Miss. If he should call."

"Thank you." Frustrated, she hung up the phone and contemplated her alternatives. There weren't any. That was the only contact number she had for him. She'd have to bide her time until he returned her call. But that didn't mean she would spend the day stuck in her hotel room waiting for the phone to ring. She decided to see some of the sights on her own, maybe even pick up a few souvenirs for Denise.

Quickly she changed out of business attire and into a capri pant set in a cool mint green, slipped on a pair of white Esprit sneakers, grabbed her straw bag and sunglasses and was ready to go. There was a wonderful art gallery in town that she and Vincent had briefly glanced at that she wanted to return to. She made that her first line of stop.

———

Even early in the day, the gallery seemed to have a steady stream of potential customers. Nina assumed the majority were tourists like herself, but was surprised to discover that the only accent in the shop was hers.

She wandered up and down the aisles admiring the hand-painted pottery, gold bangles, jewelry, exquisite fabric, sculptures and lavish paintings of tropical scenes. A very eclectic art gallery, Nina thought.

"May I help you with something, Miss?"

Nina turned toward the inquiring voice. "I was really interested in purchasing some paintings."

The young woman smiled. "Wonderful. I'm sure we have something that would interest you. Please, follow me."

Nina did as she was instructed, winding her way around display tables and chatty customers, remembering how she was once as sinewy and lithe as the woman in front of her, until she found herself inside a separate room that could easily rival the Whitney Museum in New York with its style and breathtaking artwork.

"Oh my . . ." she gushed, turning in a circle in an attempt to take everything in at once.

The young woman laughed lightly. "That is the reaction of most visitors. Feel free to look around . . . and if you would sign our guest book?" She handed Nina a leather-bound book.

Nina signed her name and continued her appraisal of the work. "Are any of these for sale?"

The woman glanced at the guest book and her entire expression changed. "Some. It would have to be arranged directly with the artist. If there's anything you need or are interested in purchasing, let me know."

Nina spun toward the woman, with a broad smile on her face. "I certainly will. Whom should I ask for?"

"Jade." Her eyes locked with Nina's.

"Thank you, Jade. I think I'll look around some more. Do you know any of the artists?"

"Yes. These are all done by the same artist."

Nina's eyes widened in amazement. "You're kidding." She stepped closer to one painting that particularly caught her attention: a portrait of an old woman framed in a window looking out onto the landscape. She bent, peered closer at the name scrawled at the bottom. "I can't quite make the name out."

"Vincent St. Michael is the artist, Ms. Benson."

Nina bolted upright, turning toward Jade. "Did you say Vincent St. Michael?"

Jade nodded once, appraising her in one sweeping look. She folded her arms.

"I've been trying to reach him today. Do you know him well?"

Jade hesitated for only a moment. "I lived with him for five years." The stunned look on Nina's face brought immense satisfaction to Jade. This was the woman he'd had dinner with, she surmised, and she was sure she was the one who'd put that distracted look in his eyes. For five years she'd tried to get Vincent to see her, really see her. He knew how she felt about him. And now here was this Yankee-come-lately with her American ways and money. She was the one sent to buy up the St. Michael land. She'd heard the rumors buzzing in the market. Well, she wouldn't make it easy for her.

"Oh," Nina finally mumbled, her mind wrestling with that last bit of information. *Lived with him?* She was no more than a child, a budding woman—obviously stunning—but young nonetheless. What kind of man was Vincent to be involved with this child? Maybe Denise was right after all. She hadn't wanted to fall prey to the tales of island men and their proclivity for an abundance of women—young, old and in-between. But this woman-child in front of her was testament to every negative thing she'd ever heard.

"Then I suppose you do know him," Nina said, softly sarcastic.

Jade smiled. *Let her think what she wants.* "You could say that." She released a breath. "I must get back to the customers up front. If you need anything—"

"Yes, I know, call you."

Jade spun away, leaving Nina surrounded by Vincent St. Michael and her disturbing thoughts.

————

Vincent prowled around the grounds of his family's estate replaying his conversation with his grandmother the night before. Nana was right. This was family land, not for sale, and it was irresponsible of him to play games with investors when he had no intention of selling. But the devil had gotten ahold of him. He wanted to string the big shots along, let them think he was some island layabout. Had Ross Burns shown up for dinner instead of Nina, his job would have been simple. "No." But when he set eyes upon Nina his perspective and all of his righteous intentions went out the window.

Slowly he sat down on the rolling crest behind the house; beyond him his young cousins played a wild game of tag. He owed it to his family to do the right thing by them. He'd simply have to tell Nina that there was no deal, and no possibility of one. It would certainly end any chance of a relationship between them . . . but what choice did he have?

"Hey, cuz."

Vincent looked up, shielding his eyes from the glare of the sun. "Sam." Samuel Covington was his favorite cousin. So close in age, they'd grown up like brothers. He was Margaret's son, Vincent's father's sister. Margaret abandoned Sam when he was only two years old to run off with some musician. Nana took him in and raised him like her own, sparing neither her love nor the switch when necessary. It was understood by everyone in the family that Margaret's name was never to be mentioned in Nana's house or in her presence. As far as Nana was concerned Margaret was dead. Which made losing Vincent's father and his wife in the freak boating accident even more devastating. Yet the tragic loss seemed to bind Vincent and Sam even more closely. At times it was as if they shared the same mind, the same heart.

"Must be a woman," Sam said, taking a seat next to his cousin. He drew his knees close and wrapped his arms around them. "Can't imagine anything else getting you out of the house at this hour to sit alone."

"Yes, it's a woman and it's even more complicated than that."

"I'm listening."

Vincent slowly explained the talks he'd been having with the Burns Corporation, and ultimately meeting Nina Benson.

"I can't explain how she makes me feel, Sam. The only word I can use to describe it is alive. I feel alive again, for the first time in longer than I can remember—since Serena."

Sam was thoughtful for a moment. "Unfortunately, you will have to tell her you're not selling."

"And she'll go back to the States and I'll never see her again."

"Perhaps. Maybe you should talk to her. Really talk to her—and not charm her," he added knowing his cousin's reputation. "Be honest."

Vincent flickered a brow. "I wanted to get to know her and her me before I said anything." He released a long breath, then turned steady eyes on Sam. "The truth of it is, Sam, that it would be an incredible investment if we allowed them to build here. The entire family would be financially secure for generations."

"Nana would never let you do it. Selling this land would kill her."

"I know," Vincent conceded. "I know."

9

Nina left the gallery more enamored of Vincent than before. Not only was he a respected businessman, he was an extremely talented artist. It would explain so much about him— his love for beautiful things, his fascination with the world around him, even his easy, unhurried manner.

Vincent St. Michael was so much more than he seemed, Nina thought as she strolled through the marketplace, checking out the beautiful fruits and vegetables that looked as if they'd just been plucked, almost too exquisite to eat. You could never get this type of quality in New York, Nina mused as she finally decided on some kiwi, green grapes and two mangos.

As she continued her stroll her thoughts drifted back to

that girl/woman Jade and her relationship with Vincent. It shouldn't bother her, she rationalized. After all, she had no interest in him other than business. What he did in his spare time was no concern of hers. Or at least it shouldn't be. But the truth was, she was attracted to the man. Very much so, and to think that he was involved with this child unsettled her.

Briefly, she snatched a glance at the brilliant diamond on her right hand. Maybe she should consider Ross' offer, or at least give it some serious consideration. She wasn't getting any younger and it wasn't as if men were beating down her door. But did she love him, could she love him? Those were the questions that plagued her. What was disturbing most of all was that there was a spot inside of her that felt that she *could* love Vincent St. Michael.

After his talk with Sam, Vincent said his good-byes to the family and headed home. He needed some time alone, yet wandering around in his spacious beach house he had to admit that he missed knowing that Jade would turn up at some point. He'd grown accustomed to her smile, her attempts to get his attention, the incident the night before she moved out the most blatant of all.

He smiled as he poured himself a drink. He had to give her credit, though; she was bold and had no doubts about her appeal. Had he been a different type of man he would have taken her up on her offer.

Who he really wanted was Nina. It was as clear to him as the waters that gently rolled to the shore. He couldn't explain it. He barely knew her. Yet he couldn't get her off his mind for more than a minute. Why couldn't circumstances be different? Still, how much would that change? She lived in New York, and he lived in Barbados, hundreds of miles apart in distance and culture. He knew he couldn't leave. He had responsibilities and so did she.

He stared out the wide glass window to the beach below, imagining Nina frolicking in the sand, her curls blowing in the island breeze, her lush body barely covered in a swimsuit, her brilliant smile and dancing eyes, daring him to join her.

Nina.

Vincent sighed deeply. He had to tell her the truth. There was no point in leading her on. And it was probably best that he get it over with as soon as possible so that she could return to the States and he could put thoughts of her behind him and get his life back.

He went to the phone and dialed her hotel room. The sooner the better, he decided as he listened to the phone ring on the other end.

Just as Nina shut the door behind her, she heard the phone ring. It was probably Ross, she surmised, wanting an update on her progress. She had nothing to tell him, and wasn't up for one of his "talks."

She put her packages on the counter in the efficiency kitchen and listened to the phone ring for the third time. Another ring or two and the service would pick it up. At least that would buy her some time until she actually spoke with Vincent.

Vincent! Maybe it was him.

She darted to the phone and snatched it up, only to hear the dial tone. She shrugged and returned the receiver to the base, only for it to ring again before she got it out of her hand.

"Hello?"

"Nina? This is Vincent . . . St. Michael."

She suddenly felt a warm flush—the mere sound of his voice did that to her. She took a breath. "Well, hello. Did you just call?"

"Actually, I did. Thought I had the wrong number and hung up."

"So you got my message?"

Vincent frowned. "No. What message?"

Nina plopped down on the side of the bed. "I left two. One at your offices and one with . . . Jade."

"Jade?" His thoughts ran in a million directions at once.

"Yes, the young girl you live with." She paused a bit,

suddenly wanting her words to sting him the way she'd been stung when she met Jade. "I visited the gallery today."

His heart slowed to normal. "Oh."

Was that relief she heard in his voice? What was he thinking?

"Yes, she works for me," he finally said, collecting his thoughts.

In how many ways? she wanted to ask him, but held her tongue. "You didn't tell me you owned the gallery when we passed it the other day."

"Didn't think it was important. Is it?"

"I don't suppose it is."

Silence.

"You also didn't mention that you were an accomplished artist."

He chuckled lightly. "Ms. Benson, I can guarantee there are countless things you don't know about me." His tone suddenly softened, sounding almost wistful. "And it would take a lifetime to reveal it all."

Her heart knocked.

"Have you ever tried . . . I mean, tried to explain it all to . . . anyone?" Why had she asked that?

"I thought I did, a very long time ago." He settled against the cushions of the couch, stretched out his long legs. "What about you? Have you ever revealed yourself to anyone? Really?"

She could be coy, say something clever, but for some reason she felt he really wanted to know—and she wanted to tell him.

"No. I haven't. There's never been anyone . . . whom I felt that kind of connection with," she said in all honesty.

"Have you wanted to?" he probed.

Nina swallowed, thought about her abbreviated adult relationships, the superficiality of them all. She thought about Ross and their relationship of sorts. "No," she finally answered. "I haven't."

Vincent released a breath. "My Nana always told me that there is one special someone for each of us. Someone who is your soul mate, the one you will share your life with, share yourself with. And when you find that someone your life will finally be complete."

"Sounds like a wise woman."

"That she is. Maybe you will have a chance to meet her . . . before you leave."

"I think I'd like that," she admitted. "Speaking of leaving, we really need to get together and talk. My boss is beginning to think he's made a mistake in sending me down here, and I assured him that I could handle it."

The topic he'd been dreading. He swallowed. "Actually, that was the reason for my call. I was hoping I could pick you up later and we could . . . go over some things."

"Absolutely. Where and what time?"

"I can meet you in the lobby of your hotel about seven."

Nina looked at the bedside clock. It was only two. "Do you always conduct business after hours?" she teased.

"Whenever I can. See you at seven." He hung up.

Slowly, Nina hung up the phone, a smile playing around her full mouth. If he thought he was going to wine and dine her again and keep them both off the subject at hand, he had another think coming. She wasn't going to jeopardize her career for this smooth-talking island man with a penchant for young girls. This was business, she affirmed.

She got up from the bed and hunted through her closet, first deciding on a suit of navy blue. But then she thought of Jade, and Rita the waitress and the countless island beauties that invariably crossed Vincent's path in one way or the other, and decided that tonight Vincent St. Michael would only have eyes for her.

10

At five minutes to seven there was a knock on Nina's door. She'd just finished putting on her lipstick and checking her purse. Turning from the bathroom mirror, she crossed the hardwood floor of her bedroom to the front of her suite. The knock came again.

"Coming."

She pulled open the door expecting a hotel employee to be on the other side.

"Vincent . . ."

A slow smile moved across his mouth. Momentarily he lowered his gaze, as if embarrassed at being caught at something naughty, then looked into her eyes.

"I hope you don't mind that I came up." He laughed nervously. "I found myself here an hour early and they were beginning to look at me suspiciously downstairs."

His dark eyes sparkled from the overhead lights of the corridor, Nina noticed. She stepped back and held the door open.

"Well, we can't have you branded as a suspicious character, now, can we? Come in, I'll only be a minute."

Vincent stepped inside, casually looked around as he headed for the couch.

Nina watched him from behind, the ease of his walk, the way his slacks hugged his rear just right. Her stomach did a slow dip as she stepped inside and shut the door behind her.

"Can I fix you a drink or something?"

He turned toward her and suddenly everything inside him went soft and warm. His pulse beat a bit faster. Right then, at that moment, Nina Benson was the most beautiful woman he'd ever seen. Not the kind of fake beauty that graces the covers of magazines: stick-figure women showcasing perfect cheekbones, brows arched to perfection, pouty lips and attached hair. This was real beauty, natural, from the inside out.

The soft pastels of sea moss green and baby girl pink of her simple dress gave her an innocence that couldn't be created with makeup and lights. It was the essence of who she was as a woman. A woman he wanted to have the chance to know, really know before the truth came out and he lost her forever.

He cleared his throat. "Nothing for me, thanks," he said, finally answering her question.

"Well, have a seat at least. I'll be right out."

Nina hurried to her bedroom and closed the door, leaning

against it for support. "And the Academy Award for best actress goes to . . ." Her legs felt as if they would give out at any moment. She pulled in long, deep breaths to steady herself. It had taken all of her willpower and savvy to maintain her cool when she opened the door and saw Vincent standing there. Her heart felt as if it had shot straight to her throat.

There was no explanation for the impact the man had on her. He made her forget her agenda, think only of good times and spending it with him, what his lips would feel like pressed against hers.

"This is crazy," she mumbled, feeling as if her body had been heated from the inside. "Got to get it together." What was it about Vincent St. Michael that made her feel as if she didn't have a brain in her head and was functioning on pure sexual adrenaline?

Unnerved by her escalating reaction to him, she crossed the room and stood in front of the dresser mirror. She expected to find his name emblazoned on her forehead, at the very least. What she did find however, was a glow, a radiance that seemed to dance off her like the sun bouncing off the ocean waves.

She shook her head. If he could have this kind of effect on her by simply stepping into a room, what would happen if he actually held her, touched her, made love to her?

"This is crazy." What she needed to do was wrap this deal up as quickly as possible so that she could return home, return to her life. She picked up her purse, took a breath of resolve and returned to join Vincent in the front room. She would keep her head, and her focus—as long as he didn't look at her, accidentally brush up against her or move those luscious lips in her direction.

"Ready?" she quizzed, stepping back into the room.

Vincent turned and flashed that smile, and all of her resolve melted like ice cream set out in the sun.

"I brought the paperwork I want to go over with you," Nina said once they were in Vincent's car.

He tapped the glass partition and the driver slowly pulled

out into the early evening traffic, then he turned to her. "We have all evening to talk business."

"That's what you said the last time, if I recall correctly. And not one word of business was discussed."

Vincent laughed lightly. "I wouldn't say that exactly. Business can take on many forms. We discussed personal business, the things we liked and didn't, what we wanted from life. I thought all those things were important."

"Why?"

"I don't know about you, but I like to know . . . who I'm getting involved with."

Nina forced herself to concentrate on her hands folded in her lap and not on his mouth. "Where are we going?" she asked, changing the direction of the conversation.

"It's a surprise. Just sit back and relax. Let go of some of that New York energy, the feeling that everything must happen immediately." The corner of his mouth turned up in a grin. "The pleasure comes in taking it slow."

Her face was on fire and her body went on full alert. He'd done no more than speak, but he could have just as well stripped her bare. This was going to be a long night.

She gazed out of the window watching the landscape turn from city to countryside, the hills and valleys spreading out before them. She was so transfixed by the beauty set against the descending sun, she didn't notice that they'd eased onto a winding road that led to a sprawling home nestled in the hills.

"We're here," Vincent announced.

"Where is here?" Nina peered out the window.

"My family home."

The driver opened the door. Vincent stepped out and extended his hand to Nina.

She gazed up at him in wide-eyed alarm. "Your family home! Why didn't you say anything? I thought this was a business dinner, not a family gathering." She knew she sounded strident. It wasn't so much that she was angry; rather, she was suddenly afraid. If this was his family home, then family lived here. What would they think of her? Was she dressed appropriately? Why did it even matter what they thought of her? she silently chastised herself as she reluctantly took Vincent's hand and alighted from the car. She wasn't here to be liked. She was here to take care of business. Then why were her knees knocking? Damn Vincent St. Michael!

They walked in silence along the shell-strewn path that led to the family enclave. Nina had to admit that it was magnificent. The house reminded her of the picture postcards that travelers send from the tropics that make you immediately wish you were there.

The house sat on a hill overlooking rolling land that settled down at the water below. Whereas most of Barbados wasn't what you would consider lush compared to some of the other islands, the St. Michael estate was a tumble of trees and flora, small ponds and cottages set back from the rambling main house.

From her position on the path she guessed that there were at least fifteen rooms, if the three stories and multitude of windows and balconies were any indication. The entire ground floor was awash in light and as they drew closer she could hear the sound of calypso music and voices raised in song and laughter.

"Is there some sort of party going on?" Nina asked.

Vincent chuckled. "You would think so. But it's just the usual Friday night gathering. My Nana insists on it." He stopped at the front door and turned to her. "I know I should have told you, but I knew you would say no."

"You should have at least given me the chance to make my own decision."

"I'll try to remember that for next time." He smiled teasingly.

"What makes you think there will be a next time?" she countered, annoyed at his game-playing and stalling tactics.

"Oh, I think there will be," he said with the greatest of confidence. He stared into her eyes for a moment, then said, "I'd be very disappointed if there wasn't."

Her heart started racing again. "Mr. . . . Vincent, I'm here on business, remember. And we haven't—"

Vincent covered her mouth with a kiss. A kiss so soft, so passionate that Nina thought she would faint from the sweetness of it. His fingers threaded through her hair and pulled her closer, deeper. She couldn't breathe, and just as suddenly as it had begun, it was over.

He brushed her bottom lip with his thumb, as her lids fluttered open. "I think my Nana will like you almost as much as I do," he said in a thick voice before taking her hand and leading her inside.

What had she gotten herself into? she wondered as she practically stumbled across the threshold, her head still spinning. A simple kiss from Vincent was more than she could have ever imagined—and the reality was, she wanted more of the same.

11

The inside of the St. Michael home was even more impressive than the outside. Hardwood floors ran throughout, with high arching ceilings, brilliant white walls and windows that seemed to go on for miles. The furnishings were simple but Nina could tell they were expensive antiques that looked to be all hand-carved, from the heavy tables, wall cabinets and side chairs, to the gleaming wood banisters that wound their way up the stairs. There were no doors to speak of, but rather archways that led from one room to the next, giving the impression of endless space and openness.

The alluring aroma of food wafted through the air and Nina's stomach involuntarily clenched in anticipation.

"My great-grandfather, Duncan St. Michael, bought this property and the surrounding land almost one hundred years ago. He and his two brothers built everything you see."

"Everything?" Nina said in awe, looking around.

"Yes. They wanted it to be a family place, where all of us could come and settle, or visit for generations to come. My grandmother is the last of the original clan and the gate-keeper." He chuckled. "She's very serious about her responsibility to the family . . . and has passed that responsibility on to me."

Nina snatched a glance at him. His expression had lost its playfulness.

"The responsibility of this family, this property and all the decisions about both . . . are mine."

"What are you saying?"

"I think you know. Now . . . let's meet the rest of the family."

They walked through the expanse of the house out to the back lawn where tents and tables filled with food were spread out as far as the eyes could see. Children ran, squealing and playing across the sloping hills, while the adults sat back drinking glasses of Mauby and rum punch. In the center of all the activity was an elderly woman who could only be described as regal.

Her hair was spun silver twisted into a braid that hung to the center of her straight back. Her skin was the color of midnight and smooth as a newborn baby's. High, sharp cheekbones defined her face and hinted at her Indian ancestry. Gold bangles ran up the length of her thin right arm, and her petite body was adorned in a pale blue flowing shift that made her look even smaller than she actually was.

"Let me introduce you to Nana." Vincent took her hand and led her to where Clotie sat, surrounded by her nieces, nephews and grandchildren.

Vincent approached, knelt down in front of the old woman and tenderly placed a kiss on her cheek. She stroked his as if he was still a little boy and Nina immediately saw the unabashed love that flowed between them. It revealed a different side of Vincent, a caring side that she'd only glimpsed on the porch.

Slowly Vincent rose from his crouched position and turned to Nina. "Nana, this is Nina Benson. Nina, my grandmother, Clotie St. Michael."

Nina extended her hand.

Clotie looked up and appraised her for several moments, and with what appeared to be reluctance to Nina, finally took her hand. "You the woman from the States who here to take me land right out from under me children," she said as calmly as if she were asking Nina if she was hungry.

Nina was totally taken aback and for a moment was at a loss for words. She flashed Vincent a scathing look, which he ignored.

Clotie still held her hand, waiting for an answer.

"I . . . my company—"

"Don't tell me about your company, child. Tell me about you. Why are *you* here?" Clotie stared at Nina with dark, all-seeing eyes.

Nina straightened her shoulders. She would either stand her ground now, or lose everything she'd worked for.

"I came here because I believe what I can offer this family for the sale of this property would benefit everyone."

"Who is this everyone? Not my family. You mean you and your company." Clotie paused for a moment. "Look around you. What you propose to do will destroy hundreds of years of hard work, love and sacrifice—a family. What do you have back home that you can call your own, child, that has meaning? What piece of history is really yours?"

Nina thought for a moment, thought about her condo, her six-figure job, her closet full of designer clothes and her car. She swallowed. All of it could be taken away. All of it. And what would she have?

The old woman smiled. "That's what I thought." She released Nina's hand. "Vincent, why don't you take your friend and get her something to eat?" She turned away, dismissing Nina without another word or a backward glance.

Nina spun away on her heel and stalked across the grass toward the entrance to the house. Vincent was right behind her.

"Nina!"

She kept going, tearing through the house to the front door and out. She ran toward the car.

"Nina!"

She tugged on the car door.

Vincent was right behind her. She tugged on the door handle again, tears of humiliation bubbling to the surface.

"Get the hell away from me. You set me up, you bastard. You set me up."

"Nina, please, just listen."

She whirled toward him. "Now you want to talk!" she shouted. "Why didn't you tell me what I was getting myself into? Why didn't you tell me that what we were trying to buy was practically holy land?" Her eyes squeezed to two slits. "You never had any intention of selling this property, did you? Did you?"

Vincent pursed his lips and lowered his gaze.

"Answer me, damn it."

He looked up, right at her. "No. I didn't," he said quietly.

"So . . . why? Why go through all this . . . why bring me here, humiliate me? Why?" Her eyes filled, but she refused to cry, she was tougher than that.

Vincent reached for her and she jerked away. "I know I should have told you when you first arrived. It was my intention. I thought Ross would be the one I was dealing with. I wanted to crush his arrogance, his belief that anything he wanted could be his for a price, even someone's heritage. Then you showed up."

Her breath caught for a moment in her chest. "And . . . ?"

"And I knew that once I told you I wouldn't sell my family property, you would leave and I wouldn't get the chance to know you," he uttered on one long breath.

Nina was all prepared for a quick retort, but his confession caught her off guard. "Me?" she finally sputtered. "You have that, that child at the gallery . . . and no doubt something with Rita at the restaurant, and who knows how many—"

He silenced her with a kiss that made her forget her name, and whatever else she was about to babble. He held her close, meshing his body with hers until it seemed as if they were one being. She felt every line of him, the muscles that strained beneath the fabric of his clothes and the undeniable erection that throbbed between his thighs.

Heat infused her from her center and shot straight to her head as his fingers danced up and down her spine. Helplessly she wrapped her arms around his waist, needing to get closer.

The tip of his tongue toyed with hers and white flashes of light burst behind her lids. An uncontrollable sigh slipped from her parted lips as Vincent eased away. His breath was sweet and warm across her face.

"The truth is I believe your offer would be a good thing for my family," he whispered, as he caressed her cheek. "But this land means so much to my grandmother. It would kill her to sell it. And, just so you know, there is no woman in my life."

"So what do we do now, Vincent?" she asked, a bit breathless.

"Can you stay . . . for a while? Give us a chance."

"A chance at what?" She needed to know.

"Maybe a chance at being happy."

"What makes you think I'm not already happy?"

"Because I know I can show you what true happiness is," he said with all the confidence of a man who knew what he was about.

Nina rested her weight against the car. "I have no reason to stay if the deal is off. I can't explain my absence to my boss."

"You could if you wanted to. It's up to you." He paused, then touched his lips to hers once again. "Haven't you ever done anything spontaneously, Nina, without a plan, and facts and figures, but just went with your heart, your feelings?"

Without even thinking about it, she knew the answer to his question. *No.* Everything she'd ever done had been based on a plan, a means to an end. She didn't have time for spontaneity.

"Vincent, I—"

"Don't think about it now. Come back with me to the house. Meet my family, enjoy the evening." He saw her hesitation. "Please."

She tipped her head to the side and gazed at him askance. "Did you really mean what you said about . . . no one in your life?"

"Not at the moment." He grinned, devilishly. "But I'm working on it."

He took her hand and led her back to the house.

This was crazy, so unlike her. How was she going to explain this to Ross? she wondered even as her heart raced with anticipation.

12

Nina had to admit that once she settled down, she actually enjoyed herself. Vincent's family was wonderful, from his myriad of cousins to his nieces and nephews. She could see by the deference and love they showed him that he was held in high regard. They looked for his approval on everything from what subjects to take up in school to dating, and everything in between. And with each request he showed patience and love, taking his time to give them thoughtful answers and encouragement.

Food and drink flowed through the night, and Nina experienced the sense of camaraderie—family. Her favorite relative of them all was Sam, who took time out from the weekly festivities to sit with her.

"We have a wild bunch, huh?" he asked, sipping a glass of rum punch.

Nina giggled. "That you do. But everyone is wonderful."

"I'm sure your family has its rituals back home," he commented.

She thought about the harried holiday gatherings, the bickering and guaranteed fight between her uncles Jason and Paul, and the arguments between her little cousins. Those events, thank heavens, she only had to endure twice a year: Thanksgiving and Christmas. And it was usually held in someone's cramped apartment, yet another ingredient for mayhem.

"Nothing like this," she finally admitted, truly appreciating the tight knit of the St. Michael clan. She only wished she could have the same with her own family. If anything, she tried to keep her distance and focus on her career.

"That's too bad. Family is so important. It's the tie that binds, that keeps you rooted and gives you a sense of purpose. We've lived on this land for a century. All of us were born right in that house. Most of us grew up in it." He chuckled lightly. "And Nana never lets us forget it, believe me."

"She's a very strong woman."

"That she is. She holds it all together. And now with her getting on in age, she's passed the torch on to Vincent."

Nina didn't respond.

Sam turned to her. "What do you think of Vincent?"

Her head snapped in his direction. "What do you mean?"

"How do you feel about him?"

"I . . . I think he's a very interesting . . . an appealing man," she murmured, her lips still hot from his kiss.

"He cares about you."

"How do you know that?"

Sam smiled. "Vincent and I are like brothers. There are no secrets between us." He took a breath. "This is very hard for Vincent. More than he will ever let on. He worships our grandmother and is bound by family love and loyalty to abide by her wishes. But he cares about you, deeply. And he's torn. It's been a long time for Vincent. A long time since he's allowed anyone to touch him."

Her eyes searched through the darkness and spotted Vincent playing a game of tag with the children. Her heart knocked in her chest.

"I'm pretty much in the same predicament," she admitted. "My boss, like your grandmother, has expectations." She glanced briefly at the diamond on her finger. "And as much as I'd like to stay and see what could happen between us, I have to go back. My life is in the States."

Sam slowly nodded his head. "That's too bad, Nina. I think you're missing out on something quite wonderful." He stood and patted her shoulder. "Enjoy the rest of your evening and your stay on the island."

Nina watched Sam walk away, even as she thought about his revelations. She couldn't just give up everything on a whim, on a maybe. She wasn't that kind of person. What if she did stay and it didn't work out, then what? She would have lost everything, and Vincent would be no worse off than he was right now.

No. She couldn't do it. She wasn't going to risk everything she'd worked so many years to attain. She'd just have to take Ross's disappointment and move on. There would be other deals. Then why did she feel so lousy?

When she focused on her surroundings, Vincent was coming her way, with a plate of sweet yellow plantains, peas and rice, stewed chicken and a slice of black cake. "Thought you might want something to take back to the hotel, for a late-night snack." He knelt down in front of her. "Have you enjoyed yourself?"

"Very much. I'm glad I stayed."

He placed his hand on her thigh. "So am I, Nina." With her sitting there, so beautiful to him, under the moonlight, he wanted to kiss her. Kiss her right there for everyone to see. His escalating feelings for Nina had him totally off balance. He didn't let women get under his skin like that. And what was most disturbing of all was that he barely knew Nina. But he desperately wanted to. At that very moment, he made a silent pledge to himself. He would have her, no matter what or how long it took.

They stood in front of her hotel room door. Vincent held her hand.

"I want to apologize again for not telling you the truth about everything from the beginning. That was wrong."

"Yes, it was." She smiled. "But I think I understand."

"Do you? Do you really?" He stepped closer. "I know you have to go back. But I only have one thing to ask of you before you leave."

She swallowed. "What?"

"Give me a week. That's all. One week of your time. Spend it with me, get to know me. Let me show you my world."

"Vincent, I . . . my job—"

"Let me deal with Ross." He cupped her cheek. "Please,

give me that much. One week, and whatever you decide after that I'll accept."

Her heart was racing madly. She barely knew this man and he was asking her to put her life, her career on the line for a lark, on a maybe.

"One week," she conceded, holding up a slender finger.

The corners of his mouth curved up in a grin. "You won't regret it. That much I promise you." He stepped closer, lowered his head until his mouth was inches away from hers. Then he captured her lips with his own, in a kiss so sweet and full of promise, it left Nina weak.

Half walking, half stumbling into her suite, she mindlessly shut the door behind her, recalling Vincent's parting words. "Pack your bags. I'll be here for you in the morning. I only have seven days to change your mind and I intend to do just that."

Oh Lord, she moaned, not unhappily, as she flopped across her bed. Seven days and nights with Vincent St. Michael. She couldn't begin to imagine what he had in store, but it was pure heaven just thinking about it.

"You're doing *what*?" Denise screeched into the phone.

"I'm packing my bags and spending the next seven days with Vincent."

"Girl, it's a damned good thing I'm sitting down. Are you crazy? You don't know this man. He could be the Boston Strangler for all you know."

Nina laughed, her heart and spirit light. "This is Barbados, and they caught him, remember?"

"Yeah, yeah, but you know perfectly well what I mean. What did this brother whip on you?"

"I wish I knew." Nina sighed and sat on the side of her bed. "I can't explain it, Denise. It's just a feeling I have. I've seen him with strangers on the street. I've seen him with his family, how he treats them, how everyone respects him. And he's not heavy-handed about it. If anything, he's gentle. I believe in my heart he's a good man, Denise. And I believe he will be good to me—for as long as it lasts." She paused for a moment. "I've always taken chances in business, leaping out there and doing what others were afraid to do. But I've never taken that chance with my own life, my future, my happiness. And I want to. I want to take that chance with him, just this once. I could be wrong. But at least I'll never have to wonder 'what if.' "

Denise blew out a long breath. "What are you going to do about Ross? He's going to have a heart attack."

"And knowing Ross, he'll pay for the best doctors, the best hospital and walk away better than new." Nina chuckled.

"You know, you're probably right. But my main concern is you, Nina. I just want you to be happy. And hey, what better place than on a tropical island with a fine, rich man whose kisses can curl your toes?"

They both roared with laughter.

13

Vincent opted to forgo his driver. He didn't want any distractions, anyone to disturb them. With Jade gone and out on her own, he had the house to himself as well. So, for the next seven days it would be him and Nina . . . getting to know each other. He helped her into the car almost without a word and drove aimlessly away from the hotel.

Nina didn't know what to anticipate for the next seven days, but what she certainly hadn't expected was an almost shy Vincent. This was not the man who took the world by its tail and shook it, who walked into a room and made it his. He was tentative with her, as if suddenly unsure why both of them were there . . . then she, too, began to question her reasoning.

"Is there some plan for today, or am I going to be left in the dark as usual?" she snapped with a bit more bite than she'd intended. But the truth was, he was making her edgy and second-guessing herself, and that was something she truly hated. She folded her arms tightly beneath her breasts and felt the rapid flutter of her racing heart. She was a hot second away from tapping her foot.

Vincent cleared his throat, knowing that he was being foolish and she had every right to be irritated. He looked both ways and veered off the main road onto the shoulder. He cut the engine and turned to her.

"Nina, before anything remotely foolish falls from my lips, let me just say first that I'm sorry."

Nina slightly loosened the hold she had on her body. "Fine," she said tightly, barely moving her lips.

"I don't know what's been happening to me lately—or should I say since I met you. I know I want to be with you. And I know that what you represent goes against everything my family sees as holy. It seems as if everything and everyone is against us even trying to see where this can take us. And I'm on a tightrope, trying not to fall off. One minute I want to hold you, kiss you and never let go, and the next I want you on the fastest plane out of here and out of my life." He saw her flinch and reached for her hand. "Because I know I can really care about you, Nina Benson, and I'm terribly afraid of what it will all mean in the end, where it will take us, how it will change everything that we have come to know about our lives."

"Vincent, I've never been one to take any kind of risk. But I'm taking one with you. And I'll be damned if I know why. After spending time with your family, seeing what your heritage and the loss of it could mean, I realize that you're putting all you know on the line and so am I. At some point we both will have a lot of answering to do." She leaned forward. "I want to be sure . . . to have plenty to tell them." She kissed him softly, letting her lips play with his.

"I think that can be arranged," he murmured.

When they arrived at Vincent's house, it was still early. The sun bathed the window-encased house in light that bounced off the hardwood floors and glass-topped tables.

Vincent gave Nina a tour and she marveled at the hot tub, the home theater on the upper level and the quiet elegance of the finely furnished rooms.

"Did you have this built?" Nina asked once they'd settled on the deck.

"About fifteen years ago, actually. At the time I thought it would be the home I would share with my wife-to-be."

"Oh," Nina mumbled, not sure how to respond.

Vincent leaned back in the chair and put his bare feet up on a vacant one. "Don't you want to know what happened?"

Nina raised her brows. "If you want to tell me."

"Her name was Serena . . ."

Slowly, Vincent told Nina of how they'd met in school and it was love at first sight. He knew he'd found the one woman who would forever make him happy. His every waking hour was devoted to making Serena happy. And six weeks before they were to walk down the aisle she told him she was in love with someone else, his best friend.

"I didn't think I'd ever get over it," he quietly admitted. "I never thought anything could hurt so much."

Nina reached across the table and took his hand. "But you did, Vincent. Look at all that you've accomplished."

He laughed derisively. "I had no other choice but to work, at my art, the family businesses, taking care of my relatives." He released a sigh. "It helped . . . somewhat. But . . ."

"But, what?"

He looked at her, the sincere expression on her face. "But it was never enough. There was always this hole inside me that never seemed to be filled, no matter how many hours, how much work, how many women I crammed into my day. There was always an emptiness."

Nina looked off toward the water, at the beauty that surrounded her, and realized just how much alike they really were. She, too, seemed to have so much . . . material things, but the things that mattered, the things that sustained a person, were missing from her life as well.

"I know how you feel. It's been the same for me."

"You must have someone who cares about you a great deal." He gazed at the diamond that sparkled on her finger. "I can't believe you bought that for yourself."

Her face heated with the truth. She straightened in her seat.

"Ross gave it to me shortly before I came here."

Vincent momentarily lowered his gaze. "I see. Does it have some special meaning?"

"I believe to him it does."

"And you?"

"I'm torn. I've known Ross for a long time. His efforts got me to where I am in my career. He's been good to me."

"And?"

"And I suppose in a way I feel obligated to him."

"Obligated to what? To do whatever he asks, whatever he wants?"

"No," she snapped. "Of course not. But I have to consider his feelings."

"What about yours, Nina?" He lowered his feet to the hardwood and leaned close to her, his eyes boring into hers. "Do you really care about him? Can you care about him the way I know you can care about me?"

Nina sprang up from her seat and turned away, giving him her back. "How do you know what I feel, what I'm capable of?" She felt his presence behind her. Her body stiffened.

Vincent placed his hands on her shoulders. He lowered his head and planted tiny kisses on the back of her neck. A tremor ran upward from her feet to her fingertips. "Because I know you, Nina Benson," he whispered hot against her neck. "I see you in my dreams, I feel you in my soul, like I've never felt another woman. Not even Serena. And I believe you feel me, too." He turned her around to face him. "Tell me it's not true. Tell me your heart doesn't flutter like mine does every time we're together. Tell me you don't think about me, feel me when I'm not there. If you can, I'll take you back to the hotel and never bother you again. I'll even take you to the airport and wish you well on your flight home." He waited a heartbeat. "Tell me, Nina."

The sudden thought of leaving him filled her with a kind of dread she'd never felt before. "I . . . I can't." Her mouth trembled and he stroked it with his thumb. Her eyes fluttered closed an instant before his mouth covered hers.

His kiss was slow and sure, exploring her by degrees, tak-

ing his time. There was no hurry, she thought, giving herself
to him, willingly allowing his strong hands to stroke the
curves of her body. They had all the time in the world. At
least, they had one week.

Nina and Vincent spent their first day together exploring the
beach, picking up shells, frolicking in the waves, relaxing on
the deck, letting the island sun bake their limbs. They talked
to each other, really talked. Shared funny stories of their
childhood, the friends they'd known, the mistakes they'd
made. Vincent told her of his life in England and the role he
played as acting head of his large family. Nina shared her
own anecdotes of city life, the hectic pace so unlike the ca-
sualness of the islands. She told of her parents and her best
friend Denise who was always trying to set her up with someone.

   They ate, they drank, they played and before long the brilliant Caribbean sun began to set over the waters and the air
seemed to still, the only sound for miles was the waves hitting
the rocks against the shoreline.

   And when night fell, they explored each other.

14

"This is yours," Vincent said, showing her to a room at the
end of the long hallway on the upper level. "I think you'll be
comfortable."

   Nina stepped inside. The canopy bed with its wicker frame
was draped in a sheer white netting. A white wicker dresser,
matching end tables and an overstuffed lounge chair filled
with floral pillows were the only furnishing. The room had a
walk-in closet and a private bath that could easily rival The
Ritz.

   She spun toward him, a brilliant smile beaming across her
face. "It's beautiful," she said on a whisper. "Like a fairy
tale."

   Vincent headed for the door. "Think of yourself as a princess." He turned toward her, his expression soft, his eyes conveying things that his lips wouldn't utter. "Rest well. I'll see you in the morning." He closed the door softly behind him.

Pulling in a deep breath, Nina sat on the side of the bed and surveyed her space, recapped her day. It had been perfect. Vincent had been perfect. If she didn't know better, she'd think it was all some fabulous dream, someone else's life. But it was hers. And she didn't want it to end.

She unpacked her suitcase, placing her lingerie in the deep drawers and her clothes in the closet. Selecting the perfect outfit, she smiled and headed for the shower.

Vincent paced the expanse of his bedroom floor. What he wanted to do was march into Nina's room and make love to her in every corner of it until the sun rose. It had taken all of his willpower not to seduce her on the beach, when her dress had clung to her body after she'd run out into the water.

Did she have any idea the effect she was having on him? Even with Jade living in his house for five years, even her blatant availability and her unquestionable sensuality had never made him feel this way—feel this need that ate at him like an insatiable hunger. How long could he stand it before he took her, had her for himself, tasted the sweetness of her womanly flesh?

He kicked off his shoes, letting them slam against the wall, a minor outlet for his frustration. Maybe what he needed was a stiff drink and a cold shower. He trotted downstairs, fixed his drink and returned to his room.

He could hear the shower waters beating against the tiles in Nina's bathroom. His imagination went wild. Before his eyes he could envision her naked body, scented soap and steamy water sliding across her luscious breasts, down the slope of her stomach, settling for a moment in the soft tangle of triangular hair, then down the soft flesh of her thighs to pool at her feet. Her hands slid across her nakedness, taunting him, begging him to replace her hands with his own.

A groan of pure agony bubbled up from his throat, the

powerful erection almost painful against the fabric of his
jeans.

He tossed down the last drops of his drink and headed for
the shower. The icy pellets of water did nothing to quell the
urge that burned inside him.

When he emerged from the shower, dripping with water
and no calmer than he was when he entered, he made up his
mind to just go to bed, try to sleep it off. He listened for the
sounds of water coming from Nina's room.

Silence.

He walked to his bedroom door and opened it.

Nina stood on the other side, a look of calm expectation
hovering in her eyes.

"Your room or mine?" she asked in a husky whisper.

It seemed as if his entire body screamed with relief. He
took her hand, pulled her inside and kicked the door shut
behind her.

The light of the moon and the glow of the stars cast an iridescent glow across Vincent's bedroom, tossing their nude
bodies into an array of erotic silhouettes against the pale
walls.

The journey along the contours of their bodies was like
finding their way across sheets of music, examining each
note, playing it to perfection, letting it build, recede and build
again until they knew that becoming one was the only way
to still the rising crescendo that rose within them like the
waves that beat outside the window. And they did, again and
again until they lay weak and spent, wrapped in each other's
arms, watching the sun ascend above the horizon.

It was near noon before they finally found their way out
of bed, laughing and giggling like children as they washed
each other in the hot tub, then went for a dip in the ocean.
Food, clothing, the world around them was forgotten. They
only had eyes and thoughts of and for each other.

"We really should get dressed at some point," Nina said
as she lay stretched out on the deck chair, totally at ease with

her nakedness, something she'd never felt comfortable with before—especially in front of a man.

"Why?" Vincent chuckled. "I love looking at you. And I think you feel the same way," he added with a wicked leer.

"You make me feel beautiful," she said, looking up at her island god.

He knelt beside her, placed a tender kiss on the underside of her breast, causing a shiver to shimmy along her body. "You are beautiful, Nina. To me you are the most beautiful woman I've ever seen. I could hold you captive here and make love with you forever."

She swallowed as the sudden reality of their situation settled within her. They didn't have forever. At some point she would leave. She would go back to the States and he would go on with his life, and their time together would soon become a distant memory.

"You know that's not possible," she said. "We can't stay here forever."

"Why not?"

She sat up. "Because . . . we can't."

Vincent straightened as well. "I suppose you're right. You do have a life to get back to."

She cleared her throat. "And so do you."

He looked away, unable to stare truth in the eye, as much as he wanted it to be otherwise. What he needed her to say, wanted her to say was that she would stay with him, give him his life back, make him whole. That she would give up her life in New York and forge a new one here with him. But he knew he was dreaming the impossible. They were from two different worlds. And if they had seven days or seven years that fact would not change. He couldn't leave, and she couldn't stay.

He stood. "I know you're right. There are some things I do want to show you while we still have some time." He turned toward the house. "Let's get dressed, then I'll take you into town."

———

They spent the next few days visiting the extensive property that Vincent owned under the family name: the art gallery, restaurant, a small bed-and-breakfast, a business school and one of the busiest vegetable and fish markets on the island.

Everywhere they went, Vincent was greeted with warmth and a large degree of deference. For all of his lighthearted, easygoing manner, Vincent St. Michael was an astute businessman, who managed the family empire with an ease Nina was unaccustomed to. She was used to Ross browbeating and intimidating his employees and competitors to get results. Vincent used his warm smile, well-chosen words and sincere compliments. And it worked.

The more time she spent with him, the more she came to admire him. And she began to realize as they lay together night after night that she was falling in love with him, and that leaving him would be the most difficult thing she'd ever have to do.

On the seventh day, as promised, Vincent drove Nina back to her hotel. The ride seemed to take forever and was conducted in relative silence.

He pulled to a stop in front of the hotel.

"Safe and sound," he said, trying and failing in his attempt at lightness.

"It's . . . it's been wonderful, Vincent. And no matter what you may think, I enjoyed every minute of it."

He wouldn't look at her. He couldn't. If he did he knew he'd make a fool of himself and beg her to stay, tell her how much he loved her and needed her in his life. But Nina had given no indication that she felt the same way. And he wouldn't be the first.

"Do you need me to help you with your bags?"

She swallowed over the knot in her throat. "No. I'll be fine. Thanks."

He nodded. "When will you be leaving?"

She pushed out a breath. "I'll call my home office today. I'm sure once I tell my boss that there's no deal, he'll demand I be on the first plane back to New York."

"I'll call Burns and explain. I'm sure everything will be fine."

"Yeah. Me, too," she added inanely, not really caring. "Well, I'd better go." She reached for her suitcase from the backseat, then turned to look at him. "Good-bye, Vincent."

"Good-bye, beautiful Nina," he said softly and was sure that his heart was breaking for the second time in his life. But he'd made the mistake of putting his emotions on his sleeve once before, he wouldn't do it again.

Nina opened the door and stepped out. She turned once and looked at him through the glass, then hurried off toward the entrance before he could see the tears brimming in her eyes.

"I love you," he whispered. "Have a safe trip home."

15

On the entire flight home, Nina felt as if she were dying inside. Before boarding she kept scanning the crowd, hoping against hope that Vincent would appear at the airport like Angela Bassett did to Taye Diggs in *How Stella Got Her Groove Back*. But that was the movies, this was real—and there was no knight in shining armor begging her to stay.

But if she thought her flight home was disastrous, it was nothing compared to the tirade she was the recipient of when she returned to work on Monday morning.

The veins in Ross' forehead looked as if they were about to burst. He paced the floor with such furious intent she was sure he would wear out the carpet.

She sat with her hands folded in her lap and just listened. What else could she do? The truth of the matter was, she really wasn't paying attention. She really didn't care. Her mind was fixed on what she'd given up.

"I knew I shouldn't have let you handle something this big," he boomed. "What the hell am I supposed to tell the contractors, my partners, for Christ's sake! I trusted you to deal with this, Nina. Trusted you and you blew it. And that . . . that St. Michael calling me as if this was no big deal," he ranted. He momentarily stopped his pacing and glared at her. "You've made a fool out of me, and out of this company. I should have taken care of this myself. But I let my emotions get in the way."

She looked at him for the first time since she'd entered his office nearly twenty minutes earlier. "Your emotions?" she asked incredulously.

"Yes. I let my feelings for you override good judgment, and now we'll all pay for it," he growled.

Suddenly she stood. "Ross, you have no more feelings for me than you do for another quick deal. I was simply something else to acquire. Something you wanted. I could have closed the deal. I could have convinced them that what we intended to do was the greatest thing since emancipation. But I didn't." She stepped up to him. "And you want to know why, Ross? Because what that land meant to that family was a helluva lot more than we could ever give. But you would never understand that." With that she spun on her heels and stormed out, leaving the door swinging on its hinges.

"So how long are you going to be miserable?" Denise asked as they sat in Nina's living room.

Nina stared out the window of her brownstone, upon the teeming streets below, envisioning the sandy beaches, the sun-splashed mornings and the man she loved and left behind.

"Huh?" she finally mumbled.

"Why don't you call him, Nina?"

She turned from the window, pain and sadness hanging around her eyes. "I can't."

"Why not? This is the millennium. A new day. Anybody with a set of eyes can see you're in love and miserable. And you won't be happy until you tell him."

Nina lowered her head. "What if he doesn't feel the same way?"

"You'll never know standing in the window looking like you just got beat up."

Nina forced a weak grin. "I do miss him, Denise. I miss

him like crazy. These past few weeks have been hell. And Ross hovering around me like a vulture waiting to strike doesn't help."

"Then tell him, girl. Take a chance. What do you have to lose . . . besides some pride?" she teased.

Nina blew out a breath, a slow smile eased across her mouth. "This isn't something you tell a person on the phone," she said, the excitement hitching her voice. "It's something you need to tell them in person. Don't you think?"

Denise laughed. "Whatever you say, girl. But this time could you see if you can hook a sister up?"

Nina was as nervous as a new bride when her plane landed at the Barbados airport. On the entire flight she thought about how foolish, how reckless this was. What if he didn't want her? What if he told her to go back home where she belonged?

But what if he didn't?

She retrieved her bags from the carousel and hurried toward the exit, intent on hailing a car to the hotel. She didn't see him until he was right on top of her, bags in hand.

"Nina—"

"Vincent—"

"What—"

"I—"

"You first," he finally said.

"I, uh, I came . . . to see you."

He put his bag down next to his feet.

"But you're . . ."

"I was coming to see you."

Her eyes snapped up to meet his. "You were?"

His smile warmed her from head to toe. "Yes, I was." He stepped up to her, cupped her cheek. "I couldn't stand another day being without you, Nina."

"Neither could I."

"I love you," they said in perfect harmony.

Vincent took her in his arms and kissed her like he'd dreamed of kissing her from the moment she'd left, and the world continued to spin around them, but the only people in it for them was each other.

"I always wanted to see you settled down before I died," Clotie said to her grandson as they sat together on the back porch of the family house. "I just never believed it would be with a Yankee."

Vincent chuckled. "Neither did I, Nana."

"You know those Yankee women want their independence, won't walk in their husband's shadow."

"I want someone who is my equal, Nana. Not some plaything. Nina is the one for me. I love her and I want you to love her, too."

Clotie sucked her teeth. "We'll see." She squinted her eyes. "You sure she not trying to ease her way into the family to get her hands on the property?"

"I know she's not. She's given up her career to be with me. That should say something."

"Well, if you love her like you say, I guess it should count for something. I didn't raise you to be no knucklehead."

"I feel better already," he joked.

"Hmm. You know if you planning a wedding, you do it the right way with the banns for three Sundays, give folks a chance to speak their piece."

"I know, Nana." He thought about the age-old custom of announcing the upcoming wedding in church for three Sundays to give anyone the opportunity to voice any objections. If it were up to him he'd marry Nina today. But custom was custom and he wanted his Nana happy.

The entire St. Michael clan pitched in to help with the wedding; from cooking every imaginable island delicacy to selecting flowers, writing invitations and repainting the house. "Won't do to have company coming and the house in disarray," Nana scoffed at her already immaculate house.

The family china and silverware that had been used by Vincent's great-grandmother and great-grandfather at their wedding was laid out on the starched white linen tablecloths.

Even Jade pitched in by going shopping with Nina to find her wedding dress.

"I always thought myself in love with Vincent, ya know," Jade confessed as she zipped up Nina's gown on her big day. "Even thought about standing up in church and telling the congregation how wrong this marriage was."

Nina turned around to face the beautiful woman dressed in a satin gown of pale sea green.

"But when I see the look in Vincent's eyes when you walk into a room, I knew he would never feel that way for me. Him loves ya. You're a lucky woman. And I hope you make him happy. Really I do."

"Thank you, Jade."

Jade sniffed. "You two gon' make some pretty little ones," she added, brushing the silk gown along Nina's hips. "And knowing Vincent, he gon' want plenty of 'em."

Nina laughed, her heart filled with joy at the possibility.

Beneath a star-dappled night sky, Nina Benson emerged from the house of St. Michael and walked regally down the white cotton rug toward her soon-to-be husband to the emotion-filled sound of the wedding march.

Denise held her train, while Nina's parents sat teary-eyed beneath the enormous tent that held the more than one hundred standing guests. This was to be her new family, her new home, her new life. Her heart raced as she approached the makeshift altar. She wanted everything to be perfect. Suddenly, she had a flash. She had followed tradition down to the letter. She had something new: her dress; something borrowed: her garter from her mother; something blue: a handkerchief from Denise. But she didn't have anything old. Panic seized her and she nearly missed her step.

Just before she reached the priest, Clotie slipped something cool and round into her hand from her aisle seat. "It was my husband's," she whispered. "It's yours now, chile." She smiled and closed Nina's hand around her gift.

Nina opened her fingers and looked down at the object in

her palm and saw the gold ring that Clotie had long ago slipped onto the finger of her husband. Nina's heart seemed to rise to her throat. She leaned down and placed a tender kiss on the soft cheek. "Thank you. I'll make him happy. I promise."

Taking a breath, she stood erect and finished the final steps to the altar and took Vincent's hand in hers.

"Dearly beloved . . ."

It was a moment that could not be put into words, the enormity of it left her light-headed. She barely heard the priest's words as she thought about what she was embarking upon. Not only were she and Vincent joining two lives, they were merging two cultures, bridging gaps. It wouldn't be easy, she knew that. There would be sacrifices to make on both their parts. But they were willing and she looked forward to the days and years ahead to her new role as partner in a flourishing business and wife to her beloved.

One day she would sit in Nana's place and she and Vincent would hand off the ring to their grandchild. She smiled as the priest asked if she would take this man.

As soon as I can get him out of here, she thought wickedly. We need to get working on those kids!

"I do," she said clearly for all who were gathered to hear. "I do!"

And Vincent greedily took his new wife into his arms and gave her a hint of what was to come, for then and always.

Southern Comfort

FRANCIS RAY

1

Charlotte Duvall was a charmer. She was the kind of woman men noticed, and women aspired to emulate. It was impossible to remain detached and impersonal once you saw her and had been graced by her eloquent presence.

Vincent Maxwell had heard the flowery accolades often from his cousin, Brian, so much so that Vincent often wondered if his young and still highly impressionable twenty-four-year-old cousin was half in love with Charlotte. Vincent hoped not. Especially since Brian had recently announced his engagement to Emma Hamilton, a rather shy kindergarten teacher.

Vincent had liked Emma immediately when Brian brought her by his office several weeks ago. Sweet-faced with a lovely smile, the woman obviously adored Brian. She even laughed at his lame jokes. They seemed so right for each other. They were the same age and attended the same church.

However, in the weeks that followed, Brian had become increasingly vocal in his adoration of Charlotte. When Vincent mentioned his concerns to Brian, he always laughingly denied any romantic interest in Charlotte and assured Vincent that he would understand once he met her. With Brian's wedding six weeks away, Vincent, as Brian's best man and eldest cousin, felt it past time for him to meet this paragon of virtue and desire.

"I'm so glad you and Charlotte's schedules have finally worked out so you can meet each other," Emma said with a smile, her nut-brown face glowing with love and happiness. "I was afraid you two wouldn't meet until the wedding rehearsal."

"So am I," Vincent said, sipping his tonic water. As tired as he was after a ten-hour day, if he drank anything alcoholic, he'd be asleep in an hour. In his briefcase, which he'd left in his car, was a three-inch stack of paperwork he needed to go

through before a meeting at eight the next morning. He'd
never been late with a report and he didn't intend to start
now. He'd pulled an all-nighter before. He could do it again.
It was in Brian's best interest that Vincent meet this Charlotte
Duvall person ASAP. Even the name sounded seductive and
mysterious.

Although Vincent hadn't been around his cousin for years,
he doubted Brian had much experience with women. Vincent
had. Women could be as vicious and as devious as men in
getting what they wanted.

His mouth tightened as he thought of Sybil Lamount.
Beautiful, cunning and heartless. A viper if ever there was
one. She could ruin a person's career and never lose a moment of sleep. Spoils of the game, she always said.

Vincent took a sip of his tonic water and found the taste
as bitter as his thoughts. *Forget her, forget the past,* he chided
himself. He had survived when others had not. His mind had
to be on one thing and one thing only: re-engineering Ora-
Tech Petroleum Company's entire financial structure. The
task was monumental, but in his three-month-old position as
vice-president of finance, it was his job, and what he had been
wooed away from Standard Securities in Boston to do. As
with every job Vincent undertook, he planned to do it and do
it well, no matter what.

"Charlotte works as hard as you do," Brian put in from
his place on the far side of Emma.

"Mmmm," was all Vincent said. He doubted that very seriously. Women simply didn't have the force of will or the
single-mindedness that a man had. Most were too easily
distracted by emotions. Of course, a few had made it to the
top, but in doing so, in Vincent's humble opinion, they had
to compromise in some way. Their path was littered with
broken relationships, rebellious children and antacid bottles.
Working sixteen hours a day or being gone ten to fifteen days
out of a month didn't go very well with caring for a family.
Something went lacking. He'd seen it happen too many times
in the past.

Or if they were as heartless as Sybil, they didn't worry

about any emotional attachments or the people they stepped on on their climb up the corporate ladder. The job was all that mattered and to hell with anything or anyone else. *That* was something of which he had personal knowledge.

"Charlotte's almost as fantastic as Emma," Brian said, his handsome face wreathed in a boyish grin.

Vincent easily shifted his thoughts back to the present. His onyx eyes narrowed on his cousin. There it was again, that open praise bordering on worshipfulness in Brian's voice.

Even as a boy Brian had been impressionable. He'd been reared by easygoing, good-natured parents who believed the best of everyone. Vincent's father, his namesake, often commented that William, his younger brother Brian's father, was every con man's dream.

Vincent's father had worried when William Maxwell moved his family from Connecticut to Dallas twenty years ago to teach philosophy at Southern Methodist University. Vincent's father, a high-powered banking executive, was pragmatic. Vincent's mother, the quintessential executive's wife with a liberal arts degree from Vassar and who could hold her own with Martha Stewart or B. Smith, was sensible. No one got to them. They had reared Vincent to be the same way.

"Oh, look. Charlotte's here."

Vincent glanced in the direction Emma was staring, but all he saw was the broad, black-tuxedoed back of the maître d'. Then the man moved and Vincent, renowned for keeping his calm in any situation, barely kept his mouth from dropping open.

Surely he wasn't seeing what he thought he was. No woman would be that bold. But as he stared all he could see was a smooth toffee-toned body draped in an oversized fringed shawl. The soft, iridescent material in shimmering bronze tones slipped off one golden brown shoulder revealing more bare skin and the lush swell of Charlotte's breasts.

A hot ball of healthy lust rolled through Vincent. It seemed he had been right to be concerned about Brian. Few men would probably be immune to such an obvious temptation.

Smiling warmly, Charlotte said something to the overly attentive maître d', then turned toward them, waved and started in their direction. For a long moment the man she walked away from stared wistfully after her, only looking away when a waiter came up to speak to him. Vincent could understand why.

The view from behind was probably just as enticing as the one in front. Her walk was a mixture of strut and saunter on impossible high-heeled leopard sandals that bared her feet and showed off trim ankles.

"Charlotte."

Charlotte glanced around at the white linen–draped table-for-two she had been about to pass, then stopped abruptly and bent to hug the matronly woman in pearls and diamonds who had greeted her. Nimbly, Charlotte scooted around the table to the gray-haired man who had risen and gave him a hug as well.

In the three months Vincent had been in Dallas he'd noticed that people in the South were high on hugging and emotionalism. Bostonians as a rule weren't so enthusiastic or demonstrative.

However, at the moment he was annoyed to find he also noticed how the deep fringe on the shawl lazily parted to provide a tantalizing glimpse of Charlotte's shapely brown leg each time she bent over. It annoyed him further that as he glanced away he saw the rapt attention of several other men in the restaurant doing the same thing. It wasn't difficult to see the open speculation in their faces as to what, if anything, lay beneath the shimmering shawl and if the material would rise further to give them the answer.

Vincent sat back against the leather booth, picked up his glass and studied the small fresh-cut floral arrangement on the table. He'd met that type of flamboyant woman before. Women like that held little interest for him. He preferred his women to be feminine and demure. Provocativeness belonged in the bedroom. Apparently no one had told Charlotte about subtlety. He would be civil to her because he had no choice.

She was Emma's maid of honor. *He* didn't have to be her new best friend.

"Hi. Sorry I'm late."

Despite his best effort to remain detached, the slow, husky Southern drawl stirred something within Vincent. It was the kind of voice lovers used when they were hot and sweaty and tangled in moonlight and each other. Because of his hectic schedule those nights were a distant memory.

"I'm just glad you're here." Laughing, Brian stood, his long, lanky arm curving affectionately around Charlotte's slim waist as he kissed her offered cheek. Vincent cut a look at Emma to see if she disapproved of her fiancé kissing a woman who wore seduction so brazenly. To his surprise, Emma was smiling warmly.

"I'm just glad you and Vincent are finally meeting each other," Emma said, her hand reaching out for Brian's. He grasped it immediately. "The wedding is only six weeks away."

"I wish it were tomorrow," Brian said, squeezing Emma's hand.

For a moment the two of them had eyes only for each other. Vincent almost breathed a small sigh of relief. Charlotte wasn't an issue as he had suspected.

"I think they've forgotten about us," Charlotte said lightly, her voice a smooth mix of silk and honey and magnolia blossoms. The pouty lower lip fit the seductive image the voice evoked—and so did the rest of the face, with its sharp cheekbones, thick black lashes over slumberous hazel eyes and dainty nose.

Emma and Brian laughed, then he finished the introductions. "Charlotte Duvall, political fund-raiser extraordinare, long-time friend of the bride and maid of honor, meet Vincent Maxwell, financial wizard and Vice-President of Finance for Ora-Tech Petroleum Company, my favorite cousin and best man."

Vincent slowly came to his feet. It had been rude not to do so earlier, but he had reached that point in his life when he followed his own dictates in his personal life. "Ms. Du-vall."

A smile spread across Charlotte's beautiful face. He no-ticed a tiny mole near the corner of her mouth. The top of her head barely reached the middle of his chest. She was smaller and daintier than he realized. More trouble. A man would feel protective toward a small woman, and he just bet Charlotte Duvall used that to her best advantage.

She held out her slender, French-manicured hand. "Please, call me Charlotte. It's a pleasure to meet you. I was afraid you were a figment of Brian's imagination."

The way she seemed to center her attention entirely on a man had probably caused many to succumb and throw them-selves at her feet. Vincent was made of sterner stuff. Cour-tesy, not interest, dictated his next movements. Her soft hand barely settled in his before he released it and stepped aside. "If you'll have a seat, we can order."

Charlotte kept the smile on her face with difficulty. She earned her living by being able to read people quickly and correctly. She'd bet the platinum card tucked in her Hermés bag that Vincent Maxwell didn't like her. The limp hand-shake, the slight curl of his sensual upper lip, the disapproving black eyes all told the story. His loss.

She reached for her shawl. His broad shoulders stiffened.

Her brows puckered, then cleared as the reason came to her. She smiled to herself. The attire was designed to draw a man's attention. It did the job extremely well and as her mother had always said, why wear something that no one noticed?

The first time she had worn the outfit at a fund-raising dinner for the Sickle Cell Anemia Foundation, she'd been inundated with requests from women to have the designer's name. She'd happily given them her sister's name and address in Charleston, but the dress was one-of-a-kind, as were most of her clothes.

Charlotte smiled into Vincent's tight face and slowly pulled the shawl from her shoulders, knowing that as she did she'd reveal her bare skin inch by inch until the light material slid over the low bodice of the leopard-print strapless dress. His eyes rounded.

After twenty-nine years she had gotten used to men's re-action when they saw her breasts: She was top-heavy, but she no longer slumped her shoulders or wore oversized tops to hide what God had given her. Women went under the knife to get what she had naturally.

Sure the disapproving expression on Vincent's face would vanish, she watched and waited expectantly. If anything, his mobile lips tightened even more. She admitted the bustier-style of the clinging dress plunged a bit, but it was in no way indecent. *Stuffed shirt*, she thought.

Only an uptight Yankee would think a Southern woman would appear in public so improperly dressed or disapprove of a little cleavage. To think, she had looked forward to fi-nally meeting him. Dismissing Vincent, Charlotte slid into the booth. "Emma, I told you the meeting might run late and to order."

Emma waved Charlotte's words aside. The two-carat round diamond on the third finger of her left hand reflected a rainbow prism from the crystal chandelier several feet away. "It's only a little past nine and since tomorrow is Friday, I can sleep in late on Saturday."

Charlotte shook her head of shoulder-length auburn curls. She hated to be the bearer of bad news, but she had to do her duty. A duty that she had performed eight times in the past four years. With difficulty she shook away the unsettling memory of people's comments at the last wedding where she had been the maid of honor, wanting to know when she was going to be a bride. She wondered the same thing.

"Saturday you and Brian are meeting at your parents' house at ten to go over the final guest list and get the wedding invitations in the mail. Then at two you meet with Pastor Bailey in his study to confirm the ceremony details."

Emma's brown eyes sparkled with humor. "Sleeping late for me is any time past eight. I get up at six on school days."

Charlotte shuddered delicately. "You always did get up with the chickens. Brian, why don't you get the waiter?" The words were barely out of her mouth before the waiter appeared. Somehow she knew the reason was the silent man sitting next to her.

"Please bring another menu," Vincent requested.

"If you all know what you want, that won't be necessary." Charlotte smiled up at the waiter. "Hi, Louis."

A flush climbed upward from the banded collar of the man's white shirt. His Adam's apple bobbed. "Good evening, Ms. Duvall. It's nice to have you dining with us again."

"Always a pleasure." Putting her elbows on the table, she linked her slender fingers. "My friends were waiting on me. Please tell Pierre I'd consider it a favor if he'd do his magic and get our orders out as soon as possible."

"Certainly, Ms. Duvall."

She sent the young man another hundred-watt smile, then turned to Emma, who had a tiny, knowing smile on her own face. "You first."

In less than a minute the waiter had hurried away to put in their orders, then returned almost immediately with Charlotte's white wine. In less than two minutes their mushroom appetizers appeared. Aware that another customer's order would be late, Charlotte guiltily speared one. But as was her understanding with the chef, the other customer's appetizer was now complimentary and the cost billed to Charlotte's account. While she enjoyed the ability to pamper her clients, she understood that the integrity and high standards of the five-star restaurant had to be maintained.

Although this wasn't business, for some perverse reason she wanted to show Mr. Stuck-up he wasn't all that. Just because he was an executive with a large firm didn't mean squat. So what if he didn't approve of her? There were plenty of people who did. She had clout, too.

But as the meal progressed and they were served their entrées, Charlotte became aware that not once had Vincent spoken directly to her. He smiled and chatted with Brian and Emma, but acted as if she wasn't there. When she tested her theory and asked him a question, he gave the answer in precise diction as if he were reciting to his English teacher. One he didn't particularly care for.

Charlotte, as the youngest of three sisters, had never taken being ignored very well. She took being judged unjustly worse. Combined, the two offenses hit her boiling point midway through her blackened catfish. The ladylike thing to do was to ignore the rude man. He was a Yankee and didn't know any better. She, on the other hand, had been raised to be hospitable, ignore offenses and never forget she was a Southern lady. But as the meal lengthened she recalled she had also been taught that if a woman were smart enough she could get her point across and remain a lady.

"Vincent." Charlotte drew out the first syllable of his name, then ended the second in a soft croon. She waited until he slowly turned to face her. She wondered briefly what that sensual mouth would look like relaxed, then dismissed the thought. "I certainly hope our hot Texas summers aren't too brutal for you. Boston's climate is so different."

Unyielding black eyes narrowed. "I was in Saudi for two years."

"Then you can take the heat. How nice," she said drolly. Dismissing Vincent, she reached for the crystal salt shaker and brushed her bare arm against the fine cotton blend of his jacket. He stiffened as if something vile had touched him.

"Excuse me, sugar," she smiled into his taut face. He certainly hadn't liked being called "sugar," but then neither did she care for being treated as if she were something repugnant.

Immediately she made up her mind—the challenge was on. For the next five minutes, she "accidentally" brushed against Vincent every chance she got and called him "sugar." Her lips twitched. If he became any stiffer, he'd crack.

A delightful prospect.

With that thought in mind, Charlotte decided a two-pronged attack was in order. She leaned toward Vincent to ask him his party affiliation. The twin assaults would surely send him over the edge. Relishing the outcome, she grinned.

Vincent chose that moment to reach for the bread basket

near Charlotte's plate. Instead of her brushing against his shoulder, his right forearm grazed her breast.

Charlotte froze out of embarrassment and the unexpected thrill of pleasure that shot through her. Her sharp intake of breath hissed through her clenched teeth.

Time stood still, then started again as she slowly faced him. The apology on her lips died under his accusing glare. Hot shame flooded her cheeks and made her speechless for one of the few times in her life.

Vincent scooted over. "Sorry, I didn't mean to crowd you."

She felt inexplicably worse by his unexpected gallantry. She opened her mouth to say it was her fault, then inwardly shrank from the anger boiling in his stormy black eyes. He thought she had done it on purpose.

Charlotte realized she had no comeback. Her childish act of teasing him had gotten her into this predicament. Mutely, she turned to Brian and Emma and was relieved to see that they were too involved with each other to see what had happened.

Vincent picked up the roll from the linen-draped silver basket with his left hand, broke the bread in half and placed it on his bread plate without taking a bite. Charlotte had the feeling he wished the crusty roll were her neck.

"Brian, should I plan to go with you and Emma to see the pastor Saturday?" Vincent asked.

Smiling, Brian shook his head. Apparently he didn't notice Vincent's strained voice. "It will be more like a counseling session to make sure we're ready."

His jaw tight, Vincent nodded solemnly. "Well, if you'll excuse me, I have some paperwork that I have to get to tonight. The bill has been taken care of."

"You haven't finished your meal," Charlotte blurted.

Cold eyes stabbed her. "I've lost my appetite."

Charlotte flinched.

"Thanks, cuz, for dinner and for coming," Brian said, then asked, "Do either of you ladies want any dessert?" At the negative shake of the women's heads, he tossed a fifty on the table. "Then we'll walk out with you. Emma was up late last night with PTA."

Emma leaned her head against his shoulder and stared worshipfully up at her fiancé. "Charlotte, I hope you find someone like Brian."

"One can always hope," Charlotte said.

A snorting sound came from the direction of Vincent, but when Charlotte looked around, his expression was bland. "Did you say something?"

"Nothing you'd want to hear."

Realizing he was probably right, Charlotte stepped in front of him and headed out of the restaurant. Outside, as luck would have it, Vincent's car arrived first from the valet. She had hoped she might get a chance to apologize. Curtly, he dipped his well-shaped head in Charlotte's direction before warmly saying good-bye to Brian and Emma. Then he went around and got in the driver's seat of his late-model Lincoln Town Car and drove off.

"I'm afraid I didn't make a very favorable impression on your cousin, Brian," Charlotte said, staring at the taillights of the luxury sedan before they disappeared as Vincent turned onto Houston Street.

Perpetually easygoing, Brian slung his free arm around Charlotte's tense shoulders. "Don't worry. I admit Vincent is the serious type, but he's an all right kind of guy. The reason he hasn't been able to meet you until now is that he's re-engineering his company's entire financial organization. He's got a lot on his mind. It'll be different the next time you meet him."

"Brian's right, Charlotte," Emma said from beside Brian, who had his other arm around her trim waist. "Vincent just has a lot on his mind. He's a great guy. Besides," she said with a grin, "there's not a man alive who's immune to you."

Charlotte smiled as Emma had intended, but it was forced. All her friends thought she was some kind of femme fatale. But Charlotte knew all too well she wasn't, just as she knew that men *were* immune to her. While her friends were getting married right and left, she was going home alone.

Hugging Emma, Charlotte went to her Lexus, tipping the attendant as she got in her car. Traffic was light in downtown Dallas and soon she was on Central Expressway heading north and home. It might have been her imagination, but every car she saw seemed to have a couple snuggled together inside.

Pulling into the garage located in the rear of her house, she went straight to her office off the kitchen and checked messages. There were seven since she had retrieved the last one before she went into the restaurant. That was light, but it wouldn't remain that way.

Her party needed money to ensure that when the time came their presidential candidate won the White House, and when he did he'd need the votes of senators and congressmen and -women he could count on. Her job, her passion, was to ensure that that happened. And that meant money, and lots of it.

By law, fund-raising could only be conducted while the Senate wasn't in session, from January to June first. It was May twenty-fifth. And although fund-raising didn't usually get into full swing until late fall, things were already happening.

Cutting off the light, Charlotte stopped by the bright kitchen done in celery green with creamy oyster accents, pulled a bottle of water from the refrigerator, then continued to her bedroom, yawning as she went. She'd been up since six working on a volunteer project for Brian's House, a home for children with AIDS. But it would be worth it. The budget would be met for the following year and then some.

Fighting back another yawn, Charlotte reached for a padded hanger in her mirrored walk-in closet. Out of the corner of her eyes she saw the rose silk taffeta maid of honor gown for Emma's wedding hanging in a thick plastic bag emblazoned with the name *Yvonne's Wedding Gowns*.

Melancholy hit Charlotte without warning. She had a beautiful, tastefully furnished, brick four-bedroom home, a nice car, a closet full of clothes for each season of the year, and a job that allowed her to work out of her home and set her own hours. And no one special to share her life with.

As a political fund-raiser, she not only helped in a small way to shape the policies of the country, but met influential and often famous people in the process. In Dallas, there was something going on every weekend and almost every night. Her social calendar was full, but her personal life was empty.

Only her immediate family was aware of how much it hurt when people continued to ask when *she* was going to walk down the aisle as the bride. She wished she knew.

Most of the men she met were either out for what they could get, already in a relationship, or thought she was too outspoken and aggressive. They wanted a woman who stayed in the background, who was nonthreatening and demure. She'd never be that.

She sighed. Those attributes, some would say faults, she admitted to herself, were what had gotten her into her present predicament. But you couldn't get political donations by being timid. Especially since she was only five-feet-two in her stocking feet. She'd learned to walk gracefully in stiletto heels because she'd been taught that a lady always wore heels, but they also added inches to her height.

To those who said she had a Napoleonic complex, she said bull. She'd just learned early to speak up for herself in a house full of women who all wanted to be heard. She often wondered how her daddy, a loving, soft-spoken man, had stood it. But he had, and he'd appeared to relish being around so many women.

Charlotte was the only one of her sisters still single. She'd absolutely refused another blind date or to be hooked up. If Mr. Right was out there, she'd wait until God placed him in her path. But patience had never been Charlotte's strong suit.

At the last wedding she'd attended as maid of honor— number eight—Ira Hadnot, a reporter for the "Lifestyle" section of the *Dallas Morning News*, had asked Charlotte about doing a story on the number of times she had been down the aisle and not married. Thankfully, Ira had been joking and why shouldn't she? Ira had a wonderful husband who adored her. She had someone to go home to; someone to wake up with.

Tossing the hanger on the king-sized bed, Charlotte unzipped her dress. She, on the other hand, woke up to the sound of an alarm clock. She was twenty-nine with no prospects. But that wasn't her biggest concern at the moment. Her biggest concern was facing Vincent Maxwell and apologizing.

She strongly believed a person should take responsibility for their own actions, even if it meant getting their head chopped off. Vincent looked as if he could chop with the best of them.

2

Vincent stepped into the chrome-and-glass elevator on the third floor of Ore-Tech Petroleum Company, nodded absently to two men he recognized from marketing, and punched nine. Vincent's mind was on the thick stack of fan-folded paper he'd just picked up from accounting.

The data he held was just another piece of the larger puzzle that was needed to complete the financial reorganization of Ore-Tech. After working sixteen-, sometimes twenty-hour days for more weeks than he cared to remember, the financial plan was finally coming together. When he and his team were finished, they'd save the company millions.

People not in the corporate world tended to think that all executives did was play golf and have five-martini lunches. If that were true, the company they worked for would go bankrupt. Truth was, they worked their butts off. They saw little of their families. The trade-off for the family was a higher standard of living.

When he wasn't traveling, there wasn't a night that he didn't take work home. However, he was well compensated for his hard work and diligence.

The high six-figure salary he earned easily went to seven figures with bonuses and profit sharing. If things went as planned he could retire in twenty more years at fifty-five, if he wanted. He didn't see that happening. He liked what he did, and if he did say so himself, he was very good at it.

The elevator door opened on the fifth floor and the men got out. Vincent's destination was the top executive floor and his corner office that looked out onto picturesque Lake Caroline that meandered through Las Colinas, an upscale office and residential complex. As the elevator door closed, Vincent's thoughts went to Brian.

His cousin wanted the high salary, the corner office, but Vincent wasn't sure the easygoing man was cut out for the stressful, hectic pace that could crush a man and his marriage. Vincent had been raised to believe that a man took care of his family. The man worked and the wife stayed home. That's what the men in Vincent's family did—until Brian.

Emma planned to continue teaching. According to Brian, she liked to cook for him, and enjoyed going to the movies. If Brian continued his climb in the marketing department of the telecommunications company he worked for, she'd be cooking for one, and the only movies they'd see would be the ones rented from a video store. Vincent couldn't remember the last time he'd seen a new release, with or without a woman.

Although he had no thoughts of getting married, when he did decide to take the plunge, he planned to follow tradition. His wife would stay at home.

Vincent liked Emma and while she seemed practical, he wondered if she could handle the pressure of being married to a man gone more than he was home. Vincent shifted the papers and wondered about something else: how a nice, sweet woman like Emma had a friend like Charlotte.

Charlotte. She was completely unacceptable, but that hadn't kept him from thinking about her. She'd been on his mind when he finally drifted off to sleep last night, then in his dreams.

His hand closed over the spot on his arm where her breast had touched. The soft imprint had burned into his flesh and left him wanting to remove the cloth barrier and place his mouth there. He scowled. He'd known she was trouble the moment he'd laid eyes on her.

His scowl deepening, Vincent bumped the closing elevator

door with his shoulder and stepped off. It wasn't like him to let a woman distract him. Not even Sybil had managed to do that.

Determined steps carried him down the wide hallway filled with contemporary art and lush tropical plants. Six offices were located on the floor. His was at the far end. Opening the heavy mahogany door to his outer office, he took two steps, then stopped abruptly. The last person he expected to see perched on the edge of his secretary's desk was Charlotte Duvall.

Her hazel eyes widened. Mulberry-painted lips parted in surprise, then she seemed to glide off the desk and onto her feet. Multiple layers of white swirled around her, then settled, but not before he'd seen those shapely legs that had helped deny him his sleep. He closed the door with a crisp snap.

"Vincent, I know we don't have an appointment and that you're a busy man, but if you'd give me five minutes I'd like to explain about last night," she said in a rush, eyeing him warily.

"You have fifteen minutes before your next appointment," Millicent informed him. "I could get you and Ms. Duvall some coffee, if you'd like."

Charlotte glanced back at the older woman and smiled. "Please, call me Charlotte."

Millicent smiled back, a real smile full of warmth and pleasure.

Vincent's gaze went from one to the other. He felt as if he was in the Twilight Zone. His secretary, Millicent Howard, was cool, crisp, and a bit remote. But obviously not with Charlotte. He'd inherited her from the previous vice-president and since his secretary in Boston hadn't wanted to relocate, he'd agreed to keep Millicent.

The first time he'd met Millicent, the diminutive sixty-year-old had politely informed him that she was a secretary, not a waitress or an errand girl. She typed 120 words per minute, spoke five languages, had an in with all the departments needed to get his reports done quickly and correctly, knew all the word processing programs, and didn't mind working late.

Aware of what his schedule was going to be like, Vincent figured he could get a housekeeper to shop and do errands for him, so he'd kept Millicent on. In the months since, not once had she ever offered to bring him coffee.

"Vincent?" his secretary questioned, peering at him from behind her tortoise-frame glasses, none of the gray hair that she wore scraped back in a tight bun out of place.

"No, thank you, Millicent." Another thing about Dallas was that all the employees seemed to be on a first-name basis. Balancing the papers in his arm, he opened the door to his office. "You have five minutes."

"Thank you." Charlotte passed him in a flutter of white, the exotic scent of jasmine trailing softly behind her.

Need nipped him in a place he didn't want to think about. He'd let her have her say and then she was out of there.

Closing his door, he nodded his head in the direction of one of the matching navy blue leather seats in front of his massive desk. Then he rounded the desk and placed the papers on the corner. His hand settled on the back of his executive swivel chair and pulled it back. He glanced up before taking his seat and discovered Charlotte, her posture rigid, still standing.

He folded his arms, uncaring that the posture was confrontational and rude. She deserved no less. "You have five minutes," he reminded her.

Her chin came up. "My behavior last night was reprehensible. There is no excuse for it and I apologize. I set out to provoke you initially, but the last incident was totally unplanned and embarrassing for both of us. I hope we can put the incident behind us for Emma and Brian's sake."

He studied her a long time. The stunning face and clenched fists. She didn't want to be here. They were even. He didn't want her here either. He'd rather keep his very low opinion of her. It was easier and safer.

He didn't have to think back to remember the hot stab of lust that touching her breast had caused or her wide-eyed stare of embarrassment. Faked, of course. But one thing he was sure of was that the imprint of her nipple pressing against her dress afterward hadn't been there before. The last thing he wanted to be aware of was that she was aware of him.

"Why would you want to provoke me?" His voice gave no quarter and usually sent those under him scurrying to get out of his way.

Charlotte's small chin inched higher. "Because you acted as if I was a contaminant, and I foolishly tried to get back at you."

Unfolding his arms, Vincent placed his hands palm down on his desk and stared across it at the woman who stirred something not quite tame in him despite his best efforts. Reluctantly he had to admire her courage. Not many people stood up to him. "Is that how you usually react when someone doesn't like you?"

The question was deliberately provoking. "No."

He kept his gaze steady. To let it wander was dangerous. The white dress draped seductively over her voluptuous body. Whoever thought white was virginal hadn't seen Charlotte in that dress that fluttered, whispered, beckoned with each graceful movement. "Then why me?"

For the first time she seemed to lose her cool and bit her lip. Something he'd very much like to do for her. He tried to look sterner, but it was difficult with this heat coursing through his veins.

"Poor judgment on my part."

Vincent straightened. If Brian was correct, poor judgment was not a characteristic people associated with Charlotte. So there had to be another reason.

There was a brief knock on his office door. There was only one person in the company who Millicent would allow to disturb him. Vincent rounded his desk. "Come in."

The words were barely out of his mouth before the door opened and the CEO of Ora-Tech and his boss, Sidney Hughes, entered. Hughes wore his sixty years well. Despite the ups and downs of the oil industry, his silver hair was as thick as it had been thirty years ago. His shoulders were arrow-straight beneath his crisp, pointed-collar white shirt. The shirt was open at the throat, the sleeves rolled up to reveal a thick gold watch on one tanned wrist.

In contrast, Vincent's blue-and-white–striped cotton shirt was buttoned, his woven silk weave tie with discreet flower motif in periwinkle was knotted precisely, his sterling silver cuff links fastened securely in the French cuffs. Beneath his gray, pinstriped double-breasted jacket were silk braces. Dressing was the one area Vincent had no intention of altering.

"Hello, Sidney."

"Hello, Vincent," Hughes greeted in his Arkansas twang. His gaze had already shifted to the woman standing just behind Vincent.

It figured, Vincent thought in rising irritation. Charlotte attracted men like a steel magnet drew metal shavings. Any man who was interested in her would always have to worry. "Charlotte Duvall, please meet Sidney Hughes."

Hughes was already reaching out his large manicured hands and smiling. "No need for the introduction, Charlotte and I are old friends." He gently squeezed her soft hands in his. "It's nice seeing you again."

"Hello, Mr. Hughes, nice to see you too," Charlotte said. "How's Mrs. Hughes?"

"Helen is bursting with happiness. That dealer in Europe finally located that antique Chippendale table and chairs she wanted."

"I love antiques! Especially Chippendale. The rich carving is bold and energetic, yet beautiful," Charlotte said.

"You said it. I warned Helen that the housekeeper might quit when she saw the chairs and table with all that fancy carving, but they trade off days dusting." Sidney shook his head in obvious puzzlement. "In any case, we're having all of the executives of the firm and their spouses over tomorrow so she can show them off."

Charlotte twisted her head to one side. The gold hoops in her ears glittered in the afternoon sun. "And you just adore her and enjoy giving her what makes her happy."

"She keeps life interesting," Hughes said, his green eyes twinkling. He looked at Vincent. "I didn't mean to interrupt."

"You didn't," Vincent reassured his boss. "Charlotte and I were finished."

Sidney's keen, intelligent eyes went from one to the other. "I didn't know you two knew each other."

"We just met last night. His cousin is marrying one of my dear friends. I'm the maid of honor and Vincent is the best man," Charlotte explained, aware that Vincent had just given her her walking papers. She might have known that the first time he said her name he'd have his nose out of joint.

"Helen can't wait for the day our children decide to settle down." Sidney shook his head. "I just got off the phone with her and promised I'd remind Vincent in person about tomorrow night. The last time, he got there when everybody was about to leave. Almost missed out on the barbecue."

"I'll be there and on time." That night he'd been caught up in finishing an analysis and lost track of time. He didn't plan for that to happen again. In the business world, socializing was a necessary part of the climb. Vincent considered it a necessary evil.

"You said that before." Sidney rubbed his chin thoughtfully and stared at his newest executive. "You still dateless?"

"Yes," Vincent answered slowly, hoping Sidney wasn't about to do what he thought he was.

"Well, then I have the perfect solution to ensure you get there." The older man smiled and turned to Charlotte. "Why don't you come with Vincent? Helen would love to see you and show off her latest acquisition."

"I'm sure she has other plans," Vincent quickly interjected. He could see why they called Sidney the Silver Fox. He had left Arkansas with nothing and had amassed a fortune in the oil industry with brain, grit, and ingenuity.

"I do have plans," Charlotte said dutifully, not meeting Vincent's gaze.

Hughes' shrewd eyes narrowed on Charlotte. "There's going to be a lot of people there. Some of them you may not have met. Fertile ground, Charlotte. Might be able to get a few donations. You know the political coffer could always use money and the excitement of new blood."

Charlotte didn't have to think long. People working in the political arena often became discouraged and fell by the wayside. If there was a chance to benefit the party, she couldn't turn her back on it. Vincent might be upset, but business was business. "I can be there later, if that's all right."

Hughes' green eyes sparkled with triumph. "We'll see you when we see you."

"Until tomorrow night, then. I won't keep you from business." Bracing herself, she turned to Vincent and almost sighed. Did he ever smile? His black eyes didn't look too happy behind his silver-rimmed glasses. "Thank you for seeing me. Good-bye."

"Good-bye."

"Good-bye, Mr. Hughes. I'll see you Saturday night."

"I'll call Helen when I get back to my office and give her the good news."

Charlotte stole another look at Vincent and caught him scowling at her. She offered him an apologetic smile. His expression didn't change.

Sighing, she walked from the office, aware that Vincent watched her with disapproval. Stopping briefly at Millicent's desk, she found out the affair was formal. Helen Hughes intended to show her eighteenth-century table and chairs off to their best advantage. Waving good-bye to Millicent, Charlotte headed for the elevator, her mind going back to Vincent.

Despite the hard gaze and occasional dark look from behind his glasses, Charlotte couldn't help but notice his handsome face and the lean, rugged body in beautifully tailored clothes. Vincent was one fine brother.

He was also trouble.

Impatient and somewhat annoyed with herself, she jabbed the elevator button. She didn't like the thoughts going around in her head or the answer to Vincent's question of why she had reacted to him the way she had. Leave it to a Yankee to cause a Southerner grief.

———

Saturday night Charlotte was typing on the computer and talking on the phone headset with the campaign manager for their party's candidate for city council when the red light by her keyboard began to flash. The doorbell.

Not for the first time did she experience mixed feelings about having the electrician install a signal light for the front doorbell. But she had a habit of tuning everything out when she was working on a project and had missed several important deliveries.

Not that there had been a chance of that happening yesterday or today. No matter how hard she tried, her mind kept straying. She knew the reason and it irritated her all the more because she knew *he* wasn't thinking about her.

She was in the middle of ten things as usual, but unlike usual she wasn't doing any of them well. Ending the phone conversation, she pulled off the headset and saved the list of possible donors to a fund-raiser for Senator William Upshaw.

The clock on the computer read 7:15. By eight-thirty she could probably get dressed and go to the Hugheses' party. She'd get there by nine-thirty, spend an hour socializing, then slip out. She didn't want to impose on Vincent's territory any more than necessary, but she had a duty to her party.

The doorbell rang just as she stepped onto the cool sandstone marble tile in the wide foyer. "Coming. Keep your shirt on."

Throwing the two dead bolts, she yanked the door open. "What is—" That was as far as she got. On her porch, in a tuxedo that sculpted his wide shoulders and long muscled legs perfectly, was the man who had distracted her all day.

She snapped her mouth shut. "Why aren't you at the Hugheses' party?"

"Because Helen and Sidney think the only way to get us both there is if we come together." His gaze unhurriedly tracked her from her mussed hair, white oversize blouse, black stretch pants and stopped at her bare feet. Her toenails were painted the same electrifying, eye-popping red as her fingernails gripping the door.

He lifted his head. "It seems she was right."

Charlotte's toes curled on the cool floor and she wished she had her heels on. It was a distinct advantage craning your neck back to stare up at a man who easily topped six feet when you wanted to stare down your nose imperiously at him. "I have never missed an engagement and not called to cancel."

"Helen asked me to stop by to pick you up to make sure. She said she had called twice and your line was busy." He slid his hand into the pockets of his black pants. "It seems you don't have call waiting."

The way he said it made it seem like an accusation. "I do on my personal line, not on my business line. A person who calls me has my undivided attention." Why did the handsome ones always have to have something wrong with them? Vincent was too rigid and too judgmental.

The phone rang. The perfect excuse. "If you'll excuse me, I need to answer that. Good night. I'll let Helen know you dropped by." She started to close the door, but his hand stopped her.

"I think you better answer that first."

"The machine will get it."

"It might be Helen."

"I'll call her back once you leave."

"You're missing the point." Vincent frowned down at Charlotte with open impatience. "She wants you there tonight. She's as determined in her own way as Sidney is when he wants something. She says you liven up a party and Mary Lou wanted you there. I'm to bring you."

Charlotte's hazel eyes widened. "Mary Lou is back from the spa?"

"Isn't that what I just said?"

Charlotte thought of giving Vincent a look that would set him back on his polished heels, but the prospect of seeing Mary Lou was too delightful. Mary Lou was Sidney's eighty-nine-year-old mother. She was a hoot and a half. Mary Lou Carlaise from Pine Bluff, Arkansas, was a diamond in the rough and a very free spirit. "Why didn't you say so earlier?

I wouldn't miss it." She started to close the door again. Again, Vincent's hand stopped her.

"You've delivered your message," she said pointedly.

His black eyes narrowed. Charlotte could almost hear his teeth grind. "As I said, I'm to escort you."

Her eyebrow went up. "Sugar, since when did vice-presidents begin to double as escorts?"

"Since now, so just get dressed and we can leave."

Folding her arms, she stared up at him. "I don't take orders very well."

"Sidney said to remind you of the fertile ground."

He'd slipped that in nicely. Charlotte could almost admire him if he didn't irritate her. "I don't need you to take me."

"I never said you did." Vincent looked at the gold watch on his wrist. "I don't like being late, please get dressed so we can leave."

"Sugar, you must be hard of hearing, because I'm not going anyplace with you."

The scowl Charlotte expected didn't materialize. "Correct me if I'm wrong, but weren't you the one who came to my office yesterday offering words of apology? Was that just talk or did you want us to be friends?"

Charlotte gazed into the black eyes watching her and felt an unmistakable tug in the region of her heart. She honestly didn't know what she wanted them to be. "I'm sure you must be a busy man."

"That didn't seem to stop you from coming to my office and getting Millicent to let you stay so you could see me."

He had her there. What the heck? "It'll take thirty minutes for me to shower and get dressed."

"I was prepared to wait forty-five." He lifted a laptop.

Charlotte burst out laughing, then stepped aside. Perhaps there was hope for Vincent to lighten up after all. "Come on in and make yourself at home. Would you like something to drink?"

"No, thanks."

"The kitchen is this way. You can set up on the dinette table." She led him through the living room of comfortable overstuffed chairs, crystal, and fresh floral arrangements. "I'd hate to see you hunched over and getting a crook in your neck."

"I'll bet."

Since he had said the words without his usual sarcasm, Charlotte let them ride. "If you change your mind about something to drink there's an assortment in the refrigerator. Glasses are in the cabinet next to it."

"I'll be fine."

"Somehow I don't doubt that. I'll call Helen and tell her we're coming." She turned away and went to get dressed.

Vincent placed the carrying case on the round glass dining table, took out the laptop, and booted it up. He didn't get much further. It was difficult to work with abstract facts and figures when he was visualizing a very full dimensional figure getting dressed.

He slipped the single button free on his tuxedo and worked his shoulders. He wished she hadn't mentioned the part about taking a shower. The other night at the restaurant he might have thought she had done it on purpose, but now he wasn't so sure. Sidney was no fool; neither was his wife—or his secretary, for that matter. A woman of loose morals would not be accepted in any of their lives.

Leaning back in the chair, he glanced around the neat celery green and creamy oyster kitchen, then into the living room that carried out the same color scheme. The house was warm and inviting. The kind that you feel comfortable in taking off your shoes and kicking back. There was nothing showy or loud.

He'd been in enough homes to know that money couldn't buy taste. There were even a couple of antique pieces of furniture, including a Queen Anne corner chair and a Hepplewhite demilune table mixed with art by Arthello Beck, Jr., and Carole Joyce. And the style worked.

She hadn't been blowing smoke when she'd said she loved antiques. Oftentimes people trying to impress you said what they thought you wanted to hear or things to ingratiate themselves or to show how intelligent they were. He was forced to admit that apparently Charlotte did none of those things.

Who was the real Charlotte Duvall?

Rubbing the back of his neck, Vincent went back to the laptop, determined to complete the financial data for the benefits programs. If there was a way to reduce costs and still give the employees excellent coverage, it would be done. If not he'd look elsewhere. A company was only as good as its employees. He wouldn't jeopardize their health.

"Thirty-seven minutes."

Vincent looked up and was suddenly glad he was sitting down. The lady packed a wallop.

She wore a long, strapless black dress that fit over her lush breasts. Her hair was pulled back, silhouetting her beautiful face. Her lips, lush and inviting, were painted the same eye-catching red as he'd seen earlier on her nails. Long black gloves that reached almost to her shoulder completed the outfit.

She was elegant and alluring—and trouble.

Vincent did the only thing he thought safe. He turned back to the laptop and concentrated on shutting it down instead of gawking at the striking woman a few feet from him. Placing the laptop back in the case, he stood, picked it up, and finally turned to Charlotte.

"Do you need a wrap?"

Her smile wavered for a split second. "In the living room."

"Shall we go?" He walked toward her, but was careful not to touch.

"Certainly, we don't want to be late." Swirling, she went to the sofa in the living room and picked up her purse and a black silk chiffon scarf.

Vincent followed, his eyes somehow straying to the easy sway of her hips. Charlotte Duvall, as he had thought, definitely looked as tempting going as she did coming.

The smooth voice of Ella Fitzgerald filled the silence in the car as Vincent drove to Sidney and Helen's home. Charlotte, usually a brilliant conversationalist, could think of nothing to say. From the overhead lights on the freeway, she snuck peeks at Vincent. She came to the same conclusion she had when she first saw him: He was a handsome brown-skinned devil. And after so many men had tried to get her attention, it rankled a bit that he didn't seem to notice her ...

There it was, she thought, finally admitting the reason for her inexcusable behavior at the restaurant. She hadn't liked being judged and dismissed by a man she found attractive. She could blame it on melancholy from Emma's impending wedding or blame it on what it was, a lapse in common sense. Vincent got to her. Of all men, why did her body have to pick a stuffed shirt? She sighed in frustration.

"You all right?"

"Yes," she quickly told him, and searched her mind for something to say to keep the conversation going.

He nodded and returned his attention to the busy traffic on Central Expressway. He drove competently and smoothly.

"You drive well," she said.

He cut his gaze to her again and Charlotte could have banged her head against the padded dash. Of course he drove well. He was from Boston. He'd have learned to drive in heavy traffic, snow, and ice. Dallas hadn't seen any appreciable snow in the five years she'd been here, and only one small ice storm that had all melted by the next afternoon. They didn't even close the public schools, much to Emma's students' dismay. Even with the infamous crazy motorists on the expressways, this was a cakewalk for him.

"Thanks," he finally said.

Charlotte had never considered herself a quitter. "We've already discussed the weather."

This time she got a small smile from him. "Yes, we have.

You probably know more than you ever want to know about me, but what about you?"

"Youngest of four daughters from Charleston. Mother was a schoolteacher who quit to have my oldest sister, Ondine. Mama went back when school started in the fall. Since Ondine was late, as she always is, she was only six weeks old. Mama cried so hard at work, my father had to go pick her up. Daddy, a Realtor, took the opportunity to turn the garage into an office and open his own business. Mother became his secretary." Charlotte twisted toward Vincent as far as the seat belt would allow and smiled at the retelling of the story.

"Turns out it was the best thing that could have happened to the Duvall family. Daddy, as they say, can sell snowshoes in hell. But he's the most honest, loving man I know. By the time my third sister arrived, Daddy had an office and a secretary with two other Realtors."

Vincent hit the signal indicator and exited the expressway onto Loop 12. "My kind of man. How did you get into politics?"

"My cousin Jeb, my mother's youngest sister's oldest son, ran for city councilman in Charleston, and we all pitched in to help. I was a senior in high school. It was fun, and I found I had a knack for selling too, but what I sold could make the world a better place for people to live. So I majored in political science."

Vincent pulled up in front of a three-story mansion. Light blazed from every window. A valet dressed in a white polo shirt and dark slacks rushed to open his door. "I take it Jeb won."

"By a landslide."

Grinning at each other, they got out of the car.

A butler opened the heavily carved front door. Almost as soon as Vincent and Charlotte stepped onto the three-story foyer with limestone and marble flooring, Sidney was there to greet them. By his side was an elderly woman with coal black hair who was even more petite than Charlotte. She was dressed in a sequined red gown. Diamonds and blood-red rubies encircled her throat, wrists, and hung in shimmering color from her ears.

" 'Bout time you got here!" she said by way of greeting.

Charlotte grinned and enveloped the small woman in a gentle hug. "Mary Lou, it's good to have you back. The spa must have been wonderful. You look sensational."

Mary Lou waved a hand. A ten-carat diamond winked. "I'm going to live until the day I die."

"Which will be a long, long time," Charlotte said, then glanced over her shoulder. "Have you met Vincent Maxwell yet?"

Sidney's mother held out her hand. "How do you do, Mr. Maxwell. Welcome to my son's home."

Vincent took the offered hand and held it as gently as he had seen Charlotte do. "Thank you. It's a pleasure." Releasing Mary Lou's hand, he leaned down to her. "Charlotte hadn't planned to come, but once she heard your name she couldn't wait to get here. I can see why."

Pleased, Mary Lou fluttered her lashes again. "Well, Sidney, it looks like you've finally found a live one. What do you do, Mr. Maxwell?"

"Please, call me Vincent." He looked at Sidney before continuing. "Your son has given me the privilege of being Vice-President of Finance, in charge of reorganizing the financial structure of Ore-Tech, among other things."

"A number cruncher." The way Mary Lou said it wasn't a compliment.

Vincent surprised Charlotte by smiling. "Someone has to see that the lights stay on."

Shrewd gray eyes stared up at him. "I bet you do it very well, don't you?"

"I do try, Mrs. Hughes."

"Call me Mary Lou." She took his arm and looped her other hand through the curve of Charlotte's arm. "You've already met the rest of the guests. Charlotte can meet them before we go in to dinner. I'm dying to tell her about the young masseur I met in Hot Springs who wanted to be my boy toy."

Sidney's mouth gaped. Mary Lou turned away and missed the indulgent smile that followed.

"You think I shocked him, Charlotte?" Mary Lou asked, her steps slow on the gleaming hardwood floor as she led them to a window seat covered in a fresh spring blue and cream plaid fabric near the stone fireplace in the living room. The other guests were enjoying before-dinner drinks on the terrace.

"Definitely," Charlotte assured. "Vincent even has his mouth open," she teased.

Mary Lou squinted at Vincent. She refused to wear her glasses and didn't trust contacts. "Must have closed it."

Vincent laughed, a rich joyful sound that curled through Charlotte and warmed her like mulled wine. Her heart thumped in her chest. *Easy, girl.*

"I like you, Vincent." Mary Lou sat on the seat. Charlotte pushed one of several tapestry footstools scattered through the room under Mary Lou's small feet. "You won't be disappointed if I didn't have a shocking story to tell, will you?"

"I'll survive."

"Good. Now, Charlotte, what's going on with the party and what can I do to help?"

Charlotte told her. Check donations from companies might be illegal, but not from relatives of people who owned the company. Mary Lou had wisely let her son reinvest her money in his company and subsequently she was worth millions.

Fifteen minutes later, Helen announced dinner, beaming proudly as the guests got their first look at her mint-condition eighteenth-century Chippendale dining table and chairs. The lavish dining room offered a beautiful view of the lighted outdoor pool and gardens beyond. The table, set with Baccarat crystal and heirloom china, sparkled as much as Helen in her silver gown. Sidney was visibly pleased and proud.

Dinner was scrumptious. And although Charlotte hadn't gotten a chance to search out potential donors, she was enjoying the evening. Vincent, sitting to her left, was a good conversationalist and not once had she felt he disapproved of her in some way.

They were almost through with dessert, a marvelous chocolate mousse that Charlotte knew she'd have to work on her StairMaster to get off her hips, when tranquility screeched to a halt. Across from her, Ashley Green, the assistant vice-president of marketing services for strategic accounts, turned green, slapped her hand over her mouth, and rushed out of the room. Her husband ran after her.

Charlotte was already pushing back her seat. Vincent and the other men stood as she did. "I'll go see if I can help."

"Thank you," Helen said, but Charlotte had already turned away.

Charlotte found the couple in the powder room off the hallway near the kitchen. Ashley's full-skirted lavender-colored taffeta gown was billowed around her. Beside her on his knees as well was her husband, holding her long auburn hair out of her face and harm's way with one hand and the other around her waist. He looked almost as pale as she did.

Charlotte wet one of the thick hand towels on the black marble vanity and knelt beside them to press the cool cloth to the woman's face in between her bouts of illness. Mutely, her husband offered his thanks.

Soon there were only dry heaves from Ashley. Still on her knees, she leaned weakly into her husband's arms. Tears coursed down her pale cheeks.

"Please don't cry," Charlotte soothed.

Tears fell faster. "I'm so sorry, Anthony."

"Shhh, you and the baby are what counts," he consoled.

"But this position is what I've worked for. I've only been assistant vice-president for a year." Ashley shook her auburn head in despair. "This shouldn't have happened. We just bought the new house—"

"It doesn't matter," he interrupted, brushing his lips tenderly against her forehead. "Things will work out."

Charlotte felt as if she were intruding on a very private moment. She pushed to her feet and stepped away from the couple. "Shall I tell the valet to bring your car around?"

"Thank you," Anthony said.

Ashley's weak voice stopped Charlotte when she was almost out the door. "Charlotte?"

She turned. "Yes?"

"Please don't tell anyone."

"Honey, they'll have to know sooner or later."

"Please," she repeated, her pleading gaze on Charlotte.

Another woman trying to break through the glass ceiling and having a rough time. "I won't."

To Ashley's obvious embarrassment, everyone came out to the car to see her off. She mumbled apologies about something she ate for lunch, then ducked her head. Her husband said nothing, but his tight lips told the story. He wasn't too pleased with his wife's not telling them she was pregnant. When they walked back inside, one of the wives mentioned that Ashley had been sick at the barbecue two weeks ago as well.

"Would anyone care for coffee?" Mary Lou asked.

"I'd love a cup," Charlotte said, catching a thankful look from Helen.

However, as the evening progressed, Charlotte sensed by the preoccupied look on the other guests' faces, and their hosts', that they were all thinking of the possible reason for Ashley's illness and coming to the same conclusion. These men were shrewd and observant. Ashley's attempt to conceal her pregnancy had probably been futile. She was only fooling herself.

Charlotte knew she was right when Sara, the wife of the vice-president of human resources, whispered, "I think she's pregnant."

Charlotte didn't have to ask why the middle-aged woman was whispering. The men were in the game room shooting billiards. Mary Lou, spotted ten points, was partnered with Vincent. Helen had gone in to see if they needed anything. The women in the enclosed terrace amid tropical plants that reached the apex of the twenty-five-foot ceiling nodded in agreement.

"Poor thing." This from Nancy, wife of the president of

business markets. She was in her mid-thirties and her balding husband looked to be in his early sixties. He seemed to be as taken with her as she was with herself.

"You make it sound as if it's the worst thing that could happen to her," Charlotte said, aware that she was the outsider here, but that had never stopped her from speaking her mind in the past.

"They live off Ashley's salary. Anthony has been trying to make a profit from that bookstore of his for years." Nancy Brisby fingered her blond hair behind her ear. The diamond in her ear was as big as a dime. "She could have done better."

Charlotte clamped down on her lower lip to keep her thoughts behind her teeth. *So could your husband.*

Sara threw Nancy an annoyed look, but the other woman was gazing in a jeweled compact mirror, putting on an unnecessary layer of plum-colored lipstick, and didn't notice. "Ashley has another child, David, the cutest three-year-old you'd ever want to see. Her husband didn't like her going back to work when David was six weeks old, but they adjusted because Ashley has always aimed to shatter the glass ceiling and thought being out longer might jeopardize her job," Sara explained.

"So, they'll adjust again," Charlotte said, but Sara and the other women looked doubtful. Remembering Ashley's words in the bathroom, Charlotte was afraid the women might be right.

They heard the clicking of Helen's heels on the hardwood flooring and Sara launched into the latest rebellious act of her thirteen-year-old: wanting to get her eyebrow pierced. Everyone laughed as the women traded stories on the trials and tribulations of parenthood, but from their smiling, proud faces none of them would change a thing.

"None of you work outside the home?" Charlotte asked, although she was reasonably sure of the answer.

They all shook their heads of perfectly coiffed hair. Their reasons were varied, but mainly it was because of the husband's job. By the nature of their man's position, they entertained a great deal, and then there were the children. There were just so many hours in a day to get things done.

Charlotte thought it was rather sad that two of the women had given up their own promising careers to be at the beck and call of their busy husbands. Although they were quick to point out they hadn't minded, Charlotte wasn't so sure.

It had been her father's suggestion but her mother's *decision* after Ondine was born to stay home. No man was going to dictate to Charlotte that she *had* to give up her career to stay at home with the children unless that was what *she* wanted.

As the conversation progressed it became abundantly clear that, though the women might empathize with Ashley, not one of them could truly understand why she just didn't chuck it all and go home to raise David and his future little brother or sister. Charlotte thought it was more than money. None of them seemed to understand that you might give up on a dream quietly, but if someone tried to take it away, you'd fight with everything to stop them.

With the exception of Ashley becoming ill, Vincent had had a surprisingly enjoyable evening. Charlotte had blended in well with the women. She had certainly been a hit with the men. Even Paul Brisby, who had recently married a much younger woman, couldn't seem to keep his eyes off Charlotte.

Men noticed Charlotte. Any man who married her would always have to wonder and worry about her, but that wasn't his problem. For him, life was good. He was settling in nicely at the firm, and he and Sidney got along well. And it appeared he was liked by Mary Lou as well. Vincent shook his dark head and chuckled.

"What?" Charlotte asked, surprised by the sudden sound of Vincent's laughter and the jittery feeling it sent through her nervous system.

"Sidney's mother is a hustler. She no more needed to be spotted ten points than the Black Widow."

"Black Widow?"

"The moniker of women's world billiard champion Jennifer Chen," he answered, then maneuvered around an SUV on the five-lane Central Expressway. "It's a good thing we weren't playing for money."

Charlotte's lips curved upward. "She likes to tease."

"She likes you. You took up a lot of time with her tonight."

"She's fun; besides, elderly people are revered in the South. And if they're a little unorthodox like Mary Lou, they give the family character and color." Charlotte chuckled. "We don't hide our relatives who are different; we enjoy and appreciate them."

"So I noticed." Vincent's friends and associates would have been horrified to have their elderly mother flirting with their business associates, then hustling them at pool. "Nothing Mary Lou did seemed to embarrass or annoy Sidney."

"Did it embarrass or annoy you?"

Vincent thought he heard a bit of censure in Charlotte's voice. A quick glance told him he wasn't mistaken. Her hazel eyes glinted. "No. As you said, she livened things up." He paused. "It was nice of you to check on Ashley." At the time he had been surprised that none of the other women who had known Ashley longer had gone to help.

"Anyone would have done the same," Charlotte said simply.

Vincent wasn't so sure. Deep in thought, he turned onto Charlotte's tree-lined street. "Ashley is top-notch at what she does. It would be a shame to lose her."

"Why would you lose her?"

Vincent favored Charlotte with a look that intelligent people bestowed on those with less than two brain cells to rub together. "The company is going through a transitional phase. We need every key person at the top of their game."

"You heard her; it was something she ate. She'll be better tomorrow." Charlotte hoped she was right. Ashley had looked so desperate.

"She's been late every day this week, and twice I've been trying to work on a report with her and she had to rush to the ladies' room," Vincent said. "Doesn't sound like it's something she ate that's the problem."

Poor Ashley, Charlotte thought. *Everyone knows.*

"She's lucky she's advanced this far. Maybe it's time she stayed home. Her little boy must miss her terribly."

"I'm sure she makes up for the time spent away from him and her husband when she's home."

"Time lost can never be regained," he said pragmatically.

"Women can work and take care of their families."

Vincent was shaking his head before Charlotte finished. "A woman's place is in the home. Women trying to prove they're as good as men in the workplace is what's contributing to the breakdown of the family."

Charlotte almost bit her tongue off trying to remain calm before speaking. "Then you believe a woman should stay at home and have a gourmet meal and well-behaved children waiting for her husband when he gets home."

"Exactly."

"Bull!"

Vincent's head whipped around so fast Charlotte thought he might get whiplash. It would serve him right for his antiquated way of thinking. "Women have just as much right to a career as men," Charlotte pointed out fiercely. "What's wrong with a man cooking a meal or changing a diaper? This isn't the Stone Age where the woman stays home to birth and raise the kids and the big, strong man protects them and drags home T. Rex's hindquarter to roast over a spit."

"Men are supposed to care for the women and the home. My mother never worked. Yours didn't after your sister was born, and neither will my wife," Vincent said heatedly.

"With that attitude you probably won't get one."

His mouth tightened. "I'm not looking for one."

"That's good, because no woman in her right mind would have a husband as antiquated and stuffy as you." Folding her arms, she turned to look at the window. *Opinionated sexist.*

She remained in their position until Vincent's car stopped in the circular driveway in front of her double doors. Charlotte didn't wait for him to open her car door. By the time he caught up with her, she was halfway up the steps.

Opening the front door, she turned, her body rigid with

indignation. "Good night, Vincent, and thank you for picking me up."

"You've never met Ashley before tonight; why are you being so difficult?"

"Injustice is injustice. I don't have to know the person," she flared. "But I guess coming from the North, you wouldn't understand."

His mouth had that pinched look again, but all he said was, "I think you should go inside before one of us says something that can't be taken back."

Her chin lifted at his annoying way of ordering her around. Light brown eyes narrowed. "Sure thing, sugar." Going inside, she flicked off the porch light and threw the dead bolts, angrier than she ever remembered being in her life. Stripping off her gloves, she headed for her bedroom. She reached the doorway and pulled up short, a sudden thought of Emma and Brian, and why she'd been trying to be nice to Vincent in the first place, coming to her.

Heck! She had done it again.

Whirling, she raced to unlock the front door, then rushed through it and straight into something hard and unmovable. A scream tore from her throat.

"Charlotte, it's me."

While her heart tried to beat out of her chest, she felt the alignment of his hard, muscular body against her, his large hands on her bare arms. Her heart then raced for an entirely different reason. Awareness shimmered though her. "I–I was afraid you'd already left."

"I was waiting until the light came on at the other end of the house."

"Oh," was all Charlotte could manage as fear turned to other more dangerous emotions.

Vincent made no move to release her. Her luscious breasts were pillowed against his chest, one of her legs sandwiched between his. Her face, tipped up to his, was shadowed by the ornamental shrubs on either side of the small porch. Someone had watered the grass recently and the smell was earthy and elemental and oddly arousing.

"You make me angrier than any person I've ever met," he finally said.

She had to moisten her lips before she could speak. "You seem to have the same effect on me."

"Why do you suppose that is?"

"You're from the North and I'm from the South?" she ventured, trying to hang on to the conversation and not keep wondering what his mouth would taste like against hers.

"Perhaps." His hand lifted to her face. She trembled beneath his touch. Her eyelids drifted closed. Vincent stared at temptation and trouble. He could afford neither. Gently he eased her away. When her eyes opened, he released her and stepped off the porch, and took a deep breath, hoping it would clear the tantalizing scent of jasmine and the wrong woman from his nostrils, from his mind.

"Was there something you wanted to say?" he asked quietly, trying to forget how warm and soft Charlotte had felt in his arms.

"I–I wanted to apologize." She couldn't see his face clearly, but she imagined his eyebrow shot up. She sighed heavily. "For Emma and Brian's sake, I hope this is the last time."

"One can always hope."

Charlotte tried not to sigh again. "One of the women tonight had some unflattering things to say about Ashley and it made me angry. I didn't say anything to her, then I jumped all over you."

He folded his arms. "Why me and not her?"

"Because I didn't want to jeopardize your standings in the company, but when we began talking about women in the workplace I got upset all over again," she explained. "You are wrong, you know."

"Never bite your tongue for me," Vincent told her. "I can take care of myself and furthermore, I'm not against women in the workplace, only those in positions that require them to be away from home more than they are there."

"Please stop." She held up both hands. "We'll be arguing again, and I'll have to apologize again."

Smiling, he unfolded his arms. "I guess we agree that we disagree and let it go at that."

"Deal."

"How long do you think this time will last?"

"Depends on how long it takes you to annoy me," she said with complete honesty.

Sudden laughter rippled from his mouth. "Charlotte, as Mary Lou said, you do liven things up."

"I'm glad we got this settled," she said.

"So am I."

She stared at him; he stared at her. "Well, I guess I'll say good night."

"Good night, Charlotte."

Charlotte hesitated for a moment longer, then went inside the house and locked the front door. Then, remembering what Vincent had said, she went to her bedroom and turned on the light. She didn't hear the sound of his car starting and wondered if he had gone, just as she wondered why he hadn't kissed her, and if the opportunity would present itself again.

Plopping on her bed, she stared up into the ceiling, a slow smile curving her lips. She certainly hoped so.

4

She was all that he desired, all that he wanted. She responded eagerly to the lightest touch of his hands, the gentlest brush of his lips. He'd fantasized, planned, and now she was in his arms, draped only in moonlight. Her breathing was as ragged as his, her need as great. He'd give them the release they both craved, but not yet. He wanted to savor the taste, the textures, the scent that was uniquely hers.

"I need you," she said, her voice low, hushed, urgent.

"I need you too," he answered, his voice tight and guttural. He reveled in the demanding nails raking his back.

"Vincent, is that you?"

Vincent came awake instantly. He stared at the phone

clutched in his fist as if he had never seen one. Groaning in part embarrassment, part disappointment, he sucked in a gulp of air and spoke into the receiver. "Yes."

"I—I didn't mean to disturb you. If you're busy I can call back when you . . . er finish . . . I mean later."

Vincent closed his eyes, then opened them and stared down at the papers scattered on the desk in his home office in his condo. He'd fallen asleep while working on them. A rarity. His body didn't usually shut off until he allowed it to do so. Instinctively he'd answered the phone while still asleep. And dreaming, a very erotic dream.

"Vincent, should I call back later?"

His eyes opened at the continued hesitancy in Charlotte's voice and realized what she must have thought when he answered the phone the way he had. His hand rubbed the back of his neck impatiently. She was the reason behind his loss of sleep for the past week. He kept dreaming that they were in bed together with nothing separating them but a thin sheen of perspiration after a marathon bout of hot sex just like tonight.

"Vincent?"

"I'm here." He took three long breaths, hoping to focus his mind elsewhere and forget about the problem below his waist. It didn't work. "What is it, Charlotte?"

They hadn't spoken or seen each other since he had dropped her off at her home last Saturday night.

"Brian and Emma had a fight. Brian is overdosing on coffee at a restaurant around the corner from her house, and Emma is probably crying her eyes out. We have to do something."

Vincent rubbed eyes burning and gritty from lack of sleep. "We?"

"You're the best man and I'm the maid of honor," she told him unnecessarily. "It's our duty to see them through any problems that may stop them from getting to the church on time and getting married."

"I'm not sure helping them over an argument qualifies." He glanced at the Seth Thomas clock on his desk. 2:15 A.M.

Just one night he'd like to get to bed before midnight.

"Anything qualifies. I should know."

"Meaning?" He waited for an answer, but none came. "You're still there?"

"I'm still here." Her voice had definitely taken on a weary note.

A frisson of unease went through Vincent. Had he been right about Brian being attracted to Charlotte? "Are you telling me everything? Why didn't Brian call me?"

"He didn't want to disturb you."

"Apparently you didn't feel the same way," he told her, feeling lighter despite the situation.

"I thought he meant paperwork. I didn't know he meant you'd have company."

Vincent was caught in a delicate dilemma. He could explain he was alone, but then he'd also have to explain why he'd answered the phone the way he did. "Never mind that. Where's Brian now?"

"At the Yellow Rose. It's off Interstate 20 and Westmoreland."

"I'll find it." Vincent came to his feet. "Go back to sleep. I'll call you in the morning."

There was a slight pause. "Thank you, Vincent, and I'm sorry about disturbing you." The line went dead.

Vincent rolled down his shirt sleeves, feeling inexplicably like a coward who had kicked a puppy.

Twenty-three minutes later, with the help of his car's navigation system, Vincent pulled up in front of the all-night restaurant. The neon sign of a single stemmed rose winked on and off. Several cars and trucks dotted the parking lot. One of them was Brian's Alfa Romero. Vincent had been hoping that his cousin had already gone home.

Getting out of the car, he activated the lock. His usual brisk steps slowed as he walked to the glass double front doors. He had no idea what he would say to Brian or if he should say anything at all. Perhaps this was for the best. Yet, somehow the obvious concern in Charlotte's voice had pulled him here as much as his love for his cousin.

Inside he scanned the Formica-topped tables looking for his cousin. A clean-shaven man in his mid-thirties with close-cropped black hair wearing a white shirt and black slacks came out from behind a glass casing filled with pies and rushed up to him. "Are you Vincent Maxwell?"

"Yes."

Relief clearly shone on the man's dark face. "Great. They're over here."

They. It appeared the lovers' tiff was over and Charlotte had gotten him here for nothing while she—

Charlotte glanced up, saw Vincent glaring at her, and her spirits plummeted even lower. They had been spiraling downhill ever since she'd called and he had a woman with him. At two in the morning, it wasn't hard to guess why.

She nudged Brian. "Vincent's here."

The young man's head came up and he stared at his cousin with misery in his brown eyes. "I don't know what to do."

Charlotte patted his lanky arm. "We'll think of something, won't we, Vincent?"

Vincent slid into the booth on the other side of Brian. "I thought you were home."

She shrugged elegant shoulders beneath a black shirt that clung to all the places Vincent had dreamed of touching. "Fred called me and here I am. But that's not important; we have to get Brian and Emma back together."

"She gave me back my ring." Brian's hand was clutched in a fist on top of the table beside a half-empty mug of coffee.

"Charlotte, can I see you for a moment?" Vincent didn't wait for an answer. He slid out of the booth and went to a corner table for two in the back of the nearly empty restaurant. Holding a chair for Charlotte, he waited while she sank onto the padded seat, then took his seat across from her, pushed his glasses up on his nose, and placed his folded hands on the table. "Explain to me why you're here?"

She started to say that wasn't of any consequence, but the stubborn set of Vincent's jaw told her she'd just be wasting her time. "Fred Bowers, the manager, is a good friend to all three of us. We go to the same church and are in the same singles group. After Brian had been here for an hour, refusing to go home, Fred called me. I called Emma, but her phone is off the hook. I got here about thirty minutes before I called you because Brian still refuses to go home. The rest you know."

"Any idea what caused the problem?"

Charlotte ran her hand through her hair. "None. Brian's not talking."

"Maybe her parents know." Vincent shook his head to the waitress who appeared. Charlotte did the same.

With a weary sigh, Charlotte leaned back against her seat. "If so, they probably won't help. Emma is an only child and adored by both parents. She's always led a sheltered, protected life. She went to school at a local university and still lives at home. Her parents made it no secret that they thought she was too young to get married and that she and Brian should wait a couple of years. Neither would object if the wedding were canceled. Especially her father."

"They *are* young," Vincent said, drumming his fingers on the table.

"But neither of them are impulsive or stupid. They love each other and what's more, they're good for each other." Arms braced on the table, she stared across at Vincent. "Except with her kindergarten class, Emma was painfully shy and had few friends. Brian introduced her to his many friends and she's helped him find the direction he needed in life. He's not just about having fun anymore, but doing something worthwhile with his life. He's mentoring at her school and has definite career goals."

"You've never had any of those doubts, worries, or hang-ups, have you?"

"No, I've been fortunate and very, very blessed," she answered, wondering where the conversation was going.

He stood. "Wait here and let me have a go at it."

"Thank you, Vincent." She bit her lower lip. "I'm sorry about disturbing you."

He stared down at her. She was beautiful, sensitive, and caring. He was coming to understand why Brian's opinion of her was so high. She'd never turn her back on a friend. Fred had known that, and Vincent finally knew it too. "I'm not."

Going back to the booth, he slid in beside his despondent cousin. Brian had his head bowed, his hands in his lap. Vincent had negotiated deals in the past and figured he'd treat this the same way he did when they hit a snag. Go for broke.

"You still love her?"

Brian nodded without lifting his head.

"Then are you going to sit here and mope all night or are you going to go back to her house and try to straighten out whatever it is that caused this?"

"She doesn't want to talk to me."

"Then just tell her to listen," Vincent said. "Negotiate. Find common ground. Your love for each other should be a good start. Apologize. Then kiss her until she gives in."

His cousin lifted his head and stared hard at Vincent.

"What?" Vincent asked, warily.

"I just never figured you had to spend time soothing women," Brian answered.

Vincent saw no reason to tell his cousin he was right. He simply didn't have time for that sort of thing. "Come on. I'll go back with you. At least, if her parents call the cops, I can post bail for you."

Vincent hadn't thought Charlotte would go home and let him and Brian go see Emma, but he had given it a good try. As he suspected, she'd adamantly refused. She could ride with him and Brian or follow in her car. His choice. Since Vincent worried about her being on the road by herself, he told her to get in the backseat and put Brian in the front.

In the end, Charlotte's presence was what saved Emma's father from calling the police and having Brian *and* Vincent arrested. Charlotte had one simple request of the irate man: Could he please see if Emma was asleep? If she was, they'd leave, but if she was still awake and as miserable as Brian, then please allow her to speak with him. Emma's happiness was what they all wanted.

Emma's father had closed the front door without commenting, but a short while later the door opened and Emma stood there in her stocking feet, her eyes red and lids swollen, her blue dress wrinkled, her shoulder-length light brown hair mussed.

Brian, took one look at the miserable picture she presented and said, "I'll die if you don't love me."

Emma turned into her waiting father's arms.

Brian's hand unclenched. The engagement ring fell from his fingers onto the sidewalk. His body wavered as if he might fall, then he turned and slowly walked back toward Vincent's car.

"Emma, if you let him get away instead of working out your problems, perhaps I was wrong about you," Charlotte said fiercely. "Perhaps you *are* too immature to know how to love a man. Running away never solved anything. Make sure this is what you want because you may not get a second chance. Once word gets out he's available, the single women in church will be all over him."

With fire in her eyes Emma whirled around. "Teresa already was."

"What?" The shocked word erupted from Vincent, Charlotte, and Emma's parents.

Midway down the sidewalk, Brian spun back around. "She came on to me at the movie theater and I told her to get lost. She saw you, and you played right into her spiteful hands."

"You were about to kiss her when I came out of the ladies' room," Emma accused, stepping away from her father in her righteous anger.

"No, I wasn't. I was trying to get her arms from around my neck. Why would I want to touch another woman, let alone kiss her, when I have you?" Brian said, coming forward until he was almost nose to nose with Emma. "I love you. Can't you get that through your stubborn head?"

Emma spluttered. "Don't you dare call me nam—" He jerked her into his arms, silencing her words with his lips.

"Take your hands off her!" Emma's father started toward them but Charlotte threw her arms around his neck. His wife grabbed him around the waist from behind. By the time he managed to untangle the arms of the determined women, Emma was clinging to Brian as desperately as he was clinging to her.

"He might make a go in labor relations after all," Vincent murmured with a pleased smile.

"He was fooling around with another woman!" Mr. Hamilton shouted.

Mrs. Hamilton touched his arm and quietly asked him, "Douglas, were you fooling around with Charlotte a moment ago?"

Much as his daughter had done earlier, he spluttered his outrage. "Melissa, you know darn well I wasn't. I was trying to get her arms from around. . . ." Understanding dawned. With one look at the embracing couple, he shook his head in obvious defeat and curved his arm around his wife's shoulder. "Looks like there's going to be a wedding after all."

"Don't you just hate it when women are right?" Vincent said with a grin. He looked at Brian and Emma still locked in each other's arms, the kiss showing no signs of ending, then thumped his cousin on the back. "There'll be enough time for that. Now, we need to find Emma's ring."

"Oh, my goodness!" Brian straightened, panic in his face.

"My ring!" Emma cried frantically, pressing the palms of her hands over her face.

"I'll get a flashlight." Emma's mother rushed back into the house.

"Oh, Daddy, we'll never find it!"

Her father lovingly patted her on the back. "Don't you worry, baby girl, we'll find your ring if we have to take up every blade of grass."

They didn't have to do that, but it did take fifteen minutes of searching on hands and knees, fingers combing through thick blades of St. Augustine grass that hadn't been cut in a week.

Vincent located the ring, stone down in the tiny crevice

between the grass and the edge of the sidewalk. "Found it."

With a cry of delight, Emma rushed over. Brian snatched the ring from Vincent's hand, gallantly went down on one knee, and slipped the ring on her finger. "I'll love you always."

"Brian, I'm so sorry," Emma said, tears in her voice and in her eyes. "I'll never doubt you or take my ring off again."

Vincent glanced at Charlotte and Emma's mother. Both were sniffing. He looked at Emma's father, who looked as perplexed and uncomfortable as he felt. He handed Charlotte his white monogrammed handkerchief with one hand, then, with the other, lifted Brian to his feet.

"Charlotte needs to get home and I doubt you want to tax the patience of your future in-laws any further. Good night, everyone."

Grinning, Brian allowed himself to be pulled away. "Thank you, Mr. and Mrs. Hamilton. Emma, I'll call you as soon as I get home."

She threw kisses and would have followed her fiancé to Vincent's car, but Charlotte caught her by her dress. "Brian lives twenty minutes from here. That'll give you just enough time to pick out a sensational outfit for church tomorrow, roll up your hair, then put some cucumber slices on your eyes. You don't want to give that shameless Teresa any reason to think her plan might have worked, do you?"

Emma turned to Charlotte. "It almost did."

Charlotte smiled. "Almost doesn't count."

"Thank you and Vincent for caring." Emma gave her a hug. "I couldn't have chosen a more perfect maid of honor."

Loneliness hit Charlotte again. Always a maid of honor and never a bride. Somehow she managed to smile, then rushed to Vincent's car and got into the backseat trying not to think of the empty house waiting for her.

When Vincent pulled up behind Charlotte's white Lexus in the circular driveway it was almost four in the morning. He met her on the sidewalk as she dug into her oversized black purse. "What are you looking for?"

"My house keys."

"They aren't on your key ring?" He frowned as she continued to rummage through her bag.

Shaking her head, she never looked up. "Too easy for some unscrupulous person in valet or the auto shop to make a duplicate. Here it is." Lifting the key, she opened the door and turned. "Well, good night and thanks again."

"You don't have an alarm system?" he questioned. From down the street came the barking of a dog.

She made a face and pushed her curly auburn hair behind her ear. "Yes, but I forgot to activate it when I left tonight."

"It wasn't on last Saturday night when I brought you home either," he said, censure in his voice. "It's senseless and careless having a system and not turning it on."

"Don't start being difficult again."

He peered down at her. "I'm never difficult."

She rolled her eyes. "Spoken like a man."

"I am a man."

She had no comeback to that. He was a man and a very tempting one at that, but he was taken. Southern women never poached. "Good night, Vincent. Your friend is probably still waiting on you." Charlotte knew she would have been.

He stepped closer, surrounding her with his arousing clean male scent. "There is no one waiting for me."

Instead of assuring her, his words had the opposite effect. "You're into one-night stands?"

The horror and accusation in her voice had him grinding his teeth. "No."

"But I—"

"I was dreaming! All right?" he practically snarled.

She blinked, then her lips curved upward in a slow sultry smile. She dreamed too. "All right."

He stared at her lips, glistening and inviting. "You're trying to tempt me, Charlotte."

"Whatever do you mean?"

Her Southern accent had thickened. He thought of long lazy nights of loving with him deep inside her and her straining to get closer. His body went as hard and as stiff as forged steel. He would have sworn neither of them moved, but somehow their faces were closer, their lips almost . . . All he had to do was . . .

Their lips touched, the gentle joining of mouths. Their bodies gradually sank together as first one tongue then the other tentatively explored the shape, the heat, the drugging desire to have more, to taste more.

On tiptoe, Charlotte wound her slender arms around Vincent's neck. One of his strong arms slid around her tiny waist and anchored her snugly against his hardness. His other hand tunneled through her thick hair. He deepened the kiss, taking them both deeper into passion, into need.

With consummate expertise he plundered her mouth and scattered her thoughts. Her body quivered like a taut bow, caught and held by the will of this man. A willing, eager participant, Charlotte pressed closer to the hard, muscular length of him. He felt good and made her feel even better.

Vincent held on to his sanity by sheer force of will. Somehow, he got them through the door and shoved it closed behind them. A kiss had never taken him under so fast or so completely.

Charlotte was fire and desire in his arms, burning out of control and he was enjoying every mind-blowing second. He couldn't get enough. Groaning, his hands slid under the black spandex top and closed over her breasts. She moaned and he moaned right along with her.

He had to see. He looked down and almost lost it. The black scrap of lacy confection didn't even try to hide the creamy swell of her lush breasts. His thumb grazed over a nipple. It pouted immediately for him. Charlotte's breath hissed through her teeth. So sensitive. Probably tasted like chocolate mixed with whipped cream.

Lips parted, his head bent. He had to taste and find out.

The phone rang.

The strident sound was like a blast of frigid air. It rang again. Eyes closed, Vincent reined in his desire with an iron will. Straightening, he withdrew his hands and pulled down her blouse, then looked up into her dazed eyes. "Should I say I'm sorry?"

She drew in a gulp of air past lips that were damp and swollen from his kisses before she could speak. "Only if you are."

For once in his short relationship with Charlotte, Vincent didn't have to ponder his answer. "No."

Relief swept across her face. "Good, because neither am I."

The answering machine activated on the fifth ring. "Charlotte, this is Emma. Brian is on the other line. We wanted to make sure you got home safely. Hope we didn't disturb you."

"Thanks again, Charlotte," Brian said. "I know Vincent made sure you got home all right, so we'll call him."

Quickly crossing the living room, Charlotte snatched up the receiver. "I'm here."

She stared back at Vincent and wished she was still in his arms, letting him drive her crazy with his mouth and hands. Who would have thought a conservative man like Vincent could kiss like the scoundrel every woman secretly dreams of finding and taming? He certainly didn't dress like one.

Tonight he wore a pink diamond-patterned shirt with a white collar and cuffs. He even had on a properly knotted tie at four in the morning. On another man, she would have thought the shirt too feminine, but on Vincent anything looked good. But she'd bet he'd look even better without anything on.

His black eyes darkened as if he knew exactly what she was thinking. The temperature of her body shot up again.

"I'm sorry, what did you say?" she asked, having no idea what either Brian or Emma had said after she answered the phone. "No. You didn't disturb me. Yes, I'm fine. Good night. I'll see you in the morning at church." She replaced the receiver, then linked her fingers and stared across the room at Vincent.

"I suppose this has happened between a maid of honor and a best man before," he said casually.

All the mellow feeling inside Charlotte shattered. "Are you making a generalization or an accusation?"

"Watch it or you'll be apologizing again," he told her, the corners of his mouth slanting upward.

"Since I hate redundancy, good night, Vincent, and thanks for your help." She went to the door, opened it, then stepped to one side. "Church starts at eight."

He didn't move. "We were doing pretty good for a while tonight. You think we'll ever make it for an entire evening without an argument?"

Because she saw amusement instead of censure, she answered honestly. "I continue to hope so."

Crossing the room, he stopped in front of her. Strong, elegant fingers lifted her chin. "So do I." His kiss was as fleeting as it was sweet. "Good night, Charlotte."

Her eyelashes slowly fluttered back upward. "Good night, Vincent."

With a gently teasing smile he stared down at her. "At the risk of starting another argument, make sure you lock the door after me."

With a reckless smile like that he could probably ask her anything, she thought. "Since you put it like that." She locked the door behind him, then raced down the hall to cut on the light in her bedroom.

Vincent was turning out to be very interesting. She couldn't wait until she saw him again, kissed him again. He'd probably call after church, maybe ask her to dinner. She couldn't wait.

Vincent didn't call Sunday or Monday. By Tuesday Charlotte vacillated between annoyance and concern. By Wednesday afternoon she knew he hadn't been unexpectedly called out of town on business nor was he lying broken in a hospital. He was well and working hard, according to Brian, who had been at Emma's house when Charlotte went by to take Emma for the final fitting of her wedding gown.

Thursday morning, Charlotte frowned down at the blue phone in her office. She was tempted to just pick it up and call, but that was as far as it went. Southern women did not chase men. It was acceptable to let them know that you were interested by a look or a comment that you hoped to see them again, but that was the extent of things. Their kiss had certainly said that and more.

Why hadn't he called? She knew when a man was interested in her. Had she done something to turn him off?

The phone rang. Her heart gave one hard knock against her rib cage before caller ID identified the call as coming from Senator Upshaw's office. Annoyed with herself *and* Vincent, she picked up the phone. She wasn't wasting another second trying to figure out why Vincent hadn't tried to contact her. Nor was she letting him stop her from doing her job.

Thirty minutes later, she hung up the phone, the date for the senator's fund-raising dinner finalized. The western-themed gala would take place downtown at the venerable Adolphus Hotel's posh grand ballroom on August eighteenth.

Spinning around, she picked up a disk with the names of businesses that had political action committees and shoved it into the disk drive. As she worked through the list of companies with PACs, Ore-Tech's name came up. Her mouth firmed, then she continued. Vincent apparently wasn't giving her a thought. She was going to do the same with him and do her job. If he came to the shower the singles group from their church was giving Emma and Brian Friday night, she'd show him a thing or two about tampering with a Southern woman's affection!

Vincent heard Charlotte's laughter before he saw her. He worked his way through the friendly crowd of young people in the sprawling ranch house of the senior pastor of their church until he was only a few feet away from her. As he had come to expect, she was surrounded by four attentive men in the spacious kitchen. In the past jealousy had never been an emotion he'd had to deal with in his personal or business life.

He was dealing with it now.

He had purposely stayed away from her since last Saturday

night. He told himself he had too much work to do, which he had. But it was also to see if he would miss Charlotte. He had. Constantly.

He had come tonight because Brian had not wanted a bachelor party and his singles group at church had decided on a joint shower for the engaged couple. Brian had informed Vincent his attendance was a necessary part of the duties as best man. However, seeing Charlotte, Vincent knew he wouldn't have been able to stay away even if he wanted to.

She had on white again. This time it was a backless ruffled silk dress that was also strapless. Fleetingly, he wondered what kept the dress up and how soon it was going to be before he found out. He started toward her.

Charlotte had seen Vincent across the room staring at her. *Good.* Despite the men surrounding her, she managed to make sure Vincent got a good look at her dress. She'd teach him not to kiss her like his life depended on it and then not call.

"Oh, Henry, sugar, you do say the funniest things." She'd known Henry for five years and the other three men almost as long. They were as safe and comfortable as a ratty bathrobe. Not like the dangerous man approaching.

"Good evening, Charlotte, gentlemen. I don't believe we've met." Vincent extended his hand to the man nearest him, and in a matter of seconds the handshakes and introductions were complete. "Do you mind if I steal Charlotte for a moment or two? As maid of honor and best man, we need to talk. Reverend Bailey said we could use the game room."

In his usual high-handed way, Vincent didn't wait for an answer. Gently encircling her upper forearm with long, lean fingers, he pulled her away from her admirer. Shivers of awareness raced up her arm from his fingertips.

Charlotte didn't want to be alone with Vincent, but she didn't wish to make a scene either. She wasn't as detached toward him as she would have wished. He looked too good in his wheat-colored suit and her body recalled too well the pleasure he could give. He closed the door to the game room behind them. Her uneasiness increased dramatically.

"What's so important that it couldn't wait?"

"This." His lips descended.

Charlotte twisted her head. His lips missed her mouth, but she trembled as they brushed across her cheek, sending an undeniable shiver of longing down her spine. "If that's all you have to say, I've heard it before," she said, hoping he didn't hear the shakiness or need straining her voice. "I'm sure this isn't what Pastor Bailey thought you had in mind."

"You're angry with me again."

Lying wasn't her style. "As a wet hen. Go kiss someone else."

"I don't want to kiss anyone else," he said, the truth sinking like tenterhooks deep into his soul. His eyes slowly ran the length of her. "You look absolutely wicked in that dress. Planned for me to suffer tonight, did you?"

Her chin went up. "The thought had entered my mind."

"You succeeded." He pulled her into his arms. "I missed you."

She lasted for one long breath, then she softened against him. "You didn't call."

"I was trying to see if I could get you out of my mind." He held her away from him, his dark eyes intense. "I couldn't."

"Does that annoy you?" she asked, afraid of the answer, but realizing she had to know before she fell any further. She was half in love with the conservative scoundrel already.

He kissed her on the tip of her nose. "Not since I walked in, heard you laugh, and wanted to punch four men I'd never met in the nose. I've accepted my fate."

She tried to appear shocked, but she was too pleased to pull it off. She'd never expected a staid man like Vincent to be jealous. "They're just friends."

His handsome face became serious. "But you were sharing your laughter and smile with them, not me."

Her bare arms looped around his neck. She tilted her face toward his. "I'm here now."

He didn't need another invitation. His mouth took possession of hers. This time there was nothing sweet about the

kiss. It was blatantly arousing, a mating of tongues, a duel of
desire where each became the victor. When Vincent finally
lifted his head they were both shaking.

He held her tightly. She was small, but gloriously built
and absolutely perfect in his arms. "I suppose we better go
back and join the party."

Still pressed against him, she stroked the curve of his jaw
with her finger. "I suppose."

Unable to resist, he nuzzled her neck and delighted in her
soft sigh that ended on a ragged moan. "Any objections to
my following you home?"

"None at all." Charlotte lifted her face. "But I have out-
of-town houseguests."

"What if I offered to put them up in a hotel?" he asked,
only half teasing.

On tiptoes, she kissed his chin. "Nice try, but since it's
two of the bridesmaids, I don't think I could do that."

"How long are they staying?"

"All weekend."

Vincent groaned.

5

Now that he had seen her, he didn't want to go the entire
weekend without seeing her again. He wasn't leaving the
game room until they had a firm date. "How about I take you
ladies to breakfast?"

"That's very sweet of you, Vincent, but Emma's mother
has already invited us over."

"Lunch?"

"We're going shopping after breakfast and I don't expect
we'll stop until either our feet or our credit cards give out."

Vincent was not a man who gave up. "Dinner?"

"I promised Beverly and Carolyn to take them to The
Place, a new dance club in Deep Ellum. They have a buffet
there."

"Just you ladies? No men?"

"Just us."

Vincent frowned. "That doesn't sound like much fun, watching other people dance."

"Finding a dance partner won't be problem for either of them." Charlotte played with the button on his jacket. "You'll understand once you meet them."

Vincent didn't think Charlotte would have any problem either. The thought of her being in some other man's arms annoyed the hell out of him. "Do you mind if I stop by?"

The pleased smile on her face came and went in a blink of an eye. Uncertainty took its place. "I don't think you'd like the music."

"It's not hip-hop or rap, is it?" he asked, the distaste clear in his Bostonian accent.

The worried expression didn't clear from her face. "No, it—" The knock on the door interrupted them. She stepped back. "Come in."

The door opened and Henry stuck his head in. "Sorry to disturb you, but Emma and Brian are about to start opening their gifts."

"My goodness." Grabbing Vincent's hand, Charlotte hurriedly left the room. "Thank you, Henry."

Vincent allowed her to lead him back to the den decorated with streamers and balloons, then assign him to his duty. He was to make sure Emma and Brian always had a gift ready to open. Charlotte would keep track of the gifts and the givers' names.

As the happy couple unwrapped gifts from the useful to the useless, Vincent caught himself laughing just as hard as everyone else and truly enjoying himself. However, occasionally when he glanced at Charlotte, she'd have a pensive look on her face. He pondered the cause behind the faraway expression. He didn't like the idea of her being unhappy when she went to such great lengths to ensure the happiness of those around her. He'd find out tomorrow night what was bothering her. Because as sure as his name was Vincent Albert Maxwell, he was going to that dance club and make sure some cowboy didn't try to make a move on Charlotte.

Deep Ellum was the undisputed avant-garde district of Dallas. In the shadows of multibillion-dollar corporations in downtown Dallas, Deep Ellum was populated with million-dollar businesses and those on the verge of bankruptcy, five-star and no-star restaurants, designers renowned and unknown, the prerequisite tattoo shops, clubs on the cutting edge or no edge. New Yorkers might have called the area "funky." Bostonians would have called the area "urban blight."

Vincent parked his car on the side street, and hoped he could call it safe.

He heard the music at the bottom of the three curved steps. His eyebrows lifted at the sound. The fast tempo of the Latin beat was easily distinguishable. He breathed a little easier. Charlotte obviously thought he wouldn't enjoy being there, so he hadn't known what to expect.

He bounded up the step under the red-and-black–striped awning and prepared himself for whatever. The room was spacious with strobe lights in the ceiling, and surprisingly smoke-free. People were pressed together at the bar, on the dance floor, and clustered around the tables circling the wooden dance floor. Arms were in the air, feet seldom were on the floor. The steps were quick and intricate.

"Vincent, over here!"

Peering through the crowd, Vincent saw Charlotte's house guests. Beverly and Carolyn were identical twins, and built like warrior princesses with the sultry beauty to match. When asked about their unidentical names he was told their mother had always been unorthodox. Shaking his head, Vincent thought the trait had passed on to the daughters, who were having the time of their lives dancing and bumping hips with two grinning guys on the dance floor.

He waved. The women hooked their thumbs over their shoulders. Nodding that he understood, he wove his way through the crowd. He didn't see Charlotte, but he did see three guys clustered around a table. With a shake of his head and a curve of his mouth, he headed over.

"Hello, Charlotte. Mind if I sit down?"

Her head whipped around. Her smile blossomed, then grew strained. "Hello, Vincent. I'd like you to meet these nice gentlemen who've been keeping me company."

Vincent's expression remained pleasant as Charlotte completed the introductions. It was obvious the three men wished he'd keel over with a coronary. It was just as obvious that Charlotte was worried about something.

"Would you like something to drink?" she asked when the three men had finally accepted that she wasn't available and moved on.

"Scotch and soda," he told her and watched in fascination as she managed against all odds to get the attention of a waiter and gave him the order.

She bit her lip, then said, "It can get rather hot in here. You want to take off your tie?"

"I'm fine," he said, then watched her sneak another glance at him. Finally, he'd had enough. He took her hand. "If my being here bothers you in some way, I'll leave."

Her hazel eyes widened with obvious distress. "It's not that."

The waiter returned and set down his drink. Vincent let go of her hand and reached for his wallet.

"That's all right, Charlotte has a running tab," the man said, then was gone.

Vincent picked up his drink, his gaze on Charlotte. "You come here a lot."

"My second time actually." She twisted the stem of her margarita glass and eyed his red silk tie with navy stripes. "You're sure you're not hot?"

"I'm fine." Vincent took a sip of his drink. Charlotte seemed to acquire friends wherever she went. The three men who had just left had struck out, but Charlotte had remained polite and cordial so they didn't feel belittled or angry. In fact, the only time he'd ever seen her irritated or annoyed was with him. Just as she was now. Interesting.

The music changed to the hot and spicy beat of the salsa. Most of the dancers moved off the floor, including Carolyn and Beverly. They slumped into their seats on the other side of Charlotte and reached for their fruity drinks.

"Would you care to dance, Charlotte?"

Charlotte, who had just turned her glass up, choked. Vincent pounded her on the back as she stared wide-eyed at him. "W-what did you say?"

"Would you care to dance?" he repeated, telling himself again that he was going to find out what was troubling her before the night was over.

Grinning, she gave him a quick kiss on the lips. "I should have known a scoundrel would know how to dance, even the salsa." Standing, she reached for his hand and led him on the floor to the loud applause and yells of the twins.

"You go, girl!"

"You were worried about me?" he asked as he curved his hand around her waist.

"I didn't want you feeling uncomfortable," she admitted.

"Thank you," he said, then he began to move to the pulsating music.

"For what?" she asked as he made a sudden stop, twisted her away then back to him.

His eyes burned down into hers. "For caring."

That's all the time they had for conversation, as Vincent moved her across the floor, first maddeningly slow, then like the onslaught of a torrent. Each movement was filled with grace and power and seduction as their bodies moved first away then back to each other, the passion raw and impetuous as they teased and coaxed each other, then offered solace once again when their bodies joined.

Only once before in her life had Charlotte felt so vibrant, so alive, and it had been in Vincent's arms as well. The dance became more than a dance. It was as if Vincent were wooing her, making love to her as he held her body and matched his steps to hers as elegantly as he matched their bodies. She lost herself to the throbbing beat of the music, lost herself to him. Where he led, she effortlessly followed, and when he spun her away, she yearned to be in his arms, held against his body.

The end came suddenly with the strum of a Spanish guitar. Applause erupted around them. Face to face, body to body,

their breathing labored, Charlotte and Vincent stared at each
other and each knew their relationship had shifted, changed
into something hot and needy.

Charlotte had always known Beverly and Carolyn were good
friends. The women proved it when Vincent and Charlotte
finally reached their table after all the congratulations, handshakes, and pats on the back from the crowd. The twins insisted they were worn out and wanted to go home. Charlotte
knew her protest was weak at best. She wanted nothing more
than to be alone with Vincent. One look at Vincent and she
knew he felt the same.

    If they didn't go someplace where they could get their
hands on each other soon, they'd both explode.

    Thankfully, on the drive to her house, Carolyn and Beverly
kept chattering. Considering they were litigation lawyers for
one of the largest law firms in Houston, they had no trouble
talking. In their church singles group before they moved, they
had lovingly been referred to as motormouths.

    Charlotte parked the car in the garage, sent the twins a
thank-you-for-understanding look, and rushed to open the
front door. Vincent was coming up the walkway.

    Charlotte rubbed her hand on the side of her red chiffon
dress. "I thought we'd sit out on the patio."

    "All right."

    Closing the door after him, she turned and caught the twins
grinning at them. "If you need anything, Vincent and I will
be outside."

    Carolyn yawned. "I'm going to bed."

    "Me, too." Beverly stretched.

    Charlotte walked through the den, then opened the French
doors leading to the back yard. Lights followed the winding
path around the yard. She kept walking until she reached the
double chaise lounge.

    She turned and was in his arms, his mouth on hers, before
she could take her next breath. It was heaven. It was hell.
The yearning was almost a physical pain.

    "I want you, Charlotte."

All she could do was whimper. She wanted him too, but both knew that was impossible.

He nipped her lower lip. "Do you think they're watching?"

"No." Her breath hitched as he used his teeth on the delicate lobe of her ear, then worked his way downward. His tongue licked the upper curve of her breast. Her legs buckled.

Picking her up, he gently placed her on the lounge chair, then came down beside her. Even in the semidarkness, she could see the fire and passion burning in his eyes. She swallowed.

"I won't take you tonight, Charlotte, but I'm going to come very, very close."

She swallowed again, thought of what a proper Southern lady should do when faced with temptation, the words of her mother and grandmother about remaining chaste until marriage, then Vincent closed his hot mouth over her nipple and she was lost.

Beverly and Carolyn had a ten-fifteen flight the next morning out of Love Field. Due to bad weather in Houston, the plane didn't leave until two hours later. When passengers in their seat rows were called, Charlotte gave them a hug, and quickly headed for the parking garage. Vincent was taking her sailing and she could hardly wait to be with him again.

He was waiting for her when she arrived home. In less than an hour they were in the water of Lake Ray Hubbard. She couldn't have asked for a more perfect day. Skies were blue and the wind gentle.

Later he'd taken her to dinner at a restaurant on the pier. They'd talked for hours, but were comfortable in their silence as well. When he'd taken her home, he'd driven her just as mad with longing as he had the night before. She knew she was tempting fate, but it felt too good to stop.

During the next couple of weeks, both of their schedules became hectic and they only saw snatches of each other. During those times, they'd often wonder which of their pagers was ringing, and who would be called away first. It became a standing joke between them, but it also made them appreciate their precious time together.

Vincent delighted in having a woman who understood his work and didn't pout if he had to cancel a date. No matter what, Charlotte always greeted him with a smile and asked how his day went. She accepted that business might interfere with their plans and never made him feel guilty. He began to look forward to being with her. He'd catch himself rereading her handwritten notes on scented stationery saying she was thinking of him. Charlotte made him feel special and he enjoyed every second of it.

However, the first time Charlotte had to cancel because of an unexpected meeting with her party chairman, Vincent took her home from the theater as grumpy as a grizzly with a thorn in his paw. Much to his increased annoyance, he'd told her how he felt the moment they walked through her front door.

"Vincent, I'm sorry," Charlotte placated, then stood on tiptoes to kiss his jutted chin. "But this couldn't be helped. I have just enough time to pack before the car picks me up."

Vincent was usually a very reasonable man, but tonight he couldn't quite seem to find that quality in himself. Not when Charlotte was standing before him in a mauve-colored, clinging slip dress, looking delectable and tempting. He had been looking forward to spending an uninterrupted evening with her. "This is Saturday night, for goodness sake. Can't you get out of it and fly down to Austin tomorrow?"

"You know as well as I do that Saturday and Sunday can be just another workday for us. Besides, could you get out of a meeting with your employer if you had key information they needed?" she asked.

"No, but I don't have to like it," he grumbled.

Charlotte laughed and kissed him again. "I do admire an honest man, but I'm afraid I have to throw you out."

"I can take you to the airport," he suggested. He didn't want to let her go. He was surprised how strong the feeling was.

She shook her head. "Thank you, but there's a car coming."

He didn't move. "How long will you be gone?"

"Probably just overnight. I'll be back before you miss me." She glanced over his shoulder as a limo pulled up behind Vincent's car. "Get going, so I can pack."

His hands fisted on the soft chiffon scarf around her neck that was almost as soft as her skin. The back of his knuckles lightly grazed her breasts. He forced himself not to increase the contact. "Would it destroy your image if I kissed you?"

Hands that weren't quite steady circled his wrists. "I'm not sure, but I'd be disappointed if you didn't."

The kiss was long and hot, leaving her breathless. "I–I'll call when I get back."

"You better." Releasing the scarf, he walked back to his car and drove away.

Vincent wasn't in a very good mood by Tuesday afternoon. After Charlotte had gone, the weekend hadn't been that much fun; since she was still gone, the week wasn't shaping up much better. Tossing the papers on his desk, he got up and went to the office window, annoyed with Charlotte and himself.

He missed her.

Slipping his hands into the pockets of his slacks, he sent an accusatory glance at the silent phone. When they'd talked last night, she'd said she'd call when she got back into town. She was returning on a private jet with a group of major political contributors. He'd bet, by the time the plane landed, Charlotte would have gotten the maximum contributions allowed.

She was a charmer. And he was enthralled by her. What was the matter with him? Women did not interfere with his work. Charlotte's fault again. She simply got to him.

It was his conversation with her that had him trying to cut Ashley some slack. At least she had stopped being sick every day and finally confessed to being pregnant. But if her department figures weren't on time in the future, he'd have to take a second hard look at the situation. But in the meantime, her performance was exemplary.

Vincent had run into her husband and their little boy one day when they came to take Ashley to lunch. They had all looked happy. Perhaps it could work for some couples.

Pulling out his chair, Vincent sat down and picked up the financial report of a new natural gas discovery in Oklahoma. When Charlotte finally came home he wanted his work done so he could spend some time with her tonight. He had an early morning flight to Atlanta for a business meeting that could last through the rest of the week. If Charlotte was delayed, he might not see her until the weekend. The thought had him snarling at the papers in his hands.

Five minutes later he was up again, pacing in front of the window behind his desk. This was Charlotte's fault. That's what came of women having jobs that took them out of town for extended periods of time. If she had a regular job, she'd be in town and he wouldn't be edgy and needy. They could have spent more than a handful of hours together so he wouldn't feel like scum if he made love to her the way their bodies craved.

The intercom buzzed and he pounced on it. "Yes?"

"Vincent, Sidney called. You were supposed to meet him at the Racquet Club ten minutes ago. If you're not there in ten minutes to play against the guy from CityCore, you lose by default. Sidney doesn't like to lose without at least playing," Millicent said.

Vincent's mood went from irritated to feral. He had won the round-robin tournament for his company and was now being pitted against other company winners for the grand championship. The real winner would be the high school students who received college scholarships from the ten thousand dollars each company donated to participate. "Tell Sidney I'm on my way."

Kevin Harris, Vincent's opponent, never posed a real threat. Vincent came out of the box like a demon and never let up. Company employees and members of the Racquet Club gathered to watch. Both men were soaked with perspiration when Vincent hit the winning shot. Kevin swung valiantly for the speeding ball and ended up sprawled on the floor.

"Game!" shouted the referee.

Breathing hard, Vincent walked over to Kevin and extended his hand. "Good game."

"Yeah, right," Kevin said, then smiled, took the offered hand and came to his feet. "Is it a woman or business that has you steamed?"

Vincent flicked a glance at the bearded man. "Why do you say that?"

"Last week you came out to have fun. This week you came out with blood in your eye." Kevin grasped the door handle. "That could only come from one of two reasons."

Vincent didn't say anything, just waited for Kevin to open the door. When he did, the first person he saw standing there was Charlotte, a wide grin on her face, pumping both fists. He didn't think, he just grabbed.

He felt her start of surprise, then the melting of her body against his. He kissed her like the starved man he was. She kissed him the same way.

Only the congratulatory thumps on the back brought Vincent back to reality. He realized what he was doing and where he was doing it. Surprise went through him. He'd never been the demonstrative type, especially in public.

Lifting his head, he slipped his arm around Charlotte's waist and felt her tremble. What they both needed was a heavy bout of hot, mindless sex. Come tonight, that was exactly what he planned for them.

Thankful she still had the car service, Charlotte left Vincent a note saying she had errands to run, then slipped away when he went to the locker room to shower and change. Still shaken from his kiss and her own desire, she hadn't been sure she would have made it home if she had to drive.

As promised, she'd called Vincent when the plane landed. On learning where he was, she'd gone to watch and cheer him on. She'd marveled at his athletic prowess and the muscular strength and coordination of his graceful body that made her want to run her hands and her lips over every inch of him.

Being conservative, he'd surprised her by wearing only white cotton shorts which, against his toasted brown skin, made him even more striking. The kiss had been another surprise. She'd hungered and thought of little else except being in his arms again while she was away.

Then what?

Vincent, as he had said, was a man. Men wanted intimacy. She had vowed to wait until marriage. With Vincent, she was seriously thinking of abandoning that vow . . . if he loved her. For she was no longer falling in love, she was *in* love. If he loved her, if there was a chance for them, she'd take the risk that what they felt for each other was forever.

Curling up on the four-poster, she tried to shut out the little voice that warned her that when you compromised one principle, others would surely follow. Unsuccessful, she threw back the quilt her grandmother had made for her, and dressed in her jogging shorts, sweatshirt and tennis shoes. Time to stop feeling sorry for herself and do something that she'd been putting off for weeks: get back into her exercise regime. Clipping the front door key to the special loop on the waistband of her shorts, she left.

Although it was after six, the sun remained fierce, reminding her that she had forgotten her shades and sun visor. She never slackened her stride. Perhaps the run would clear her head. She needed to know what to do. The kiss had told her that the next time they were alone, Vincent wouldn't want to stop until they'd made love. Could she give him what he wanted?

Passing neighbors cutting the lawn, walking dogs, or out jogging like herself, she waved. She'd made a place for herself her in the quiet residential neighborhood since she moved there three years ago.

At that time, she'd already been maid of honor twice and, although there was no one special in her life, she had believed that surely her time would soon come. With the rising cost of housing and knowing single men seldom if ever purchased a house, she'd asked her father's help in finding a house in hopes that she'd share it with a husband and family one day. Now, she had to face reality. That day might never come. If Vincent wasn't the one, she wasn't sure she'd ever want anyone again like she wanted him.

She'd never been a whimsical woman. She devoted her all to whatever held her interest. Her family, her friends, her church, her party. Now that included Vincent. She couldn't imagine loving anyone else so completely, nor did she want to.

She barely noticed the sound of a honking horn. It was common for teenagers to blow at the women joggers. She didn't realize it was Vincent until he pulled a half block in front of her and got out of his car.

Her stride shortened until she was walking. She wanted nothing more than to run into his arms. The thought scared her. Each time she saw him, the need for him grew. When he walked out of her life, and he would, she'd be torn to pieces.

"Hello, Vincent."

Hands on his hips, he studied the weariness in her face. This wasn't the woman who had burned so hotly in his arms a scant two hours ago. "Hello, Charlotte."

"I'd stop, but I don't want to cramp up," she said as she passed him.

"No problem." Vincent activated the lock on his car and fell into step beside her.

She threw him a quick look. "You aren't dressed for this. You'll have a heatstroke."

He loosened the stone gray silk tie and kept walking. "You finish with your errands all right?"

Her strides lengthened. "Yes, thank you."

In Vincent's association with women, exaggerated politeness usually meant annoyance or anger. As Charlotte started up a sharp incline, he regretted again his reckless behavior at the Racquet Club.

"I'm sorry if the kiss embarrassed you."

Her smooth stride faltered. "It was just a kiss."

Vincent's eyes narrowed. Now he knew he was in trouble. Thunder rumbled. "Perhaps we should go back to the car."

"I don't mind the rain." She pulled ahead of him. "You go ahead. I'll call later."

"Hello, Charlotte."

Never slowing, she waved at the gray-haired woman wearing a straw hat who was watering her bed of begonias. "Good evening, Mrs. Allister."

"Good evening, young man."

"Good evening, Mrs. Allister," Vincent called and easily pulled alongside Charlotte.

Thunder grew closer and more ominous. "Vincent, if you get rained on, you're going to ruin your clothes."

"I have others."

Her mouth firmed, but she didn't say anything else, just kept jogging. When they turned the block onto Charlotte's street, the rain started to fall. Drops turned to a torrent in seconds.

"I told you," she stopped to yell at him.

She looked close to tears, standing there with her small fists balled, glaring at him. She was hurting. He stepped toward her. She backed up. He kept coming until he closed his arms around her. He thought she would fight, but her hands clutched the lapels of his suit jacket. He felt her body shaking and wished he knew the cause.

"Honey, don't cry, please. Just tell me what it is and I'll fix it. Please don't cry," he soothed, then realized it was ridiculous for them to stand in the rain. He picked her up and started for her house.

This time she reacted. "Put me down," she demanded, pushing against his chest.

He kept walking. "Hush. I have you and I'm not letting go."

Immediately she stilled. He looked down into her face. His heart clenched when tears streamed down her cheek. Gathering her closer, he continued to her house. "Whatever it is, I'll fix it."

Charlotte had almost pulled herself together by the time

Vincent reached her house and stood her on her feet. "You can dry off, and then I'll drive you back to your car," she told him.

Vincent silently followed her down the hall. There was nothing he could do about the trail of water he left. In the guest bath, she handed him a large bath towel and a robe. "Your pants and shirt are probably ruined anyway, so the dryer can't do much worse to them. I'll be in the kitchen making coffee."

He caught her arm. "You need to get out of those wet clothes."

Her fist clenched. "I'll be fine."

"Take them off or I'll do it for you," he warned.

Because she so badly wanted to pick a fight with him and take the cowardly way out, she went to her room, changed, and blew her hair dry. She was reaching for her lipstick when she realized what she had been about to do. Make herself pretty for Vincent. Placing the tube on the vanity, she left her bedroom.

None of the women in her family would ever dream of letting a man other than their father see them without at least lipstick and mascara on. Another Southern tradition. She'd break that one, but no others. She had made her decision.

She heard the drone of the clothes dryer as she emerged from the hall. *Vincent.* Drawing a deep breath, she continued to the kitchen, steeling herself against seeing him again.

It did no good. He simply caused her heart to beat faster, the lower region of her body to pulse with need and desire. He wore the white terry-cloth robe she had given him. Underneath his skin would be warm and bare. She stuck her hands in the pockets of her slacks. "Since you've made the coffee, I'll get the cups."

He stepped in front of her as she was about to pass him. He watched her as she quickly staggered back. "What's going on, Charlotte?"

She couldn't meet his eyes. "Nothing."

"What happened between this afternoon at the racket match and now? It had to be more than the kiss."

This was it, the moment she had dreaded and couldn't avoid. "I decided that we should just be friends and forget about anything else."

Vincent's eyes stabbed into her. "You mean forget how it feels to have my hands and mouth all over your body and that—"

With a strangled cry, she pressed her hand to his lips. "Please, don't."

Strong, unrelenting hands grasped her upper forearms. "Talk to me. Tell me what it is, so I can fix it."

"The only way you can fix this is to destroy it."

He shook his head. A drop of water rolled down from his forehead. He ignored it. "What are you talking about?"

"I've never been with a man and I don't plan to until my wedding night."

Vincent's mouth fell open and his hands dropped.

6

"You mean. . . ."

Her chin lifted. "Yes."

"But . . ." He stared at Charlotte, lush and beautiful. Even now, with her face free of makeup, she was still the most gorgeous woman he had ever met. The first time he'd seen her he'd wanted her and the wanting had only grown more intense since then. "Men follow behind you like birds following a path of bread crumbs."

"So?" The uncertainty in her eyes changed in a heartbeat to anger. "Where there's smoke there's fire?"

Vincent thought of all the fiery passion in Charlotte, but he didn't think he should point it out at the moment. A virgin. And every time he saw her, he wanted to be inside her. "I think I need to sit down." He did, eyeing her wearily. She didn't look any steadier than he did. "Maybe you'd better sit down."

"I'm fine."

His eyes narrowed a fraction. Charlotte pulled out a tub

chair across from Vincent in the breakfast nook and stared
out the window at the rain and the jasmine climbing up the
redwood trellis of her neighbor's house.

"Is this what's been bothering you since Brian and Emma's
shower?"

Surprise had her turning her head toward him. She hadn't
thought he or anyone else had noticed. "No." The coffee began to drip into the carafe and she got up to get the cups.

"Charlotte, talk to me, help me to understand," he said
quietly.

Since she had been all over him every chance she got,
giving him every indication that she wanted what he wanted,
she felt he deserved an explanation. Taking a wooden tray
from the cabinet, she placed cloth napkins, spoons, cream and
sugar, and the cups on top, then brought everything back to
the table and sat down.

"I was raised in a loving Christian home and taught that
intimacy meant a commitment. At the same time, I was taught
to be a Southern lady and that meant charm, grace, femininity,
and a deep responsibility to family and the community." Her
hand trembled as she poured cream into her coffee and added
sugar. "The men I've met in the past have never wanted what
I wanted, a home and family." Her hands clutched around the
delicate china cup. She lifted her gaze to his.

"I was melancholy at the shower, because Emma and
Brian's wedding will be my ninth as a maid of honor. Men
see the outside and are turned on, but none want me, the
person that I am on the inside, enough to stay around once I
say no." She lifted the cup to her lips. The liquid scalded as
much as the unshed tears stinging her eyes. In the past, she'd
had no trouble telling shortsighted men good-bye. Easy to
understand why. She hadn't loved them.

She set the cup down, looked over Vincent's shoulder at
the copper teakettle on the stove, then rose. "I have some
business calls to make. I'll drive you back to your car when
your clothes are dry."

She started to turn toward her office in the back near the
kitchen, then realized she'd be too close to Vincent. "I'll be

in my room. For Brian and Emma's sake, I hope we can remain civil toward one another."

She escaped; that was the only way to describe her hasty departure. In her bedroom, head bowed, she sat on the bed. First one, then a second teardrop splashed on the clasped hands in her lap. Her chest hurt. No wonder Brian and Emma had been so miserable that night. It felt as if someone had ripped her heart out. But they loved each other and had made up. That wouldn't happen for her.

Vincent watched Charlotte go. He didn't know what to say or do. He hadn't expected this. His eyes closed, then opened. He was known as the "fixer" by his contemporaries. If there was a problem, call Maxwell, he'd fix it.

His hand rubbed over his face as he thought of what Charlotte had said. "The only way to fix it is to destroy it."

Pushing to his feet, he pulled off the bathrobe and went to the dryer. He was getting out of there. He had learned to control his zipper early in life. He knew how to court a woman, but in the back of his mind there was always the knowledge that eventually they'd become intimate. For Charlotte intimacy meant marriage.

He jerked the door open and pulled on his still-damp briefs. No woman's body was worth being tied down and all the resulting responsibilities. He liked his life the way it was, being able to go and come as he pleased, and take off at a moment's notice for business or pleasure.

Charlotte wouldn't be the first woman to use sex as a lever. She withheld hers, while Sybil had never said no. Whenever and wherever, she'd been willing. At the time, he hadn't known it was to help her on her climb to a vice-presidency of the company he'd worked for in Boston.

He'd had the ear of the president and CEO of the company and she'd known it. She'd used the same method in the past, but he hadn't found that out until later. Women used sex.

He wasn't going to make the same mistake again.

Charlotte woke with a headache and dried tears on her cheeks. Accepting that there would be more before she was completely over Vincent, she rolled from the bed and glanced at the clock on her bedside. 7:13. Weak light poured though the arched half window in her bedroom. The rain had stopped. Apparently, Vincent had preferred walking to his car rather than seeing her again. She hadn't looked forward to seeing him again either.

No, that was a lie. What she hadn't wanted to see was the accusation in his face. She should have told him sooner she couldn't be what he wanted. She couldn't blame him for not sticking around. She just hoped, as she had told him earlier, that they could be civil. Not for anything would she cause Emma and Brian's wedding to be less than perfect for them.

Pulling off her shirt and pants, she went to take a bath. The world didn't stop because she was miserable. She had a charity auction to attend. Children were depending on her, no matter how much her head was hurting.

Some time later, she stepped out of the oversized tub. After toweling dry, she rubbed her favorite jasmine-scented lotion over her body. Each movement an effort, she pulled on lacy purple lingerie trimmed in black, a garter belt, and sheer black stockings. Next came her makeup. By the time she'd applied her lipstick, the pounding in her head was excruciating. Rubbing her temple, she started to the kitchen for an aspirin.

Her head down, out of the corner of her eyes she saw a shadow move. She screamed.

"Charlotte, it's me," Vincent said, stepping away from the French doors to cut on the lamp on the end table.

Her heart pounding, she simply stared at him. As she had predicted, the combination of rain and the clothes dryer had shrunk his clothes a bit. He was almost comical with his high-water pants. "I–I thought you had gone."

His open mouth snapped shut. For some odd reason he seemed to have difficulty swallowing. "I–I wanted to make sure you were all right."

Warmth she couldn't suppress filled her. If only . . . "That was nice of you."

"Charlotte, could you please put on a robe?"

Her hazel eyes widened. She gasped, glanced down, and tore back to her room.

Vincent closed his eyes, but he could still see her in the wicked lingerie, the string bikini with lace inserts that he could very well imagine investigating with his tongue. Shoving both hands over his head, he headed for the refrigerator. He grabbed the first thing he saw, bottled water, and chugged it down.

"Vincent."

He spun around. Charlotte was dressed, but she was in a long purple gown trimmed in black lace . . . just as her lingerie had been. He chugged the water again. "I want you, Charlotte."

"But do you love me?" she asked quietly.

In her expressive face he saw a mixture of misery and hope. "I don't know. I think about you more than I should and I worry about you."

Her eyes blinked rapidly as if she were battling tears. "I worry about my friends also. I'd like to have you as a friend."

His hand clenched on the plastic bottle, causing it to make a popping sound. "What I want to do to you and with you has nothing to do with friendship."

She gulped and glanced away. "You shouldn't say things like that."

Watching her, he took another swig of water. She was trembling. She was as aware of him as he was of her. "What would happen if I kissed you?"

Her eyes jumped back to him. "I–I . . . wish you wouldn't."

Placing the bottle on the counter, he walked to her, his gaze never leaving her. "I'm not other men, Charlotte. I see you. I see the charming, caring woman you are, but I've also tasted the passion on your mouth and on your skin." His fingertip grazed her nipple. It hardened immediately. Closing his hand into a fist, he stepped back. "How can I not want to make love to you knowing you want me to?"

She fought hard to control her desire for Vincent and answer his question. "Because you have honor and integrity. Because you're not the kind of man to take advantage of a woman. Because I care for you and I wouldn't care for a man who would use my feelings against me."

"I wouldn't be so sure," he said tightly. "Where are you going?"

"To a charity auction."

"You're one of the items?"

She blushed. "No, I'm an auctioneer."

His hot gaze ran over her, remembering. "You'll do very well. Good-bye." Pulling his suit jacket from the back of the chair in the kitchen, he walked past her.

"Vincent, you can't go out looking like that," she called. "Please, I insist on driving you."

He looked over his shoulder. "Scared I'd be picked up before I reached my car?"

The only way she could handle this was to find humor in the situation. "You do look pretty awful."

"And you look lovely."

"Thank you. I'll get my purse and you better be here when I get back." Picking up her skirts, she ran past him. In her bedroom, she snatched up her shawl, fumbled to transfer her necessary items into an evening bag the size of her hand, then rushed back out. He was still there, arms folded, leaning against the counter in the kitchen.

"Don't forget to set the alarm this time." Pushing away from the counter, he walked out the door.

Charlotte activated the alarm and followed. In less than three minutes she pulled up behind Vincent's car. A lump formed in her throat. "Good-bye, Vincent."

"Is this a private auction or can anyone attend?"

Excitement and hope rushing through her, Charlotte opened the glove compartment and handed Vincent an invitation. "This will get you in."

He got out of the car. "I'm not making any promises."

"I know." Charlotte pulled away from the curb, unable to stop herself from glancing at her rear-view mirror. Vincent stood on the sidewalk, watching her just as she was watching him.

In the back of Vincent's mind he'd always known he
wouldn't be able to stay away. The auction was being held
at a billionaire's estate. The grounds and mansion were spectacular, with ten fireplaces, an indoor and outdoor pool, a lake
for boating, a pond for fishing, a tennis court, two libraries,
and every marvel known to man. However, to Vincent, the
real marvel was standing on a small raised platform, shimmering and beautiful beneath a Waterford chandelier. Charlotte.

With charm and grace Charlotte worked her magic on the
crowd, gently coaxing them to go just a little bit higher for
the sake of the children's hospital. She smiled, winked, flattered, and bedazzled. Men and women lapped it up like
whipped cream. But she could also be a steel magnolia, if
needed.

Once she hadn't gotten the price she thought acceptable
for a weekend getaway package for two at the Crescent Court
Hotel, a five-star hotel in Dallas, and she had refused to let
it go. Since she couldn't change the auction rules of highest
bid winning, she simply took a seat, crossed her legs, and
waited for the bidding to go higher.

Not wanting to see her embarrassed if no one bid, Vincent
had lifted his number. The smile she sent him was more potent than hundred-proof whiskey. Other bidders jumped in.
Vincent found his hand going up again and again until he
won the bid. Mary Lou, who was there with Helen, had
winked and nodded approvingly at him.

Vincent was rather dazed when a young woman came up
to him and handed him his claim ticket. He didn't need a
weekend package for two. Then he glanced at Charlotte and
admitted the truth. She simply dazzled him. He'd do anything
for her. It remained to be seen if that included not doing what
he wanted to do *to* her.

A white-jacketed waiter passed and Vincent plucked a
glass of champagne from his tray. Of all the available women
in the Southwest, he had to be attracted to one with deep

Southern roots and morality. He'd been celibate before, but he had never wanted a woman as much before.

Charlotte had expected Vincent to insist on following her home, but had not a clue what to expect afterward. Walking through the house from the garage, she never remembered being so nervous or filled with such anticipation. She opened the front door and he was there. Dark and dangerous and so desirable. Moonbeams draped over his broad shoulders.

Neither spoke, simply looked at the other for long endless moments.

As if coming to a decision, Vincent stepped closer until the warmth of their breaths and bodies mingled. "I can't imagine not wanting you, but neither can I imagine walking away."

Her breath and words trembled over her lips. "I feel the same way."

He took another step. Their bodies touched, breasts to chest, thigh to thigh. "I'll try, but I'm not making any promises."

"I know." She had come to her own decision. "Would you like to come in?"

He shook his head. "Too far. I need to kiss you now."

With the raw passion simmering just beneath the surface of his voice, Charlotte expected the kiss to be rough and demanding. Instead it was a gentle exploration of reassurance that gradually deepened into something rich and deep and arousing. Feeling her control slipping, Charlotte eased back and placed her head on Vincent's chest. His heart beat erratically, but his arms were locked around her as if he'd never let her go.

"I have to go out of town for a few days, but I'll be back Saturday. You want to go sailing?" he asked, his voice thick and tight.

Despite the needs clawing at her, she leaned her head back and smiled up at him. "That's certainly better than weeding the flower bed, as I'd planned."

"We can do both," he said, enjoying the feel of her in his

arms as much as the quick emotions that flashed across her face.

"Somehow I can't imagine you on your hands and knees in the dirt," she told him.

"My mother has a flower garden and I used to help her." As he remembered, gardening was hard, tiring work. Good. "Eight early enough?"

"I'll fix breakfast."

"See you Saturday." Opening the door behind her, he gently pushed her inside and closed the door.

Vincent amazed Charlotte again. He'd shown up Saturday morning casually dressed in faded jeans and a melon-colored polo shirt, ready to work. The dandelions hadn't stood a chance. When she'd mentioned she wanted more flowers on the patio in pots, he'd insisted that they forgo sailing and go to the nursery. It wasn't until later in the afternoon that she realized he might have an ulterior motive for working so hard: Both of them would be too tired to think about sex.

If she hadn't been already in love with him, she would have fallen.

After they'd cleaned up, she'd grilled steaks and they'd enjoyed their meal on the patio surrounded by blooming flowers in Mexican urns, clay pots, and baskets hanging from the wrought-iron posts Vincent had installed. Only once or twice did she think of how wonderful it would be to have him as a husband and there all the time with her.

But he hadn't made any promises. He might leave today and never return. Even as the thought saddened her, she refused to give up hope.

The kiss that night was brief. They had looked at each other and realized that no matter how tired their bodies were, they still wanted each other.

The next day at church Charlotte noticed that Emma and Brian were nervous wrecks, worrying that a catastrophe was waiting for them. After services Charlotte called Vincent and asked him to meet them at Emma's house. He was there within the hour.

With his help, they had gone over every detail, reassured the anxious couple, then double-checked the checklist. Charlotte would contact the guests who had not responded, go with Emma on Monday to meet with the wedding photographer and the videographer. Vincent would go with Brian the same day to pick up the wedding rings and check the engraved inscriptions on them, and check on the entertainment.

When Emma and Brian had finally calmed and had been reassured of a wonderful wedding, Charlotte had glanced up to see Vincent watching her with a curious expression on his face. She had frowned at him, but he had shaken his head and suggested he take everyone, including Emma's and Brian's parents, sailing and then out to dinner.

Everyone accepted. They'd had a wonderful time. Sailing had soothed the frayed nerves of anxious parents and edgy children. As the evening progressed, Charlotte also felt a lessening of the tension in her own body.

When Vincent let her take the wheel of the speedboat, he stepped behind her to guide and help. She felt alive instead of nervous. With his arms around her, the wind in her hair, she tossed him a grin over her shoulder.

"Watch where you're going," he said, but he was smiling too.

Facing forward, Charlotte smiled. She was seeing another more playful side of Vincent and she heartily approved.

In the days that followed, she approved even more. She and Vincent saw each other almost daily. He said he was making sure she didn't let his plants die. She replied that she babied them shamefully. That earned her a kiss. It wasn't easy pulling back then or after the other kisses that followed, but they managed.

Two days before the wedding, Vincent had to go out of town. Since the wedding rehearsal and dinner were the next evening, and he wasn't sure how long he'd be away, he'd only told Charlotte. As much as he had been against the wedding in the beginning, he had finally realized how much Brian and Emma loved each other and he was happy for them. He had also come to realize that loving a person meant putting your needs behind what was best for them.

"First-class passengers may now board Flight 1222 for Chicago, Illinois."

Grabbing his garment bag and laptop, Vincent stood and followed the other first-class passengers onto the plane. On board, he handed the stewardess the bag and his suit jacket, and took his seat.

Instead of opening his laptop to work, he stared out the window and remembered Charlotte's smile and infectious laughter, the disappointment that she couldn't hide because he wouldn't be there tonight to go to his first political rally with her. He remembered her warm body and how good it felt curled trustingly against his on her sofa last night as they watched a comedy.

He twisted in his seat as his body again made him vividly aware of his long bout of sexual denial. He wasn't sure how much longer he could do this. A couple of times he was aware that if he pushed Charlotte just a little harder, she would have given herself to him. He hadn't wanted that. He wanted her there with him every step of the way. Besides, he'd never do anything to destroy her faith in him. So what was the answer? He honestly didn't know.

Charlotte was in a quandary. The wedding consultant, the officiating minister, Brian and Emma, and their parents had been asking where Vincent was for the past twenty minutes. They all were clustered in front of the podium with no best man. Charlotte considered confessing that he was out of town when the main doors to the sanctuary opened.

"Hello, everyone. Sorry I'm late," Vincent greeted, his long legs quickly carrying him down the aisle.

"I'm just glad you're here," Brian said, relief etched on his face as he reached out to shake the extended hand of his cousin. "Working late as usual, I see. I've already warned Emma my hours are going to get crazier at work."

Emma smiled up at her fiancé. "I'll miss you, but I understand it's important to you."

"Now that the best man is here, let's get started," said the wedding consultant as she hustled the bridesmaids and groomsmen back down the aisle of the church, Charlotte with them. She hadn't even gotten a chance to speak with Vincent.

Impatiently, Charlotte listened to the instructions she knew as well as the consultant. Her face must have said as much for the woman gave her a stern look of disapproval and said, "I know *some* of you have gone through this many times before, but others have not."

All of the other women except Emma looked at Charlotte. She'd never felt more keenly that she'd never be a bride.

"I'm sure you're right, Mrs. Phillips," Emma said in the ensuing silence. "But good manners are never out of place."

Charlotte blinked at the ready defense by Emma. Mrs. Phillips, however, lifted her pointed nose higher at the rebuke.

"Brian and I want our wedding to be absolutely perfect, Mrs. Phillips, that's why we chose you. You're the best at what you do. We know we won't be disappointed," Emma continued.

Mrs. Phillips preened. "No, you shan't. Groomsmen, line up by height as I instructed earlier."

The paired men started down the aisle, followed by each bridesmaid. Seeing Mrs. Phillips' attention elsewhere, Charlotte felt it safe to whisper to Emma, "Thanks, and very well done."

Emma's smile was impish. "After watching you all these years I should know how to get my point across."

"You learned well. My turn." Charlotte stepped out and started down the aisle and saw Vincent standing beside Brian. Love washed over her, and something close to fear. Her steps faltered, then she continued despite the pain deep in her chest. Would he ever love her?

Never a bride. Never a bride. Never Vincent's bride.

The taunting beat replayed itself over and over in her head as she walked slowly down the aisle when she wanted to run out of the church. Instead she dutifully took her place to the right of the minister aware that she might never stand before him with the man she loved.

Vincent had never seen Charlotte look so sad or so hauntingly beautiful. Whether by accident or design, she'd worn an ankle-length sleeveless white sheath. She might have been a bride herself. The thought brought him up short.

Charlotte had made it no secret that she wanted to get married, planned to get married. One day a man would come along who would win her. A mixture of jealousy and anger swept through Vincent at the thought of any man touching her, kissing her, making love to her.

"Isn't she beautiful?"

Vincent pulled his unsettling thoughts back to the present. His narrowed gaze went from Brian to Emma, on the arm of her father, slowly coming down the aisle. She was beautiful. From her radiant expression it was obvious she knew that she was loved, cherished, and wanted. Beside Vincent, Brian's face split into a wide, proud grin. He had done well for himself. He might be young, but he apparently knew what he wanted and how to get it.

Vincent on the other hand was still floundering. He craned his neck to see Charlotte and couldn't. Then, seeing the eagle-eyed consultant's attention on Emma, Vincent moved back until he saw Charlotte, her head slightly bent. His heart turned over.

She looked up and straight into his eyes. Vincent felt as though the world had dropped away from his feet. No, he quickly amended, he was looking at his world. *Charlotte.* As the realization sank in, his heart pounded, his legs felt wobbly. It couldn't be.

"Vincent, are you all right?" Brian asked.

Vincent didn't know how to answer. Somehow he finally managed to answer, "I'm fine. I shouldn't have skipped lunch."

Brian slapped him lightly on the shoulder. "When we finish here we're having the rehearsal dinner, so just hang in there."

Vincent was hanging, all right, and the rope was unraveling fast.

Charlotte was miserable. Each time she'd catch Vincent's attention at the rehearsal dinner, he'd quickly look away. To make matters worse, they were dining at Fish and one of Brian's groomsmen, a man she'd never met before, was trying to hit on her.

She'd tried ignoring him, gave him warning looks, but nothing seemed to dent his thick skull. The only thing that saved the overbearing man from a drink dumped in his lap to cool him off was the fact he kept his hands to himself and she didn't want to ruin the evening for Brian and Emma.

By ten she was more than ready to go home. However, as maid of honor she had to wait until all the others had gone. Finally, there was only her and Vincent waiting for the valet to bring their cars.

"Charlotte, I realize you're tired, but do you mind coming back to my place? I'd like to ask your opinion about something," Vincent said.

Charlotte was about to say no when he added, "It's about the wedding. It won't take long."

Charlotte bit her lower lip as indecision and regret held her still. Vincent lived downtown in the new and chic town homes on Turtle Creek. And he had never asked her to his home before. Foolishly she wished that the first time hadn't been for the sake of someone else.

The valet pulled up with her car. Vincent's arrived seconds later. She pushed her earlier thoughts aside. This was for Brian and Emma's sake. "All right."

"Just follow me." Tipping her valet, then his, he got in his car and drove away.

Charlotte followed, determined to hear what Vincent had to say, then leave. Determined not to let one tear fall.

The residential building was as posh as the upscale address implied with a rose marble entryway, an immense flower arrangement in the center of the rotunda, curved stairway, and sparkling chandelier. As she followed him inside his home, Charlotte fleetingly noted the hardwood floor and tasteful furnishings.

"Would you like a glass of wine?"

"No, thank you." She sat on the sofa and rested her purse in her lap. She didn't plan to stay long. "What about the wedding? Is there some problem I don't know about?"

Vincent scooted the magazines and silk flower arrangement over on the coffee table, then sat facing her. "Yes."

"What?"

"I'm in love with you. Will you marry me?"

Charlotte's mouth opened, but nothing came out.

Vincent stared into her shocked face and talked fast. "I didn't expect it either. I knew I wanted you, but then I saw you walking down the aisle, and it began to sink in. I love you."

Her eyes closed and when they opened they were filled with accusation and pain. "How could you do this to me?"

"I lo—"

"Don't lie!" She came to her feet. "You want to sleep with me and you think the way to do it is to offer a fake proposal."

Vincent had risen with her. "Fake proposal! What kind of man do you think I am?"

"Obviously one I only *thought* I knew." She gripped her bag. "Good night."

She got two steps before he caught her by the forearms and pulled her toward him. "Now you listen to me. I said I love you and I darn well mean it. I never said that to another woman in my life, not even to that scheming Sybil."

Charlotte stopped struggling. Fire flashed in her eyes. "Who's Sybil?"

"An unscrupulous woman who thought to use me to advance in the company I worked for and was fired instead," he told her.

"You had an affair with her," Charlotte guessed, and although it had been in the past it still hurt. The woman had shared with Vincent what Charlotte might never have the chance to experience.

For a moment she didn't think he would answer, then he did. "Yes. Unlike you, she used her looks to get her what she wanted. When I found out about her duplicity I fired her."

"I'm sorry."

"Don't be. It taught me a lesson about sex and women."
He sighed. "At least I thought it did until I met you. You're
nothing like I thought and everything I could have wished
for."

"I didn't expect you to stay after I told you," she said
softly.

His thumb stroked her arms. "Neither did I."

"Why did you?"

"Probably a combination of a lot of things," he said, thinking as he went. "I enjoyed being with you, hearing your
laughter, watching you enjoy life. Your kisses also nearly
blew the top of my head off. The little sounds you used to
make when you were clinging to me nearly drove me crazy.
We both know I didn't have to propose to get you to sleep
with me."

She gasped and he kept talking. "You know why I stopped
every time? It was because I'd rather cut off my right arm
than hurt you."

Since there were times she would have given in, all Charlotte could do was glare.

Vincent wasn't finished. "Do you think I wanted to fall in
love with a career woman who I'll have to get on her calendar
to see? I missed you like crazy while you were in Austin."

Charlotte felt herself softening, but felt compelled to point
out, "A woman has just as much a right to a career as a man."

"A woman's place is in the home, caring for her family."
He released her, then raked his hand over his head in frustra-
tion. "I cut Ashley some slack because of what you said, but
I'm not the husband and family she's missing time with.
There'll be times when you're gone almost as much as I am.
I don't have any illusions that will change. I don't like that!"

"I believe in what I'm doing just as much as you do," she
told him, wanting him to understand.

"I know," he said, his voice softening. "Helping people
and trying to make a difference in their lives is as much a
part of you as breathing. I finally figured out that's one of the

reasons people are so drawn to you." Black eyes narrowed. "Men especially. I wanted to punch James in the nose tonight. I would have, if I hadn't thought it would upset you."

Charlotte felt her resistance fade a little bit more. "I can take care of myself."

"I realize that as well. You also have very strong moral principles and I trust you implicitly. I'll always be waiting for you to come back home to me." A slow, teasing smile came over his face as his hands settled on her waist. "It will be my pleasure to ensure that you can't wait to get home."

She pushed at his chest. "I'm still upset with you."

"I know, but I'm working on getting you over it." He kissed the curve of her jaw, her lips. "I brought you here so you couldn't toss me out until I convinced you how much I love you."

Her voice trembled. "Vincent, are you sure?"

His head lifted and he stared down at her with love in his eyes. "I love you more than life itself. You opened my eyes to what a real marriage is: trust, love, commitment, and sharing. I found my Southern comfort and I have no intention of letting her get away."

Her arms circled his neck. "I love you. Together we'll make it work."

He pulled her closer. "I figure if I can learn calculus, I can learn how to fix a meal and change a diaper."

Her heart glowed. "I'm sure of it."

"Then your answer is yes?"

"Yes, forever and always, my conservative scoundrel."

Epilogue

The bride wore white. Chantilly lace, tulle, and silk-satin were used to create an elegant gown with a sweeping train and veil for the formal December wedding. In her white-gloved hand was a cluster of calla lilies. As she made her way up the aisle on the arm of her beaming father, a hush fell over the packed, flower-filled sanctuary. She didn't notice; her gaze was locked on the man in the gray morning coat who would soon be her husband, just as his was on her.

As they had done so many times in the past six months since their engagement, they communicated with their eyes.

I'll love you always.

I'll love you right back.

Then she was standing beside him in front of the minister, her hand resting trustingly in his. There wasn't a shred of doubt in her mind that he would always be there for her, nor were there any doubts in his mind about her.

We made it.

We certainly did.

Soon.

Soon.

The ceremony proceeded with the solemn lighting of candles, the exchange of vows and giving of rings, then the moment each had waited for. "I now pronounce you man and wife. You may kiss the bride."

The kiss was a brief brush of lips, then hand-in-hand they were rushing down the aisle to the waiting limousine that would take them to the reception at the posh Crescent Court Hotel. Exactly an hour later, the couple slipped away, leaving their best man and maid of honor to ensure that all the guests had a wonderful time.

"Hurry," she said impatiently, crowding him as he tried to unlock the door to their honeymoon suite in the Crescent Court. Neither had wanted to wait to start their honeymoon.

"The key card is—there!" The green light blinked on. Turning, he lifted her up in his arms and stepped inside, then kicked the door closed. He didn't stop until he was in the lavishly decorated bedroom of the suite. Vintage champagne, a huge fruit basket, and finger food waited. Neither noticed. All that mattered was the turned-down, king-sized bed.

"Please put me down and help me out of this dress." Lifting her cathedral crown off her head she tossed it and

his coat he'd taken off in the elevator in the direction of the
love seat.

He set her on her feet, then breathed a sigh of relief that
there were only five satin-covered buttons. "My hands are
shaking."

"My entire body is shaking," she said.

They both laughed, but it was nervous laughter. The last
button slipped free. "Done."

She reached to pull the dress off her shoulders. He helped,
then sucked in his breath as the dress slid down her body.
She stood in yards of tulle and satin-silk wearing a white lace
bustier, delicate lace bikini panties, and sheer white lace-top
thigh-highs.

"You simply take my breath away." His hands spanned
her tiny waist and lifted her out of the gown.

Her hands rested on his broad shoulders as she stared up
into his intense black eyes. "I plan to do a lot more to you
before we leave this room again."

He grinned. "Charlotte, I do love you."

"I love you too, Vincent. Thanks for giving me this," she
said, her hands coming up to cup his face. "Now, it's my time
to give." Her lips nipped his, then she traced the seam of his
mouth with her tongue.

He shuddered. His hands tightened. His eyes narrowed to
slits. "Why don't we give to each other?"

In his usual way, he didn't wait for her consent, but fastened his mouth on hers. The kiss was bold, erotic, and mind-
bending. Her little moans and whimpers told him she was in
complete agreement with his idea.

Vincent fell back on the bed, carrying Charlotte with him.
He rolled and she was on the bottom. "Unbutton my shirt
while I act out a fantasy."

She reached for the first pearl button with shaky hands.
Vincent's tongue rimmed the bustier, its deep center. Her
body quivered. The pleasure was unbelievably erotic. The
only way she completed the task was that she wanted to do
the same thing to him.

Vincent found the zipper in the bustier and slowly drew it down, revealing lush breasts and pebble-hard nipples that begged for his attention. Not yet. He wanted to rush, but for Charlotte it would be the first time and, if he could keep his sanity, it would be one that she would always remember and cherish.

His hand drifted over the flesh he had uncovered, as gentle as a butterfly's wing, as thorough as a cat licking cream, and that was exactly what he planned next. The tip of his tongue stroked first one turgid brown point, then the other.

Beneath him, Charlotte twisted. A slow heat was building between her thighs. Her legs moved restlessly. "Vincent?"

"I'm here." His hand cupped her womanhood. She whimpered. Then he dipped one long finger inside her. Her hips came off the bed.

He stared into her eyes, eyes that were hot as his. She leaned forward and curled her tongue around his nipple. Vincent couldn't hold back a moan nor did he try to. However, when her hand closed around his manhood and stroked the length of him, he gritted his teeth and gently pushed her hand away.

"I did it wrong?"

"You did it too right."

Her smile purely feminine, she went back to driving him crazy with her sweet mouth and nimble tongue, removing his clothes while he took enormous pleasure in acting out another fantasy in the way he got rid of her panties.

Flesh to flesh, heart to heart, they explored each other and loved each other on the way to the intimate bonding both had waited months to share.

Poised above her, he stared down at her and was gratified that he saw no hesitation, only love and desire. "I love you."

"I love you."

His hips moved to bring them together for the first time, then he was surrounded by her velvet heat. The fit was snug; the sensations exquisite. He loved her not only with his body, but with his heart and soul. She loved him back the same way. When her cry of fulfillment came, he was there with her, holding her as he always would.

The Southern lady had married her conservative Yankee scoundrel, and the fit was perfect.

TURN THE PAGE FOR AN EXCERPT FROM
DONNA HILL'S LATEST BOOK

Rhythms

AVAILABLE SOON IN HARDCOVER
FROM ST. MARTIN'S PRESS

Down in the Delta, somewhere just beyond Alligator, Mississippi, rests the colored section of Rudell. A community of less than five hundred, divided unequally by race, wealth and religion by the Left Hand River. It was named such because from the top of the highest tree in Rudell the rippling river looked like a man's left hand. Yes, it sure did.

Well, today all the folks, black and white alike, moved heat-snake slow along the dusty unpaved roads, pressed down by the heavy hand of the July sun.

Towering yellow pines raised their angry fists toward the blinding white sky, demanding a long cool drink. Mosquitoes buzzed and bit, zealous in their hunt for sweet, moist flesh. Especially the plump legs of little brown baby boys and girls. Good chewing grass, razor-thin, glistened like emerald fire, fanning out as far as the eye could see.

Funny, how nature plays its tricks. Earlier that same year, the spring of 1927, the mighty Mississippi River rose higher than ever before in its history. Before its floods were over, the river had turned the Delta valley into lakes of despair. Dikes and levees crumbled while the river swallowed whole towns and farms with an insatiable appetite that could not be stopped by man.

The war between man and nature rode the ever-increasing tide. Still, months after the devastation, lost land and lost lives, recovery was a slow and painful process. The Father of Waters had spared no one, colored or white. But, times being what they were, the coloreds who already had so little now had even less.

Yet, even the oppressive, relentless heat and untold tragedy couldn't stop the parishioners of First Baptist Church from stomping and shouting on this Sunday morning just as on any other.

The white clapboard building, put together plank by plank

by the men of Rudell, offered them little refuge as the steam
ascended from the momentum of the congregation bunched
together along the crowded wooden pews.

The sun streamed in through the hand-blown windows,
casting rays of shimmering color across the woolly heads of
the congregation, to explode in a ball of brilliant light that
gleamed off the ten-foot cross of Christ. The strongest members of First Baptist, male and female, had carried that cross
in through the narrow door, five years ago, piece by piece,
nailing it together in silent reverence. It stood in proud testament of all they had endured. And they were grateful.

Today, more than ever, they had much to be thankful for.
They'd been spared.

"We done seen the wrath of the Lord," Reverend Joshua
Harvey ebbed and flowed, his voice an instrument of persua-
sion. "His mighty hand swept the Mississippi from Arkansas
to the Gulf of Mexico. Wiped out sinners and non-believers
with a puff of his breath."

"Amen! Yes, Lord," shouted the pulsing throng.

"The great flood of '27 we hear tell it called. I say it be
the great cleanser. The Lord's way of riddin' this earth of
those who continya ta do us harm." He stretched out his arm
and passed it over the packed room. "And y'all know who
I'm talkin' 'bout."

"Praise the Lord!"

"But many of our innocent sistahs and brothas have suf-
fered, too. They been left with even less than the nothin' they
had."

"That's why we's here t'day, Reverend," shouted Deacon
Earl, looking round to see the nods of assent.

"Amen," again came the response.

"I knows y'all don't have much," the Reverend continued.
"You works hard to feed yo' families from sunrise till set.
But it's up to us who have little to share with those who have
less."

Government relief had come to those stricken by the devastation of the flood. But it was slow coming, if at all, to
some of the colored sections along the Delta.

Joshua gazed out at his congregation, the beaten, the downtrodden. His dark all-seeing eyes peered into their souls, his heart heard their prayers. He witnessed the unflinching pride in the bent backs, the clawed hands and leather-like faces. Sorrow shadowed their eyes, but hope hung on their lids. In each one he saw strength from a people who had seen much for any one lifetime. Still, he knew he could ask for more.

"I knows what I'm askin' is gon' be hard for the lot of ya. But I needs ya to dig deeper than yo' pockets. I needs ya to dig inta yo' hearts to help those who cain't help themselves. We here in Rudell gotta come together once again as a community and as a people." He paused to let his words rest a spell. "The doors ta the church gon' be open all day. Brang what chu kin. Deacon Earl gon' be in charge of collectin' whatever y'all kin brang."

Cora sat in the front line of the choir. The flick of her slender wrist moved the circular cardboard fan in a steady flow in front of her face. She gazed out at the rows of black bodies, a melody of color, size and shape. They were hypnotized by the power of her daddy. Pride puffed her chest. Papa Daddy could do anything. He could make you believe the impossible, give you strength when you had none. He made it so easy for her to lift her voice in praise, as much for him as she did for the Lord. She wanted to do them both proud.

Like so many colored communities, the heart and soul of Rudell could be found in the church. Reverend Joshua Harvey was the bedrock upon which Rudell was built. Their lightning rod. The calm during the storm. It was to him that the white folks came when they had trouble with their coloreds, Cora thought. Daddy always found ways to make the peace. But, of course, he made them think it was their own doing. He knew white folks in a way few coloreds did in those parts. He spoke their language, knew the power of their words as well as those of his flock. Daddy carried the weight for all of Rudell on his back.

While he was not seen as the equal of the whites, something in Daddy's bearing made them tolerate his uppity ways. He was like the esteemed Booker T. Washington with the powerful white folks up North. Daddy was just like that. White folks feared as much as respected him and the quiet power he held over the town. His church was the visual symbol of that power.

"I want y'all to stand now and join our choir in song." Joshua turned briefly toward his daughter, a smile of pride on his thick lips. "Lift yo' voices to the Almighty in thanks."

The choir stood in unison and Cora stepped forward.

David Mackey stood out on the dusty road, his starch-white, high-button shirt clinging to his moist back. Even his sweat tried to find a place to hide from the beating sun, securing sanctuary beneath his stiff shirt collar.

He whipped out a spotless white handkerchief from the pocket of his blue serge pants and mopped his brow, then set his straw hat squarely atop his close-cropped head.

He'd fretted for hours about what to wear, wanting to make the best impression. His customary work pants and clean but frayed shirts were fine for visiting his sick and laid-low patients, but not today. Today was special.

David drew up a deep breath and checked his scarred gold pocket watch, a gift from his father.

Service would be over directly, he calculated, and then he'd see her again. As a matter-o-fact, if he shut his eyes he could see her face plain as the day is long, as he was sure it would appear while she led the choir through the strains of "Swing Low, Sweet Chariot." Her powerful contralto voice poured out of her tiny body, entered the soul, grabbed and shook it.

The age-old cry of the weary souls seeped through the walls of the one-room building. But it was Cora Harvey's rapturous voice that soared above them all.

Cora Harvey. She was something else. A right pretty thing. He'd spotted her months ago and upon discreet inquiries he'd found out who she was. That discovery compelled him to keep his distance as much as he wanted to do otherwise. Since then, they'd passed each other on several occasions when she made her monthly shopping trips into town. However, up until the other afternoon, she'd never paid him no never mind other than a passing wave or flashing that smile of hers. Then they'd run into each other at Sam's market earlier that week and she'd given him his first look of encouragement. Of course her daddy wasn't looking. But he dared not approach her, not with the good Reverend close at hand.

David sighed. They came from different sides of town, one divided among itself by more than just the Left Hand River, but by race, wealth and religion. Cora Harvey was the daughter of a sharecropper turned preacher-man who worshipped in the Baptist church. He, on the other hand, was the one and only colored doctor in Rudell, the surviving son of the now-prosperous Mackey family, who paid his homage—at least some of the time—at the Episcopal Church on the other side of the dividing line.

It shouldn't matter none, he mused, but it did. The Baptists were considered common, while the Episcopals were made of the few educated coloreds, those with a bit of money. As much as colored folk had endured since they were brought in chains from Africa, and stuffed like garbage into the bowels of death ships, one would think that now they would band together. That was not to be. It wasn't enough that the white folks made no secret of their disdain for the coloreds. The coloreds did it to themselves.

David snapped out of his woolgathering at the sound of voices surging through the now-opened church doors. He took a quick look at his shoes—which still held their shine—wiped his face one last time, and walked forward.

Cora stood on the plank-wood steps of the church, flanked on either side by her parents, Pearl and Joshua. She looked so soft and beautiful in her pale-peach cotton dress, David thought, just like one of those dolls he'd once seen in the *Sears and Roebuck* catalogue. Her smooth pecan-colored skin with undertones of red glowed as if lit by an inner sunbeam. Her thick, neatly plaited hair was pulled back in one braid that fell to the center of her back, protected by a sun bonnet that matched her dress. She sure did look pretty.

She shook hands with each of the church-goers, accepting their praises of her singing with grace and the right amount of humility.

"Sister Cora, that voice of yours gon' take you straight to heaven, chile. Lordhammercy! Mark my words," professed Lucinda Carver, as the sweat rolled in waves down her plump face.

"Thank you, Sister Carver. I sure hope so."

"You just make sho' you hold open them pearly gates for this old sister," she chuckled, patting Cora heartily on the arm.

"See you tomorrow, Cora," Maybelle said, giving her friend a kiss on the cheek. "I's goin' to meet Little Jake at the river," she whispered in Cora's ear, before running down the steps.

Sassy, Cora's friend since they were both in diapers, stepped up beside her. "That girl gon' get herself in a heap of trouble if her Mama ever finds out." Then Sassy giggled. "Harold Jr. say he gon' come by and sit on the porch later when it cool down some. I'll see you later." Sassy, it wasn't her real name, but that's what she was always called, skipped down the stairs.

Cora watched her two friends leave and wished she had someone waiting on her, eager to see her under the stars.

When the last of the parishioners filed out, Joshua slipped into his role as father, husband and protector. "Come along, ladies. We best be gettin' on outta this here heat," he instructed.

Pearl eased up 'long side her towering husband and slipped her arm through his.

"Comin', Daddy." Cora took a step down when movement across the road captured her attention. She felt the muscles in her heart expand and contract, creating a moment of light-headedness. It was him, that handsome, quiet doctor who made her stomach feel funny inside.

Pearl's eyes followed the trail of her daughter's. "Oh,

Joshua, here come that nice young doctor." She gave his arm a "come on" squeeze, and a quick wink to Cora.

"How nice kin he be ifn he thinks he's too good to worship in a Baptist Church? Humph."

"Joshua," Pearl hissed in warning as David crossed the first step.

"Afternoon, Mrs. Harvey, Reverend." David tipped his hat and looked at Cora. "Miss Cora."

"Doctor Mackey." Cora gave him her sweetest smile and wished her mother and father would leave her be.

Silence hung between the quartet as heavy as the heat. The poor boy looked so nervous from the glare Joshua was hurling his way, that Pearl's maternal instincts leaped to his rescue. "What brings you to First Baptist this hot day, Doctor?" Pearl asked, finally breaking the silence.

"Well, ma'am," he paused and looked from one parent to the other, wishing that his heart would stop hammering long enough for him to take a breath. "I was hoping you'd allow me to take Miss Cora here over to Joe's for a soft drink, maybe some ice cream." He swallowed down the last of his fear and plunged on. "That's if Miss Cora is willing." He snatched a quick look at Cora. "I have my auto-mo-bile right 'cross the road. I'd have her back in plenty of time for supper. I—"

"What 'chu know 'bout what time we has supper?" Joshua pulled his black, wide-brimmed hat a little further down on his brow with the intention of giving his dark features an even more ominous look.

Cora's face was afire, and it had nothing to do with the heat. She was mortified. Here she was seventeen years old, almost eighteen in six months, and her daddy was treating her like a knee-high. When would she ever be able to court like the other girls she knew? Daddy was always preaching 'bout how she needs to settle down. How was she ever supposed to do that if he wouldn't let no respectable man near her? Not that marriage was her goal no how. It was just the whole notion of having someone interested in her. Especially a doctor. All the girls would be green with envy.

She wanted to know what it felt like, wanted to know what

she'd heard some of the girls of the church whisper about. She had yet to be kissed. How could her daddy embarrass her this way? Maybe the earth would just open up like she'd read about in the picture books and swallow her whole.

"Joshua, for heaven's sake, let the young man speak his piece," Pearl cajoled, seeing the possibilities in the union. "That sounds right nice that he wants to take Cora for a soft drink. Matter a fact, I could use a long, cool glass of lemonade myself." She looked at Cora who flashed her a smile of thankful relief. "You ought to take the good doctor up on his offer, Cora. Don't you think so?"

"Sounds invitin', Doctor Mackey. Is it all right, Daddy?"

Joshua heard the soft plea in his daughter's voice and saw the eagerness shining in her eyes. In that instant he remembered all too clearly what it felt like to be young. What it felt like when he met his Pearl. He weren't nothin' more than a paid slave workin' the cotton fields. When he'd drag his weary body home after a day under the Mississippi sun, Pearl would run down the road from her beaverboard shack and bring him a tin of water and a piece of dried beef or a biscuit.

"I figured you'd be thirsty," she'd always say.

"Right kind of you," he'd answer.

She'd walk with him part way down the road till he finished his water.

"Thank you much, Miss Pearl."

She'd duck her head all shy. "Tomorrow," she'd whisper and run off.

That musta gone on for months. That and things they didn't talk about no more, till Joshua said the two of them would do much better as one.

"Whatchu sayin'?" Pearl asked, taking a seat on the top of a flat rock.

Joshua squeezed his hat in his hands, trying to find the right words. He shifted from one foot to the next.

"You what I look for at the end of the day, Pearl," he finally said. "Thinkin' 'bout you out in dem fields makes me remember I's still a man, not some pack mule like Mistah

Jackson make me out to be. I kin be somethin', Pearl. Somebody. You believe that?"

"I knowed it from the first time I saw you hitchin' down that road yonder."

"I got dreams, Pearl. I want to have my own church one day, preach the Word. I–I want you to be a part of that."

"That yo' fancy way of askin' me to jump the broom wit' you?"

Joshua grinned like a young boy, seeing the challenge in her eyes. "I s'pose."

"Then I s'pose I will."

And she'd been by his side ever since, sunup to down. Never complaining, no matter how bad times had gotten. Pearl was his strength, his reason for everything. Her faith in him, her unwavering love was his joy. And Cora was just like her.

Truth be known, he'd like nothing better than to see his strong-willed Cora married off and secure. It would sho'nuff make Pearl happy. A good, solid husband may just be the thing Cora needed to tame her willful ways. But that didn't mean he had to make it easy for any man who thought he was good enough to come a-courtin' his baby girl. Especially an Episcopal doctor—and one from the other side of Rudell at that.

"I s'pose," he grumbled. "We have Sunday supper at four o'clock sharp."

Pearl briefly lowered her bonneted head to hide her smile. "You might think about joining us, Doctor. I fix a fine table."

Joshua threw her a cutting glance, but kept his own counsel.

"I just might, ma'am. Thank you." He looked at Joshua who gave an imperceptible nod of approval. The day was beginning to look better every minute, David thought.

Cora gave her mother and father each a peck on their cheek and stepped down.

"I'll be sure to have her back in plenty of time for supper, Reverend."

"Be sho' you do," Joshua added for good measure.

Cora couldn't believe her luck as she walked side-by-side down the church steps out onto the road. The saints must surely be with her today, she mused, tossing up a silent prayer of thanks. Her father had never so much as entertained the notion of her courting, even though all the other girls her age had a steady beau. "You're not other girls," Joshua Harvey would boom in his preacher voice. "You the daughter of the reverend of this town and you ain't gon' be seen with just anybody."

Well, Doctor David Mackey must sure be somebody, she thought, delighted.

"I'm right happy your folks let me take you out for a spell, Miss Cora," David said in a hushed voice as they crossed the road to his Model-T.

She looked up into his dark face, eyes like polished black opals, and her young heart panged in her chest. "So am I, Doctor Mackey." She batted her eyes demurely as she'd seen some of her church-going sisters do and she would have sworn David blushed beneath his roasted chestnut complexion.

Strong, large hands caught her waist as David helped her step up into the seat, and Cora was no longer sure if it was the force of the blazing sun, or a fire that had been lit inside of her that caused the surge of heat to run amok through her body. Settling herself against the soft, cushioned seat, she adjusted her hat while David rounded the hood and hopped up beside her.

"All set?"

Cora nodded, suddenly unsure of herself.

The Model-T bucked, chugged, coughed up some smoke and finally pulled off down the rutty road, bouncing and bumping all the way. As they drove by the rows of makeshift shacks, half-nude children playing in the river and old wrinkled women smoking corn pipes all stopped and stared at the handsome couple in the automobile. To see colored folks driving was rarer than having meat for dinner once a month.

But instead of feeling like a specimen under glass, Cora

felt like royalty. She smiled and waved to everyone who came out on the road, wide-eyed to greet them. Little children ran alongside the car until they grew weary and the old Model-T chugged out of sight.

"Did you go to Sunday service today, Doctor Mackey?" Cora asked, needing to break the train of silence that hung between them like clothes drying on a line.

David cleared his throat. "No. Not today." He shrugged, then chuckled lightly. "Truth be told, it's a while since I been to church."

Cora angled her head in his direction, surprise widening her sparkling brown eyes. "Why? Don't you have anything to be thankful for?"

"Sure I do. Except I don't think you need to set up in a building to give thanks. I believe that God can hear my prayers and my thanks from wherever I am."

Cora frowned, tossing around this new idea. What David was saying may well have been Greek for all the sense it made to her. It never occurred to her not to attend Sunday service. She'd been brought up and reared in the church. All of her friends attended. They had social functions, did things for the community, helped each other out in crisis. Why just the other week, the sisters got together and took turns sitting with old Miss Riley who'd been feeling poorly for months. She didn't know what she'd do if she didn't have her church and her church family. Besides, on Sunday mornings, she could do what she loved more than anything, raise her voice in song.

"But—it's more than that," she protested, convinced that she was right. "It's about belonging to something that has meaning, being a part of something."

"That may be, Miss Cora, and I don't fault no one for going. I don't want you to get me wrong. I do set foot in from time to time, just not right regular." He turned briefly to her, hoping that his revelation hadn't put her off, especially with her being the preacher's daughter and all. But the reality was, he wanted to be honest with her.

"If Christians are supposed to love all men, then what's

the difference between your church and mine? What makes one better than the other—the amount of money you put in the collection basket, how large the congregation, what side of town you worship on?" he asked with honest sincerity.

Cora crossed her arms beneath her small breasts. She listened to what he said. Secretly she wondered the same things, but she'd never dared to voice her concerns, ask her questions.

"You're a very interesting man, Doctor Mackey," she said, still unwilling to give in. "You've put something on my head to ponder."

"That's a start," he said, turning to her with a grin.

It was then that she noticed the deep dimple in his right cheek and knew, that barring everything else, whatever differences may separate them, she wanted to see more of him, hear his strange thoughts and maybe become exposed to a side of life she'd never known existed.

Shortly, they arrived in the center of town and pulled to a stop in front of Joe's. David quickly hurried around and helped Cora from her seat. She immediately felt the curious gazes from the townspeople as they went about their Sunday business, the surprised looks from friends of her father and mother as she took David's arm and walked toward the shop.

Voice by voice, conversation ceased as heads turned toward the open door. The heat stood like a man between them, separating them from the brown, tan and black bodies, then was buffeted about by the slow, swirling ceiling fan—the only one in town.

The interior was dim and it took Cora a moment to adjust her eyes from the glare of the outside.

David glanced down the narrow aisle and cleared his throat. "There's a table in the back," he said, indicating the vacancy with a stretch of his arm.

They proceeded through the gauntlet of probing eyes.

Cora's gaze faltered for a moment, then darted briefly about, a taut smile drawing her mouth into a thin line.

"Afternoon, Miss Wheeler," Cora, said, remembering her

manners as she recognized her nosey neighbor from down the road.

"Cora Harvey," Sarah Wheeler droned, long as the quitting whistle at the cotton mill. "I didn't know the good Reverend let you keep comp'ny." Her tiny eyes skipped across David's face. "Doctor Mackey. Ain't you lookin' fine this bright day."

"Comp'ny in general, or me in particular, Mrs. Wheeler?" David asked with a tip of his hat, and an extra drawl, his smile fixed and direct as his stare.

An ungloved hand fluttered to her chest. "I . . . I just meant . . . she, Miss Cora seems so young still. Well I recall when she was just a bitty thing." Sarah's forced laugh flapped like the wings of a feeble bird.

"She seems all grown up to me," David replied smoothly.